The Burning Jacket

The Burning Jacket

Nel Rand

DANCING MOON PRESS
NEWPORT, OREGON

The Burning Jacket
copyright © 2010 by Nel Rand
All rights reserved
www.nelrand.com

This book is a work of fiction. The characters, incidents, and dialogue are drawn from the author's imagination and are not to be construed as real. Any resemblance to actual events or persons, living or dead, is entirely coincidental.

No part of this book may be used or reproduced or transmitted in any form, or by any means, electronic or mechanical, including photocopy, recording, or any information storage and retrieval system, without written permission from the author, except in the case of brief quotations embedded in critical articles or reviews. For information, address your inquiry to nelrand@yahoo.com.

ISBN-13: 978-1-892076-74-8
Library of Congress Control Number: 2010922650

Rand, Nel
The Burning Jacket/
1. Title; 2. Fiction; 3. Young Adult Fiction; 4. Women's Fiction;
5. Ecology

Manufactured in the United States of America
Book design: Carla Perry
Cover design and production: Dan Mandish, Mandish Design

DANCING MOON PRESS
P.O. Box 832, Newport, OR 97365
541-574-7708
www.dancingmoonpress.com
info@dancingmoonpress.com

FIRST EDITION

Praise for the award-winning first novel
Mississippi Flyway
by Nel Rand
2007 Foreword Magazine Book of the Year Award finalist

"A compelling story told by natural storyteller. Author, Nel Rand, takes the reader on a gripping, and at times painfully rich voyage of self-discovery in *Mississippi Flyway*. She peopled her story with characters that leap off the page and her prose has an opulent nuance that places the readers firmly in the scenes. Her evocative, descriptive passages are excellent and serve to set the stage. This complex and emotional novel is beautifully published with an eye-catching cover photograph and appealing covers. Rand's deft characterization, gift for natural dialogue and compelling storyline will linger with the reader long after the final page. *Mississippi Flyway* is a tremendous story from a talented new comer."
—*Judge's comment from Writer's Digest 15th Annual International Self-Published Book Award*

"… The real strength of this book is the relationship between Tiny and Ellie. It's evident why father and daughter are estranged; so clear, in fact, that some readers may balk when Ellie agrees to leave with her father. But Rand has created strong, compelling characters in Tiny and Ellie and you want to keep reading, keep rooting for them, even when you suspect what they face will not be pleasant.

A brief interview with the author is included at the end of the novel, along with discussion questions for book clubs. Even if you read it on your own, *Mississippi Flyway* is book that is sure to stir up emotions."   —*Katerie Prior, Clarion Review*

"A woman takes a road trip through the South with her estranged father, trailed by a rogue sheriff bent on revenge. The author's style, rich with unforced detail, expertly conjures very different places— the sour air in a den where men have been gambling for days, the muddy, punishing waters of the Mississippi, the cool veranda of an antebellum building.… An absorbing well-written novel about coming to terms with personal demons."   —*Kirkus Discoveries*

**Additional copies of *The Burning Jacket*
and Nel Rand's first novel, *Mississippi Flyway*
can be ordered through
www.nelrand.com**

Dedication

This book is dedicated to the preservation of the Desert Tortoise.

The Desert Tortoise is a threatened species under the California State Endangered Species Act of 1989 and the Federal Endangered Species Act of 1990.

The population of the Desert Tortoise in the Mojave Desert has gone down 90 percent since 1980. The status of the Desert Tortoise is a bellwether for the health of our deserts.

This book is also dedicated to our planet
and to all of us who dwell upon it.

Acknowledgments

Thanks to my teacher and mentor, Meg Jensen.
And thanks to my manuscript readers: Pam Patrie, Darlene Key, Margaret Rand Corbett, Carole Isis—who also was a godsend with the first edit, Heather Gonzales, and Susan Pasarow. Thanks also to Scott Ryon, my friend and retired homicide detective, for his expertise about guns and what they do.

Finally, I give much thanks to Carla Perry, owner of Dancing Moon Press, for a great job of editing and designing in her own unique and elegant style.
Thanks to Dan Mandish for the great cover design and thanks to my publicist Lena Burdett for her website design and expert help getting the book out into the world.

ONE

Chapter One

Raynie: February 2000.

Erma Geddon woke up today, a month too early. She's a California Desert Tortoise, and my best friend. We have four major things in common.
    1. We are both girls.
    2. Today is our birthdays. It's Valentine's Day. We don't know the real day or year of Erma's birth so I share my big day with her. She was rescued out on a highway near Palm Springs and the turtle rescue people decided that she's around fifty years old. I was born in Anaheim Memorial Hospital just after midnight on February 14, 1989.
    3. Erma is on the endangered species list. And so is my sorry eleven-year-old ass.
    4. We both have scientific names. Her name is *Gopherus agassizii*, mine is *Homo stupid*.

I memorized Erma's official moniker when I was five and a half. My dad, Ray (I prefer to call him Ray, now that he's gone), used to quiz me in front of company to show off how smart I was. He would lift me onto a table and I would stand Indian tall, like my Granny Tooley, and recite, "Class: *Reptilia*, Order: *Chelonia*, Suborder: *Cryptodira*. Super Family: *Testudinoidea*, Family: *Testudinidae*, Genus: *Gopherus*, Species: *agassizii*."

From Granny Tooley I learned the importance of naming things, like the animals and plants that live on the earth, birds that fly in the sky, learning the names of one's ancestors, or hard ones like naming a wrong that needs righted. I use Erma's genus and species now that I'm older, and have nothing to prove. I love the way it sounds, *Gopherus agassizii*.

The words set my mind adrift on a silver sea, in a pea-green boat with billowing sails, in the company of the Owl and the Pussycat. We land in a place of long ago and far away where people live simple lives, laugh, and dance around bonfires, and never have to worry about nuclear war and clean air. A place where it's safe for kids to play and roam without fear that some pervert will snatch them from their front yards. A place where all the plants and animals, including humans, speak the same language and nobody kills off other species because they don't understand them. A place where the people you love never go away and leave you.

"Don't dawdle, Raynie. Get dressed."

I'm glad Mom interrupts my thoughts. I've boarded this downhill train too many times, as Ray would say, and it always ends with me wheezing and then sucking on my inhaler.

As you know, today is my birthday and I'm out in the garage getting my clothes out of the dryer. I plan to wear them to the La Brea Tar Pits, the place I chose to go for my celebration, if you want to call it that, and that's when I see Erma Geddon poke her head out between the wooden slats of her box, her eyes at half-mast. I miss her when she's asleep, and hope, for selfish reasons, that she will wake up.

My birthday falls on Monday this year and Mom got special permission from my school to take me and True on a field trip to the tar pits. True's brother, Jason, is going with us, minus official permission. He's playing hooky.

Ray used to take me to the tar pits all the time. He knows I love learning about how the world used to be thousands of years ago. But he didn't even call to wish me happy birthday today, not that I blame him. I probably wouldn't either if I were him.

THE BURNING JACKET

I hate to cry worse than I hate falling down and skinning a knee, but the tears come like a cloudburst of unexpected rain. I blow my nose on a dirty towel in the laundry pile of things to be washed as I steady myself. I can feel Ray lifting my chin with a fist and saying, 'Zip it up, little soldier.'

Mom took the day off from the bakery she half owns. I don't want to disappoint her more than I have already.

Birthdays are special days to honor our journey on Earth. That's what Granny Tooley says. She sent me a card, a watercolor of a bunny rabbit sitting under a Douglas fir tree. She made it herself.

I'm one week older than True. Last Saturday her mom, Ashanti, threw a big shindig for our birthdays at the South Coast Country Club complete with clowns, jugglers, and mimes. There were eight of us kids and we rode around in a white limousine all afternoon, waving balloons out of the window in the roof. The party ended early because of Jason. He ate too much ice cream and cake and barfed chocolate toxic waste all over the white leather back seats of the limo.

The Shandaras moved to a fancy house in Irvine three months ago. When Ashanti told True their family was moving from Anaheim to Irvine and she would be changing schools, True staged one of her famous tantrums in front of the moving men. She has a flair for the dramatic. She can throw her voice to China in a high-pitched scream that sounds like a female cougar in distress. Ray says she sounds like a dying diva in an opera. He calls her *La Trueviata*. And she never stops until her mother caves in to her demands. I timed "the changing school" scene. It took forty-seven minutes before Ashanti threw in the towel. I am eternally grateful that God gave True a powerful voice and the courage to use it.

True uses her grandmother's Anaheim address as her place of residence, and Ashanti drives her back and forth every day from Irvine. A bonus is that Jason decided to go to a school in Irvine, and we don't have to put up with his out-of-control bodily fluids behavior anymore. He used to spit and try to wipe buggers from his nose on us when we passed him in the hall.

Mom couldn't believe Ashanti would drive so far every day, at least forty minutes each way—sometimes more than an hour, depending on freeway traffic. Ashanti told my mom they moved to get away from all the Mexican immigrants in the schools in Anaheim, which seems odd to me as Ashanti and her husband, Rudi, are immigrants from India and should understand what it's like not living in the country where you were born.

I don't deserve any special treatment from my mom even if it is my birthday. I'm lucky she doesn't kick me out. I could be, at this very moment, sleeping under a bush with the homeless people down by the dry riverbed under the freeway where Ray used to jog every morning. Maybe he's joined the list of the endangered along with Erma and yours truly. He could be down there now, hungry and hiding under a bush.

I think of Marilyn who lives on the corner out in front of Starbucks Coffee in Orange. Ray and I used to go and talk to her sometimes. She always dresses in the same retro, low-cut black cocktail dress that shows her boobs, and wears a big floppy black hat and white gloves, even on the hottest of days. She sits all slathered in suntan oil on the edge of the red brick island that's filled with pink impatiens. Looking like a faded beauty queen, Marilyn soaks her feet in a plastic tub of water that matches the pink of the impatiens. When you ask her questions, she points to a big sign she made that says she was strangled by the Anaheim killer when she was a child and he destroyed her vocal chords. Ray said that's just one of her many stories; Marilyn changes them every year or so. He said she lost her voice because she smoked too many cigarettes. He always gives her a five-dollar bill, and for that she'll haul out old, yellowed, dog-eared photos of a young blond lady, who could be anybody. She points to the photos and then to herself. She won't let you touch them though.

One picture is of a smiling beauty with white teeth, her head poking through a giant Life Saver. Even at my age I'm not foolish enough to believe that if you suck on Life Savers you'll be beautiful and have white teeth. Marilyn has a couple of suitcases with all her earthly belongings tied together and perched on top of a wagon with a handle so she can pull it around. No one knows for sure where she sleeps at night.

I look for Ray every time Mom and I drive by Marilyn's corner. I'm always a little disappointed when I don't see him out there in the hot sun soaking his feet in that pink tub with Marilyn. I worry about Ray. He doesn't have a great work history.

Ray's the one who put Erma Geddon out in the garage on the shelf this past November (one of the last things he did before the big blow-up) next to all the rock polishing equipment he spent a fortune on a few years ago and hardly ever used, and the boxes of brand new toys that have never been opened, stacked from floor to ceiling. Ray says the toys are collectors' items and will be worth a fortune someday down the road.

I see sand slowly sifting out of Erma's bed onto the concrete floor. Mom yelled at Ray for filling the box so full because she would be the one to clean it up, not him. According to Mom, Ray never does anything right, or keeps his word. He left right after that.

Correction: Mom kicked him out. That was shortly after she looked me in the eyes and demanded I tell her the truth. Of course, I cracked immediately under the pressure and confessed how I came to have the large sum of money she found in my sock drawer, a story that I do not care to talk about at this time.

I watched through a blur of tears as Ray wheeled out a

suitcase that was a dead ringer for one of Marilyn's, and got into a yellow cab. I chased him down the street and around the block, the sharp glittery pieces of stars in the sidewalk digging into the soles of my bare feet. I chased him until the taxi turned and entered the busy traffic on Magnolia Avenue. That was the last I saw of him. It's been almost four months. He hasn't even called me one time. Not even a ho, ho, ho at Christmastime. I hope he doesn't hate me, but I think he does.

The first month after he left, I used to drag my blanket and pillow into his office every night after Mom went to bed. The leathery smell of the old catcher's mitt he used to play ball with helped me pretend he was just away for an out-of-town game. But then one day he came while I was at school and got all his stuff, except for the things in the garage. When I saw the imprint of the rings on the carpet where his desk used to sit, it really hit home that he was gone and wasn't coming back. I sort of went hysterical and broke a lot of Mom's old 78 and 45 rpm recordings of Miles Davis and then locked myself in Ray's office and wouldn't come out for half a day and a whole night.

Erma Geddon had been moving real slow and sleeping a lot by mid-November, just before Ray left. One day she slept all day under the azalea bush in the backyard and didn't come out to see me when I came home from school, so Ray decided it was time for her big sleep, as he called it. He's the one who named her.

Ashanti told True and me that the name was taken from the bible, from the Book of Revelation. She says that the United States today is the place where the final battle between good and evil, Armageddon, will be fought, and only good Christian people will be saved. She's always talking about The Rapture. Ray says that's a lot of baloney and I shouldn't pay any attention to it. He says that the Shandaras are the most fanatical of all Christians—the born again kind. Hinduism was their religion when they lived in New Delhi but they converted to Christianity when they became citizens of the Unites States. Ray says it's ironic because the Hindus are tolerant of all other religions and teach that all spiritual practices can lead to self-realization. The Christians, on the other hand, according to Ray, say you have to believe that Jesus died for your sins in order to be saved.

And the thing is, True has started quoting the Bible lately. Her eyes take on a glow like the phenomenon called foxfire, a greenish luminescence caused by fungi growing on rotting wood. I saw it one night in the forest at Granny Tooley's place. True stares straight ahead, like she's looking right through you. Her body gets stiff and shakes like a cat having a fit. Then, in this otherworldly voice, she says things like, 'The Lord will descend from Heaven and we who are in Christ shall rise to meet him in the air.' I don't know if she's for real or just fooling around with me. She says I won't be able to rise up in the air unless I take Christ as my personal savior and she's worried that we'll get separated and won't see each other anymore. Just in case True is right, I ask God, just before I go to sleep at night, if he could put in a good word with his son, Jesus, to save Erma Geddon, my mom and Granny Tooley, and please save Ray and me. God knows the two of us need it.

Ray says the reason he named my tortoise Erma Geddon is because her natural habitat, the Mojave Desert, is being destroyed by off-road vehicles and lots of other things. I start wheezing when I think about all of those glorious tortoises being crushed in their burrows in the sand.

I have asthma pretty bad sometimes. It's worse when I get stressed. I've had it since I was a little kid. That's when Ray started calling me *Wheezer*. He's the only one who calls me that. He has a nickname for everybody. He calls Mom *Olive Oyl* instead of Molly because she's skinny as a stick and has a big head, according to him. I think she has the greatest smile in the world. She's beautiful when she smiles. She hasn't done much of that lately though. She calls Ray *King Ko*ng because he's big and loud. I find his size comforting and even when you're not in the same room with him, you usually always know where he is. Correction: where he was.

They say that during hibernation (it's called brumation when tortoises go to sleep) they don't hear anything, but I wonder if Erma heard all the yelling that went on between Mom and Ray. The sight of Erma has a calming effect on me. I come out to the garage when I'm upset and wheezing, and pull up a chair to sit next to her all snuggled in her sandbox asleep. I stare at her motionless shell (it's called a carapace). The pattern on her back reminds me of the Labyrinth out in the Anaheim Hills where Ray takes me on Halloween. Correction: took me. Erma Geddon looks like she's dead but Ray said her heart is still beating, only real slow.

When Erma's awake, I draw lots of pictures of her, particularly the pattern on her back, in different variations and colors. Her shell reminds me of something Granny Tooley told me. She said the whole history of the world since it was first created is written in Erma Geddon's shell. She said the *I Ching*, an ancient Chinese Oracle that can tell people's fortunes, was figured out eons ago by the wisest men in the world by studying the patterns on the backs of turtles. She said Erma is a *bodhisattva*, a being who has attained enlightenment and could leave this troubled world and be free, but hangs around on earth to help others deal with their suffering. Granny Tooley knows everything, but according to Mom, a lot of what Tooley knows she makes up in her own head. Ray calls her *Dancing with Lies.*

"Are you ready? We need to leave now or we're going to be late picking up True and Jason. And help me load this stuff into the car."

I can hear the rustle of plastic bags filled with bottles of water, a *must have* item for traveling in case you get stuck in traffic on the freeways, and peanut butter sandwiches that I helped make, with lots of homemade grapefruit marmalade. Our neighbor, Marsha, picks the grapefruits from her own tree to make it. I can smell oranges that Mom picked from our tree in the front yard. She made my favorite cake, chocolate marble, with dark chocolate frosting for my birthday party.

We have a brand new Ford SUV. Ray bought it without asking Mom, just before he left. She said it was a gas hog and polluted the air too much, and she went berserk when she found out how much it cost, because she was the one who would be responsible for the payments. Now you have to pry her out of it. She comes home from work at night and sits out there for a long time in the driveway, like Erma when she hides inside her shell. I think Mom does it to get away from me. I know she is real mad at me for breaking her Miles Davis records, and I remind her of my namesake, whom I know she is mad at. And the worst thing is the money I took and all, and how I lied to protect Ray. My mother hates liars. She said if I only knew what it was like growing up around Granny Tooley's fibs I would understand how important it is to tell the truth. Personally, I love Tooley's stories. And if she bends the truth sometimes, it's usually for a good reason. It's called artistic license.

"Mom, Erma's awake. Can we take her with us?" I lift Erma carefully out of her bed, legs paddling the air, and put her down on the cool concrete floor. She darts her head back into her shell for a second, and then pokes it out again and looks up at me with sleepy, loving eyes. You have to be careful about picking up tortoises. If they get scared, like out on a road or in the desert, they could pee and lose precious water that they keep stored up in their bladder for when they need it, and then they could die.

"Hello, my darling. I'm so glad you are awake." I kneel down and kiss the back of her head. She smells like the building blocks of cookie-making: chocolate chips and vanilla. "Let's go out back and get you some food." I open the garage door that leads to the fenced-in back patio and yard and step out, Erma paddling close behind me.

"She's supposed to be sleeping." Mom's voice sounds surprised but not in a good way. As if what a person is supposed to do has anything to do with what they really do.

The air smells of bougainvillea and oranges after yesterday's rain. I love the rain. I don't usually wheeze for at least a day afterwards, unless I'm upset about something, but today I can barely see the snow-dusted mountains peaking up above the high adobe-colored fence that divides our yard from the Gonzales's. Their German shepherd, Percy, sounds like he would tear you limb from limb if he ever got his teeth into you. I climb up on the ladder and look at him through the lacy concrete pattern at the top of the wall. I've only seen the Gonzales's a few times. They've lived there about a year but they work all day. I haven't heard any children's voices in the yard.

I pick some dandelion petals, Erma's favorite dining delight, and lick the yellow pollen from my fingers. It tastes a little like spinach. The sun catches little sparkles of raindrops on the still-wet grass. I sit down on it with Erma by my side. She sniffs my offering, but doesn't seem to be very hungry.

"Why did you take her out of her box?" Mom stands on the patio watching us, cupping a hand over her forehead to keep the sun out of her eyes. It looks as if she's trying to smile but can't.

"She was moving around like she wanted to get out," I said, shrugging my shoulders in a gesture that I inherited from Ray. He used to shrug a lot when he was being accused of something; like whatever it was, was out of his hands…a natural disaster, or an act of God or something. "I can't go and leave her alone the first day she's awake." I rub my chest, feeling a wheeze forming deep in my lungs.

The Burning Jacket

"She'll be fine out here in the yard. She's used to being alone. We've already made plans and shouldn't break them now. And besides, you've been pestering me to go to the tar pits. I've taken the day off." Her voice softens and her face manages a half-smile. "We'll have fun. We hardly spend time together anymore. And it's your birthday." She comes over and puts her arm around my shoulder and kisses the top of my head.

I know it's true about Erma being all right without me. According to a book I read, her species spends ninety-five percent of their time huddled down in burrows, alone. After all, she has succeeded in living nearly a half-century without me. I guess she can survive another day.

My mother's kiss has let loose a landslide of guilt inside of me. I start to say something about how sorry I am for the mess I made, but the words feel like a wadded up message stuck in the neck of a bottle that has bumped around in the ocean for a godzillion years. Nothing comes out but a faint, high-pitched wheeze and some more tears that run down and tickle my neck.

One of Ray's duties, since he rarely had a real job, was to pick me up at school in the afternoons and bring me home, and stay with me until Mom got home around six. He made a secret deal with me to take a taxi home every day and to have the cab stop about a block from the house, and I would walk home from there. Then he would come home about fifteen minutes before Mom did.

He would give me cab money every day and a twenty-dollar bill as a bonus to keep my mouth shut. I don't know where he got the money and I didn't ask. I had a fat roll of portraits of Andrew Jackson tucked down under my collection of reptile socks. (They're not socks for reptiles. They're decorated with frogs and crocodiles and turtles and stuff.) I became as rich as Mrs. Astor. I started carrying a lot of money around in my ugly pink pillbox purse with shiny black plastic straps that True and I found at the Goodwill. The purse appealed to my darker side. On one banjo-flat side in big, black, shiny letters was the message, "You can't afford me." Word got around that I carried a lot of cash in that purse, and I became quite popular at school. Of course I shared fistfuls with True. We spent it on things we aren't allowed to use, like lipsticks and eye shadow, and True bought a new CD of the Hanson brothers, *The Middle of Nowhere*. She thinks they're cute. We lived high on the hog for a while, until True's mom, Ashanti, discovered a pile of bills and a ton of makeup hidden in her daughter's underwear drawer. True was smart enough to know that all the twitching, eye rolling, and screeching in the world wouldn't save her this time. She caved under the pressure of burning in hell for all of eternity, and told how we got the money. Ashanti hot-pedaled it over to the bakery in her new red Porsche and told Mom the whole sordid story. I was caught red-handed getting out of the taxi a block away from home and was relieved of my fortune along with a mighty burden of guilt.

Erma Geddon looks up at me and winks and then lights out with her spread-out flat, muscular legs and strong claws, paddling over to one of the tunnels she has dug to her favorite burrow under the floor of the tool shed. She understands that I have to go, and this is her way of telling me that she'll be all right on her own, and that I'll be all right too.

I receive her message as a warm breeze of relief until reality rushes back in like the Santa Ana winds gusting through the great divide of my broken heart.

I feel a wheeze coming on.

Chapter Two

Molly: February 2000.

Raynie and I are on Highway 57 going to True and Jason's house. It's Raynie's birthday and we're heading for the La Brea tar pits. I can see the concrete buildings spread out below the freeway near the chalky dry riverbed of the Santa Ana River. The plain no-nonsense structures look like illegal squatters, interrupted by the steel angel of the Anaheim Stadium with its dippy halo. I can only assume the architect who designed the sculpture intended it to be a symbol of hope and invincibility, but today it seems like a bad joke, a monument to rotten air.

    A familiar acrid smell fills my nostrils. I feel a tickle in the viscous fluid of my left eye, a wriggling brown worm that leaves zig-zaggy castings in my vision. I can see all right to drive. The doctor said it's nothing to worry about, just an allergic reaction to traffic pollutants. Raynie's allergies are worse; she has asthma.

    The smog sneaked back after the rain, a thief stealing the oxygen from the air. It formed a curtain that looks like melted Gouda cheese across the sky, layering itself between Anaheim and the San Clemente mountains. I hold my breath as long as I can in protest. At sunrise this morning, after last night's rain, I could still make out the shape of the mountains as they pushed against the bell jar of an orange sherbet sky. Now the once clear images are a memory.

I remember when I was a kid and lived in the Anaheim Hills with my dad, Carl, you could see clear out to Santa Catalina Island eighty miles away.

"Mom, will Erma really be all right without me?" Raynie's soft, hesitant voice brings me back to the task at hand, driving in a winding ribbon of traffic on the freeway.

I look over at Raynie. What she seems to be really asking is, "Will we be all right?" Will she and I ever be all right with each other? Will we be all right without Ray?

"Yes, Erma will be just fine, and so will we." I pat her on the knee in a gesture of reassurance, even though I'm not sure about anything.

Raynie doesn't talk much about her father. She hangs out in the room he called his office. He would go in there, lock the door, and shut out the world, saying he had work to do. The only work done in that room was surfing the net for pornography sites, drinking beer and smoking dope.

He came and emptied the room last week while I was at the bakery and Raynie was at school. I found Raynie sitting in there yesterday, on the floor with the door closed, her mood as blue as the carpet, staring at a drawing in black ink she had just completed: a picture of Erma Geddon flanked by a larger desert tortoise on one side and a smaller more feminine looking one on the other. They were holding flippers with brave smiles on their faces that, somehow, conveyed the opposite of hope. The background was a wallpaper of frogs, splayed and plastered on the page like pinned specimens, a dark cloud that rained teardrops of messy ink-blobs running diagonally from the top right corner to the bottom left. The picture was a sinister departure from her usually sun-filled, intensely colored drawings. I think she is talented. She has a strong sense of composition and color.

My thoughts turn to the dream I had last night. I started having the dream when I was around sixteen. I seem to walk in

The Burning Jacket

on it as it's running, like a scene in a movie. Sometimes I catch the beginning, sometimes the middle, but I've never seen the ending. I'm not sure where to place last night's scene. It seems to be close to the end. I write bits and pieces down when I wake up but can't organize them in any cohesive way.

I'm walking through newly plowed fields. The clods of earth smell like wild mushrooms. A man wearing a white linen toga instructs me to pay attention to the hues of the soil underfoot because the umber, burnt sienna, and shades of violet are the exact tones I need when mixing the pigments that make the colors for glazing pots. The man radiates strength of character and kindness. I am overjoyed to see him. I've met him many times before. He is my teacher.

It's autumn, and a slight breeze gifts my nostrils with the musty smell of grapes growing on the mountainside, heavy and ready for harvest like the fruit ripening inside of me. Then, riding on a breeze, there is a slight smell of something new, an intrusive odor of rotten eggs. I put my hand on my rounding belly and rub little circles in a gesture of comfort. I look up at the mountain. It looks peaceful against a cerulean sky. I worry, nonetheless.

For a second, the Highway 57 sign is transformed into a woven tapestry of the intensely saturated earth colors of my dream. A daydream about Raynie dances in my head. *She and I are walking hand in hand, laughing and singing a song in a language I don't understand. It could be Latin, although I've never heard it spoken. A woody, sweet, familiar odor of violets fills my senses: an unexpected gift of grace.* Since that first dream when I was a teenager, this fragrance has embraced me from time to time, out of the blue, while day-dreaming, or doing the most ordinary of things.

The lingering colors of the fields in my dream remind me of a poncho I bought long ago, in Mexico, when Ray and I were first together and Raynie was a small transparent pearl in my womb. At that time my life was full and my heart was a compass pointed straight ahead toward promises neither Ray nor I could fulfill: to love one another forever. I loved that poncho. Accidentally it got mixed in with some old clothes I gave to Goodwill. When I realized what I'd done, I went back to the store but it was already gone.

Raynie has stopped playing the piano since Ray left. Before, you couldn't keep her away from practicing for hours on end. Her teacher, Mr. Harrison, who a few months ago was excited about her progress and said she showed great promise, is threatening to drop her as a student. I called him on the phone and pleaded with him to give her some more time to recover from the shock of the family splitting up, but he wasn't sympathetic. He's newly married with no children yet. I don't think he understands how hard it is on a child when the parents separate. He said he would give her a month to get herself together and start practicing.

I glance over at her again as I drive. If I were to mix the color of my daughter's eyes on a palette, I would squeeze from the tube a glob of aquamarine blue and add a touch of smoky Payne's Gray. She has grown rangy in the last year, like a juvenile coyote… taller than any of her friends and most of the boys her age.

Since Ray left, Raynie has abandoned her straight forward "here I am world" stance, a posture that she inherited from her Granny Tooley, my mother. She's slouched down in the car seat with her arms and legs all twisted in knots. It looks painful. She is a beautiful child with Tooley's high cheekbones, much to my envy. I got stuck with Dad's round full-moon face. Tooley insists that her high cheekbones came from her father who was a Coast Range Indian. At least that's what she tells everybody. I don't think there is anyone alive who knows her true biological

The Burning Jacket

heritage, not even Tooley herself. When I was a child, she told me conflicting stories about my ancestors. I felt like a kite with no tether, flying all alone in the air without a past and no destination, betrayed by her lies.

My throbbing knee rubs against my jeans and reminds me of the fall I took when I stepped off the curb in front of the bakery yesterday. I've fallen three times since Ray left. I don't want Raynie to know. I tend to lose my footing when life falls apart.

Last month, the rug was literally yanked from under me. I came home from work and found my prized oriental carpet missing from the living-room floor. I paid two hundred dollars for it thirteen years ago at a garage sale before I met Ray, in those bittersweet days when I was young, independent, and full of hope.

Those were glorious days mixed with intense grief. Dad was killed in 1986 while crossing the Grapevine coming into Los Angeles in a pile-up during a freak snowstorm. He hadn't amassed a fortune making dentures for a living, but he left me enough money to buy the house outright and start the bakery with my partner Duchess. Dad was the steady, reliable parent during my childhood.

Just before I met Ray, I was painting in the studio every day. The bakery had been open for two years and was coming into its own, finally discovered by local pastry gourmands. Tooley even came to the grand opening along with her friend, The Chief. I never knew his real name. Everyone assumed he was Native American but he had a dark swarthy look, like the gypsies I saw in Spain when Dad surprised me with a trip to Europe for my college graduation from UCLA. The Chief was my mother's benefactor. I don't think they were ever lovers. They never slept in the same bed as far as I knew. The Chief slept out in the woods a lot of the time when I lived with them in the cabin near Roseburg, Oregon, when I was little, before my real father threatened to call the authorities on Tooley for keeping me out of school. She let me go without a fuss, not willing to move into town and be "on the grid" as she called it.

I was six when I moved to the Anaheim Hills to attend regular school. I remember feeling reborn from an alien world to one of safety, comfort, and light. It seemed like magic to turn on a faucet and hot water would flow out, to have instant heat by moving up the red needle on the thermostat, and to cook food without first gathering wood and building a fire. What I liked most was going to the bathroom inside without getting cold or wet. I felt like a queen on a throne sitting on a comfortable toilet seat that flushed with a flick of the wrist

Despite the fact that my mother never had the luxury of a formal education, she speaks with the eloquence of a poet. She taught herself to read and speak correctly. She says there is no excuse for anyone to use poor grammar, whatever their circumstances.

I don't know anything about The Chief's background except he is a throwaway from a war no one wants to remember.

I think about The Chief. I'm sure Tooley loved him. He was like a father to me. What I remember about him was that his head touched the sky and his eyes were wild and shone yellow at night like those of a wolf. He would sometimes pace the cabin like a caged animal and then disappear into the woods for days. I always wondered how he stayed warm at night. Sometimes I could hear him cry, nearby, at the edge of the trees. Other times he would howl and moan. Tooley told me that he wrestled with his demons and to leave him alone and stay clear of him during those times.

The Chief taught me to carve animals from pieces of wood. I used to help him build deer and elk skin drums to sell at the Saturday Market in Eugene. He and Tooley used to play duets to the plants and animals, she on the wooden flute and he on a drum.

Tooley tried to teach me things, like how to spin wool and build a fire, but I resisted learning from her and she would quickly get impatient and stop trying. Spinning wool seemed to me, and still does, a waste of time when you can walk into a store and buy yarn from anywhere in the world.

The Chief had a commanding presence. He didn't speak often and when he did, everyone listened, expecting pearls of wisdom to flow from lips that were hidden by a mass of black curly hair. But instead, in a thunderous voice, he would repeat slogans he learned in the Marine Corps. Things like, "Death smiles at everyone, Marines smile back." And, "You will die, I will die a Marine."

For the grand opening of the bakery, Tooley and The Chief drove down in their Ford truck, Dorothy Ann, and performed a special ceremony to banish negative vibrations from the building. In her typical theatrical style, Tooley, with sweeping waves of her arms, held bundles of burning sage and whirled around the room chanting something unintelligible while The Chief beat a slow rhythm on his drum to call forth propitious spirits that would lead the bakery to financial success.

After the long drive, they wouldn't come home with us to spend the night. Tooley told me that The Chief was uncomfortable in enclosed spaces. They drove away into the night in Dorothy Ann, immediately after their smoke and mirrors performance. The Chief disappeared into thin air a year after the christening of the bakery according to Tooley, at a Harmonic Conversion ceremony at Mount Shasta.

Things were going well for me when I bought the bakery, and then I met Ray and lost my sanity. A huge part of me wishes we'd never met. But then I wouldn't have Raynie. And I can't imagine living without her.

Ray and I had the Oriental rug he stole from me appraised last year. Turns out it's a silk picture rug from Persia, made especially for a couple for their wedding. The appraiser told us it would bring around twenty thousand on today's market. I'm sure Ray has already sold it. When I called the police about the matter, they told me their hands were tied. As long as Ray and I are still married, Ray owns half of everything. That's when I had the locks to the front and back door changed.

My magic carpet. My prayer rug. My Before Ray Rug. The rich reds and deep blues would send me into a trance while I sat, limber as a gymnast, in lotus position, and coaxed the sun from its slumber. Afterwards I would take my morning cup of coffee out to the garage—it was my studio then, before Ray filled it up with expensive junk he compulsively purchased. I would paint for three hours before relieving Duchess at the bakery. I had begun to exhibit my work, even had an article written about me in the Anaheim *Register*. Then I got pregnant and married Ray, and it all ended.

Duchess had warned me about Ray, more than once. I remember the Tarot reading she had done for me during the early days of our courtship. Ray has a big, clumsy body and his captivating smile could render me speechless in those days. The fuzz on my arms and legs stood on end when he walked into a room, and the sight of his hairy chest triggered warm, moist tremors deep inside the awakening volcano between my thighs.

"Don't throw your pearls before swine, Queenie," Duchess said in her nasal New York accent; her quick, brown eyes troubled. Duchess was buxom, with dark auburn hair that fell to her waist but was kept imprisoned in braids for the sake of bakery hygiene. At night, it flowed in Rapunzel-like waves, just daring some handsome prince to try to climb the tower she had built around her heart. Duchess was tough. Grew up in a Jewish ghetto in Brooklyn. Knew her way around the streets and could sniff out a fake in the blink of an eye. A throwback to the seventies, she wore Birkenstocks, long skirts, smelled of patchouli oil, and rocked, while kneading bread, to her favorite music. Usually Marvin Gaye's "Let's Get It On."

"There's the damned Knight of Swords again," Duchess had said, looking at the cards. "He seems to show up in all of your layouts lately. And coupled with the Three of Swords, I don't know, but that spells danger." She shook her head causing her braids to swing from side to side like a pendulum.

I looked at the bloody heart with three swords thrust through it. How could I take the reading seriously? My Ray was heaven on earth. The cards were wrong.

"The Knight of Swords is reversed." An angry looking young man in full armor rode a white horse into what looked like a rainstorm brandishing a sword, ready for battle. Dark jagged clouds filled the background. "Reversed, it means indiscreet, extravagant, foolish, unfaithful. He's trouble. I'm telling you." Duchess rubbed the pale violet amethyst crystal that hung like a bullet on a silver chain around her neck.

Duchess confessed to me later that Ray tried to hit on her more than once while he was dating me. He told her then that he preferred large women. I should have seen the warning signs. She should have told me. But would I have listened?

Duchess and I met in an existential literature class at UCLA. We used to read Camus and Sartre out loud to each other and ponder the nature of human existence. We've been fast friends ever since. She is the foundation of the bakery. I'm the icing. She creates earthy loaves of our now famous flaxseed and sunflower sprout bread, honey raisin whole wheat, and crackly-crusted round loaves studded with olives and pepper. I nicknamed her the Duchess of Loaves, and she dubbed me the Queen of Cupcakes, shortened to Duchess and Queenie. Her given name is Laurie.

I handle all the sweet stuff. The bakery is named after my special coffee cake, Orange County Sunrise, a rich concoction of flour, butter, sour cream, orange juice and lots of orange zest, iced with a cream cheese and honey spread. It took some time to perfect. Now it's a favorite on breakfast tables and restaurants all over Anaheim, Los Angeles, and as far south as San Diego.

If only I had heeded Duchess's warnings. I ignored my own instincts as well.

After Raynie's forced confession about Ray bribing her with lots of money (where the hell was he getting it?) and leaving her alone at home for three hours every afternoon, I took a day off work, borrowed my neighbor Marsha's car and followed him.

First stop was the Rio Real Liquor store on Lincoln. He was in a huddle out in front of the store with several greasy teenagers of Hispanic ethnicity. After about a half an hour it looked like they had come to some agreement that involved laughter and a high-five to each other. Then Ray went into the liquor store and came out with a brown paper bag stuffed with what looked to be the size and shape of a fifth of something. I thought he was buying alcohol for the boys but they had already left. He tucked the bag under his arm, got into the SUV and headed down Lincoln to Beach Boulevard and Stanton, parked at a sleazy motel in front of room 121, and got out carrying the bag. I sat in the car for what seemed like an eternity and listened to Deepak Chopra tapes that Duchess had loaned me on how to attain peace and enlightenment. My head pounded and I was hyperventilating despite Chopra's calm nasal voice.

Finally, they came out of the room together. Ray and a fat, pimply-faced blond, who looked to be around sixteen, dressed in pink pedal pushers, a spaghetti strap, low-cut T-shirt that revealed cleavage as deep as the Grand Canyon, with the words "I'm Bitchin" written across her chest. Her stomach cascaded down over the pedal pushers like toxic waste, and her belly button sported a stud that sparkled like a gold filling in a pimp's mouth as it caught the sun. They were hugging and laughing. She got into a blue Toyota and drove away. I cut Ray off before he got into the new SUV he enjoyed, thanks to my hard-earned money. I resisted the urge to smash him against the car with the Honda but then remembered it was borrowed and I still had payments on the SUV. Reason kicked in, but rage and hurt kicked Ray out of my heart that day.

I am so lost in my thoughts that I don't remember when Raynie and I changed freeways to Interstate-5. I turn my right blinker on and move to exit at the Culver Drive ramp. We circle around the block to True's house, a large, stucco, Spanish-style structure surrounded by a high wrought-iron fence covered in jacarandas. The gate is open and we drive up the wide, circular driveway. True and Jason run out from the front entrance, which is flanked on either side by two large terracotta planters filled with red geraniums. Ashanti waves and comes around to the driver's side as her children jump into the back seat.

"Hey. How are you? I've been meaning to call to see how you're doing, but I was so busy with Christmas and church stuff." Her words, heavy with a punctuated accent, and guilt, roam several octaves on the scale from high to low. Ashanti is beautiful, with dark eyes and silky, long black hair held back in a chignon. Few of my old friends have called me in the last few months since Ray left. Not that Ashanti is really a friend. We don't socialize together other than coordinating picking up the girls or dropping them off somewhere.

She pokes her head in the back window. "You two behave now, and don't give Molly any trouble." Ashanti looks like a graceful doe gazing at her children. She often wears beautiful silk saris but today she has on white shorts, a T-shirt and spotless white tennis shoes, the contrast showcasing her dark, smooth skin.

I glance in the rear view mirror at her children. True is dark, petite, pretty, with almond-shaped eyes, the same age as

Raynie. She was adopted from a missionary orphanage in Indonesia when she was two years old. And Jason, True's brother, is twelve. Jason was adopted a few years ago from an agency in Los Angeles. His mother had been hooked on amphetamines when he was born and he spent most of his early years bouncing around foster homes. He looks like a typical pubescent boy, with a face full of ripe pimples and hair that covers most of his eyes. He grunts a reluctant hello, and slouches down in the seat, plugged in at the ears to a portable CD player. He wears a constant frown, speaks in monosyllables, and his face is perennially flushed.

The Shandaras have a twenty-one year old son, Delmar, born to them in India. I have seen him only a few times, during holidays. He was attending a Christian college somewhere out of state and recently quit. Raynie said he was being forced by his parents to be a minister. True told Raynie that their folks still think he is attending school but he has secret plans to join the Marine Corps. She made me swear under oath that I would not tell Ashanti. But now I'm feeling guilty about the promise and may have to break my word.

"Sorry I can't go with you." Ashanti seems in a hurry to have us gone, orchestrating directions with sweeping hands and fire-engine red acrylic fingernails that get overhauled every two weeks by a Vietnamese lady at one of numerous beauty salons tucked into almost every commercial complex in southern California.

"Just get back on the Santa Ana North, take the Santa Monica West, get off at Exit 8 and turn right, then right again onto La Brea, make a left on Wilshire Boulevard. You can't miss it, there's a big sign that says Page Museum." She waves us off before I even start the engine.

* * *

The parking lot at the museum is full of cars and school buses. I take the ice chest with the picnic lunch out of the back of the SUV and carry it in with me. I don't want the icing on the cake to melt in the hot car. The lady who sells us tickets says she will be glad to stash it behind the counter in the air-conditioned building.

"If we get separated after the lecture and movie, we'll all meet here by the entrance to the auditorium in one hour for lunch, okay?"

I'm saying this mostly for Jason's benefit, he has a tendency to get lost, like a dog off his leash. I plan to stick close to the girls even though they race ahead to get seats on the bottom tier in the auditorium. They're oblivious to everyone around them, giggling and practically sitting on top of one another. Raynie, all arms and legs, looks even taller next to tiny True, who can't be more than four and a half feet. The place is abuzz with the voices of excited children. Jason climbs to the top tier, looking surly and lost without his safety blanket. The docent made him hand over his CD player and earphones.

The lights dim and a sun rises through a soft haze on the big screen. The trumpeting voice of what sounds like an elephant fills the suddenly silent theater. Two American mastodons emerge from the mist, a mother and her six-year-old daughter we are told. They're trapped, side-by-side, horror on their faces, struggling to free themselves from the sticky tar. Their real bones were recovered intact from Pit 91 and are on display in the museum. I feel the anguish of the mother on the screen trying desperately to protect her offspring. I think about the dream I had last night. Life stirred in my dream womb. I had felt endangered by an unnamable threat.

Since the birth of Raynie I have had conflicted dreams about being free, without the heavy burden motherhood imposes, and at the same time loving Raynie intensely and feeling the need to protect my child from all harm.

The narrator continues his drone. I feel like a time-traveler shuttling back and forth through a warp.

"In the four-and-a-half billion-year history of the Earth, the fossils from Rancho La Brea were formed anywhere from nine thousand to forty thousand years ago, and have defined an interval of time—the *Rancholabrean* Land Mammal Age, which represents the last five hundred thousand years of the late Pleistocene Epoch. If the Earth's history was reduced to a twenty-four day, the La Brea fossils would have been deposited in what is now downtown Los Angeles three-fourths of a second before the end of the day."[1]

I look over at Raynie and True. Their shoulders touch as they lean in to one another, almost imitating the same gesture of caring as the two mastodons on the screen. My throat tightens. How do I show Raynie how much I love her and still convey to her that she must be responsible for the consequences of her actions? How do I let her know that, even though I'm still angry about her covering for Ray, I will always protect her, and feel her as a constant bright presence in my heart forever, through all of space and time?

After the presentation I stroll around the museum shadowing Raynie and True. True seems more interested in orbiting Raynie than looking at the exhibits. Raynie, on the other hand, looks totally absorbed by the fossils on display—mastodons, bison, camels, American lions, mammoths, and ancient species of horses, tigers, and dire wolves. There are also replicas of birds of prey, reptiles, fish, and even skeletons of fleas and iridescent beetles, all victims of the tar pits. Raynie seems particularly interested in the reptile exhibits. *No surprise*.

We rendezvous with Jason at noon. He is waiting by the theater door, red-faced and silent, but on time. Raynie hops up

---

[1] Terra, Vol. 38, No. 2. June 2001.

and down and holds out her wrist to show me the silver turtle for her charm bracelet that True gave her for a birthday present. I haven't seen her this happy since Ray's departure.

I go back to the front desk and pick up the ice chest and follow the girls outside with Jason bringing up the rear. We sit in a cathedral of cypress and pepper trees, next to the pools of bubbling tar, guarded by a giant casting of a mastodon while eating our peanut butter sandwiches and drinking lemonade from paper cups.

The smell of methane gas bubbles up from Pit 91 and mingles with the sharp oily odor of tar, rivaling the brown, sulfuric emissions of present-day traffic.

A ribbon of cars and trucks snake by on Wilshire Boulevard less than a football field away. The immensity of this juxtaposition is stunning. I shiver, grow limp with wonder and fear as I silently shout *Bravo! Beware!*

I stand and clap an ovation to the endurance and vulnerability of all forms of life.

I light the candles on my daughter's birthday cake.

She makes a silent wish.

Her youthful joy fills my heart.

All of time and space merge into one as she blows out eleven candles on her cake with a single breath.

Chapter Three

Tooley: Early March 2000, Southern Oregon.

"Well, hello Miss Tooley. Haven't seen you since hell froze over. Been hidin' in the woods?" Ed Dice rearranges his ample bottom on the high wooden stool behind the counter. Like a puffed up tomcat grooming himself for an encounter with a female from the feline species, he runs his fingers through his hair that is now little more than a whispered prayer. He takes the toothpick out of his mouth, licks his lips, and winks at me like I'm a fat mouse he's about to devour.

With the exception of Ed Dice, I love everything about the Feed and Seed Exchange in Roseburg. The acrid smell of burlap gunny sacks rolled back at the openings like turned down cuffs on hand-knitted socks, filled with seed potatoes, sulfurous smelling red, white, and yellow onion bulbs, various grains, and grass seeds are like a ceremonial welcome to spring. The gardener within me quickens. I want to rush home and get out the rototiller even though the ground is still too wet.

As I near the counter I see only a one-gallon jar left of my herbal tea concoction: peppermint, lemon balm, raspberry leaves, and elderberry flowers that look like tiny snowflakes. Pride fills me to see the jar is almost empty, nearly sold out at a dollar an ounce. The mixture looks festive, like Christmas confetti with the dried red rosehips mixed with the green herbs. I peddle it to the locals as an infusion to ward off colds, sore throats, and flu. Don't have hard evidence to prove that it doesn't work. Next month it'll be time to once again start gathering the early harvest: wild nettle, and Oregon grape leaves in the woods around my cabin.

I catch my dead mother's joy, a palpable presence, as I unscrew the lid of the jar and inhale, flying on the wings of scent straight back to her arms, a child again, without a care, weightless, dancing in circles around her.

Every day spent with Mama was a time of lightness and grace. I was five when she died but I remember her lessons. She taught me that the first cuttings have the most power to heal. She walks beside me in spirit as I gather herbs from the bountiful earth and we celebrate the brief time we had together.

We are in the potting shed where she dries the wild herbs she collects in the woods and down by the river. I feel safe with her as she bundles the perfumed plants to dry. "Make sure you gather the nettle in the early spring when the leaves are young and tender. When they are older the oils will burn your skin." I hear her soft voice.

"What do you need today besides a big old bear hug from Ed Dice?"

Ed's voice makes my body stiffen. I ignore the remark. It's best to nip in the bud any fantasies he may have about me. He's a horny old man, and nosy to boot. "I need a hundred pounds of dog food and eighty pounds of chicken feed," I say.

"Hold on there. What's the big rush? Always dartin' around the store like a hummingbird. You never light anywhere for even a minute." Then he smiles and sticks his tongue through the gap where his upper front teeth once called home.

"I got five dozen fresh eggs out in the truck if you want them," I say gruffly, ignoring his questions and the lascivious gyrations of his tongue.

"Yeah, sure, I'll take anything you got. Your eggs are the

best. They sell real good. And you got the prettiest eyes in the world. You sellin' them too?" He laughs and puts his hands over the family jewels as if the gesture will ignite my passion.

I pull three plastic bags from the roller by the counter, and put a scoop full of each color of onion in their respective bags.

"Them's real good yellow seed potatoes. New this year. Supposed to be better than Yukon Gold. Here let me get you some to try. On the house." He sidles up beside me, his left arm touching my right, as he bends over to scoop the potatoes. I jump back, feeling the boundary that has been breached.

"I don't want any seed potatoes. Got plenty. Get my dog food and chicken feed. I'll go out and get the eggs." I make a beeline for the door.

Ed is behind the counter when I come back.

"Looks like I owe you money. Sold all of your eggs and tea from last month. I owe you fifty dollars." He opens the till. With a sideways Sylvester Pussy Cat smile he says, "Hold out your hand." I don't, and he counts out two twenties and a ten onto the counter top.

"Why don't you let me deliver the stuff you need once a month out to your place? It'll save you from coming all the way in to town. I know you don't like to hobnob much with the local yokels, but Ed Dice will be glad to help you out."

He always talks about himself in the third person like he's a visiting celebrity, or maybe it's his way of detaching himself from the consequences of his obnoxious behavior. He has a wife of forty some odd years at home.

"You know all I got for you is a post office box here in Roseburg. I need your real address. Just write it on this sales slip."

"You got all the information you need. Why would you ever need my address?" I feel like an exposed hermit crab frantically trying to find a new home in which to hide.

"Tax purposes. That's what." He stands there thrusting the sales slip and a pen my way.

"Ed Dice, you are so full of shit it's coming out your ears. I'm not giving you my address. Just get my stuff and I'll be gone. If you bother me again I'll just have to shop at the feed store at the other end of town." I shoo him away as I would an unruly rooster. Without a word he follows me out to the truck and loads my feed: the dog food in twenty-pound bags, and the chicken feed in two bags of forty pounds so I can unload them by myself at home.

"You forgot hay."

"Don't need any."

Ed comes right up to the truck as I get in, slam the door, and lock it. He puts his hands, flat-palmed on the driver's window, and says something I can't understand.

"Get your god-dammed hands off my truck."

I pray that Dorothy Ann will start without a push as I pump the gas pedal and hope I don't flood the engine. She needs a start in the mornings like I do. She's been a reliable companion for more years than I can remember, back when The Chief gave her to me.

The Chief. I watched him disappear before my eyes in a ray of pink light on August 17, 1987, during a drumming ceremony on Mount Shasta at the Harmonic Convergence among a gathering of thousands. Bless his tortured soul. I've tried, but have not been able to contact his spirit.

Dorothy Ann does not disappoint. She jerks forward with a cough of the engine.

"You ornery old woman! What the hell is the matter with you?" Ed shakes one fist in the air while grooming the latent fur on his head with the other, ever hopeful. I give him the finger and mouth "asshole," gritting my teeth as Dorothy Ann lurches again and then warms to a purr.

Chapter Four

Raynie: March 2000.

"Open the door. I know you're in there, bitch! How dare you change the locks. We're still legally married, you know. And when the divorce is final half of everything is mine, including our daughter." Bang! Bang! Bang "I could come and take her away and you'd never see her again. Come on open up. All I want to do is see Wheezer and wish her happy birthday."

"You're a month too late for that. Go away or I'll call the police and get a restraining order against you. Leave us alone, and stop shouting. You'll scare Raynie."

My mom's voice sounds small and creaky like the old wooden floor in Granny Tooley's cabin.

I'm under my bed trying to calm Erma Geddon. She hid when she heard all the yelling. Ray sounds like he's trying to break down the door. Erma doesn't like loud noises. Her muscles get tight when she's scared and she tucks her head into her shell.

It's Saturday morning. Normally I would be on the computer e-mailing True, but Ray came and stole my computer out of the bedroom yesterday while Mom and I were gone. At least Mom thinks it was Ray's doing. But I'm not convinced that he would be mean enough to steal my computer. Whoever did it came through my window. There was shattered glass all over the floor. Mom had the window replaced right away, with double panes and a strong lock. I'm glad Erma was okay. I would die if anybody hurt her or took her away. I'm not sure Ray was the culprit who stole Mom's prayer rug either.

I'm torn. Part of me is afraid of Ray, and part of me wants to go and open the door and give him a big hug, but Mom ordered me to stay in my room with the door locked when she heard him hollering and banging on the door.

A few months ago, Ray started calling in the middle of the night. Mom said he sounded drunk or high on drugs, or both, saying things like, "I'm coming to get my daughter and you'll never see her again!"

One night last week he came to the door about three in the morning and said he had a gun and wouldn't hesitate to use it if I didn't come with him right then. Thank God, Mom had the locks changed after he stole her rug. She threatened to call the police and he ran away.

I'd call True but my cell phone is in the living room and Mom will have a fit if I go out and get it.

"You're a filthy bitch with a capital B," he yells.

Now it sounds like he's trying to kick down the front door with his feet.

"I know people. I could put a hit on you anytime I want, bitch!"

"Ray, please go away and leave us alone. I know you've been drinking and don't mean what you're saying, but for Raynie's sake, go home."

"Home? I have no home because of you. You don't have a clue about what I've been through. My credit's no good. I just got evicted from my apartment. I can't get into my storage unit because I haven't been able to pay the rent. If you could just give me enough money for that I could get that travel trailer out and park it in the backyard and live here for a while until I get a job and get on my feet." I hear loud belching. "Come on, Molly. What do you say?" His voice is soft and pleading.

"Get some money from your rich parents and stop bothering me."

I hear Mom talking on the phone. I assume she has called the police.

"I can't get hold of them. They're flitting around Europe somewhere. Nobody cares about me. I want to see my Wheezer." More loud kicking and yelling.

"It's bad enough that you stole my prayer rug but to steal your daughter's computer is inexcusable." Mom is crying.

"We aren't divorced yet. And when we are, half of everything is mine, including my daughter. And why haven't you even filed for divorce yet if you want to get rid of me so bad?"

"Believe me I will do just that Monday morning. And that rug was mine before I even met you, so you had no right to take it."

Erma's head is still tucked inside her shell. I wish I had a shell to hide in. I feel hot and cold at the same time. I want to be out of my skin. Out of my body.

"At least loan me a hundred dollars. I don't even have enough money for food. And what's all this talk about a restraining order? I don't even have a place to stay where they can serve it on me."

"Don't worry. I know where you get your mail. I'll have the marshal deliver it there."

"Well, if you think a damn restraining order is going to keep me away, you are mistaken!"

The knocking sounds compete with the screams of sirens. A moment of silence and then I hear the police knock at the door.

"He ran away when he heard you coming," I hear my mother say to the police.

When the police leave, I unlock the door and go to the

living room, relieved that it's all over, but sad that I didn't get to see Ray. I could have maybe talked him into not yelling, and being nice to Mom, and make him stop calling her bad names. Mom gives me a hug and we cry together.

    I go back in the bedroom, shut the door, pull the blanket off the bed, and drag it under the bed where Erma is waiting for me. I have a first class headache, with chills and fever. Think I'm getting the flu.

Chapter Five

Tooley: March 2000, Southern Oregon.

Raynie is perched on the edge of the weathered wooden bench by the Greyhound bus station, feet resting on top of her red scotch plaid suitcase, when I pull up to the curb in Dorothy Ann. No one else around. I must have gotten the arrival time wrong.

She looks abandoned save for the dappled sunlight from the great oak tree that dances a blessing on her features in a gentle doting way. She sees Dorothy Ann and me, a smile of relief brightens her face. She rushes over to the curb with arms outstretched as I get out of the truck.

"How long have you been sitting here? I'm sorry I'm late." I look at my wrist as if consulting a watch, a reflexive gesture that surprises me since I've never worn a watch. It seems bizarre to strap on one's arm a constant reminder of life marching forward, in tiny goose-stepping tick-tocks toward its inescapable conclusion. The arthritis in my bones is reminder enough that time is running out. My hold on the earth seems more tenuous by the day.

"How are Kachina and Kevin and Gattita? Has Annie had her baby yet? And have the hens hatched any baby chicks? Erma Geddon woke up early. I wanted to bring her but she wouldn't like the rain and cold weather. And the bus ride probably would have scared her." Raynie stops for breath. She is a whirlwind of energy eager to suck up all the news from the farm and tell me about her life since our visit last summer. She pauses long enough for me to kiss her on her cheek.

"Annie had a boy. Looks like his fleece is going to be prize. He's out in the barn waiting for you to name him. And all the dogs and cats are fine. And the chickens can't wait to see you." I sling Raynie's suitcase in the back of the truck, the movement eliciting a twinge of pain in my right shoulder as I look up at a clear sky.

"Your stuff will be all right in the back. It's not going to rain today." We get into the truck. "Are you hungry? Want to stop for one of Alisha's veggie burgers over at the Liar's Café?" An exaggerated nod in the affirmative is her answer.

* * *

There is a late-afternoon lull in the café. The bulk of the customers are loggers who come at daybreak for breakfast. Every morning a free breakfast is given to a logger who can tell the tallest tale. One lone man in overalls and heavy boots sits at the counter eating apple pie and drinking coffee. Raynie makes a beeline for the red-topped stools at the counter and twirls herself around a few times, then sets a few more stools spinning with her hand. She notices my hesitation. I feel a familiar panic in my gut and a prickling up my spine at the thought of sitting with my back to the open door, leaving me vulnerable.

"It's all right, Granny Tooley. We can sit at a table. You can sit over here." Raynie directs me to a chair in front of a solid brick wall. "Always cover your back," she winks at me.

A boy who looks to be little older than Raynie (I don't recognize him) comes to the table. He is like a puppet come to life at the sight of her. Raynie orders without consulting a menu. "I want a veggie burger and a chocolate hazelnut milkshake."

"Where's Alisha?" I ask the boy. I'm aware of a deep

furrowing in my forehead despite my efforts to stop the gesture.

"Oh, she's taken the day off. I'm her nephew. My name's Ralph," he says to reassure me.

"I'll have exactly what she's having," I say, trying my hardest to smile back at him with a face that has stiffened without consent from my mind. I expected to see Alisha and I don't take well to sudden changes.

When the waiter walks away Raynie pats my arm with a comforting gesture "Granny Tooley, you're an animal person, not a people person. You're like me. I'd rather be with Erma Geddon than anybody I know, except, maybe you, and True." Raynie sighs.

Her once innocent clear eyes, placid as a remote mountain lake, now reflect turbulence, a hurt I've not seen before. Molly had mentioned in her letter that Ray had moved out and they were getting a divorce and Raynie was having a hard time of it. Ray reminds me of a fat forest slug, slow and slimy, but I know that Raynie adores her father, and for that reason I hope he and Molly can work things out.

Raynie is taller than when I saw her last summer. She's beginning to lose her stick-like shape in favor of an hourglass figure. Her breasts are budding.

I long to hold back time. She is not yet interested in boys and doesn't understand the effect she has on them. Raynie retains a charming unselfconscious peace with her body. She has on a brand new sweater of California weight, not nearly warm enough for Oregon in early spring. I have just finished knitting a handmade one for her, from Annie's wool.

It was a crystal late spring day and a bit nippy last year when I sheared dear Annie. She seemed to know she was sacrificing her warm coat to make someone she loved a warm and comfy sweater. She stood straight and still and I sheered in long ripples of cuts. I spun the soft merino fleece into wool over the long rainy winter days until I had enough skeins of yarn for the project.

I had traded some wool at the Saturday market for a washtub full of black walnuts, tub and all. I put the tub on the porch by the front door and covered the walnuts with water. Every time I remembered, I peed in the tub so the color would become fast and penetrate the yarn. The dark brown was to be the background color of the sweater with accents inspired by forest foliage and red onionskins, which provided a rose color to match the rosehips left hanging on leafless bushes. The mugwort I planted in last year's garden gave a yellow green like the new growth on the tips of Douglas fir trees in the early spring, and the light green was provided by a surprise find, some lovely soft lichen that the coyote I was tailing led me to, up the hill and to the right about a mile or so. A wind had blown down an abundance of the lichen from the big fir trees. You would have thought I had struck gold. I yipped and danced around in circles trying to call the coyote closer to thank him for leading me to this treasure. He hadn't come any closer but he hadn't run away either. He stood on the ridge of the hill and looked down at me.

I look down at Raynie's lightweight tennis shoes, and then at my sturdy Danner boots, mud crusted on the sides. If this weather holds, she won't need more than tennis shoes.

I look up at a sky empty of clouds or rain. The rain is like a nourishing mother, my surrogate mother. The lack of it is felt as a space around my heart that not even my radiant, enthusiastic granddaughter can completely fill.

Chapter Six

Raynie: March 2000, Southern Oregon.

"Raynie, you are a well-stirred stew."

Tooley pokes the fire with her willow stick. The two of us are perched on a giant Douglas fir stump. There are six of them cross cut and arranged in a circle around a bonfire out in the open field behind Tooley's cabin, next to her fenced in garden. It's the only place where we can build a fire and not burn down the forest. The trees in this spot were felled years earlier, before Tooley moved in. If you haven't been to Tooley's place before you probably would never find it, tucked away in the middle of an old-growth forest. The cabin was built by Tooley's friend, the legendary Chief. He left or died before I was born.

I overheard Mom tell Ray that Tooley and The Chief were illegal squatters on the land, that it belonged to a big timber company. Tooley says the land doesn't belong to any one person, that we are all caretakers of the earth.

Tooley calls this place where the trees were cut *the gathering of the fallen*, or *the conclave of chiefs*. In honor of the slain trees, Tooley plants circles of nasturtiums around the stumps every spring.

As if reading my mind about the fallen trees, Tooley begins to talk about the thing that most breaks her heart.

"The dignity of the land is violated, and Mother Earth and all the creatures that live in the forest are betrayed each time an old-growth tree falls at the hands of the loggers." She pokes harder at the fire with her stick.

Tooley believes that the trees have souls and the spirits are still alive in the stumps and deserve to be heard. When the wind blows through the treetops it sounds like woody whispers and the bark crackles and moans. So far, I think only Tooley can understand what the trees say, and maybe the dogs.

Kachina and Kevin look like Mutt and Jeff with similar colors and markings. Kachina is a German Shepherd, and Kevin is a Corgi. Every once in a while they roust themselves from a deep sleep, jump up and howl like they've heard a ghost.

"When we cut all the trees, and the earth is flat, the souls of all the people and the animals will fly away in the air to another place." Tooley looks solemn.

"What about your cabin? Isn't that built of wood? Don't people need the trees to build their houses? And where will all the animals and people go? And will only the Christians rise up in the air?" I ask in one breath. We're performing our usual spring cleansing ritual, the burning of garden debris and bags of trash that couldn't be disposed of all winter in the cabin's wood stove. We also have a personal spring-cleaning. Tooley says it's good for the soul to reflect on the year just gone by.

We write out our personal agenda of things to get rid of in our minds on brown paper grocery bags, not to be shared with anyone, unless we want to. We write down habits we want to shed, things we regret having said or done, and a list of things we want to do in the future.

I wrote so long my hand started buzzing, and then got a cramp in it, so I quit before the list was finished. They were mostly things for which I wanted to be forgiven. And the things I want to accomplish this year, like grow boobs and get my belly button pierced. Well, those are really True's recent aspirations, but since she's my best friend, I'll go along with her.

My real goal is to save the world. Mostly I want to save the animals, like Erma Geddon, from becoming extinct because of what we humans do in the name of progress. Sometimes it's hard for people to know what to do to help, and I want to teach them.

After unburdening myself of three pages of sins, I am savoring a marshmallow toasted to perfection, charred on the outside and runny on the inside. I've participated in this sacred rite of spring since before I could read or write. Tooley had a dream one night that told her we should do this every year. The tree stumps feel a little softer each year, and there are little piles of sawdust where bugs have slowly eaten away at the wood. Everything changes with time.

The trillium, wild currant, and scotch broom that edge the clearing are in full bloom. Erma Geddon would love this place if it were only warmer. A cold gust of wind sounds like an old woman moaning as it blows in and whips the blaze to a frenzy causing little sparks to dance circles in the air.

"Speak, Sister Wind," Tooley says.

She's standing, holding up her stick, and addressing the air. She sits back down on her own special stump. She is not as straight as last summer; her eggshell body is cocooned like a butterfly larva in the burning jacket, a heavy, felted monstrosity the color of urine, spotted with black rimmed-craters where wayward sparks from past fires have burned through the dense wool. It smells like sour milk and lanolin, like Annie and her new lamb, which I have named Raoul in honor of his Spanish heritage. He is bred from merino sheep first brought to Spain by the Moors. The sheep are prized for their fine fleece for spinning.

Tooley taught me that bit of history, and she is going to teach me to spin this week. First with a hand spindle, then I'll graduate to the two-peddled wheel that The Chief made for her a long time ago.

The Burning Jacket

At night, when the rain falls on the tin roof of the cabin, Tooley sits and cards the unwashed fleece into roving. That means she combs the fleece and when she takes it off the comb it rolls up like big sausages ready to spin and these are called roving. Then she spins the carded roving into yarn. She calls it "spinning in the grease." I love the smell of lanolin and the way the wool twists itself on the spindle of the big wheel as she peddles with her feet, keeping pace with the falling rain.

Granny Tooley chooses to ignore my questions about how people build houses without wood, and if only the Christians get to rise in the air and leave when the planet is destroyed by clear-cutting, natural disasters, or atomic bombs.

Her white braid looks like a rope of giant hand-spun yarn as it trellises down her back to just above her waist. She stares into the fire. I look sideways at her. Winter gray rings circle the speckled blue irises of her eyes that are the exact color of robin's eggs. Once I found the shell of a robin's egg in the forest not far from here and it took my breath away with surprise, the same way Tooley's eyes do when I first look into them after I haven't seen her for a while. They remind me of Erma Geddon's eyes—kind, wise, and sad, yet ever watchful. They seem to hold a great mystery that can't be spoken. I've learned from Tooley that not everything can be named and classified like I want it to be.

"You come from the pioneers; steady, honest, hard-working, self-reliant God-fearing people, with a vision of a new land, a hope for new life in their hearts, mixed with stubborn, Indian, coyote-trickster blood that will serve to wriggle your way out of any mess. You remember that. You can only know who you are by those who came before you."

Tooley spins stories like she spins fleece. She's telling me the history of the burning jacket, how it was first made and then passed down, along the matriarchal line, from one generation to the next. I haven't heard this version before.

"Is this a true story?" I ask. Not sure how much I want to get invested in it, although I seem to absorb all of her stories like a thirsty sponge that has been out in the desert for a long time and is suddenly thrown into a big puddle of water. Tooley is in her best story-telling mode while huddled around a fire, wrapped in her tatty old burning jacket. It almost doesn't matter what she says, the magic is in the telling.

"Oh pooh. Who cares? What is truth anyway?" Tooley says. "Truth is like an ocean with forever shifting tides and unfathomable depths." She waves her hand in the air, the hand not holding the stick. "Sometimes you have to grab a thought out of thin air and make it true to suit the needs of the time." She seems disgruntled by my questions.

"Back to the story. Your great-great-great grandmother Olive had been married six months shy of her seventeenth birthday but her husband got the wanderlust and uprooted her from her home and family in Nebraska when she was three months pregnant with your great-great grandmother, Cecilia, to follow a pipe dream out west along the Oregon Trail. Olive fashioned this jacket from scratch, starting with the shearing of the sheep in the spring of 1860." A faint smell of lanolin still lingers in the burning jacket, binding the present with the past as the story unfolds.

"Olive's scissors snipped away at the heavy coat the animal had grown to withstand the harsh Nebraska winters. The jacket was to be a surprise gift for her husband, Dandrun Fox, for the long journey to the great Northwest. He had told her stories about the majesty of the country, the high snow-capped mountains of the Sierras, the giant trees that formed natural cathedrals flanking the great Pacific Ocean."

Tooley pauses a moment and looks deep into the fire.

"After skirting the bottom part of the fleece, cutting away the edges that drag along the ground, collecting cockle burs and various grass seeds along with bits of excrement, she washed the fleece in a large tin tub with a goodly amount of soap she'd made by rendering hog fat and lye, then soaked and rinsed the thick mat of wool a few times, careful to leave enough lanolin in to keep the material well-insulated. In an empty feed trough, Olive stretched out the fleece, built a fire nearby, and fed it the rubbish left from clearing a patch of land intended to be her flower and herb garden."

Tooley blows on a toasted marshmallow and pops it into her mouth. "Intermittently throwing ladles of boiling water on the fleece in the trough, and pounding it with a thick hickory branch, the wool follicles interlocked forming a thick felt. In this way, she fashioned the front, the back, and a piece for each sleeve. Then she made two large rectangles for the pockets. She pulled up dandelions and yarrow from the unplowed fields and put them in a big tub of water out by the back door, into which she peed every time she thought about it. After piecing the jacket together with an awl and yarn, she put it in the tub of weeds, water, and urine and left it until the color suited her. It took about two weeks."

That explains the yellow color.

"Tooley, why did Great-Great-Great-Grandmother Olive pee in the tub? Isn't it wrong to pee in a tub with clothes in it?"

"Oh, well, that was back in the old days, when they didn't have easy access to commercial mordants to dye wool."

"What's a mordant?" I ask, threading the last marshmallow in the bag onto my willow stick and holding it in the fire.

"A mordant is a chemical. It means to bite," she said, making a silhouette with her hand of a biting mouth. "The acid in the chemical opens the wool follicles and allows the colors from the plants to stay in the wool and not wash out. The acid in the urine allows that to happen. The Indians used their pee all the time for mordant."

Thinking of my mother's warnings to take Tooley's stories with a grain of salt, I am dubious about the peeing in the tub part. Tooley stares into the fire, trance-like, for what seems an eternity with dancing flames of salamanders reflected in her eyes. A tree falls in the woods somewhere behind the burning circle. We hear and feel the soft thud, a slight shudder under our feet.

"Another sentry of the forest, another child of nature, falls back into its mother's arms," Tooley says with sorrow in her voice, her stick raised straight up toward the sky. "Must have been that skinny widow-maker up by where we found the chanterelles last August. I've been waiting for that one to go down for some time now." She breathes out little steamy puffs of regret, as if she has lost a child.

Tooley says she never gets lonely out here. She says that the plants, birds and animals are better company than humans. They don't break your heart like people do. I believe that myself. I'd rather be with Erma Geddon than anybody. Granny and True are close seconds.

Yesterday, down near the creek, I heard Tooley talking to the apricot tree that had dressed itself that very day in white blossoms. "Aren't you smart," she said to the tree. "You've gussied yourself up for your coming out this year."

We had a picnic to honor the spring debut of the tree's blossoming and Tooley played a special tune that she made up on the spot on her wooden flute. As a thank you, the tree reigned down her soft white petals in a gentle kiss. Everybody showed up—the raccoons, all the dogs and cats, the chickens, and even a mother deer and her fawn. Coyote came and stood at the edge of the trees and watched. Tooley says the coyote is the animal spirit of The Chief. He watches over her, and will come to take her home when the time comes.

Tooley makes up special songs for all the animals and

plants. The songs come to her in dreams. She talks to the dogs like they are people. Once I heard her tell Sassy, her old sheep dog who was having trouble getting around and finally died a few years ago, a story about the wonderful place old dogs went to live after they died. How easy it was going to be to just let go and stop breathing. How Sassy would grow beautiful white wings and fly to a place where she would go back in time and be able to run like a puppy again, chase chickens to her heart's content, and eat bones chunky with meat, filled with tasty marrow.

Tooley calls her place "the farm" but it's not really a farm, it's a small cabin carved out of the forest. Around the cabin where the big trees were cut long ago, grow maple, hazelnut, cottonwood, yew, and a giant oak tree. Besides the cabin she lives in, there is a wood shed, a vegetable, flower, and herb garden out front, fenced in so the deer and chickens won't eat it all, a chicken coop where the chickens only go to roost at night, a shed for the sheep, and an out-house. The chickens roam free during the day, laying their eggs wherever they want. I help Tooley gather eggs to sell when I visit. It's like Easter Sunday every morning, tromping through the woods looking for the white, brown, and sometimes green eggs nested in the salal and other low-growing brush.

Every day around ten o'clock in the morning, Snooky, a big Rhode Island Red, lays her egg in a hole next to the garden fence. She announces the event with a "baak baak baak, assshoooo, yuaak yuaak yuaak" and waits by the egg for Kachina to saunter over and gently take the egg out of the hole and eat it. Kachina gives Snooky a thank you nudge, and Snooky gives Kachina a love-peck on the nose. Kachina is faithful to Snooky; she hasn't cozied up to the other hens, nor does she eat their eggs. Sometimes Snooky stands watch over Kachina while she naps in the shade of the apple tree over by the woodshed.

Tooley built me a tree house last year, high up in the arms of the big oak tree. I have tea parties up there with my friends, a family of peace-loving raccoons who devour eggs, dog food and apples that I haul up the ladder for them. Tooley says I spoil them, and when I'm gone they show up on her doorstep every evening waiting to be fed.

The fire crackles and leaps toward us, whipped liked a whirling dervish into a frantic dance by the increasing wind as we feed it the last of the dead plant material.

Tooley looks warm and insulated in the jacket. My hands are cold but my body is warm in the new sweater Tooley knitted for me, all dyed with woodsy colors. When I wear it I blend into the forest and feel like I all but disappear to the outside world. It will be too heavy to wear in California. She made it big so I can leave it here and wear it for the next few springs, at least, or maybe it will still fit when I grow up. I'm suddenly sad that I don't get to spend more time here with her.

After awhile Tooley says, "Now, where were we?"

I remind her. "Great-Great-Great-Grandmother Olive made the jacket for Great-Great-Great-Grandfather Dandrun Fox for their trip out west. Did she give him the jacket? Did they go?"

"Oh they went alright. Dandrun didn't get to wear the jacket for very long. And he never got to see the big trees or the Pacific Ocean. Somewhere west of the Mississippi River, just east of the ridge of the Rockies, he took a chill in the cold and died from pneumonia. Olive buried him in a shallow grave of moraine formed from ancient glaciers, and sent him to heaven along with the prayers from all the members of the wagon-train party, but not before she took from him the jacket she had made. That was the transfer of the patriarchal rule of our family to the women. She would need the jacket to stay strong in the face of unknown dangers on those cold lonely nights without him. She would need it to keep her unborn child warm and from harm.

The Burning Jacket

The women in the family were the strong ones, the caretakers of the children and the custodians of Mother Earth and all her creatures. These women were the keepers of the fire, and the ones who passed the stories down from one generation to the next." Tooley paused to sip coffee as black and thick as the bubbling pits at La Brea.

"Olive pushed westward with the others, walking beside the wagon to ease the burden for the horses until she was too big to walk and had to ride in the wagon. Your great-great-grandmother Cecilia Sierra Patton was born while crossing the final mountain range, the snow-covered Sierras, that winter of 1860. That is how you got your middle name, Raynie Sierra Winters Rogers." Tooley spoke my full name as though she were proud of me. A seed swelled and quickened inside my heart.

"What happened then?"

Tooley paused so long I thought the story was over.

"Well, let's see. Cecilia Sierra Patton grew up and married John Wright. They lived not far from here, out toward the coast. Cecilia gave birth to four sons with John. When the boys grew up they all went in search of gold. They scattered themselves from Alaska to California and were never heard of again. It's a shame." Tooley shook her head. "Anyway, one day Cecilia up and left her husband. She ran away with an Indian named Winter Bear. Let's see, she would have been around forty-four and a half when that happened because she gave birth to your great-grandmother Juanita, in the early nineteen hundreds. She never married the Indian, he was from a northwest coastal tribe, but she shortened his name to Winters and made it her own."

Tooley pulls out a faded, dog-eared sepia photo from the pocket of the burning jacket. A young woman in a flowered dress smiles at us, a vision from heaven. She looks like Tooley, straight and tall, with high cheekbones. She's holding an infant. I'm surprised to see it's the same photo Tooley used to keep in a fancy silver frame on the chest by her bed, which is tucked into a tiny space under the stairs that lead to the loft.

When I was young, Tooley used to let me sleep with her. I felt safe in the warm cubbyhole wrapped in her arms during a storm when the wind howled and the walls of the cabin rattled and creaked in the wind. Every night before going to bed she would kiss the photo and say, 'Goodnight Fanny, wherever you are.' In the past when I asked her who the woman was, she would always ignore the question.

"Now this child, Juanita, nicknamed Fanny, being half-Indian, knew the ways of nature and the art of dreaming. She was a seer, and was also fortified with the stoic spirit of the pioneers. She always seemed to know what was going to happen before it actually did. This girl you see in the picture is my mother, Juanita Fanny Wright Winters."

The air held its breath with me.

"You are a great deal like her, as am I," Tooley says.

"What happened to her? Did she give you the jacket? And why did you call her Fanny instead of Mother?" I ask, unable to take a breath. I reach for my inhaler for the first time since I've been here.

Tooley seems to be counting on her fingers. "Well, just before Olive died, she gave the jacket to her daughter, Cecilia, and then when Cecilia died the jacket was passed down to her daughter, your great grandmother Juanita Fanny Winters and yes, she gave me the jacket before she died. That's why my last name is Winters." Tooley said this as though she wasn't sure of her accounting of the facts.

"Why did you kiss her picture every night? Mom says you told her you never really knew your mother and that you were raised by your father, Jeb, and that he died when you were fifteen."

I ask too many questions. I hope Tooley will keep talking.

The Burning Jacket

Mom said never to mention Jeb around Tooley. If his name were spoken, she would open all the doors and windows and say that it smelled like something had died and rotted inside. She would light her sage bundles and cleanse the energy of the cabin. Sometimes she wouldn't eat or speak for several days after the naming.

Tooley sips away at her coffee for a long time and stares into the fire. She has gone somewhere I cannot follow. The wind has stopped. The only sound is the hissing of the fire and an occasional snore from one of the dogs, a ripping sound like Tooley's rototiller when it first starts up.

Finally, she comes back to me and says in a low voice, "She died way before her time, my mother. I called her Mama, but Fanny was what everybody else called her. I remember twirling in circles together. She laughed a lot and taught me how to harvest medicinal plants and weeds."

"Mom says you never told her anything about your mother."

"Your mother has never wanted to know about my past. Better she doesn't know about the things that broke my heart." Tooley sighs and stands up.

The wind returns on cue with a force. I feel sad like I did the first time I saw the movie *Bambi*. The movie is over and the credits are rolling. You don't want it to be over. You want to change the ending and not have Bambi's mother die. I was surprised when Tooley spoke again.

"Jeb was not my father." She spat on the ground. "My real father was an Indian, member of the Chinook tribe. I was born under a full moon in a tepee out in the woods, near the ocean, one cold December night. I remember my birth. A coyote echoed my howls when I hit the world feet first. It was a hard birth for my mother. She named me Tallulah after the famous actress with a husky voice, and my father named me Coyote. My full name is

Tallulah Coyote Running Bear Winters. I couldn't pronounce my own name so I shortened it to Tooley. I remember that much."

The frown lines on Tooley's forehead loosen their grip a little. She straightens up tall, like she used to be, as her name hits the air like bubbles of champagne at a party. We both say it together as we hold hands. "Tallulah Coyote Running Bear Winters."

"What happened to your real father, and how did Je…" I stop myself. "What happened to your real father?"

I was fighting back the urge to pee, but afraid that if I did, Tooley might take the interruption as a stopping point. So, I suck it up and hold it. I'm surprised when she continues.

"My father was participating in a sacred ceremony when he was struck by lightning."

"Mom told me that J-E-B…" I spell the name rather than say it, "… was struck by lightning, according to what you told her. Were they both struck by lightning?" I feel my mind making giant leaps over imaginary canyons.

"No. J-E-B was hit in the head with a meteorite. There's a big difference you know." Her voice turned bitter, like the muddy coffee she was drinking. "You've seen that hunk of rock on the shelf by the wood stove? That's a piece of the meteorite that landed on him. It just fell, flaming from the sky one day when he was out plowing the field. He never knew what hit him. He was smoking when we found him." A smile scurries across Tooley's face, and is gone in a blink of the eye.

"How did you get the burning jacket from your mother if she died when you were little?" I ask, regretting never having had the opportunity to meet my great-grandmother who foretold the future and birthed such a remarkable woman as my grandmother, Tallulah Coyote Winters.

"She left it in the back of the closet in my room where Jeb wouldn't find it. She told me all about it and said I should never let it out of my sight, or lose it. She attached a note to the jacket that read, 'As caretaker of the earth and all its creatures, may my daughter, Tooley, build her fires carefully and put them out properly when the time comes for endings, with passion, humor and compassion toward all others and herself.'"

I want to ask one more question. I want to ask if I would inherit the burning jacket from my mother. Would my mother take seriously the responsibility of the burning jacket, or would she treat it as a rag and sell it at one of her garage sales?

The fire has burned to ashes. There would be no more stories today. I run behind a tree and finally relieve myself. The sun is setting; the cold comes fast with the dying of the fire.

As if reading my mind, Tooley opens a wing of the jacket, and invites me in. I feel safe like a baby bird nesting in my mother's feathery down.

"One day you will inherit this jacket from your mother as I did from mine," she says as we hobble toward the cabin together, bundled as one in the heavy warmth of my dowry, dogs trailing close behind.

"Your ancestors have a history of being brave and knowing how to survive. These traits were pounded into the wool by your great-great-great-grandmother Olive; a piece of clothing made in love for her husband, your Grandfather thrice removed, Dandrun Fox. When your time comes to wear the jacket it will protect you and keep you strong as it has me, and all of the women before me."

"Will the jacket protect Erma Geddon too? Will it keep her species from becoming extinct? And will it help the frogs to survive? And will it keep the people I love safe?"

Tooley looks sad but determined.

"Yes," she says. "All in good time. All in good time."

Chapter Seven

Molly: April 2000, Anaheim, California.

The dream I had early this morning has already filled two pages of my dream journal. It unfolds like a great love story, one that I relive as I write.

The earth stayed green last fall and winter, continuing into this spring and summer. The boy and I are convinced it is a renascence brought about by our lovemaking. Grace flows through us, into everything we touch, and gilds the hot July afternoon with golden butterflies that land on us en masse; they tickle our skin until we laugh and shoo them away. Our passion blesses the earth and slows the relentless rush of time that cuts away at crazy love, a kind of love that only youth is foolish enough or brave enough to endure.

We are a contrast in light and dark; the boy's swarthy gypsy skin and long black hair mingles with my honey hair and cream-colored skin; my mother was from the north where people are light skinned, and blonde. The two of us together reminds me of the figures on a beautiful Etruscan pot on a table in the portico of my father's house. My name is Julia, after my father Julius. I turn sixteen next month, in August.

A slight breeze spirals down from the peak of Vesuvius, cools us, and causes us to look up. Grapevines have woven a cloak of green around the mountain. The vines are producing a record amount of grapes. The workers will pick the grapes soon to make wine, and the people of Pompeii will fill their casks and call it a good year.

The cooling carpet of mint, crushed beneath our bodies, tries in vain to put out the raging fire that welds us together as one. We lay down by the stream, our bodies spent from lust, in a tangle of ecstasy. The air is thick and pungent with the odor of mint, honeysuckle and violets, the smells so sweet they are a measurable dimension.

Smiling, the boy says to me, 'We have mastered time and therefore death, you know. We can live in this moment forever if we will only remember.'

"Four, five, six, seven ...." My neighbor, Marsha, brings me back to a jarring reality with her exuberant countdown to eight o'clock when she will press the remote control that opens the door on one of our famous mutual garage sales. The whole world is waiting on the other side.

The door rises on the present play of reality to a clear sunny day, thanks to the blowing Santa Ana winds.

"Will you look at all those Mexicans getting out of that little car?" Looks like a circus clown routine."

I resent Marsha's imposition upon my fantasy. Her nasal, salty voice drags me kicking and screaming back to reality, unwilling to let go of the images and the euphoric feeling of the kind of love that only happens in dreams. I lean out from myself into an afterglow scent of wood violets dappled with peppermint. As I was writing, I was aware of translating from Latin to English. I've never studied Latin, and have heard it only once when I went to a Catholic funeral Mass for one of my dad's friends when I was seven. The chanting struck a chord in me. It was as if it could have been at one time my native language. I feel the words now, exciting and alive inside of me.

The dreams started again just after I kicked Ray out, six

months ago. I haven't seen him since that screaming match we had a few weeks back. He tried to call me from jail the other night but I didn't accept the call. When I called the jail they told me he had been caught driving under the influence. Since it was his first offense, he won't be in there for long. I'm sure Grandma and Gramps Rogers bailed him out.

I got a restraining order against Ray in case he comes back here raising hell. I sent Raynie to Granny Tooley's for spring break so I'm resting better at night knowing that she is safe. At least she's in the hands of the lesser of two evils.

My dreams fill my thoughts again. Maybe I'm lonely, and the dreams fulfill a need. A leitmotif that runs through all of the dreams is the lingering smell of wood violets and mint that drifts through the curtain that divides reality and reverie. The scent clings to me for a few hours and then fades. Others are able to smell it as well. Both Raynie and my bakery partner, Duchess, asked me about my new perfume the other day after a particularly detailed dream that felt more real and interesting than any of my waking dramas. I could kick myself for not writing it down immediately. The details flew away before I opened my eyes.

In my waking state I'm not particularly comfortable with fantasy, or daydreams, preferring to live in the here and now. I hardly ever read fiction. Yet these dreams about the young woman who lived in Pompeii are so real. I would be interested in Tooley's take on the meaning of the dreams but they are sacred to me and I'm not sure I can trust her with them.

In art classes there was pressure to do nonobjective art, to mimic the Abstract Expressionists, but I could never break through to that level of letting go. I was stuck in realism… clichéd still-lives with Chianti bottles and fruit. Later, I graduated to landscapes and live nude studies.

After experiencing one of the dreams I feel like I'm living

in a dual reality and could possibly open up at those times to a looser painting style, one that does not require foreground or background, subject or object.

Part of me sits on a folding chair in a garage in Anaheim, California, in the year 2000 and another me lives as Julia in ancient Pompeii, madly in love with a swarthy young man. Writing about Julia is like ghostwriting. It reminds me of *pentimento.* Other lives lay hidden underneath the painting on the surface of the canvas, in layers.

One of the reasons for having a garage sale, other than to get rid of any reminders of Ray, is to clean out the space and get my studio set up again. Maybe the act of painting will sublimate my primitive desires about a gypsy boy in Pompeii into works of art. My left-brain tells me it's only a dream, while the solid memory of his smile and smell haunts me with a love that feels like truth I've never felt in this lifetime, not even in those first months of falling in love with Ray. Is there such a thing as a soul mate, and how does one know when one finds him? How do we make love last beyond the falling in love stage?

"What were you writing? You looked lost in thought," Marsha says.

She looks disapprovingly at the "Mexicans." She says she's not prejudiced, but she is. She calls all people of Latin American descent Mexicans, and hassles our neighbors, the Gonzales family, all the time about stealing grapefruit from her tree. Does she expect them to pick the fruit and pass it back over the fence when the branches hang heavy to the breaking point over into their yard?

"*Buenos dias! Cómo está?*" Marsha smiles as if she speaks Spanish fluently, and then looks confused when they fire questions back at her that sound like vowels rushing over a waterfall. They look at her expectantly and she waves her hand impatiently and says, "Speak English. You live in the United

States now." She turns to me and says, "When they all start chattering it sounds like a whole village vomiting in unison."

I scrunch down in my chair like Raynie does, wishing I could go back into the dream.

Earlier this morning, I parked the SUV on the street to make room in the driveway for two of the four long folding Bingo tables that Marsha borrowed from her church. The other two are set up in the garage. The Santa Ana winds have been blowing the last few days so we put all the stuff that could fly away inside the garage—mostly baby clothes outgrown by Marsha's grandchildren and Raynie's hand-me-downs. She seems to grow an inch every month. Her feet have increased two shoe sizes this year.

Marsha's items are tagged with round orange stickers and mine, blue. We have one table where all items are twenty-five cents. We'll put the money earned from that table in a Mason jar and buy pizza for dinner at the end of the day.

Marsha Fratello is in her late sixties, frumpy in an old-fashioned housedress, support stockings, and old lady shoes. Her hair is the color and texture of blue-gray steel wool. She looks like a throwback to how grandmothers dressed pre-1960s. I don't envy her life. She and her husband had just celebrated their fiftieth wedding anniversary last year when he died from a sudden heart attack, leaving her a not-too-substantial life insurance policy and a howling loneliness that could only be partially appeased by playing Bingo at St. Boniface Church over on Euclid four nights a week. Occasionally I join her and marvel at her luck. I usually manage to drop at least a hundred dollars while Marsha cleans up, sometimes winning as much as five hundred dollars a night.

Eddie, her husband, was from the old school, and strict rules and roles were in place about what a wife was allowed to do or not do. I used to hear him cursing and screaming at her but

The Burning Jacket

I never once heard her raise her voice to him. She used to complain to me about his rough demeanor. It's funny how death erases all faults. She sees him as some kind of saint now. They had married when she was eighteen and she's never had a job outside the home. Even though Eddie had parents that were the pillars of society, her oldest son, Eddie Junior, was arrested several months ago for selling methamphetamine to high school students, his third offense. He is in Chino Hills prison for life with no chance of parole. Eddie Junior's son, John, who seems to be a nice, respectful, thirteen-year-old kid despite what he's been through, has come to live with his grandmother. John's mother overdosed on heroin and died three years ago.

Marsha has three other children scattered around the globe, none of whom come to see her. They call on holidays to say hello but made themselves scarcer then hens teeth when they learned that Eddie Junior got arrested and his son needed a place to live. I would hate to be a mother to a teenager when I'm sixty-nine. I barely have the energy for it now at age forty. I admire Marsha for taking on the job, and help her in little ways when I can, like keeping her supplied in leftover bread from the bakery, and running errands for her. She can drive but the freeways make her nervous.

When John moved in with Marsha several months ago, Raynie invited him over to play or watch a movie several times but he refused. According to Marsha, the boy is a loner and stays in his room hunched over his computer.

I look around the garage at our combined items on display and observe how a person's stuff says a lot about them. Marsha and I are so different. Her things are more every-day, plastic, and symmetrical. At the cost of sounding snobbish, I have to say I abhor symmetry. That was the one thing I was critical of about Dad. His idea of a pleasing décor was matching end tables with matching lamps and cheap reproductions of trendy landscape paintings. I did a pretty good job of fitting in to a symmetrical life when I lived with him, blending in with the pseudo-Valley Girl scene in high school. I was even a cheerleader, but I guess some wayward seeds of my renegade mother implanted themselves deep within my psyche. Tooley can't even bring herself to knit a pair of socks that match. I guess I'm a contradiction of sorts. I'm more comfortable with logic than fantasy (except for the dreams), but I prefer things to be asymmetrical.

Most kids want their parents to live together under one roof but I knew, even before I could talk, that it was impossible for Tooley and Dad to coexist; they were too different.

Their romance was little more than a one-night-stand from what I gleaned from Dad. He met Tooley while on a rafting trip with some of his executive friends near the Umpqua River. They actually met on a street corner in Roseburg where she sold her handmade beaded jewelry. Dad thought she was the most exotic woman he'd ever seen, with her flow of black hair and pale wild eyes. He said she was dressed in deerskin pants and a plaid wool shirt, and what looked like handmade leather boots. He squatted next to her blanket on the ground, the display of jewelry sparkling in the sunshine. They talked all afternoon, and somehow for a few magical hours two very different worlds met and joined as one. I can see what the appeal would have been for his attraction to her, but what attracted Tooley to my father? Was there, at that time in her life, a nesting instinct, a yearning to have a child and live a normal life like other people? I can't imagine my mother would ever want that, although I know my father must have come across to her as reliable and steady.

One time when I asked Tooley about her feelings toward Dad, she told me that she loved him as she did all living creatures but felt stifled by his cozy, boring lifestyle. At the time I loathed her for saying that. The truth is I understand her feelings. I loved my father with all my heart, but he was a bit boring. I wonder if that's why I chose to marry a bad boy, someone totally opposite from my father.

The night of the day they met, my mother went to his campfire with strips of dried smoked salmon and made tea from a string of *Yerba Buena*, commonly known as Oregon Tea, which she wore in a strand around her neck. They made love, and I am the result of their brief union.

Marsha's four artificial Christmas trees with white flocking that make me feel not too hopeful for the future of the human race, are being hauled out to the little car that had been filled with the Latinos. They bought all of the Christmas decorations: boxes of lights, shiny balls of red, blue, and green, and bags of silver tinsel. They tie the trees to the top of the car, get in, and drive away to Marsha's *Hasta la vista!* She pronounces the 'H.'

I've never been one to hang on to objects that outlive their usefulness. Most of the things for sale were Ray's—toys, Batman comic books, yellowed newspapers from around the world dated the day Elvis died. Old Halloween costumes Ray bought for himself and Raynie to go trick or treating—Smurf suits, a monk costume, a gypsy blouse and skirt and pirate paraphernalia. Ray loved wearing costumes. He said it gave him perspective on his own life when he could disguise himself as somebody else. Then there's Ray's sports trophies, his collection of miniature cars, and the rock hounding equipment.

My contribution is several dozen quart-size canning jars from a lifetime ago when I felt domestic, and a pair of crutches from when I fell and sprained my ankle on our honeymoon.

How did it all come to this? What happened to the person with whom I fell in love, and in whom I entrusted the rest of my life? He turned into his evil twin. Why? Was it because his parents lavished him with material things and abandoned him to teenage, bubble gum chewing babysitters while they traveled the world? Was it my fault because I nagged him? Honestly, I couldn't help myself. When did we stop feeling that special bond of love for one another? Maybe love isn't something you feel; maybe it's something you do. Maybe I should have forgiven him and tried harder?

The one good thing to come out of our union is Raynie.

"I'll give you fifty dollars for all the trophies over there."

A short, fat man who looks like Al Capone peels off two twenties and a ten from the top of a bankroll and puts the bills in front of me on the table. I feel a lump of guilt in my throat. These were Ray's baseball awards that he received from the time spanning Little League through his third year in college. They stand proud—miniature silver men with legs apart, swinging bats, lonely jewels of a brighter Ray. He tried, at times, to make something of himself, almost graduated from college with a degree in Physical Education. He wanted to be a coach. But for lack of fortitude, too many parties and booze, he didn't finish his final year. I hesitate, and then think of Ray screwing the fat chick and nod my head in the affirmative.

"Here I'll put them in a box for you." I smile and mean it.

The man who called about Ray's collection of little Tyco automobiles is here. Without even seeing them, he offered me five hundred dollars over the phone. I counted fifty boxes, all brand new, never taken out of their wrappings. Ray paid around a dollar apiece for them a long time ago. I tried to research how much they were worth on the Internet, but lost patience with the whole project and told the man he could have them all for five hundred.

He saunters in, face hidden under a long red beard, but his snatchy little eyes are aglow with the fire of success like he's getting the steal of the century. I wish I had done more research, but I've already made the deal. He slowly counts out five one-hundred-dollar bills into my hand, and I put the toys in several big cardboard boxes and tell him to enjoy. I feel conflicted, but what is done is done.

My legs are going wobbly. Hope I don't fall again. I vow to charge more money for the rock-hounding equipment and keep every penny of it since I bought it all with my hard-earned money.

Ray became consumed with rocks and gemstones and with making jewelry when Raynie was four. This hobby, like all his others, was short-lived. It lasted for just one summer but we had fun taking Raynie on weekend trips to rock quarries and flea markets in search of colorful, interesting rocks.

A bucket filled with the treasures that bind family memories like photos in an album sits on the floor by the table, too heavy for me to lift. Moonstone moss agates, pink quartz, thunder eggs from Eastern Oregon, shiny black obsidian we chipped from the cliffs of Heart Mountain, and apache tears from Arizona.

The rock tumbler sits mute on the table. The silence saddens me. After I got used to it, the constancy of the sound of rocks tossing around and around was comforting, like the sound of the ocean, or the more subtle sound of mountains being formed. A steady, reliable sound. It takes a long time to smooth rough edges of stone. Maybe I should have given Ray a second chance.

A tall, thin man with silver hair wearing khaki shorts and a white T-shirt with green lettering that reads 5-K Run, Anaheim Memorial, May 1, 1999, throws a smile across the garage at me. My face feels hot and rubbery. *What the hell is going on with me? I've got to get out more.*

"How much you want for the diamond saw?" His eyes are a tumble of shapes and colors, an ever-changing kaleidoscope. When he leans in towards the table I smell a hint of violets, or do I smell the shards of my dream? My skin prickles and the hairs on my arms stand at attention. I'm glad I wore a long-sleeved shirt this morning. He picks a fire agate Ray bought in Mexico out of the bucket of rocks and holds it up to the light.

"A river of flame runs through it. Here look." He hands me the rock. It feels radiant in the palm of my hand. Words cannot escape beyond the prison gate of my lips. He seems to sense my discomfort.

"How much for all of it?" He sweeps his arm and hand like a magic wand over all the paraphernalia on the table.

I hesitate. I don't know what to do. I want to hang on to the last traces of the old Ray, who, for a brief season, spun straw into gold and polished dull rocks to burnished bits of beauty. The last hope for getting Ray back in our lives will walk out of the garage with the rock equipment.

"I'm sorry. I really shouldn't have put this stuff out here. It belongs to my estranged husband," I croak.

"That's all right. I understand. Letting go of someone you love or loved isn't easy, regardless of the circumstances." The pattern of colors in his eyes has slowed to a dense blue, like calm water in a secret mountain lake.

"You sound as if you know from experience." *What a dorky thing to say to him.*

"My wife died three years ago. Just this last month my son and I had the courage to clean out her closet and take all the stuff to the Goodwill. It wasn't easy." He shook his head. "Here's my card if and when you're ready." He smiles at me again. My face suddenly blooms with a red tide. "I mean…if or when you're ready to sell the equipment," he says.

Am I imagining a slight rouging of his cheeks? He turns and walks out of the garage and down the driveway with a backward wave of his hand.

"Well, that was interesting. That man was flirting with you." Marsha wipes her hands on her garage-sale apron with deep pockets, already bulging with coins. She wipes her hands on her apron every time she handles money, like the coins and bills were a dirty but necessary thing. I look at the plain white card with black print the man with the kaleidoscope eyes gave me. Dr. John Graham, Cardiologist. And a phone number with a 714 prefix.

"He's a doctor. I don't need to look at a card to tell that," Marsha says. "He's got that 'I'm better-than-God' look. You may be exchanging one trouble for another if you get involved with him." Marsha was ready with unasked advice.

"He wasn't flirting with me. He wanted to buy the rock equipment. I decided not to sell it so he gave me his card to call him in case I change my mind." I don't know why I feel the need to explain anything to her.

An early 1980s Mogen David wine-colored Dodge van sporting an airbrushed psychedelic phoenix surrounded by orange flames that spread out of control around the body of the car pulls up to the curb and parks dangerously close behind my SUV. The driver revs the motor once and gets out, leaving it running. It's Ray.

A van pulls up behind him and two young men get out. Both look Hispanic. One is wearing chinos with a "wife beater" T-shirt-like Marlon Brando wore in *Streetcar Named Desire*. His right bicep bulges with a tattoo of the Blessed Virgin Mary in blue ink. The other boy wears jeans and a short-sleeved plaid shirt with only the top button fastened. They wear red bandannas low on their foreheads; both have on new black sneakers with silver stripes and the initials B. K. sewn on the sides. I recognize the boys from the day I followed Ray to the liquor place. They were the kids he was hanging with on the corner in front of the store. They look like they could be gang members.

I feel in my apron pocket for my cell phone. It isn't there. I must have left it in the house. I manage to hand Marsha the restraining order I carry on me at all times and signal her to go inside and call the police.

Ray's parents had given him toys instead of love and attention when he was a child. I think that's why he crammed the garage with toys, trying to fill the emptiness inside. He hasn't really learned how to love himself or others. I know that now. The realization makes me feel nauseated about having sold his stuff.

I'm afraid he might try to kill me.

I barely sleep at night since the threats, and I try to keep a tighter leash on Raynie. I bought her a cell phone so she could check in with me when she's not at school, and I alerted the school to never let her leave with her father. I drive her there and pick her up every day. She comes with me to the bakery in the afternoons until closing time.

She does her homework and I'm teaching her how to make bread, and whittle animals from wood just like The Chief taught me. She carves busts of Erma Geddon, and exotic creatures like Komodo Dragons (she's quick to recite their Latin name, *varanus komodoensis*, and to tell me that they live only in the East Indies). And more recently, Dire Wolves and Saber-toothed tigers, after another visit to the Tar Pits just a few weeks ago with her eighth grade class.

"Hello, Olive Oyl. How are you?" Ray staggers in looking like a pit-bull on speed. His bare, hairy gut reminds me of his fat girlfriend's jewel-encrusted belly. He's unshaven and looks as if he's aged at least twenty years since I last saw him.

"Where's my stuff? I want my stuff."

Instead of slurring his words, he pronounces every vowel and consonant in an exaggerated manner. His voice sounds swollen and his face has attained the deep bruised color of calf's liver. *Thank God I didn't sell the rock collection.*

"Here. Take it all. You can have it. I didn't think you were coming back for it, and God knows you owe me all the money I would get for it."

"Load everything on the table into the van," Ray directs his two sleazy associates. "Just take the whole damn table."

"Yo, Jefe," the one with the Blessed Virgin tattoo says. They jump at his words and start hauling away the table and everything on it, one man on each end. They load the van with the remaining bits and pieces of the old Ray's life. Then they fold the legs of the bingo table and load that into the van as well.

"Hey, that table belongs to the church. Leave it here," I protest in vain. They pretend they don't hear me.

"Hey, Cholo, we're out of here. Catch you later bro." They get into the van and drive away just as a police car stops in the middle of the street in front of the house and two officers get out.

"What the hell is this all about?" Ray looks at me with a hurt look, like he was Jesus and I was Judas, betraying him.

"Are you Ray Rogers? Let me see your driver's license," the younger of the two officers says. Ray takes his driver's license out of his billfold as he mummers "Son of a bitch" and "Shit, I haven't done anything." You'll have to come with us, sir. Put your hands behind your back."

Ray resists slightly, and the older officer jerks Ray's hands back, cuffs him, and starts reading his rights.

"I didn't do anything wrong. I just came to get my stuff. She has no right to sell any of my stuff. It's worth a lot of money."

"You violated your restraining order. You are not allowed to come within a thousand feet of Molly or Raynie Rogers at any time."

"This is pure bullshit. Something she concocted to keep me away from my daughter." Ray is crying and his nose is running. One cop puts his hand on Ray's head and firmly places him in the back seat of the police car. The other cop comes over to me with a paper to sign.

"I don't know how long we can hold him. That will be up to the judge, but he'll probably be eligible for bail in twenty-four hours. My advice to you, ma'am, is to buy a gun and learn how to use it. Good luck." He shrugs his shoulders, walks away, and gets in the car. Not exactly an endorsement for the effectiveness of restraining orders.

Any sentimental attachment or lingering hope I may have been harboring for a possible reconciliation with Ray vanishes with the red brake lights of the police car as it turns at the corner.

Ray's boys left behind the bucket of rocks that sit on the floor. I pick up the fire agate just handled by Dr. John Graham and hold it up to the light. Inside is a miniature prehistoric river of fire flowing through a space unsullied by human thought or deed. The gem seems to deliquesce in my hand, releasing into the air a sense of timelessness, the way a seashell echoes the ocean's roar in never-ending cycles.

Perhaps life is a continuous dream.

Chapter Eight

Raynie: March 2000.

I dream I'm in Mom's bakery. What I call "me" is scattered into a million grains of wheat being fed into a big machine. At first I panic, feeling as though I will lose myself, that special something that makes me Raynie, but when what I called 'I' is blended with the smooth warm milk, butter, and yeast it all becomes 'we' as it is churned by a big paddle. Now 'we' are a giant loaf of bread being gently kneaded by a pair of unseen hands in rhythm to softly falling rain.

  The yeasty smell of freshly baked bread awakens my nose before the rest of my body regains consciousness. That must be why I dreamed I was a loaf of bread. The feeling of being a million little pieces, part of everything, and then coming back together again as one makes me think of Erma Geddon, as most good things do.

  The rain falling on Granny Tooley's metal roof is one of my favorite things in the whole world. I open my eyes and see the rafter beams above. The angles create purple shadows with halos of orange around the outer edges where the dark meets the light, like shadow angels that protect Granny and her place. The deep corners shelter cobwebs and mysteries that the light never reaches.

  Yesterday, when I asked her if she ever got tired of living in Oregon where it's dark and rainy most of the time, Tooley said that the dark gives depth to life, that being in constant light would be as meaningless as going to heaven and floating around on a cloud playing a harp all day.

When I squint, rainbows appear in the triangles of shadows. If I were a barn owl, or any bird, I would like to build my nest up there on a ledge where it's warm and dark and dry.

Tooley is downstairs feeding the fire. The creaky sound of the wood stove door as it opens and closes, and the thud and crackle of a new log being tossed in, are also among my favorite things.

The cabin has just one room downstairs but The Chief built a loft for more space. Tooley has a trunk filled with her personal possessions: wool she spun and dyed in glorious colors; a variety of knitting needles, sweaters, caps and scarves she made to sell at the Saturday market in Eugene; her few items of clothing. All her stuff put together would take up half the closet in my bedroom at home. A big black plastic bag of fleece ready to spin stands in the corner by the trunk. On top of the trunk sits her wooden flute and one of The Chief's handmade drums left behind when he vanished into the rosy light on the Harmonic Convergence.

Tooley is singing one of her favorite songs. *"Moon River, wider than a mile, I'm crossing you in style some day."* No matter what she sings, Tooley's voice sounds misty, like early morning fog in the forest. She likes songs from the 1950s.

Tooley says those were the best days, when she was young and the country was still together, when the average citizen still had a voice in how things would go. She says that things have gotten way out of hand and we're divided in such a way that we may never be a strong nation again. She's always worrying that the government will do bad things, like getting us into more senseless wars, and that the loggers will cut down all the trees, and the spotted owls won't have any place to live, not to mention all the other plants and animals in the forest. I guess I'm a lot like her in that way. I wish we could wrap them all inside the burning jacket and keep them safe.

Tooley contradicts herself a lot about her life. She also told me that she's glad she isn't young again, that those were the hardest times for her, when she was homeless and constantly looking for a place to stay warm and dry.

Drowsiness turns off my thinking button and I snuggle into fluffy down, content and cozy as I thank the geese that gave up their feathers so I could stay warm. I had raised a fit a few years ago about the poor geese, until Tooley reassured me that they had died of natural causes before their feathers were plucked.

I wake up again. The rain forms iridescent blue drops behind my closed eyelids—soft tinsel jingling bells in smooth glissando, and then hard staccato dots, accompanied by the brushing, whooshing of the fir trees swaying in the wind. The sounds remind me of my piano teacher, Mr. Harrison.

Because of him, I could translate the songs of nature into man-made music, and even name them in a foreign language, Italian. He would get excited about the "quality of touch and tone" as I played simple pieces such as *Twinkle Twinkle Little Star*, which he said was not to be taken lightly since it was a Mozart masterpiece. He would say, *pianissimo, pianissimo,* and put his finger over his lips and say, *shuuuussh, shuuuush*, and then, *legato, legato*, moving his arms and hands like he was conducting a symphony. His eyes would get big and his voice would get louder, *crescendo, crescendo,* on the "how I wonder what you are" part, and then yell at the top of his lungs, *fortissimo! fortissimo!* as I would bring it all home with a hefty C-chord that made my hands dance, as I quickly jerked them away from the keys when it was all over, like the professional concert pianists I watch on OPB-TV. I miss the piano lessons.

The white-gloved hands of the Mickey Mouse wind-up

clock that Tooley bought to teach me to tell time when I was four read twelve minutes to ten. I throw back the covers, luxuriating in the fact that I don't have to make my bed as soon as I jump out of it like at Grandma Roger's house. That's one of her many "pet peeves," as she calls them. If she doesn't like something you've done she turns to my Grandpa Sam, or whoever else is in the room, and says things like, 'Don't you just hate it when a person doesn't make their bed?' Tooley says if you don't want to make your bed that's your prerogative, and if a person doesn't like it they don't have to go in your bedroom and look at it.

The one and only time that Tooley stayed all night at our house in Anaheim, Grandma and Grandpa Rogers drove over, unexpectedly, in their motor home from Bullhead City for a few days.

Tooley's table manners did not escape Grandma Roger's watchful eye. She said to my mother, not looking at Tooley at all, 'Don't you just hate it when someone heaps a load of butter and jam on their toast?'

Tooley grabbed another piece of toast and plopped even more butter and jam on it. She ate both pieces, giving Grandma Rogers the hawk eye. Finally, Grandma Rogers looked back and Tooley locked eyes with her until Grandma Rogers looked away first. Tooley told me that you can't expect to be the alpha dog if you are the first one to look away.

Grandma and Grandpa Rogers bought a place next to the Colorado River when they retired. I went to visit them once but it made me sad. I wanted to free the river. It was enclosed with concrete on both sides.

Their idea of a good life is to hang out at the casinos across the river in Laughlin and gamble all day. They left me with a babysitter who smoked cigarettes that made me wheeze. She talked on the phone all day. I got homesick and chose not to visit again. Not that they would ever ask me again now that Ray has moved out. He said they were never around much while he was growing up, always off on some adventure without him. Since he left, they won't even talk to me or Mom on the phone.

The sound of the rain makes my thoughts return to Mr. Harrison and the piano lessons. I was eavesdropping when I heard him tell Mom that she was wasting her money and his time.

"This child isn't interested in music anymore. It was just a passing fancy with her. It's what happens to children who don't have the true calling."

It still hurts. I feel my eyes stinging with tears. I may not have "the calling," but I love playing the piano. I just felt bad that I should like it so much after the lies I told for Ray, and the money I took, and all that mess.

Ray used to play duets with me, sometimes "Heart and Soul," mostly "Chopsticks." We would play them over and over, faster each time until we would laugh so hard we couldn't play anymore. It didn't seem right that I should be enjoying something so much while he was homeless and maybe out hiding under a bush somewhere.

How can anyone stay sad with the smell of homemade bread filling the cabin? When I climb down from the loft Tooley has her rocking chair pulled up close to the stove, with her feet resting on the brick hearth. Two brown loaves of bread on the warmer shelf all plumped up remind me of Moses, Tooley's rooster, who puffs his chest up at the hens and tries to make them lay eggs where he directs them to. They never follow his orders.

Tooley is reading *Back to Eden,* an old dog-eared and yellowed paperback about herbal remedies. She has three books; the other two are a book on how to build houses out of mud and straw, coke bottles and other recycled stuff, and *The Prophet*, by

Kahlil Gibran. She smiles when she sees me, and opens her arms for a good morning hug.

"Just catching up on my reading. Looks like we're staying in today, unless you don't mind getting soaked. We could put on our boots and tromp around in the woods for a while. It's a little early for the spring morels to be up, but I'm game for whatever you decide." Tooley's smile is so big it splits her face in half. "That's what I like about Oregon. One day it's sunny, the next day it's rainy. Balance. That's what it's all about, balance."

She runs her fingers through my unbrushed hair. "I've made some whole-wheat sunflower seed bread, your favorite, and we can open the last jar of red raspberry jam. I've been saving it for your visit."

I think about these things all at once:

1. My need to be warm and comfy right now outweighs my wanting to explore the woods.

2. There will be no fire outside today with marshmallows and stories, but there may be stories inside gathered around the wood stove.

3. I have only a few days of vacation left and don't want to miss anything.

4. I have to pee and don't want to get wet and cold running to the outhouse.

As if reading my mind or maybe she knows by my fidgeting, Tooley says, "The pee bucket is still back under the stairs by my bed. I haven't emptied it yet. Use that. If you have to do number two, I can't help you. You'll have to brave the elements."

Grateful for the reprieve I take her up on the invitation to pee in her bucket, and wonder if we should save all our pee for mordant to make the colors bite into the wool Tooley dyes.

Tooley fries two eggs sunny side up, cuts the bread, slathers it with butter, and plops a big dollop of jam on the plate.

The Burning Jacket

The smell of hot chocolate in the blue enamel pot on the stove reminds me how hungry I am. She makes it with canned milk, something I would never drink at home but it tastes delicious here.

I pull the willow chair The Chief made up close to the fire. Moss grows from the lacy side twigs like a green slipcover. The color goes well with the flowery seat cushion. I was with Tooley last summer when she traded a hand knit cap for the cushion at the Saturday market.

Lunch and dinner simmers in an iron pot filled with pinto beans and a ham hock on top of the wood stove. The odor is glorious. Tooley preaches all the time about how wrong it is to eat animals, but she does like a good ham hock in her beans on special occasions and it feels good to know that my being here is a special occasion. She says that rules wouldn't mean much if they weren't broken sometimes. She eats mostly beans, brown rice, eggs from her chickens, canned vegetables and fruit from her summer harvest, and whatever she trades in town. There are a lot of candles and a few kerosene lamps around the Big Room, as she calls the small one-room cabin. My mom says that's just another example of how Tooley distorts the truth. Ray says to hear her talk you'd think she lived in a mansion.

Tooley used to make her own candles but she trades for them now. She says time is getting away from her and she needs to save it for the more important things, like spinning and knitting, gardening, canning, and walking through the woods with the dogs, and last but not least, singing and playing the flute. She reminds me of a tribe of Aborigines in Australia I once read about who went on walkabouts to sing the earth back into existence. If they didn't walk their paths and sing their songs along their designated song lines, that part of the earth would disappear.

Tooley sings the forest into existence every day.

Kevin and Kachina are asleep at Tooley's feet. They have just come in from the rain and their wet fur smells like moldy cheese. Tooley's pot of coffee burps a slow perk as if it suffers indigestion from its own bitterness.

"Would you like that lesson in spinning today?" Tooley gets up from her rocking chair and I join her at the picnic table. "I could teach you how to make a drop spindle in case you ever get caught somewhere where you need yarn or thread and can't buy it."

"What if I don't have any fleece to spin?" I imagine myself shipwrecked on an island.

"You can spin lots of different fibers. For instance, if you have a dog with long hair you could spin that." The thought of using old stinky wet dog hair does not appeal, but the thought of being stranded on an island with only a dog for company does somewhat excite my sense of adventure. And Erma Geddon would be there of course. And Ray wouldn't be there scaring me and Mom.

"Or you can use plants, ones with pliable big leaves like some desert plants, Agave, for example."

I wrote a paper last year in Biology class on the many uses of Agave in Mexico.

"You can weave the leaves. You don't even have to spin them."

"Tooley, why don't you just buy some of the things you need like everybody else does? Mom says as long as we live in a technologically advanced country we may as well take advantage of some of its time-saving perks."

My words don't set well with Tooley. She bristles stiff.

"I want no part of a society that does not respect life; I mean all living things. All the big kahunas running the show are greedy and can't see beyond the dollar sign. They are ruining the earth. I prefer to stay off the grid and not contribute to their foolish destruction of Mother Earth." Her usually pale face is red and puckered. I'm sorry her feathers are ruffled.

To end the conversation she goes over to the trunk at the foot of her bed and brings back a wooden dowel, some rubber grommets (she named them), a small cup-shaped hook, and two compact disks. She showed me how to slip the grommets' grooves into the rubber, over the dowel. Then she put two disks together and placed them in the grooves to anchor them to the dowel. She screwed a cup hook into the top of the dowel.

"Why are we using CDs? And how would we find those on a desert island?"

"The key word is 'improvise.' The key to sane living is recycling. Always utilize what you have already. Might as well use some of the trash we create for another purpose, other than throwing it away. I found those CDs in a waste can in the post office. You can use shells of coconuts or anything that's around to weight your stick and keep it spinning."

Tooley ties a piece of yarn around the dowel a few inches below the disks, and threads the yarn over the disc and through the cup hook on top of the dowel. "There you have it. All ready to spin. You want to catch the wool on the yarn to get started." She rolls the dowel against her leg to start it spinning and then lets it go while she feeds the wool onto the dowel. It looks easy when she does it.

It isn't easy. When I try, I have trouble keeping the dowel spinning long enough to draft the wool onto the spindle. After about an hour of stops and starts, it gets easier. I finally relax into the rhythm of the spinning disk and the falling rain. Before I know it, there is a bundle of yarn on the dowel. Even though it's uneven in width, and lumpy, I'm proud of it.

"It's important that you make something for yourself with the first yarn you spin. Tomorrow I'll teach you how to knit yourself a scarf."

Tooley and I have spun around with the earth together another day. The light fades as she banks the fire, turns up the kerosene lamp, lights more candles on the picnic table, and dishes up beans and bread along with a round of goat cheese she bartered for at the Saturday Market.

After dinner, I climb the stairs to my comfy bed in the loft, proud of what I learned today. Ray and Mom and all my problems seem far away here at Granny's place.

* * *

Little did I know that I wouldn't be able to visit my Granny in her woods ever again, or that I would never again talk to my father, Ray, or receive his bear hugs.

A year later I reread the lessons I wrote down that night before I went to sleep for the last time in my comfy nook in Granny's loft.

1. Take advantage of chances to learn something new, especially from someone as wise as Granny Tooley.

2. This same moment will never come again. You never have a second chance to live it again.

3. Cherish each moment with the people you love because they won't be with you forever. I silently kiss the night and pretend it is the back of my darling Erma Geddon's head.

TWO

Chapter Nine

> At last they killed you and broke you in pieces while your sound kept lingering on in lions and boulders, in trees and in birds. There you are still singing.
> The Sonnet to Orpheus XXVI *by Rainer Maria Rilke, Touchstone Book, translated by Stephen Mitchell, p.69.*

Tooley: April 2001, Oregon.

The loggers come in the first light of dawn, as I knew someday they would. I hear them up on the hill, a deadly army with heavy artillery, buzzing the hillside where my old dog, Sassy, is buried amid the old-growth Douglas fir trees. I drugged Kevin and Kachina with capsules of valerian root to calm them down so they won't bark or run out to chase the bulldozers. I'll let them do their business inside the house and clean it up later.

"Cock-a-doddle-do," the Judas rooster crows. I hope the drone of the engines and the chain saws have covered his morning wake-up call.

A wounded sun rises and bleeds out into a fleshy gray fog. Liquid yellow flashes of trucks and a bulldozer dart through lacy gaps in the trees like an unexpected jaundiced tide rushing in, and a glimpse of a man with a red cap sitting high in the driver's seat of the bulldozer brings up a gush of bile into my throat.

These lumberjacks are mere foot soldiers, the henchmen to lumber moguls, sent out into battle, never realizing they have choices, not understanding the consequences of their actions. They march, for a pittance of the proceeds, to meaningless slogans, as the youth of the world do when sent to die in wars with trumped up causes, to fatten the pockets of those in control. The real reason lies in the pockets of the CEOs of huge corporations. I feel a familiar helplessness well up in me from a distant, dark place and then a tide of thirst for blood and revenge. A wild fire ignites in my heart, threatening to burn out of control.

I listen and watch all day, huddled by the cold stove, pretending there is warmth in the lifeless ashes, wrapped in the burning jacket, rocking in a vain attempt to soothe the stabbing pains in my heart. Nothing can insulate me from an icy dread that my life is over. The only way I know and want to live is coming to an end. Like the loggers, I see no other choices. The dogs are by my side. Still under the influence of the drug, they are both sound asleep.

My arms and legs feel like bloody stumps as I stiffly fill the stove with wood. I won't light the fire until the loggers leave. Yes, I am burning the trees but only the ones that fall on their own, the ones that die a natural death, not ones murdered by the great guillotine of progress. In the silence I can still hear the sharp cracking shrieks of protest and the dull reverberating boom as the giants fall to earth. The sound creates a tsunami inside me. I run for the back door and heave into the Oregon grape bushes. My gut growls in protest. I've had nothing to eat today.

The sky is clouding up and it's getting dark. Thank God. They will leave soon, and I can strike a match to the wood in the stove, light some candles and cook some food. My head feels like a throbbing tooth being hollowed out by an overzealous dentist. I need a cup of hot coffee.

I sneaked out earlier and locked Annie and her baby Raoul in the shed with lots of hay. So far, they haven't bleated and given us away, and I didn't let the chickens out to roam free today. I don't know where the cats are hiding, except for Gattita, who is snoozing with the dogs by the cold hearth.

The chainsaws have stopped but the harsh raspy screams linger and reverberate through the dead branches. The sounds are closing in, getting closer. By the end of the day tomorrow, they will be near enough to discover us if they continue cutting in our direction.

I must arm myself for war against an enemy I know in my heart cannot be defeated: greed. *They* will count the wooden bodies and refer to the fallen as lumber, just as they name the killing of people in war "casualties," or more recently, "collateral damage." Logs will be sold to Japan. The fallen trees will not be honored in their own country. They will not provide shelter to the people who need it most. They will only make men who are ever-greedy for more money richer and richer, until all the trees are gone. There will be no more oxygen to breathe, and the land and hearts of the people will be barren.

* * *

All the animals have been fed. I drank a cup of coffee and ate a peanut butter and honey sandwich. It tasted like sawdust. Now we must go and assess the damage. Kevin and Kachina, with Gattita following, lead the way as we walk in silent mourning, single-file like for a funeral procession, to the top of the hill. We walk the newly-made road, stepping gingerly in the valleys between the ridges made by the bulldozer's wheels. I lean on my walking stick to support my right knee. It's been aching all week. The cherry wood staff feels solid and gives me courage to trek up the hill to a scene I dread viewing.

I remember that time so long ago, when I was running, confused and afraid, not knowing in what direction to turn, when I met The Chief. I was sixteen and he gave me this stick. He blessed it and said it was a talisman that would always guide my way in the world, that it was a reminder to use the natural resources of nature in a kind way, taking only what I need to survive.

"This way you will be able to walk tall and with much grace throughout life, with the blessing of the Great Spirit, needing little support from a society gone mad from always wanting more," he had said. He gave me the wooden flute as well, and taught me how to listen to the voice of nature and translate it into human song.

We reach the top of the hill. I sit on a stump to catch my breath. My old friends are bleeding sap, and it sticks to my jacket. I vomit again. Despite all the glib talk about replanting and managing tree farms, these heroes of the forest can never be replaced, not in my lifetime, nor, I suspect, will they be allowed to grow to full size ever again for future generations.

In what, yesterday, was a stand of saplings, the bulldozer sits like a mad Cerberus guarding the gates of hell. The driver of this devil machine had made a bold, unnecessarily wide turnaround, like a wild boy at destructive play. With one giant pass he wiped out a litany of sacred plants: the trillium in bloom, lady slippers, the oxalis, the Oregon grape, the wild huckleberry that the deer so love, the yerba buena—healing herb of the ancient ones, the flowering mullein that makes poultices for sore throats and soothes the sting of poison oak, foxglove for failing hearts, hawthorn, evening primrose—which I dry and sell as tea to help women endure hot flashes during the change of life. Thimbleberry that makes great jam, wild rose, St. John's wort—valuable when steeped in olive oil to make a lotion for varicose veins.

My dog Sassy's grave, clearly marked by a prayer arrow with brightly colored yarn planted in the earth to help speed on her gentle spirit with love and guidance, has been desecrated. The prayer arrow lies broken in a heap of crushed limbs and dying plants. *It's only underbrush to you. To me it is what gives meaning to life.*

We are joined by eight white-tailed deer. They stand wide-eyed and stunned at the edge of the rubble that yesterday was their home. The dogs are still. They do not chase them.

I take the drum and sage bundles from my backpack and go about my work of beginning the healing process. I draw an imaginary circle and step into it as I spin around with my smoldering bundle of sage to purify the space and smoke out the negative energy of the destroyers as the trees lie bleeding on the ground. Then I invoke with drumbeat, a slow tai chi of my inner creation, the spirits of the four directions by facing each one and tuning in to the special rhythm of their energies. The North, slow yet strong like the heartbeat of a hibernating bear; the East, an awakening call, like a thunder bolt, loud and staccato; the South a fiery fandango; and the West, a muted elegy that turns into a keening lament and forces me to my knees. My sobs send the deer running and set the dogs howling.

After the wave of purging, I take out my flute and kneel in the circle as a gentle rain begins to fall. The trees have been silenced, nevermore to join their brothers and sisters in the unique harmonies of a balanced forest. I must sing their song for them, and let the flute chant their eulogy. The wind will carry their song in all directions so that they may never be forgotten. My flute prays through my cold, wet lips until I can no longer feel my body. Time passes without my awareness. Finally, I open my eyes.

The rain is on break. The sky is moonless and a black velvet blanket covers the woods. I am at home in the dark. The Chief once said I had the keen vision and ability to detect motion in the dark like a sight hound. The dogs and I often walk up to the top of the hill at night, particularly in the summer, to watch the stars. The Chief and I used to spend nights up here during the height of the Perseids meteor shower during August 8 to the 14 every year. The sky is usually as clear as a deep mountain lake in late summer, and more entertaining to watch than fireworks on the Fourth of July. Through the cathedral of trees we'd see hundreds of shooting stars and small pieces of cosmic dust enter the earth's atmosphere at extremely high speeds. It reminded me how vast the universe is and how we are all a part of it.

I am suddenly so taken over with grief again that I can no longer kneel. I fall prone in the mud facing the night. I miss him so.

I remember the day The Chief and I met. I was a scared kid of sixteen on the run for a year, sleeping tucked into log fortresses that people had built around campfire pits on the beaches in summer, pitching a tent in the woods in winter to stay dry. He was down on the beach at low tide, digging clams. The salty, cold wind stung my eyes and made my nose run. I was hungry. After his bucket bulged with clams, he walked up the beach and saw me huddled on a log.

"I'll trade you these clams for your jacket," he said. "I'll bet it really keeps you warm, huh?" In fear, I hugged it even tighter around me. I would die before I gave up my burning jacket no matter how hungry I was. It was my inheritance, the only thing left from my mother.

"Don't worry, I was just kidding. I don't want your jacket. I will share my clams with you though. Can't eat all these before they go bad, and you look like you could use a good feed."

I was bone tired. I'd become expert at reading faces, making snap decisions about first impressions, trying to respond appropriate to my best interests to sudden, seemingly friendly invitations.

The Chief was tall and muscular. He would have been in his late thirties at the time. His face was hidden behind a bushy beard, but I was able to read his dark gypsy eyes like a Tarot layout (a skill I'd picked up on the road). In him, I recognized a twin soul. His eyes were both feral and soft, like a fox. I sensed an unspeakable hurt had sent him on the run like it had me. At some point the enemy had probably stopped chasing us but neither of us could stop running. We had become fugitives from internalized demons; imaginary landslides constantly threatened our peace of mind.

I followed him back to a camp in the woods he shared with two of his Korean War misfits—Earl, a skinny, little man with darting weasel eyes; and Big Skunk, a giant who stayed drunk and cried most of the time. His name preceded him. The only time I got close enough to shake his hand was during our introduction. He smelled like dead fish and rotten eggs.

That night the four of us feasted on steamed clams in real butter, wild pigweed, and skillet corn bread. An impromptu duet with Earl on harmonica and The Chief on wooden flute provided a perfect dessert to the evening festivities.

He invited me to spread out my sleeping bag around the fire with a promise to keep me from harm. With The Chief near, I didn't dread the impending night as I had most of my life since my mother's death. Before meeting him, I would catnap during the day when given the opportunity, and after dark was super vigilant, a night creature pumping adrenalin, shaking in terror of unseen predators. I let go of my fears and slept until the sun shone warm on my face, waking to a gentle day. I'd had healing dreams that night even though I couldn't remember them.

I never left The Chief's side after that. He became my protector. He and his buddies were my family. He was the alpha male in the ever-changing mongrel pack of shell-shocked veterans who wandered in and out of camp. He made it clear that if one of them even looked like they were going to touch me, he would do worse than kill them.

We never were lovers, although the attraction was strong at

times, at least on my part. Occasionally he brought other women home to the camp—sometimes for a day, sometimes longer. I never once felt jealous or threatened by them. I knew his first loyalty was to me. Not having had the guiding hand of a mother since my early childhood, I benefited from the presence of these other women.

It was Ruthie (she was much older than The Chief) who taught me how to spin wool with a hand spindle. She had seen Gandhi on a newsreel sitting in prison and spinning cotton thread and decided to learn. Ruthie also taught me how to knit sweaters and socks. After she'd been with us for six months, she went to live with her daughter in San Francisco. She left me her spindle, yarn, and knitting needles. We never heard from her again. I still think of her and miss her.

Through the years I sometimes ventured into town for romantic encounters, but they never lasted. The truth be known, I was in love with The Chief. I offered myself to him from time to time in vulnerable moments but he always refused. We both knew at some level that our soul bond could not withstand the complications of a sexual relationship. Our wounds were too deep, our egos too fragile.

When I was in my early thirties, I met Carl and got pregnant with Molly. I never thought once of leaving The Chief to go live with Carl in Anaheim. That's when The Chief decided it was time to move and find a more permanent home. He located a clearing in a beautiful forest of fir trees inland from the coast, and he and his buddies built us the cabin. We named this place The Farm. The Chief even delivered my kicking and screaming healthy baby daughter on a sleeping bag by the wood stove. I named her Molly, for Molly Malone in the song about mussels. The only part that I remember is the line about the fishmonger singing *mussels, and cockles, my Molly Malone*. I liked the song. The Chief sang it in his good moods.

The Burning Jacket

When Molly was five, her father found us and insisted that she go to live with him in Anaheim and attend public school. He had a few college degrees and faith in only an academic kind of learning. Molly actually wanted to leave. I think she missed being around other children even though she had all the creatures of the forest with which to play. I felt as though Molly had never really bonded with me. No matter how hard I tried, I could never do anything right for her. I guess I was not a good mother to a human baby. I missed her terribly though, and couldn't wait for her summer visits. She stopped visiting when she turned sixteen.

I sensed her disappointment in me. She wanted me to be like other moms. Living with few worldly goods, not knowing much about the commercial world in which she lived with her father, I would embellish, enrich everyday life with vivid stories in an attempt to entertain her when she came to visit. I tried to tell her about the burning jacket, not the real story, it would have been overwhelming and unbelievable, but a softer version—how she would one day inherit it and keep the continuity of the matriarchy alive. She misconstrued my stories as lies. So, I saved my fairy tales for my beautiful granddaughter who soaks them up like a sponge.

In all the time we were together I never knew The Chief's real name. His wife came to visit one day while we were still at the camp near Coos Bay. She called him Chuck. She stayed only a few hours and left crying. We broke camp and moved farther south that very day.

The Chief stayed drunk for a month after that unexpected visit. So did his friends, in sympathy I suppose. I always knew to stay clear of them when they were purging their demons on cheap wine. I made the trips to town for food, booze, and cigarettes. I cooked big pots of stew and skillet bread, and left them to warm by the fire. None of the men had the stomach for food during those times when the memories of what they had endured and what they had lost overwhelmed them. They could not force food into their shell-shocked bodies.

In time, they would snap out of it and be tolerable to live with again, until something else would set them off. It could be as simple a thing as an elk walking through the brush, cracking a twig underfoot.

The Chief went off the wagon only three times while I was with him: when his wife came to visit, when a letter was delivered at the Roseburg post office saying his daughter had been killed in a car accident, and when we went to San Francisco to hear the Grateful Dead. That was about a year before he disappeared.

Jerry Garcia was a cultural hero to The Chief. It was August, hot as blazes. We had no air conditioning in the truck. We hauled the dogs with us, at that time it was Puff and Clover, and drove to Golden Gate Park for the outdoor concert. Thousands of friends and fans were there—singing, dancing, and drumming. I had never been around so many people before. I wasn't afraid with The Chief by my side.

I had asked The Chief once about his name and he said, "It doesn't matter what my given name is, that man is dead." I wish he were here now. He would know what to do about the logging of the trees.

Even though I saw him disappear into a pink light at the Harmonic Convergence on Mount Shasta, I still look for him to this day, in the woods. A week or two weeks after his disappearance, when I went into town for supplies, I started asking questions at his usual haunts, the Liar's Café and the Wolf's Den Tavern.

Ben Kruger, an old drunk who was a permanent fixture at the bar, and whose word is questionable, said he saw The Chief hop on a bus headed for Portland. He said his skin was gray as ashes and he was staggering. That was the last I heard about The Chief. It made sense in a way. If he was drunk and confused he might have gone to Portland where his wife and family lived.

The dogs' eyes shine green in the dark, bringing me back from my reverie. They stand guard at the outer edge of the mourning circle. I don't see Gattita. She probably went home to get warm and dry.

I can hardly get up. The muddy jacket and the heavy black sky keeps me pinned to the earth. I'm soaked to the bone, muddy and cold. When I am finally able to stand, I bow in blessing to the spirits of the four directions and listen for their final words. It comes to me—a cry in the wind. I know what must be done. I step out of the circle and seal it closed behind me with a tracing in the earth using my walking stick.

The solid black turns to gray lattice as the forest awakens. Soft chirpings can be heard from the surrounding brush. The loggers will return soon. I must hurry.

I take the weapon from my knapsack, a five-pound bag of sugar, which I have hauled up here in anticipation of what must be done. The gas cap of the bulldozer doesn't want to come off. I bang it with a stick to loosen it, unscrew it, and pour in the lethal injection—the whole bag. When they come and start the engine, it will be coated with sticky shellac that will destroy the motor. I learned the sugar trick from The Chief and his buddy Earl when they were on a rampage to save an old-growth forest farther up the coast near Tillamook. It stopped the bastards for only a little while.

The rain returns with the light. We walk in the drizzle, single-file, down the hill. The leaves seem more intense today, in saturated colors of yellow, green, red. As if in defiance of the destruction, Mother Nature speaks through the leaves. "I will not dress myself in mourning colors. You will not defeat me."

We walk down the newly made road in stillness. The

silence is different than during the earlier journey up. It's not an anxious, fearful silence of what will be found; there is still hope in that kind of hush. This quiet is heavy and final. Like a gunshot to the head, it holds no possibilities.

Kachina and Kevin are in no hurry to play tag or race to see who will be the first one home. They seem to know that this is the last time that we will ever walk this path.

Chapter Ten

Tooley: April 2001.

Gattita is sitting on the porch waiting for me. With ears alert for the sound of the logging trucks, I dry off the dogs with a towel kept for that purpose on the porch. We run to Dorothy Ann and open the old truck's door. With tails wagging, the dogs jump inside and lie down in their usual spots in the back seat. They love to go for rides.

The chickens cluck and flap their wings as I turn them loose and scatter feed for them. They have a better chance of survival free in the woods than locked in their coop. No time to cry now. My eyes are as dry as my burning heart.

I lead Annie and Raoul out to the truck and tether them in the back, hoping that Alisha at the Liar's Café will want to take them. She told me one time that she always wanted to raise sheep. In the barn I fill three bowls with the rest of the cat food for Gattita and the other feral cats. Gattita can't go with us, she goes crazy when she has to ride in the truck. She purrs now and rubs against my legs as I scratch between her ears and say goodbye.

"You'll turn feral and fend for yourself. You'll be fine here with all the mice and birds to eat." My face aches from trying to hold back the tears. I fail in my attempt. A wall of water falls brittle and cold, like shattered glass.

"When the loggers are finished I'll come back and find

you. I'll bring a cat carrier so you won't be afraid to ride in the truck," I lie to her, and to myself.

I grab a plastic bag and throw in an unopened jar of peanut butter, huckleberry jam, honey, a bread knife, and the last of the loaf of homemade bread from a few days ago. In another bag, I place toothpaste and toothbrush, soap, candles and matches. In a large garbage bag goes the dog food, water, and eating bowls.

I go to the trunk at the foot of my bed and into a second big garbage bag and stuff the remnants of my life: three hand-knitted sweaters, socks, hats, and scarves, including the sweater made for Raynie, a bag of wooden knitting needles in assorted sizes, some underwear and a pair of blue jeans, along with my wooden flute, drum, and some sage bundles, and the picture of my mother, Fanny Juanita Winter Bear. Behind the canned tomatoes is a gallon coffee can full of coins that gets tossed uncounted into the bag. The double-bagged black garbage bag filled with bills is heavy and hard to drag out from under the bed. It's as if it doesn't want to leave its hiding place. I haven't counted it in a long time, but there is plenty of money to last for a while. I hoist the bag on my shoulder, stumble out to the truck, and stuff it in the back seat causing the dogs to wake long enough for rearranging around the bag.

My spinning wheel is too bulky to fit into the already crowded truck. It is a handcrafted masterpiece. The Chief said it was his best work. He was so proud of it he polished and oiled it compulsively. At the Saturday Market in Eugene he had bartered a drum and flute for the exotic wood from Brazil. When he finished his oeuvre he said, "There you are my princess, now you can spin flax into gold."

I take a last look around. *I must keep it together. No time to think too much.* I dash for Dorothy Ann, and heave the other two plastic garbage bags in the passenger seat. Annie and Raoul are bleating. They look miserable and scared. I feel like Noah in his

The Burning Jacket

ark as I jump into the driver's seat.

I forgot my sleeping bag. I get out and run back to the cabin that looks already abandoned and small. The day before yesterday it seemed large with life. Now the cabin looks stooped and old from betrayal. I wish I could gather it up in my arms and bring it with me. I grab my sleeping bag and stuff it in its bright red case. My pocket edition of *The Prophet* is on the floor by the bed. I stuff it into the pocket of the burning jacket.

On second thought, I grab the spinning wheel and wrap it in a black garbage bag and crowd it into the back with Annie and Raoul. They start to bleat. I know they are uncomfortable and scared but they don't have far to ride.

Gattita is still sitting on the porch. I go back to say a last goodbye. She comes to me to be petted, her rear-end skyward.

The wind has picked up. I hug the heavy and muddy jacket around me, and feel my mother reaching out through time and space to hold me. For an instant I forget where I am, until reality bears down like gravity whirling in a centrifuge of pain.

Bits of color catch my eye, as I take final inventory of a life that has been abruptly interrupted. The makeshift gadget I rigged up for plying two different colors of yarn together is in the corner of the porch; two dowels with spindles on top sticking through chicken wire wrapped around the top of an old rusted-out bucket and each anchored into a potato at the bottom. Both spindles are full of red and blue yarn that was spun to make a sweater for a customer in Roseburg. I'm tempted to salvage the yarn but decide against it. I have to get out of here before the loggers come back.

I dash back to the truck and start the engine. Dorothy Ann cooperates on the first try.

I will carry with me forever the image of Gattita sitting on the porch with legs planted like stable columns, her toes flowering out at the bottom like petals on a furry blossom. I will not let myself feel my heart breaking. I'm tempted to scoop her up and bring her with us, but she would hiss and screech and claw at me while I'm driving, not to mention irritate the dogs to fits of barking. I blow her a Judah's kiss and wave goodbye.

She grew a thick coat this last winter, perhaps in anticipation of what was to come. She'll be warm. She'll go through the cat door and stay sheltered for a while, until her food gives out and the loggers come.

The truck rocks violently, a helpless cradle in the wind as the rain falls in sideways sheets of ubiquitous gray cataracts, blurring my vision. The storm mimics my pain and anger.

Finally, we reach the highway where cars and trucks go about the business of getting to their destinations. I feel as though I have entered another dimension, one where I am visible and vulnerable. All those years with The Chief, and the years after he left, missing him but standing strong in the memory of him, was a reprieve that has now been revoked. Old familiar ghosts return to haunt me, laying claim to my peace of mind.

Chapter Eleven

> No other creature displays so exquisite an adaptation to the tidal rhythm as the grunion, a small, shimmering fish about as long as a man's hand ... the grunion has come to know not only the daily rhythm of the tides, but the monthly cycle by which certain tides sweep higher on the beaches than others.
>
> The Sea Around Us, *by Rachel Carlson, Oxford University Press, New York, 1951, p. 164.*

Raynie: August 2001.

Starring Attraction: Mr. Drake and the science club of Benito Juarez Middle School versus the Mighty Grunions of Newport Beach.

Setting: The Pacific Ocean, high tide, (third night after the official full moon).

Time: 12:47 a.m., August 2001.

Cast: A mixture of eighth grade brainiacs and maniacs, Frank Norton being the leading maniac. True's big brother, Delmar. He is an unwilling chaperone for this wonder of nature. Ashanti volunteered his time. She doesn't know he quit school to enlist in the Marine Corps. His life isn't going the way she planned. Mr. Drake, the director, is the eighth grade science teacher. The stars are, of course, the grunions. As a class, we decided to meet for one last grunion run even though school is out and we have all graduated to South Junior High this fall.

Action: Mr. Drake and Delmar are warming themselves by a bonfire far back from the tide line. The class runs up and down the sand brandishing gunnysacks and flashlights like weapons. The beach is crowded with people who have come to watch the grunions flop around on the beach and lay their eggs in the sand.

True and I tip-walk near the shore, singing at the top of our lungs, trying to avoid looking at Mr. Drake who is calling us all to come over near the fire for instructions. He has his flashlight beamed at his own face and looks remarkably like Freddy Krueger in *Nightmare on Elm Street.* Ray took me to see it when I was an impressionable five-year-old. We had to leave in the middle because I was wheezing so bad the sound disturbed the other people. The movie scared me so much I didn't sleep for a godzillion years afterwards.

In case you don't know what tip-walking is, it's when you hold hands (with your best friend preferably) and lean out as far as you can toward the sand without falling. You should try it sometime when you are sad or bored; it gives you a whole new slant on life. When we were younger, True and I used to tip-walk on sidewalks and in the malls, and sing our special tip-walking song, *The Age of Aquarius:*

> When the moon is in the Seventh House
> And Jupiter aligns with Mars
> Then peace will guide the planets
> And love will steer the stars.
> This is the dawning of the Age of Aquarius
> The Age of Aquarius
> Aquarius! Aquarius! Aquarius! Aquarius!

One summer when True and I went up to Oregon together to visit Granny Tooley, she taught us the lyrics from the musical *Hair,* declaring it the most important piece of American music ever created. She said it was The Chief's favorite. She dubbed *Aquarius* our special song since Aquarius is True's and my birth sign. Aquarius—the Water Bearer. She made us proud of our astrological good fortune, saying that we embodied the best of the old and new age. We didn't really know what to do with this information but it made us feel proud to be Aquarians.

Speaking of Granny Tooley, I'm worried about her. Mom says not to worry, that Tooley is a master of survival, but I'm not so convinced she can get by without the protection of her forest.

About four months ago, I received a large package with "Fragile" stamped on the box and no return address. It was Granny Tooley's spinning wheel with a note for me to take good care of it until she came to get it. She said she was on an adventure and would come see me when she was ready.

I miss her so much and I miss going to see her at her cabin in the woods.

Alisha at Liar's Cafe called Mom and told her that Tooley stopped by and left Annie and Raoul with her last April, when the loggers came and bulldozed Tooley's cabin.

Why didn't she come and stay here or at least call or write to tell us where she was? Mom says that's the way she is. Tooley is so independent that she won't ask for help.

I don't understand why Mom isn't more worried about her. I'm going to launch a search of my own if she doesn't contact me soon. I can't believe that she doesn't want to see me. Alisha told Mom that Kachina and Kevin had been with her. Thank God Tooley is not alone.

I haven't seen Ray for almost a year. I called Gram and Gramps Rogers and they told me that Ray was living down in Mexico. Mom didn't know where to have the divorce papers served so she got an uncontested divorce and sole custody of yours truly. I still miss him. When he first left, it was like a rash that itched all over my body. Now you can't see it from the surface and I don't scratch it all the time, but it is a hurt that I feel deep, around my heart.

Back to tip-walking. It's better to tip-walk on the beach with your bare feet, but Mr. Drake won't let us take our shoes off. He said the school doesn't want to be responsible if kids step on something in the dark and hurt themselves.

"Class, listen up now. I want you all to be respectful of one another and the other people on the beach, but most importantly show some respect for the grunions. This is an opportunity to learn something about these incredible fish. They jump up on the beach to lay their eggs. They do this under special conditions. Does anyone know what these conditions are?"

Mr. Drake's roaming gaze keeps coming back to me. I hide behind Jackson P, the tallest boy in the eighth grade, but he's not as tall as I am. True says he's had a crush on me ever since the birthday party at Patty Dean's house where we played spin-the-bottle and his spin landed on me. We went in the closet and he pressed his teeth hard against my lips and it hurt. I can live without kisses if that's what it feels like to kiss a boy.

Mr. Drake sees me and points in my direction.

So much for keeping a low profile in this drooling bunch of idiots.

True and I are the only girls here tonight.

"Raynie Rogers, why don't you tell us what you know about the grunions?"

I take a deep breath and manage not to wheeze.

"One, they spawn from February through August along the coast of southern California and northern Baja, only at night. However, there is a breed farther up the coast that spawns during the day. Two, the females will jump ashore only when seven or eight males are with her to squirt their melt on her to fertilize the eggs. Three, they know exactly when to jump, which is after the tide has reached flood stage, has slackened, and is beginning to ebb. They stay on the beach about an hour and then jump back in the ocean."

I hear Frank Norton giggling and whispering to John Bradshaw.

The Burning Jacket

"Well, get ready. They should be coming in any time now." Mr. Drake shines his flashlight on his wristwatch. As an afterthought he asks, "Does anyone know the biological name of the grunion?"

Without waiting for the goonballs to stop and look at me I say, *"Leuresthes tenuis."*

Frank Norton pops his gunnysack in my direction. "Hey, Roy Rogers, think you're so smart? Why don't you let me spray my melt on you so you can lay some eggs?"

All the boys giggle and look at me instead of the tide line. True and I both kick sand on Frank.

"Why don't you hold hands with me instead of your skinny towel-head girlfriend? I see you two, always together, always holding hands."

The other boys all laugh. Except Jackson P. He just looks at Frank and shakes his head.

Mr. Drake is out of earshot, but True's older brother, Delmar, hears the ethnic slur and grabs Frank by the back of the neck.

Delmar is the natural son of his parents. He was born in New Delhi and came to live in the United States when he was three years old. His look is exotic—dark and handsome—but he speaks and acts like any kid born in America. Delmar must live in a gym. He's bulging with muscles. True told me that Delmar quit going to his classes and just hangs out smoking dope. She found a stash in his closet and has been blackmailing him to supplement her monthly allowance. She is wicked. I guess he thought it would be better to join the Marines and get away from home rather than tell Ashanti face-to-face that he didn't want to study to be a minister.

"Don't call my sister a towel-head or you'll have to deal with me!" Delmar flexes his muscles to bring home his point."

"I don't care," Frank barks. "I want to go home. I don't

want to watch a bunch of stupid fish having sex anyway." Frank runs back toward the parking lot.

"Here they come," says Mr. Drake, excitement in his voice.

Ooohs and aaahs from a crowd of spectators rival in numbers the grunion that are leaping on shore; silver streaks shaped like commas catch the moonlight in their curves as they jump. The beach is suddenly alive with thousands of writhing fish.

People are frantically grabbing the slippery creatures with their hands and stuffing them into gunnysacks. I think it's gross and cruel to kill fish that are only trying to reproduce and keep their species alive, but the state of California says otherwise. People can catch all they want as long as they have a fishing license, and only use their hands to catch them, so I guess it is okay as long as they eat them.

True and I walk closer to the rolling waves of silver. The females dig in the sand with their tails to lay eggs in the holes they make. The males are frantically squirting gelatinous milky goo all over the female's body as she lays the eggs. The eggs will be safe for two weeks until the next highest tide of the month comes to wash them out to sea, which is when they will hatch and swim away as soon as they hit the water.

When the ritual orgy of reproduction is over, the flashes of moonlight hurl themselves back into the ocean. Human-made bonfires are put out and the crowd thins rapidly.

Then it is still, like the aftermath of a volcanic eruption. Only the waves lapping against the shore can be heard. The stillness holds the ocean breeze at bay as the grunion eggs settle down to incubate in the sand. Mr. Drake rounds us up and we head for the school bus that will take us back. Delmar's car is waiting in the school parking lot.

I'm spending the night at True's house. She wants to tip-walk back to the bus but I'm tired. I've got cramps in my stomach and have had enough excitement for one night. It's three o'clock on the morning and the moon has traveled to the other side of the ocean.

* * *

"Raynie, wake up. Wake up!"

I can't open my eyes. I'm rolling around in thick gooey stuff. It's all over me and in my nose and throat. I can't suck in air.

"Raynie, wake up! Breathe! You're having a bad dream."

"Help! You can't make me do this! Don't squirt your melt on me!"

I'm aware of noises in the back of my throat trying to get out and be heard. I open my eyes expecting to be writhing in the sand, encased in a mass of jelly, but I see True's face. She looks worried and then she laughs.

"You nutcase. You were having a bad dream. You scared me to death." She hands me my inhaler. I take a few puffs and the wheezing stops. I have a headache and my stomach aches in a way it never has before. When I turn over on my side, I feel sticky warmth between my legs. I put my hand down there and bring it up, fingertips red with blood.

"I'm bleeding."

Even though my mother explained in great detail and drew pictures of the female reproductive organs, complete with an egg being released into a fallopian tube using an eighteen by twenty-four-inch piece of her expensive drawing paper, making the beginning of the menstrual period more dramatic and romantic than the health teacher's chart, it is still a shock to feel the dark warm blood. I see the stains in my pajama bottoms like red, ragged-edged peonies blossoming. True comes back and throws me a Kotex and a towel with which to wipe.

"You just started your first menstrual period. You have become a woman my pretty pet," True says in a Wicked Witch of the West voice. "You have joined the great sisterhood and must pay the price." She throws her head back and performs her evil laugh. True started menstruating about six months ago. "Now you must undergo initiation."

"True, stop. You're scaring me." True started her first period in Math class. She told me she had to go see the school nurse right in the middle of class. The girl who sat behind her noticed that True had blood on the back of her skirt and volunteered to walk behind her. As her best friend, I should have been there for her, and would have been if she hadn't changed schools.

True's voice changes into what sounds like a nutty professor with a German accent. She jumps off the bed and picks up her tennis racket.

"Now over here," she bats at the right side of the wall, "vee haf da female reproductive organs. Und over here," she hits the other side of the wall hard, "Vee haf da male penis, shtichking out und ready to fertilize, mid his spermatozoa, de eggs that are in the oooooovaries." She makes a yodeling sound. I'm doubled over laughing. "Oh, you don't like that?" she says, really into her role now. "Vell, if you prefer, we can do it mitout the shtupid schticking out penis, by a process of 'budding'."

True runs over to the bed and grabs a pillow and puts it on her head. "Got in himmel, vas is dis? Another tiny offspring of True?" She throws the pillow onto the ground and points her finger at it. "Now go and reproduce yourself across the land, my little clone." True jumps up on the bed and starts hitting me with her pillow. I jump up and retaliate and we bounce around on the bed until we both fall down laughing.

In one motion, as natural as a sunrise, she leans over and kisses me on the lips.

The Burning Jacket

Her lips are soft. A perfect kiss.

I think of the frantic, grinding kiss with Jackson P, his body stiff and pressed hard against mine. I don't want to grow up.

I feel a warm clot of blood ooze from my body and know that I cannot hold back the enemy Time. Yesterday I was a child. Today I am officially a woman.

Chapter Twelve

Molly: August 2001.

Duchess and I sit out on the back patio by the pool in our bikinis eating quiche that she whipped up with whatever she happened to find in my refrigerator this morning. We lucked out big time with the Portobello mushrooms I had intended to stuff with Dungeness crab but never got around to it, and a piece of slightly moldy Fontina cheese. She scraped off the mold. And *voila!* Another Duchess masterpiece.

  The air conditioner in her house is on the fritz and she spent the night here. The sun that warmed my body to a slow calm just ten minutes ago has turned a scorching traitor, chasing us under the patio roof, and it's only nine o'clock in the morning. The weatherman promised a triple digit repeat of yesterday.

  The usual neighborhood weekend smells and sounds form a funky concerto: the suction of the pool filters, a ticking metronome that sets the beat for the bass growls of lawn mowers, the altos and sopranos of barking dogs. The complex melody is held by trilling larks and cooing doves that look down on us from overhead power lines.

  We are on our new summer schedule of closing the bakery on Sundays. Taking a whole day off is a luxury we discovered we could afford. We've even hired a new baker, a young man named James. He's quiet and eager to learn. He seems to have a flair for pastries, which makes my job a lot easier, and a twinkle in his eye for Duchess. She thinks he has the potential to be a great baker. He starts the ovens at 2 a.m. and bakes until 6 a.m. when Duchess comes to relieve him. This works out well for me because I've been taking Raynie to school in the morning and coming back home to work in the studio until noon. I go to the bakery and stay until six when Duchess comes back and closes for the night at eight.

I haven't seen Ray for a year. I hear he moved down south, but I still keep a watchful eye on Raynie. True's mom, Ashanti, gives Raynie a ride to the bakery after school most of the time. The days she has to walk, she calls me on her cell phone during the journey, at my insistence. There are four long blocks from school to the bakery, which is located in the East Anaheim shopping center.

I had the home phone changed to an unlisted number last year after Ray started calling every hour on the hour after midnight and on weekends. I would see his car and hear him drive by gunning his engine and squealing his breaks in that freaky truck he drove with the painted flaming Phoenix.

It had been weeks since I'd had a good night's sleep so I decided to follow the police officer's suggestion that I get a gun. Qualifying for a license to carry was easy enough because I own a business and carry cash back and forth to the bank. Self-protection from a crazed husband high on drugs and booze all the time wasn't a legitimate enough reason.

I bought a nasty little pug-nosed .38 caliber Smith and Wesson and learned to shoot at an indoor range over by the stadium, then took sixteen hours of classroom safety rules over in Brea, fifteen minutes up Highway 57. The last and final part of the training was shooting eighty rounds with my left hand, then my right hand, and finally in a squatting position.

I've always had an aversion to guns, but I surprised myself

how quickly I learned to enjoy shooting holes right through the hearts and heads of paper men moving menacingly toward me. Even holding the gun gave me a sense of power I had never experienced. I still keep the gun in my purse for reassurance, not that I would ever use it. And Ray may be gone for good. His mother told me that he loved it down in Mexico. She wouldn't tell me his location.

Raynie stayed at True's last night. She stays over there some weekends but the girls have been seeing less of each other since the move, which is fine with me. I worry about Raynie when she's out of my sight.

Duchess is feeding lettuce to Erma Geddon. I found her sleeping under Raynie's empty bed this morning. I think Erma misses Raynie when she sleeps over at True's. Erma comes and goes through the doggie door Ray installed prematurely, when he was hot to buy a puppy for Raynie. He hadn't thought to consult me. I squelched the idea immediately. I'm allergic to dogs. But we kept the door in place for Erma.

Before Duchess decided to spend the night last night, my goal had been to get up early, grab a cup of coffee in delicious silence, and go to work in the studio with no distractions. The garage is a perfect space for painting since I cleaned out the junk and had a skylight put in. With the windows and sometimes the garage door open and a fan for circulation, it works out well.

I've begun a project that has a lot of internal buzz around it. I feel like a hound dog on the scent of a new prey.

Don't think about it too much; just let it happen.

I did still life painting when I was heavy-duty into art back before Ray appeared and complicated my life. Placing shapes and colors in interesting spatial arrangements seems superficial and meaningless now. Those studies had their value in teaching me about composition, negative and positive space, how to mix color and apply it, but somewhere in my psyche I've made a giant leap. I've outgrown that period. I feel as though I'm on the cusp of something vital, something that urges on a gritty courage in my gut.

No more delays and excuses.

I've been doing careful, slow, contour drawings with pencil using my collection of seashells gathered as souvenirs during walks on beaches in Waikiki, the Bahamas, and Mexico. It had seemed of great importance to gather each shell, carefully, ones that echoed the depths of the ocean from which they came.

Once, when I was twenty-one, I had a mystical experience while walking in the sand along the shore at Huntington Beach. For a split second I became one with the ocean. I became the world's authority, and could have filled volumes with my knowledge of every creature, grass, and grain of sand in the water, but only for a moment. The experience altered me in ways I cannot even fathom or describe with words. Maybe I could nail down a tiny bit of that ecstasy on paper or canvas, use an illusion to capture the whole enchilada.

Maybe Raynie gets her love of the sea from me.

As I draw, I follow the rhythm of the shells in my whole body, continuous curving lines. With pencil tip touching paper, and not looking at the paper, I focus on the astonishing chalky wonders, not worried about the outcome. The process is the important thing.

Form follows function.

The phrase keeps chanting itself in my mind like a mantra, a puzzle I need to solve. I can hear the ceaseless wash of ocean waves that smoothed, through time, the curved edges of the shells, moving in a single-minded circular motion, a rhythm of wholeness with no straight lines or harsh angles.

I could sit for hours doing these contour drawings. I suppose I'm trying to recapture that moment of wholeness that came unbidden, out of the blue, on Huntington Beach. I know one cannot force a state of grace for it is a gift, but I long to experience that feeling again, if only for the time it takes a heart to beat one time. The memory of that moment of bliss is always in the back of my mind.

When finished with the drawings, I look at them carefully. Even though they are not accurate representations, as I would have been tempted to make them had I looked at the paper while drawing, they seem vulnerable in their naked awkwardness, compelling in a way I cannot describe. Newly born into a strange land, they hold a numinous quality the way the fresh light in a baby's eyes reflects the place that she/he has just left, a place soon forgotten in a world that hustles us along to the end of days. Do we then return to that place of pure being?

The coming and going of ocean waves in never-ending cycles.

The lines on paper hold a sensitive promise I can't ignore. With a soft watercolor brush, I add washes of sepia ink in the inside places where the shells hold the dark. In the past, I've had trouble with *chiaroscuro*, the fall of light on objects in space, afraid to add deep shadows, afraid it would make holes that I could fall into. Something is changing. I am beginning to invite in the darkness.

Bring it on. Let's get to the bottom of this. But no hurry. This kind of miracle takes time to unfold itself. One must be patient and have faith in the process.

After I do the contour drawings, I put them aside until they mature in my mind from babies into rebellious teenagers wanting independence. From memory, I do large drawings with chunky vines of charcoal, on big sheets of paper laid down on the floor. I move, as in a dance, feeling the movement of the ocean and the essence of the shells within my body.

I've commissioned my neighbor Marsha's grandson John, who loves to build things with wood, to make a dozen eight-by-ten-feet stretcher bars for me, and I ordered a roll of wide canvas. The tube of cloth arrived yesterday, a giant manicotti sitting next to a can of white gesso there on the concrete floor of my studio.

My ego seems to be less caught up in the mystique of being an artist and more focused on the process. Although I still find it hard to resist the urge to smoke cigarettes. I remember seeing a film about the Abstract Expressionists at work in their New York studios—sloppy with paint, an all male cast except for Helen Frankenthaler, all chain-smoking as they strutted around their canvases like exotic birds in some kind of serious mating ritual.

The next step is to translate the charcoal drawings into large grown-up paintings. I don't yet know what this process will entail, but my limitations are the size of the canvases and the use of acrylic paint.

Maybe I'll use brooms, trowels, and commercial paintbrushes.

I haven't shown Duchess, or anybody else, what I'm working on. If I name it or share it prematurely, I'm afraid the urgency to see it in paint will be lost.

Duchess's rattlings in the kitchen this morning woke me from an intense dream, not my usual dream. It was a nightmare of sorts, but one strangely without emotion, which made it even scarier. I've written down the dream and shown it to Duchess. She reads it out loud as we sip our mimosas.

I dive into a lake. Wolves live under the water. They seem wild and dangerous but they have collars around their necks. A man dressed in a black tuxedo dives down and brings one back up to show me. He says I should pet it. I do, and it doesn't bite. Then a little girl with long black hair dives in and swims away with the wolves. I want them to stay, so I tell them if they don't leave me I will take them to a better place to swim: the ocean. They just laugh at me. 'You can't tame us with bribes,' they say.

'You have to truly love us.'

The scene switches to a bathroom in a nunnery. *There is a baby girl sitting on the edge of the bathtub. She looks like a doll, not crying but patiently waiting for me to come and rescue her. I'm afraid she will fall backwards into the tub and hurt herself, but I can't get to her, the passage is flooded with water and I can't swim. I try to swim but a nun tells me I'm not allowed back there, that I haven't gotten permission from the authorities. This stops me. I rationalize that this is a nunnery and I cannot invade their private and holy space, and the little girl is not my responsibility. I don't even know who she is. I let the nun's words and the water, which is actually shallow enough to wade through, stop me from saving the baby.*

"What do you think it means?" I ask.

"Well, Queenie, this one's a no-brainer," Duchess is quick to reply. The baby represents your creativity and your need to express yourself through painting. You let small inconsequential things come between you and taking your inner needs seriously. Your barriers to what you want are really easy to overcome, like the shallow water, a small inconvenience, but you've convinced yourself that the water is over your head and you can't swim. You make mountains out of molehills in your struggle to get what you truly want." Duchess shrugs, proud of her analysis. She takes another sip of her mimosa.

"What about the wolves that live under the water and won't be bribed?" I ask.

"You can't tame your shadow with bribes. In fact, you can't tame your shadow at all. The dark is the source of your creativity. You need to learn to love it. The wolves have collars on to show you that they will work with you if left to their own methods. They will not be told how and where to swim. Also, I think the collars around their necks represent your need for attachments, and at the same time you are longing to be free of them."

Somehow, the analysis of the dream feels like an invasion of a sacred and private world, even though I asked for it. I go into the kitchen and make another batch of mimosas, pouring the delicious mixture of orange juice and champagne into two chilled flutes that Ray's parents had gifted us with at our wedding. I haven't used them for years.

I take a giant gulp for fortification before returning to the patio; I'm not into the game of self-improvement this morning. I want to either kick back and lounge in the shade, or go bury myself in the studio, but it's too hot out there now, even with the fans on.

Should I tell Duchess about my silly romantic dreams about a past life in Pompeii? Should I mention the doctor who came to the garage sale and that I can't get him out of my mind? I want to consult with her, but I'm afraid her answers won't be the ones I want to hear.

Is there such a thing as a soul mate that endures from one lifetime to the next? Or is it all just chemistry?

At times, I dream of a knight on the proverbial white horse who comes and scoops me up in his strong arms and happily rides off with me into the sunset. So much for all those *Women's Studies* classes I took in college that taught life is not a fairytale nor a romance novel.

Duchess laid out a Tarot spread on the patio table while I was gone. "Your Tarot readings are changing. You still have the three of swords hanging over your head indicating betrayal and separation, but something has shifted since you got rid of ButtFace. It shows in the cards. They never lie."

Sometimes Duchess goes over the top with the "let's fix you" mumbo-jumbo. I should have nipped it in the bud when she started reading my daily horoscope to me at the bakery.

Shades of my mother, Tooley, and her rituals.

Speaking of whom, I don't know her whereabouts. Last

April Tooley mailed Raynie her spinning wheel and then a few days ago a sweater Tooley made for Raynie arrived. It is really quite beautiful with muted colors and loamy smells of the woods. The postmark was from Coos Bay but there was no address and no phone number inside.

Back in April, when I talked to Alisha at the Liar's Café, she said that Tooley had come by in the pouring rain with all her belongings piled in the truck and had left her sheep there, with Alisha. Tooley had given her directions to the cabin and asked her to check on her cat, Gattita. Alisha said that she had gone out there where the cabin once stood and called for the cat. Gattita came out of the underbrush and was so glad to see Alisha that she jumped right up into her arms, purring like an outboard motor. Gattita quickly became the mascot for the Café and was a fearless hunter of mice and the occasional chipmunk that dared enter her sanctuary. Alisha said that the J&R Timber Company had bulldozed Tooley's cabin and clear-cut the surrounding forest.

That was three months ago. Raynie was supposed to spend a few weeks with her, but summer is almost over, and school starts soon. Last week Duchess and I asked the Ouija board where Tooley was, and it kept circling Goodbye. I find myself getting angry at my mother for being so inconsiderate as to not let me know where she is… just one more thing for me to worry about. Why the hell doesn't Tooley just call and tell us where she is?

I called Alisha again and she said she has not heard from Tooley.

Duchess finds it profoundly interesting that the first card in the Tarot layout, my "significator," is the Queen of Wands. "This represents you, Queenie. It indicates the qualities of constancy, loyalty, and creative vision. This is growth for you. It means you are in the process of meeting these attributes within yourself."

"I'm rid of ButtFace now, but I'm not quite ready to grow by leaps and bounds. I just want to be left alone and wallow in this conflicted web of misery I've woven." My tongue, thick from mimosas, feels like a bee that's been traipsing around in sweet sticky blossoms.

Duchess has a beautiful, blue, ankle-length hand-dyed batik sarong draped around her lower body and tied at the waist. The material flares out at the bottom giving her the look of a mermaid with a tail fin. She never shows her legs above ankle length to anyone. Her legs are her Achilles heel. I've known her for fifteen years and I've never seen them. She says she has cellulite. This seems like a contradiction of character—she's such a strong, independent woman who doesn't seem to care what people think of her. But I've never broached this topic.

"This is fun. When was the last time you just sat back here and relaxed with no commiments for a whole day?" Duchess's face stretches into a rubbery smile. "I mean, no *commitments* for the rest of the day?"

"Somebody's had too many mimosas," I say. We both giggle. "Idle hands are the devil's workshop, Duchess," I finally manage after the giggling subsides.

"Ida hands are the deva's worshop," she repeats. "Boy, what a twing twister." Our giggles turn into painful belly laughs.

"The Queen a Wans does na chase affer rainbows. She keeps ha feet plan-ned firmly on the ground." Duchess persists with the reading in a slurry voice. I stand and mess the Tarot layout with both palms, pull Duchess to her feet, and march her to the edge of the pool. She resists, but laughs. I push and she falls in, sarong and all. The cold water is delicious as I jump in after her, both of us squealing. We thrash the water at each other and for a moment I forget about the wolves that live deep in the waters of my mind. The god of wine and playfulness takes over.

Chapter Thirteen

Mike went up to his room, closed the door, got on the bed, assumed the fetal position, rolled up his eyes, swallowed his tongue, and slowed his heart.
Stranger in a Strange Land *by Robert Heinlein*
Ace Books, New York, p. 263.

Raynie: September 11, 2001.

Bubbles rise as I descend. My skin feels hot and rubbery, like Jell-O that melts and re-jells. The only thing holding my insides together is my wetsuit. It's eighty degrees out and the sun is probing the pool doggedly as if in search of a lost piece of itself that chinked off and fell to earth. I'm not supposed to be scuba diving back here when it's this hot, and never without a diving buddy, but this is a day when all rules have been thrown out the window. I don't have any homework, can't focus on reading, and I don't want to glue myself in front of the boob-tube like everybody else is doing.

Erma Geddon is in her burrow. She wouldn't come out to see me when I got home from school even though I coaxed her with rose petals. She must know that something is up, like the event for which she is named, the end of the world. She is probably disgusted with the human race.

Mom called me at school. She sounded like she'd been crying. Judy, the secretary in the principal's office, came and got me out of History class where we were all watching the Twin Towers fall over and over again. I was surprised and a little embarrassed to be singled out in front of a classroom of kids to take a phone call. Most of the kids have cell phones. We're usually not allowed to use them in class, but today is an exception. I had forgotten mine today. As it turned out everybody was so into watching the destruction and fall of the Free World that they didn't even look over at me when my name was called.

On the phone, Mom said she loved me, and that Marsha, our neighbor, would pick me up after school. Mom said she has a doctor's appointment this afternoon. Somehow, it's reassuring to know that life goes on.

Marsha is in the living room as we speak, watching a repeat of today's events. The Twin Towers video is the only thing on TV except one channel is showing cartoons to keep the little kids happy.

I wish True was here. Until this point, we have always shared important moments in our lives side-by-side. But her parents decided that she should go to a middle school in her own neighborhood. "A better class of students goes there," True had informed me without a rumor of a joking smile to follow, and in a voice that sounded hauntingly like her mother's. I don't blame True's mom for not wanting to drive on the freeways all day just so her daughter could go to school with her best friend, but this snobby attitude is something new. I tried to call her today but she isn't answering her phone.

I wish Mom would come home.

I sure could use a call from Ray on a day like this. He could call from Mexico. I wonder if he still has his old cell phone number. I'm tempted to call him and leave a message, but he probably wouldn't return my call. I've written several letters and sent drawings of Erma Geddon to him via Gram Rogers, but she sent them all back unopened. I got the idea a long time ago that Gram and Grampa Rogers weren't into having me around.

They like to live what they call "the good life." That means gambling, drinking, and smoking cigarettes in a stinky casino, or seeing the world from a tourist bus.

I feel tingly pulsations in my ribcage like I'm growing gills and turning into a fish, which could be an advantage if the air becomes too polluted for human life or if I ever need to hide from the enemy. It's my ace in the hole, like being fluent in another language.

I wonder how long Erma Geddon can stay under water.

An image that I saw this afternoon on TV flashes through my mind and causes me to shrink inside my wetsuit. It was a group of women in some Arabic country all dressed in their burkas and chirping like wild turkeys, ululating in celebration of the suicide bombings today, dancing in the streets and shouting, "Death to America!" It makes me sad to think that people in other countries hate me when they don't even know me.

The motor of the pool cleaner spits out the sentence, 'I think therefore I am,' over and over, mesmerizing me by its constant rhythm, sucking every leaf and bug into its giant, wormy mouth as it swims in short, jerky motions around the pool. I think Descartes was off base. His premise should not be 'I think therefore I am,' but rather 'I pretend therefore I am.' Isn't it all a big lie anyway? An illusion?

Today our history teacher said that people interpret historical events in whatever slanted way they wish to support their own views and beliefs. He said the wise thing is to get the facts from all sides and then come to your own conclusions. He didn't tell me anything I didn't already know. I've had lots of practice when it comes to sorting out truths from lies with a father like Ray, a friend like True, and a granny like Tooley.

I'm worried about Tooley. It breaks my heart to think of her roaming around out there in the world without her home and animals. I have to admit part of it is pure selfishness. I can't

The Burning Jacket

even fathom not visiting her and the animals anymore. Why doesn't she call me? She sent the sweater she made for me in the mail with no return address. It's too hot to wear, but I sleep with it at night and bury my face in the soft wool. It smells like her cabin, wild mushrooms, and wet dog. For my own sanity, I imagine her in a beautiful place with Kevin and Kachina, protected by the burning jacket.

Please call me, Granny Tooley.

I forgot to brush my teeth before I put on my gear, and the smell of half-digested pizza from lunch mixed with a slightly smoky flavor, like smoked oysters simmering in a chlorine broth in my mouthpiece, makes me feel like a human dump site.

True and I watched the movie, *The Secret of Roan Inish,* at her house last weekend. It was about a seal that came ashore and shed her skin. She fell in love with a human. Big mistake. The man hid her skin so she could never leave him to return to the sea. In mythology these half seal, half humans are called *Silkies*. I felt so sorry for the silkie that I couldn't stop crying. Ashanti was worried about me and asked if I wanted to go home. Since I didn't really want to be anywhere, I stayed where I already was, at True's.

I pretend therefore I am.

I am a Silkie in the sea. My wetsuit is my skin, my passport to the deep. I must never take it off. I'm getting all weepy again thinking of the poor Silkie. I don't think it would be a good idea to cry into my facemask. But how could a mortal do that to someone he loved? How could you not want the person you love to be happy? Even if it meant they wouldn't be with you. I think of Erma Geddon. Should I take her back to the desert and let her go? Would she be happier there, and safer, if the suicide bombers come to Anaheim?

Why do so many people want to kill us?

'Never judge someone until you've walked a mile in their

shoes.' I can hear Tooley's voice bubbling through the water.

'I pretend therefore I am,' burps the pool cleaner.

I am poor drowned Ophelia, not laid out resigned in death with folded arms across my chest and hands together. (That's how she was portrayed in my English Lit book from last year. Yes, I know kids don't usually study Shakespeare until high school, but True and I were in an accelerated Lit class for years.) Instead of a crown of flowers on my head, I'm spread out, face down in the water like a giant octopus with one bulging basketball eye that sees everything. I have been scorned by my true love. I'm surprised by the outrage I've conjured up at Hamlet for not returning Ophelia's love. My arms and legs thrash the water; each strand of my long, undulating hair is a deadly whip lashing out. I scare myself sometimes.

True's pure sweet kiss of last month comes to mind. We have never talked about it, but deep in my heart I wish she would kiss me again.

Adjusting my depth regulator, I sink to the bottom of the pool. Now I'm the man from Mars, Valentine Michael Smith, in *Stranger in a Strange Land.* True's brother, Jason, slipped it to me on the sly. Ashanti would have a fit if she knew Jason had read the book. I thought the novel was great and the gesture bumped Jason up to the top ten on my favorite people list. He's growing into an interesting person. He has even stopped slobbering all over me and True. I have always felt like Michael Valentine Smith did, that I was from a different planet, and the stork had dropped me here on earth by mistake. Jason told me he feels the same way. So we have three things in common.

1. We both like to read.
2. We both feel like aliens.
3. We both love True.

I wish I could just hang out at the bottom of the pool in my scuba gear forever, just grokking, like the Man from Mars, taking everything in, but I know that sooner or later the oxygen will be gone and that my gills are not yet fully developed, so I will have to ascend. Besides, Mom will drag me out when she gets home. She's really adamant about enforcing the buddy system rule. Thank God Marsha doesn't know about it.

I can hear Mr. Reiss, my diving instructor (everybody calls him Bud) as he reviews, in a husky salt-water voice, the three reasons for always diving with a partner:

1. To have someone to help you put on your gear.
2. To be there if you get into trouble during the dive.
3. To have someone with whom to share the excitement.

If push came to shove, I'm not sure Stan, my diving buddy in class, would be of help. He's not the sharpest knife in the drawer, as Ray would say. Stan is a golden California boy with folks as rich as Midas and he lives in a fancy house down in Laguna where I take classes at the South Coast Scuba Diving School. Stan drives a blue Porsche convertible.

True had no interest in learning to dive until she got an eye full of Stan when he dropped me off at her house last Saturday after scuba class. Mom was busy doing something else. True pranced around Stan's shiny car like a show pony. When he left True pestered Ashanti to sign her up for diving lessons in *my* class so she could be with *me*. Ashanti can be so naive sometimes.

Wake up and smell the coffee!

Ashanti tried to get True enrolled but it was too late. She had already missed too many of the basics. True lost all interest in scuba diving when she was told she'd have to go to a beginner class and couldn't be with Stan.

True and I have been drifting apart lately. All she wants to do is hang out at the mall and shop, shop, shop. When she isn't spending money, she's glued to the Internet surfing chat rooms, talking to boys and other girls, the ones who wear designer clothes and lots of makeup. I don't know why I bother going over there anymore, just to have her ignore me. The other day True said I had turtle breath from kissing Erma Geddon and she called me a fashion disaster because I wear combat pants and tennis shoes just about everywhere. She said my clothes made her LOL. That's email slang for "laugh out loud."

True thinks it's tacky and uncouth that I have to wear uniforms to school: brown khaki pants and green school shirts. I got my issue last week and it suits me fine not to have to think about what to put on every morning. Green is my favorite color anyway. We were told never to come to school in red. Some kid got shot last year because he was mistaken for a gang member.

True wants to go out with boys but Ashanti told her she would get put in a private girl's boarding school if she was caught getting into a boy's car. Ashanti told True that the subject of dating could not be discussed again for another year. I doubt that Molly will ever let me go on a date, given her experiences with men. Not that I want to.

I'm beginning to feel claustrophobic down here all folded up in my wetsuit. I adjust my regulator and surface to muggy air. I have made a mental list of urgent things that need to be tackled:

1. Look for Tooley.

2. Find a way to help those poor people in New York who got attacked today.

3. Try to call Ray again and tell him that I love him. And how sorry I am for telling Mom about our secret and getting him kicked out of the house even though there has been a lot of water under the bridge since then. And to let him know that Erma Geddon loves him and misses him, which I know she does.

I sit down next to Marsha on the sofa and dry my hair with a towel. Marsha's eyes are red and she blows her nose into a

THE BURNING JACKET

Kleenex. With a shaky voice, Peter Jennings sums up, once again, the events of the day:

"Today, nineteen members of al-Qaida, a militant Islam group, hi-jacked four commercial aircraft. American Airlines Flight Eleven crashed into the north side of the north tower of the World Trade Center in Manhattan, at 8:46:40 a.m. Eastern Standard Time. With nearly twenty-four thousand gallons of jet fuel aboard, the aircraft became a flying incendiary bomb. At 9:03 a.m. United Airlines Flight One-seventy-five crashed into the south tower causing the towers to collapse." Jennings pauses and his face looks like it wants to cry.

"American Airlines Flight Seventy-seven crashed into the U.S. Department of Defense headquarters at the Pentagon at 9:37 a.m., and a fourth plane, United Airlines Flight Ninety-three, crashed in a field near Shanksville and Stony Creek Township in Somerset County, Pennsylvania, at 10:03 a.m." Jennings' voice lowers to a whisper. "The estimated damage and amount of dead and injured are unknown."

I want to reach through the TV and comfort Peter Jennings for having the job of telling the world about this terrible day.

I put my arm around Marsha. She's shaking like an eight-point earthquake. I pat her back.

I hope Granny Tooley is safe, wrapped in her burning jacket, and with her animals, wherever they all are.

Chapter Fourteen

> ...I say that even as the holy and the righteous cannot rise beyond the highest which is in each one of you, so the wicked and the weak cannot fall lower than the lowest, which is in you also.
>
> The Prophet by *Kahlil Gibran*
> *Alfred Knopf, 1961, New York, page 43.*

Tooley: Tuesday, September 11, 2001.

Where am I? Sounds swarm in my throat, like bees, and form twisted hives of babble that sizzle in the dry desert air. The bees hurl their burnt corpses back at me to be explained.

I remember. I'm not still out in the desert. I'm in an air-conditioned building in a history class for elders at the community college in Bullhead City.

Kevin and Kachina sleep peacefully at my feet.

I scrunch down in the uncomfortable fold-up chair, my back to the wall. A spasm in my right calf prompts me to stand and jump up and down to relieve the pain, but I resist the urge. I didn't sleep well last night... was disturbed by nightmares of bulldozers replacing tall trees with swaying skyscrapers all around me. I stretch my legs out over the bodies of the sleeping dogs, but the position only creates a new distraction, a pain in the small of my back. I am a landslide of aches and pains today.

"Why am I here?"

Did I say those words out loud? I'm not embarrassed. I'm too old and tired for that kind of self-indulgence. I just don't want to disrupt the class.

"Lonah, would you like to take a break? Stretch your legs and walk your dogs?"

I must have spoken while half-snoozing. My eyes adjust to the light and I see the young blond instructor hovering over me looking fresh as a buttercup, dressed in a yellow flowered sundress held up over her firm upper body by spaghetti straps. She's probably in her early thirties, and obviously spends much of her time working out.

I've interrupted her lecture. Why did she call me Lonah? Is that my new name? It seems to fit. *Loooonaaah. Aloooonaah... a moan in my mind, a reflection in a coyote's eye.*

I remember now. The dogs and I had stopped to camp for the night, a few days ago or maybe a few weeks, or months. Since I've been on the road time floats in the air, like my untethered thoughts, at the mercy of any chance breeze.

I go through my recent meanderings chronologically to get my bearings.

I had parked Dorothy Ann behind Roy's Restaurant and Motel, an abandoned landmark along old Route 66 in Amboy, California. Stars and planets, punctuation marks that define the plot of my new life, had been like shiny dots in a clear indigo sky. It was chilly and I made a campfire out of dried sage tumbles and a few candy bar wrappers that littered the sand. It wasn't much of a fire, not like the bonfire I built in the backyard at Molly's in-laws, the Rogers, a few nights ago.

I went to visit them and they weren't home so I burned a pile of wood in the backyard and toasted marshmallows. It didn't turn out so well... I don't want to think about it now. Let's just say if the dogs and I hadn't fled the scene before the cops arrived, I would probably be sitting in jail right now.

The desert at Amboy was devoid of lushness and had brought out the packrat in me; any little piece of shiny glitter seemed like a gift. I looked for clues about lives in the trash people leave behind: shredded tires, soda and beer cans, plastic bags.

The debris glowed in the moonlight like sacred objects discarded on the surface of a dead planet, artifacts from a civilization long extinct. What motivates human beings to come to a place like the desert and leave traces of their lives behind? Do they do it to be remembered by future generations? Or is it carelessness? The desert a convenient dumping ground?

I wondered about the child who lost a red tennis shoe. Was he or she grown up now? A rusty, empty gasoline can sat next to a beat up mattress that looked to be in pretty good shape, except for stray pieces of stuffing scattered on the sand like dried cottage cheese. I wrapped myself in the burning jacket and lay down on the mattress. It felt good to stretch my body out full length instead of folded up like a jointed puppet in the truck.

I fell asleep. When I awoke, the dogs were baying at a barefaced moon that was on the morning-side of the sky. I joined in and the sounds came out in a long continuous moan I couldn't control. *Alooooona. Looooona. I'm all alooonaa. Lonaaaah.* I sucked in air and we cried out again and again until all three of our voices gave out. I fell asleep again to dreams of spinning fleece and rocking in my chair by a warm fire. Gattita was in my lap, purring to the sway of tall trees in the wind.

When I woke up the sun had just risen above the horizon to christen me, along with the new day. I was a different person, one without dreams of a future, with a new name that embodied all that I had battled, all that I had lost, all that I had become: Lonah Jones. I had been stripped of my mostly made-up, heritage. No more high-flying lies, no fancy names like Tallulah Running Bear Winters. I am simply Lonah Jones.

In my mind I am still out in the desert, an animal digging a burrow in the sand, in which to hide from the merciless glare of an unforgiving sun. The hot grains of sand, like thoughts, sift down the sides of the basin of my brain, sifting through the crevices. I need a simple hole with some depth to it, one that will hold my life in some meaningful way.

I am an old dog driven by instinct to dig my own grave.

I had a dog once that did just that. Chevy was the Chief's favorite dog. He was a gentle giant; part Chow, part Rottweiler. Chevy dug a big hole under a thimbleberry bush. It took him all summer. When it was deep enough, he laid down in it and died. Clean and easy. No fuss. All we had to do was cover him with dirt. That's the way I want to go.

The teacher, I can't remember her name, has gone back to her desk to continue the lecture, seemingly reassured that I am somewhat of sound mind. She is almost up to World War I in the chaos of European history.

I circle my tongue around my blistered lips, and then draw it in like a turtle retreating into its shell. My tongue circumnavigates the cavity of my still-parched mouth that water does not seem to appease. I realize I forgot to brush my teeth this morning.

I look down. The dogs are snuggled around my feet, asleep, contented, glad to be out of the blowing sand that stings their eyes.

There are five of us senior students seated at a long rectangular fold-up table. The room is in one of those thrown-up-overnight pre-fab units with low ceilings. It is a place without soul, much like a tree farm re-planted on a clear-cut, devoid of the richness of a long-standing ecosystem. This whole wing of the campus looks disposable, like tents in a caravan that could be rapidly dismantled in the night with no trace of any habitation to be found the next morning. The history of those who came before instantly erased by the sand and wind.

I had stopped here at Mojave Community College in

Bullhead City after my bonfire incident at the Rogers. I needed to use the bathroom, wash up, and refill the water bottles I had just emptied into Kachina and Kevin's water bowl. It seems to take all my energy just to get enough fluids into the three of us.

"Are you here for the Elder Hostel class, The Influence of the Hapsburgs on European History?" a pleasant female voice asked when I entered the lobby. I couldn't locate her at first because my eyes where adjusting from the assault of the sun's glare to the muted lighting inside the building. Splotches of muddy colors with pinpoints of red, after-images of stuffed olives with pimentos seared against my eyeballs.

I located the person to whom the voice belonged sitting at the front desk. My every pore sucked in the blessed cool air. Mankind was good for several inventions: air-conditioning had now bumped the spinning wheel as number one on my top-ten chart.

I think the woman at the desk knew by looking at me that my immediate "yes" to her question was prompted not by a burning scholarly desire to learn about the Hapsburgs, but rather one of survival.

The Chief had planned my education, which had focused heavily on survival—learning the use of every plant in the forest, how to stay warm and dry, how to forage for food. My cultural curriculum relied heavily on the music of The Grateful Dead and poetry of Leonard Cohen supplemented by a wide variety of dog-eared, yellowed novels The Chief bought for a nickel at the Goodwill store. I made sure I learned proper grammar on my own. I had a thing for using the English language correctly even though I had no formal education.

"I have to bring my dogs in with me. They can't stay outside. They're not used to this kind of heat," I told the woman at the front desk. When she looked hesitant, I pleaded. "I drove a long way to take the class. The Hapsburgs have been a long-standing passion of mine," I lied, not even trying to hide my desperation.

I had tried checking us into a motel, but had a panic attack in the boxy little room. The place reeked of a sickening sweet deodorizer sprayed to cover the odor of cigarette smoke, causing me to sneeze and wheeze like Raynie does during an asthma attack. Sadness fills me when I think of how my granddaughter suffers at the hands of the aerosols of progress.

I must get in touch with her soon. I just don't want Molly to come and find me and pressure me to go and live with them. I'm afraid she will try to civilize me, try to saddle and shoe me.

The manager at the motel had seen me sneak the dogs into the room and promptly knocked on my door and asked me to leave. What kind of world is this where dogs are not allowed inside of a building to cool off from the burning sun?

After a brief phone call to obtain permission for Kachina and Kevin to come with me to class, the lady at the front desk said I could go on to room 115A. The class had started fifteen minutes ago, and would meet every day from eight in the morning until noon, for two weeks. That would keep us cool for a while, at least part of the day, but not the hottest part.

The woman at the front desk at the college said her name was Anna. *Anna the Good Samaritan.* She winked at me and said if I needed anything to let her know. Then in a whisper, she said if I wanted I could take showers in the gym, and as a registered student I could use the swimming pool, as long as I didn't let the dogs go for a swim. She didn't charge me any money. She said the class was free for senior citizens. Then she opened her purse and pulled out a five-dollar bill, laid it on the counter and nudged it toward me. The gesture reminded me of an old mama cat I had a long time ago. She carried her litter of babies to me one by one, carrying them in her teeth, and laid them at my feet, nudging them toward me with her head.

The woman pointed in the direction of the food vending machines. I didn't really need the money. Taking her money made me feel guilty knowing that I have the key to a bounty of riches sewn into the hem of the burning jacket; something I hadn't given much thought to as yet. But I took the money anyway. It seemed to make her happy. I bought two Snickers bars and gulped them down as I walked down the hall to find my classroom. I hadn't realized I was so hungry.

I look around the classroom. These nomads in the drought of old age have come to warm their bones before death takes them. Are they drawn to the desert like moths to light?

Is that why I came? To subject myself to this final fire that allows no shadows in which to rest or hide? To be buried in the unforgiving sand that can only provide a shallow grave that, at best, will eventually uproot my unredeemed bones to blow forever with the tumbling sage? I am denied a deep and peaceful grave in my rich forest loam. There my body would become worm castings to mingle with and nourish the roots of my beloved trees. How I long for the trees and the soothing rain.

No more whining and feeling sorry for myself. After all, I chose to come to the desert. No more bullshit about why I am here. It's time to come clean.

I've been roaming for half a year. I went to the old campground down by Coos Bay to see if Skunk and Big Earl were around, but it's been years since I've seen them. They may not still be alive. The forest had covered all traces of any old campfires. The Chief taught Skunk and Big Earl to leave nothing of themselves behind. I saw no familiar faces in Coos Bay, no one to ask about the whereabouts of two old throwaway war veterans. I bought a tent and a camp stove and camped out in the woods for the spring and summer. I got the wanderlust, broke camp, and decided to go and have a look at the Colorado River.

The Burning Jacket

The Colorado River had been one of The Chief's favorite places in all the world. I wanted to experience it the way the way The Chief had described it. He told of setting up camp by the river, just west of the Grand Canyon. He spoke of how the water, a rippling deep cobalt blue, touched the scumbled reds and pinks and yellows of sunrise across the sky.

He said he had found a hallucinogenic morning glory that grew in abundance by the river and occasionally took trips to paradise or relived the hell of the Korean War, whichever wanted to surface from his unconscious mind at the time.

So, I had come here to honor The Chief and try to see the river as he had seen it—minus the magic morning glories.

That is why I went to the Roger's house... to get a good view of the river. My heart stopped beating due to sadness for a moment when I saw it. Engineers in charge of controlling rivers and directing their flow had entombed the great watery flow in a concrete crypt. No more wild shores in which the morning glories could thrive. No more freedom for the river to follow its natural course.

That is why I went to the Rogers' backyard and built a fire. The river needed a ceremony of cleansing. On my flute I played a pavane for a dying river. I played until I heard the police sirens. Apparently, someone reported an illegal fire at the Rogers' place.

My thoughts abruptly return to the present.

There are no windows in this classroom, but in my mind's eye I can see the mobile homes and trailers of my classmates. The vehicles look like snail shells glued by heat to the concrete parking lot.

The camper with the logo of a big silver Chinook salmon jumping in the air belongs to the couple from Canada. I am curious about them. Jon, the husband, invited me to go across the bridge to Nevada with them last night to play Bingo in one of the casinos. I declined with the legitimate excuse that I had no cool place for the dogs to stay. The truth be known, I would rather gnaw off my foot than step into a gambling casino. I did concede to having a gin and tonic with them in their big white air-conditioned fish. They even invited the dogs in to cool off.

While sipping on the pleasantly bitter taste of tonic with gin, I learned they have four children and seven grandchildren. They proudly showed me pictures of the whole family and recited each name and date of birth while pointing to a plethora of photos.

Whitney, Jon's wife, is a homemaker, Jon a retired fireman. With a chuckle, he volunteered that his most daring rescue had been saving a mother cat and her newly born kittens from a burning warehouse.

They had bought their mobile home five years ago on the occasion of their fiftieth wedding anniversary with a plan to spend their golden winters away from the cold and windy plains of Saskatchewan. They wanted to bask in the warm Arizona sun.

I was intrigued by their cozy domesticity and devotion to one another. The way they perched themselves side by side like lovebirds in a gilded cage, and leaned into each other as though magnetized by the other's energy. Something they said triggered a memory of The Chief. That happens a lot when I listen to other people.

The tan van with the tinted windows belongs to the jogger who sits a few seats down the table from me, on the left. A woman with a wide jaw. She has a German accent and a long foreign name that is hard to remember and even harder to pronounce. I call her Adidas, after the shoes she wears. Her skin and sports clothes are the same color tan as her van and the desert sand. She lives here in Bullhead City year round. No surprise. She looks like a native lizard I saw yesterday, or was it the day before? It was almost invisible but for the tracks it left in the sand.

The Burning Jacket

Adidas has a burnt smell about her, like a piece of clothing scorched by a hot iron. Her sad gray-brown eyes remind me of smoked oysters. I remember when I loved these colors, in the woods when I dyed wool in various warm shades of browns and ochre. After these few days of this all-pervasive color of desert, I swear I will never again use them. I have to give Adidas credit, she looks ancient, but she hasn't thrown in the towel. She gets up at the dawn's first light and runs three miles before breakfast.

Tex, the loud-mouthed retired oilman with emphysema has parked his white elephant of a mobile home across two spaces. He seems to be in a constant state of upheaval. He has a serious sunburn on his face and bald head, adding to the sense of turbulence that whirls around him. He reminds me of a walking brouhaha.

I made the mistake of sitting next to him in the cafeteria this morning. He was chastising Jon, the snowbird, for a negative remark the Canadian had made about George Bush. Jon said Bush was a puppet for a corrupt regime that wanted to make trouble in the Middle East to gain control of their oil supplies. Tex responded with a tirade that almost blew us to Oz, preceded by wheezing coughs and deep breaths from his oxygen mask.

"Ah, Hell's bells!" Tex said. "What the hell do you know about it? If you don't like our president, go home to your own country. What the hell do you know about the politics of oil? I've been an oilman all my life."

I made a note to distance myself from Tex's toxic spewing at lunchtime.

Della, the petite lady who dresses in flowered muumuus, sits directly across from me. Her fine strands of hair look like spun silver, done up in a knot on top of her head. It reminds me of a twisted skein of yarn and my spinning wheel, which I mailed off to Raynie for safekeeping.

Della wears a plastic comb on either side of her head with

fake orchids cascading down, framing her constantly smiling, cherub-like face. She smiles even through the bloodiest battles of European history. She rarely interrupts her smile with speech. I asked her if she was from Hawaii and she said, "Oh no, I'm from Kansas, but I've always wanted to go there." What better time than now, while you are alive, I think to myself.

The onsite over-night parking privilege is granted only to *golden-agers* enrolled in classes we were told by our bright-eyed young teacher. I cringe whenever she uses the euphemism *golden-agers*. It takes the dignity out of growing old, which is yet another euphemism. Where is the dignity of living in a deteriorating body containing a heart that breaks a little more every day?

My truck, Dorothy Ann, is parked a distance from the other vehicles. She needs her space.

I park at the school lot only during the day. I found an abandoned construction site just off Interstate 95, a few blocks east of the famous Bullhead City scarecrow, a mysterious stuffed effigy of a woman who gets a change of clothes every week, by an unknown dresser. She is currently dressed in blue taffeta, adorned with red high-heeled shoes and an old-fashioned red bonnet that ties under her chin so she won't lose her hat during the frequent sand storms here in the desert. At night, I park the truck behind a half-constructed building, which somewhat protects us from the wind and the eyes of strangers. The mattress I found in the desert in Roy is still in the back of the pick-up, providing grateful padding against the hard metal of the truck bed, for myself and the dogs.

A balding middle-aged man with thick glasses bursts into the classroom without knocking, bringing me back again to present reality. He interrupts the lovely blond teacher who is lecturing on the Battle of Verdun, the longest battle in history. It lasted ten months.

"Maria, turn on the TV! We are at war!" he shouts.

Maria falls into her chair when she sees, on the screen, airplanes crashing into two tall buildings. The images remind me of a King Kong movie I saw at the Roseburg Cinema. A moving prompt running at the bottom of the television screen states that this is a replay of a live broadcast from the World Trade Center in New York.

"Oh, my God," Adidas cries.

Suddenly the room feels like a battleground where the beloved body of our country is being torn apart before our eyes. Even though we don't have the facts, the images are enough to know something terrible and irreversible has happened. Great sorrow fills the room.

"I thought never could this happen in America. In the old country, yes, but not here in the land of the free," Adidas wails in her German accent.

Tex watches the screen with blood-red face. "Ah. Hell's bells, what's happening to my country? I wouldn't be surprised if some crazy liberals had something to do with this. Ah, Hell's bells! It's probably a hoax, a joke by the media, like when Orson Wells did *War of the Worlds* on the radio and sent everybody into a panic. I was just a little boy and my mother took me down to the root cellar to hide." He shakes his head in disbelief.

The snowbirds from Canada, Jon and Whitney, look as if they saw a ghost. "I think we'd better pack up and leave these people to their own wars. I don't want to get caught in the middle of this," Jon whispered to his wife."

I was next to them and overheard.

The TV screen switches to a smoking building with a gaping hole. Dan Rather, I've seen him before on the TV at the Liar's Cafe, says in a solemn voice that American Airlines Flight 77 crashed into the U.S. Department of Defense at Arlington County, Virginia, headquarters at the Pentagon, at 9:37 a.m.

Della's perennial smile has vanished.

Overtaken by an attack of claustrophobia, I stand, wake the dogs and exit without a word, clutching the key to the truck, followed by the Canadians.

This is no time to be sitting comfortably in an air-conditioned room while my country's men and women are burning to ashes in high towers.

I need to go and sit by the river and play my flute.

* * *

No sign of life around the Rogers' place—no cars out in front, window shades are down. I walk, the dogs run, down to the dock. We all jump into the river and float downstream to a public boat launching dock. We get out of the water and walk back to the Rogers' house. After a half dozen forays downstream, we are droopy with fatigue. The river is cold and refreshing but the trek back in the hot wind is torture.

I sit down at the round table shaded by a big umbrella in the backyard near the dock and attempt to play my flute, but only squeaks and shrill whistles come out. The discordant sounds cause the dogs to bark, so I stop, not wanting to call attention to our presence.

My head throbs. The dogs look at me expectantly. They want food but I'm too tired to walk back up to the truck to get their chow. I'll have to go soon. I'm thirsty and unlike the dogs, I cannot bring myself to drink river water. My plan is to wait until sunset.

"What will happen to the two of you if I keel over?" I ask the dogs. They look at me and lie down at my feet.

The river rises to meet me. The last thing I remember is dancing with The Chief while cool, clear water rushes over us.

"I'm glad you came to join me. I have missed you."

Chapter Fifteen

Molly: September 11, 2001.

I switched shifts at the bakery with Duchess today. I'm doing the early one because I have an appointment later this morning for a repeat mammogram and ultrasound. The lab called last Friday and said the radiologist had found something that looked suspicious. They asked me to come in this morning.

"It's probably nothing but the radiologist wants to make sure," the cheery receptionist on the other end of the phone line lied.

I'll have it checked so it doesn't fester in my mind to a full-blown death sentence. My life is too busy now to get sick.

Jose, from the Mexican vegetable and fruit market on the corner of the mall, ran in about an hour ago wearing a look of horror and told me to turn on the TV. It's been so long since I've watched TV that I had to think about how to turn it on. The set is mounted high in the corner of the kitchen, bolted there to entertain whoever is baking at night so they'll stay awake. I usually make my coffeecakes and sweet rolls before I leave in the evening, or I relegate that duty to the new baker, James.

Despite the images of the burning towers in Manhattan, or maybe because of them, business has been lively this morning. I'm out of Orange Sunrise coffeecake, and down to the last dozen cinnamon rolls. But I've sold only three loaves of bread.

It seems on this bitter day in America, people want

something sweet. It's not a "business as usual day." Routines are suspended. People's faces show fear, disbelief, grief. The strong emotions seem to call for strong, yet comforting, flavors to counteract what is happening on the television screen.

I hear and see the images but I don't feel anything. The reality of what happened hasn't caught up with my emotions. Or maybe I'm overwhelmed with my own fear about having breast cancer and can't deal with it all.

"You're here early," I say.

I look at the clock on the wall and then at my watch when I see Duchess walk through the front door during a lull. The bakery is empty except for the figures on the TV screen running from a cloud of smoking debris.

"I thought you could use a little moral support this morning. Besides I'd rather be here with you and the customers than at home watching the chaos on TV by myself." Duchess's sigh sounds like a rushing waterfall.

"Thanks for being so thoughtful. I guess I am on overload this morning. I just wish the damn mammogram was over and I was being told that everything is okay. Do you mind if I head out early? I need to get out of here and go for a walk or something." I grab my purse.

"Of course." Duchess comes and makes gentle circles on my upper back with the palm of her hand. A gesture that has the opposite effect of soothing me. I pull away.

"Besides, my appointment is in an hour and there may be traffic on the freeway."

I lie. My appointment isn't for another hour and a half, and the hospital is a fifteen-minute drive. Duchess frowns her concern. She knows I'm lying, but I know that she understands my anxiety.

"Hey, why don't we just close the bakery? We've got a legitimate excuse, like the beginning of World War III. I'll go with you and then we'll have lunch."

"No, I appreciate it, Duchess, but I want to do this alone. Thanks."

"What about Raynie? Do you need somebody to pick her up?"

"No, I called the school and they think it best to keep to a normal routine. Raynie is walking home after school and Marsha will be there. She's at my house anyway watching TV, hers isn't working. She has the key to the back door. I'll stop by here after my appointment and check in with you. Do you think you'll close early?" I ask as I head for the door.

"No, I think I'll stick it out here. I'm going in the back and pretend I'm you and make some cupcakes and cinnamon rolls." She walks over and turns off the TV and gives me a backward wave as she heads for the kitchen.

* * *

I'm on the 91 heading north. The freeway has less traffic than usual this morning, and the sky is strangely silent and empty of air traffic. I turn into the parking lot of Ralph's Grocery and sit in the car with the sun warming my face.

The SUV is my comfort zone. It's like a tank shielding me from outside attacks, but doesn't protect me from my own thoughts. How I wish this day was over.

I feel myself relaxing in the warmth of the sun and falling into a romantic reverie. This time it's about the doctor I met at the garage sale, not the dark handsome youth from Pompeii. I realize my fantasy is an escape from reality, but what's wrong with that? I could use alcohol or drugs. Daydreaming seems harmless by comparison.

It disgusts me that I fall back into the role of the weaker sex wanting to be swept away by a handsome prince on a white horse. Some fairy tales are hard to outlive.

I lean back and feel the fix like sweet water from a deep well running through my veins.

I remember Duchess's last Tarot reading:

The Queen of Wands is an ancient image of a more contemporary figure: Wonder Woman. She has it all—a loving husband and family, and is strong in her own right. She does her own thing. Marriage works for her because she doesn't need to have a man to be fulfilled in this world. She makes a choice. This is what you want in your life—the loving husband and family, the bakery, and the career as an artist.

Your challenge is to learn to balance it all.

The thought of such a juggling act puts my nerves on edge again. I don't think balance is something I can achieve in this lifetime.

* * *

I leave the parking lot and get on Harbor, go left and take a right on La Palma. My anxiety level rises as Anaheim Memorial Hospital and the lab parking lot come into view. *It's just a routine follow-up. It's nothing.* Still my heart quickens and my palms are sweaty.

Now I wish I had taken Duchess up on her offer to come with me. I could call her cell but I know I won't.

The aroma of coffee and sweet rolls, my rolls at that, takes some of the anxiety away as I enter the building. The hospital venders have been steady customers of the bakery for several years.

I'm aware of my gait. It feels stiff and slow as I cross the expanse of soft blue carpet and turn the corner to the x-ray and mammogram department.

A TV is mounted high on the wall with images of smoke

The Burning Jacket

and destruction. Fire trucks are on the scene. These are different images than the Twin Towers.

The lab waiting room is empty save for one woman. She has a flowered scarf wrapped around her head and large gold hoop earrings, the kind we wore in the seventies. I am guessing (projecting really) that compared with her personal battle, the struggle unfolding on the national scene must seem like a stupid game to her. It's funny how the crisis of an immediate personal tragedy seems to take precedence over global ones.

The woman who checks me in is crying. "They struck again," she says. "A third plane hit the Pentagon."

The images of flames, smoke, and chaos make me dizzy. I'm falling backwards into a different time and place, a *déjà vu* enduring a fiery death somewhere in the deep ocean of the past. I pinch my arm. *Yes, I'm still here.*

"Are you all right?" asks the woman at the desk. "You look a little pale. Would you like a glass of water?"

"No, I'm fine. Thanks. I'll be all right."

Despite the bedlam on TV, I smile at the woman seated in the waiting room with the scarf wrapped around her head. She must be waiting for chemotherapy treatments. She smiles back and nods. The light in her eyes compels me to sit next to her. I've seen this kind of grace in people's eyes before. It's the light that emanates from someone who remembers who they are no matter the circumstances.

Before I can say anything to the woman, the nurse calls my name. I stand and follow her like a prisoner to the guillotine, glancing back once at the woman, wanting something from her. I know not what.

Still smiling, she raises her hand as if in blessing.

Chapter Sixteen

Molly: September 14, 2001, Hospital, Bullhead City, Arizona.

The rock in the palm of my hand throbs with energy and wakes me from a deep and dreamless sleep.

I pulled away at first when Tooley woke up just long enough to pass me the rock from her trembling hand. It wasn't a conscious act of repulsion, just an involuntary reaction, a default safety mode, this shrinking that my body resorts to without my conscious consent when I'm around Tooley.

The stone looks like a river rock, smooth and slate colored. It has a pulsing rhythm that seems to echo the beat of Tooley's heart, which is mainlined through a machine with continuously blinking flashes of green. Obviously, the gesture of giving me the stone had been made with great effort and no doubt, the unspoken message meant something profound for Tooley.

I'm ashamed of my feelings of resentment toward my failing mother.

Now is not the time to be judgmental, for God's sake. She may not pull out of this.

The stone is the size of a walnut, about four times larger than the lump the ultrasound found in my left breast last Tuesday, the day my life was altered, perhaps forever. The day the towers collapsed and America was changed forever. I knew something was up when our family doctor's receptionist called the afternoon after the ultrasound and said the doctor had made time to see me as his last patient of the day. The lump was already palpable to touch.

"Why hadn't you noticed it?" he asked, with a somewhat accusing tone. "Don't you do routine breast exams on yourself?"

The only time these babies ever get touched since Ray left is when I wash them in the shower. That was the response I wanted to give, but instead I shrugged my shoulders like Ray and Raynie do when they're in a tight spot and don't have a ready answer. The truth is I had felt it, several months ago, when it was a tiny kernel, the size of a sunflower seed. The spot was tender. After a while, it had stopped hurting so I forgot about it.

Tuesday seems like light-years ago, a triple-whammy day: the suicide bombings and the news I may have breast cancer.

I don't know how long I'll be here in Bullhead City with Tooley. I tried to call Gram and Grampa Rogers but got no answer at their home.

Two images superimpose themselves in my mind: the serene face and eyes of the woman with the scarf in the waiting room having time to weigh all her options about a course of action concerning her future, and the people trapped in the Twin Towers, who had no time to reflect. One image of a woman standing at the window high in the tower reminded me of The Tower card in the Tarot deck. The cameras zoomed in on her face, a mask of terror, as she made the choice to jump to her death rather than be consumed by the flames that licked around her.

The thought of having the time to make decisions, should I have cancer, eases my mind somewhat and gives me a certain feeling of control over the situation. My biggest concern is, who will take care of Raynie if I die? Duchess comes to mind, but it doesn't seem a likely fit; Duchess can be a bulldog if she doesn't get her way, and Raynie needs a softer touch.

I don't want Ray anywhere near Raynie even if I could find

him. And if he's in Mexico, I'd rather she grow up here. And, God forbid, what will happen if Tooley dies now? Raynie adores her grandmother. Even if Tooley recovers, would she be capable of raising a child?

The scene with Dr. Phelps repeats itself over and over in my mind. His empty waiting room is filled with plants and a waterfall cascading over rocks. I sit next to the waterfall, hoping the negative ions will eradicate any hint of cancer that may inhabit my body; my hand held over the traitorous left breast.

The receptionist informs me that she is leaving for the day and that Dr. Phelps will be with me shortly. A young man in a black raincoat and holding a black umbrella, incongruous attire for southern California, exits the inner sanctum into the waiting room. There is an air of grim reaper doom about him, and the room seems to shiver as he passes me. Dr. Phelps trails him through the door with outstretched arms and hugs for me. He is comforting to look at, a round, smooth boulder of a man.

"We'll get you scheduled as soon as we can, for a biopsy. It will probably be next week before they can work you in, but go to the lab Friday morning and get your blood work done." Dr. Phelps writes something on a pad and hands it to me. "You'll need a chest x-ray and an EKG as well." He smiles, not the same reassuring and invincible smile from the lady with the scarf in the waiting room. The doctor's smile is a 'let's wait and see' kind of expression.

"What happens next if the results show it is malignant," I ask, not believing it is me saying those words.

"We'll leave it up to you and your oncologist as to the best treatment. Sometimes a lumpectomy, and/or a round of radiation are enough, or you may need a mastectomy, chemotherapy as well, depending on how aggressive the cancer is. But let's not jump ahead until we have all the facts. It could be benign. Try not to worry until we know something."

THE BURNING JACKET

With his hand on the small of my back, Dr. Phelps ushers me to the door with a certain sense of haste. It's late. He wants to go home to his family, or to the hospital to do rounds, or whatever he does when he leaves the office.

He has never walked me to the door before, even when Raynie broke her arm a few years ago playing crack the whip with Julio, a neighbor who is a senior in high school now and much more interested in driving around in his beat-up Chevy than playing silly games with the little girl down the street.

Tooley's hospital room is cold. I pull the side of my face away from the ersatz leather of the hospital chair, slowly, as if removing a sticky bandage that pulls on the fine hairs of my cheek.

I look around the hospital room. My watch reads 6 p.m. I hope I haven't slept through the doctor's rounds. The information the desk nurse gave me was merely that Tooley had suffered a heat stroke. I stumbled into the hospital four hours ago, dead tired from the drive and not having slept for the better part of three nights. The biopsy is scheduled for Wednesday.

Sleep overtook me as soon as I hit the chair, just after Tooley reached out and gave me the stone.

I was in the lab this morning waiting to have my blood drawn when I got the call from the hospital here in Bullhead City.

"Do you know a Tallulah Running Bear Winters?" The female voice sounded both amused by the name and concerned. "We're not sure, but we think this same person enrolled in a history class at the community college here under the name of Lonah Jones, unless Tallulah was driving someone else's truck, or it was stolen. Do you know either of these people?"

When they said Bullhead City, I thought at first they meant Gram Rogers, but how did Tooley's truck appear at the college? And who is Lonah Jones? Why is she in the hospital? Is she all right?

I'm so tired I wonder if this whole conversation is just one of my dreams.

"She had a heat stroke. We found Tallulah Running Bear Winter's truck registration in a 1980 white Ford Ranger, along with a letter from a Raynie Rogers with your return address. She also has two dogs with her. One is a corgi, and the other looks like a German shepherd mix. The dogs are being sheltered temporarily at the humane society."

It took a few minutes for my brain to register the facts. The lab technician was calling my name to get the blood work done.

"She's my mother. I'll have to call you right back. I have your ID number on my cell phone. I'll call you back as soon as I can."

Just like Tooley, to horn in on all the action, even from her hospital bed she upstages me. My possible cancer sounds trivial next to her heat stroke.

The voice on the phone had said that Gram and Grampa Rogers' neighbor had become suspicious of the old white truck parked in front of the house all night Tuesday, and the next morning had gone over to investigate. He found her on the boat dock, unconscious, and badly dehydrated, cradled by her two dogs.

I yawn and long to go back to sleep. The hushed bustle of the hospital personnel that supports convalescence seems to nurture me as well, an invitation to slip into a much-needed coma. The truth is, it's been months since I've had a good night's sleep. Even though Ray has supposedly moved to Mexico, I don't trust the information. He could be lurking around, waiting for his chance to steal Raynie away. On those nights when the thoughts of Ray invade my mind, my eyes stayed glued open in vigilance until the sun rises.

I squint at my mother through my swollen eyelids as she lies in the bed, helpless and ashen, motionless, on smooth white sheets, her arms tucked in tight at the sides. The nurse had battened her down like an old ship tossing in a storm just after Tooley gave me the stone. She had been tossing and turning and pinching herself, which had caused bruising on her arms.

Tooley's eyes are closed and she mumbles something unintelligible. Her lips that had once been so full in her younger days are now shriveled like a dry mushroom. Her hair looks like dead corn stalks in late Autumn.

Through a slurry of tears, I look again at the stone in my hand. A surprise smile makes my face crack like dried caked mud disturbed by my involuntary smile. What message was she trying to convey to me? Be strong, like a rock? It could be a gift that begs forgiveness, or it could be part of a quirky rite of passage, a gesture to help her get through her final hours on earth. At some level, I envy her ability to cope, her use of ceremony. Ritual is the way Tooley keeps the wolves from the door, her way to open the channel to her God or gods.

I shouldn't throw stones. Isn't my attempt to make art a ritual to channel the "spirit," the "unknown?" And, of course, the dreams. We all have our ways of coping with this ordinary existence. I think of the woman in the flowered scarf in the waiting room again.

The gauze held down with a Band-Aid strip on my right arm, a reminder of my trip to the lab this morning, rips off with one hard pull. This morning seems like forever ago. Things are moving too fast for me. It's hard to focus my eyes on the faded body on the bed. My eyes want to shut it all out again and close with sleep.

It's my fault she's here. I should have made the effort to look for her. I should have taken the time.

I should call Raynie. She'll be over at Marsha's having dinner now. How am I going to tell her that Tooley may die? Something Raynie said about Tooley a few years ago comes to mind. 'Mom, when Granny Tooley's around, everyday is like Christmas.'

I feel like a pouting child whose candy has been stolen. I had longed for that kind of closeness with Tooley. She hadn't been dependable like my dad. She would tell me outlandish lies and embarrass me in front of others, or expect me to naively believe her. Even now, in what may be her final hours, the barriers are up.

I want her to comfort me. I want to tell her I'm afraid I may have cancer and that I'm afraid to die. And I want her to hold me and tell me everything will be all right.

The nurse comes in to look at Tooley and check all the bells and whistles on the monitors to which she is attached. The nurse opens a box of Kleenex, hands it to me, and pats me on the shoulder. Salty tears burn my eyes and cascade down my cheeks to pool in the indentations of my collarbone. The front of my blouse is soaked.

"I know it's hard. I lost my mother last year. I just thank God I had her all those years."

Her words send me diving into a river of regret and guilt. My body is racked with deep sobs. The nurse tries to comfort me, which makes me feel even worse. I'm not crying because I might lose her. I'm crying because I might lose me.

Damn you, Tooley. Don't die. I need you. You're the only mother I've got.

Chapter Seventeen

> Slowly the evening changes into clothes
> Held for it by a row of ancient trees;
> You look: and two worlds now separate from you,
> One ascending to heaven, another, that falls;
> *"Evening," stanza one, by Rainer Maria Rilke.*

Tooley: September 14, 2001.

The key. Mustn't drop the key. Hang on... give to Raynie. Burning my hand. Don't let go.

My head doesn't hurt anymore. Thank God. I remember being hot and then cold. Dogs... the dogs. They kept me warm. Where are they? Then a blinding headache and a titanic thirst; needed the burning jacket to keep me warm. Where is it? Then something struck me down from behind. Like a tree in a withered forest, I was felled, by the hand of an unseen woodsman.

Had it all been a dream? Is this yet another dream?

I remember reaching for the pendant shaped like a key that lay near a cactus in a pot. The map is hidden in the pendant. I remember thinking it strange that there should be a cactus growing in a pot in the thick of the forest amid trees that are at once leafy and lush with life, and dry as bleached skeletons against a burning sky. I had to keep the pendant safe until it was placed safely in Raynie's hands. If Molly got it first she might dismiss it as a foolish game and throw it away, as she had wanted so many times to dispose of the burning jacket.

Where is my jacket? I reach down and pinch dry skin between my fingers. I'm not wearing it.

Where is the jacket? I must pass it on to Raynie... her legacy. The pendant with the map inside that was sewn into the hem. The pendant that was under the cactus plant.

Riding fast the fiery tail of a comet, high in the star-filled sky, is The Chief. Is he coming to take me home? I must give the key to Raynie before leaving.

With little more than a thought, the pendant key has been delivered, disguised as a perfect stone, round and smooth like a miniature moon in a concave sky.

"Now we can lift off." I turn to The Chief.

I am by nature a selfish person; I tend to horde the treasures of the heart and mind, but the right thing has been done here. My granddaughter's inheritance has been placed in her hands. We are one and the same, forged from the same earth and sky, and I know she will endure and survive all trials as long as the key and the burning jacket are with her.

The woman dressed in white has shackled me, tethered me like an old goat, to something cold and hard. Tears that burn well up behind my weighted eyelids and trickle down the cracked, hard, dry canyons of my cheeks.

What have I done to deserve this punishment other than to get old and take a few trips to the moon along the way? And yet I know down deep there is more that must be done here.

I have done something that is yet unspeakable. The thought blooms at night in my dreams like an evil flower.

The pendant with the secret map has been delivered. What more needs to be done? What more do they want of me? I feel burning saltwater run down my face and pool in the parched lunar crater that joins my neck and shoulders. Haven't I proven there is water on the moon, that my life substance rushes, a deluge, to fill a grateful sea? Someone is here beside me. I feel

The Burning Jacket

her reproach as pin pricks on my skin. How dare she hold me in contempt for past mistakes, for living my life as I was forced to do.

Yet, I know there is more. I must confess the unthinkable.

"What have I done to make you hate me?"

My voice impales itself on jagged pieces of barbed wire embedded in my throat that tries to keep the words from escaping. The words sound syncopated, like corny lyrics of an old country song.

"Mom, I don't hate you. Everyone here only wants to help you. I've been so worried about you. We all have. I didn't know where you were. I thought you'd wandered off back to Oregon. I was about to call the police when the hospital called."

The ragged, uneven voice of the woman has named me 'Mom.'

Hold on! Batten down the hatches. I'm on a bed, inside the recovery cone, hovering just above the ocean, awaiting confirmation to land. The 'beep, beep, beep' seems to come from somewhere inside of me. I remember. I've been orbiting the planets, dancing on the moon with The Chief, and now I'm back, alone and without him. He is the one who gave me my wings. We have soared over unnamed spaces together. And now I'm back, in this cold, hard, manmade box that has little compassion for sinners, allows no forgiveness.

"Why did you bring me back?" I asked, betrayed.

You must not leave things unfinished. The Chief urges me to stay.

"Mom, you're in a hospital in Bullhead City. Why didn't you tell me you were coming to Arizona? I didn't know where you were until the hospital called and said you'd had heatstroke." The voice is contradictory. It both cries in concern and accuses me.

Did you know that at one time there was life on Earth?

I try to smile at her in reassurance. Heatstroke? Yes. Hot and then cold. My eyelids feel like singed butterfly wings, the delicate tissues pump the air in an attempt to take flight, but they are grounded. The light is excruciating.

"Where am I?"

A carousel of white and silver encircles me in a blur of motion. Everything slows and then stops abruptly, leaving me dizzy. The face of a woman comes into focus in a room that's all white, with a sickening afterglow. Halos of mother of pearl surround the objects in the room making them look distorted and alive.

I'm bound and gagged. I've got something in my nose and throat. It feels like a snake. A machine has leached itself onto my heart, ticking out heartbeats. Is it breathing me or am I keeping it alive with my breathing? I follow the course of an irrigation hose that hangs from a stand by the bed and flows into the back of my hand. Moon drops. They are feeding me moon drops that I brought back from my recent adventure.

The woman who calls me Mom is hovering now. She looks to be in her early forties, although it's hard to tell anyone's age these days. Anyone under seventy looks young. She's dressed in a brown skirt and a short-sleeved blouse with a Peter Pan collar—an uninspired print of tiny flowers in yellow, orange, and brown. An unflattering line for someone with such a skinny neck and round face. And an unflattering haircut as well—short, not tapered, with bangs cut straight across. I don't know what's gotten into me. I'm rarely critical of what another person wears. What is important to notice is the way they walk and carry themselves; this information belies their honesty or insincerity. And the most important is, what do their eyes say? Are they capable of caring, or do their eyes betray hatred and disloyalty?

This woman is hard to read. She is trying hard to control her emotions but tiny sobs heave from her, like escapees from a prison. She looks dazed, and somehow betrayed.

What does she want from me?

"What do you want from me?" I can hear the snake in my throat hissing.

The woman moans, "Oh, no." She shakes her head, and cries again, those exhausted little sobs.

Now I've made the poor dear cry. The woman had called me Mom. Didn't that mean something? How could I be so insensitive when this sobbing woman only wants to help me? She thinks I'm her long lost mother.

A deep response akin to lactation wells up within me and makes my dried nipples itch. They hurt and I can't rub them with my hands tied down. I feel moon drops pooling in the corners of my aching eyes again. I want so very much to give this woman some moon-drops. I would give her the Moon itself if only I could.

"Don't cry dear, everything will be all right. I'll help you find your mother." I struggle to free my arms and hands but cannot. I want to touch her.

"Did you know that I danced on the moon during an eclipse? The Earth passed between the sun and the full moon. Everything became dark and silent while the Earth's shadow cloaked me in quicksilver."

I hope these words will cheer her up. I feel the muscles in my face trying to smile.

The young woman leans over the railing, her fear and grief are palpable. She kisses me on the cheek.

"I hope you are feeling better now," I say. I just want her to stop crying, to be happy.

"Did you know that scientists believe the moon to be barren, with no atmosphere or water? It isn't true you know. I was there and swam in the crater of Apollo. I can do an impersonation of water flowing on the moon if you like."

I'm not sure the woman has heard a word I've said. She cries harder and blows her nose loudly into a Kleenex.

Oh dear, I'm making things worse, and I'm too old to try and fix it. All I want to do is close my eyes and sleep. I'm so tired. It's too late.

Have I given her the pendant key? Yes. I think I have. I had felt my hand fly open, had felt my fingers fan out. I had offered her the key and she had accepted. The important task has been accomplished without any dramatic last-minute reforms. No time. All that is left are remains: burned ashes.

My life ended long ago, on that terrible day, the day Jeb wrenched my mother from my arms when I needed her most. She had been my sun, warming me with a love complete. I could do nothing to protect her. He kept hitting her until she stopped screaming, until she was bloody and silent.

From that moment on, I had no star to orbit until The Chief came along. My sun had been struck from the sky leaving my childhood world a dark and bloody battleground. I became invisible to all but an inner fury and vowed revenge one day on the man who had snatched the life out of my mother in such a brutal way.

Neighbors heard Jeb's story and sympathized with him, lowered their eyes and voices to whispers when I was present, so that I wouldn't hear about the mother who ran away and abandoned me, according to Jeb. But the truth was branded on my heart, a silent burning.

I grew from a deprived little girl who watched as her mother was swaddled in a quilt of many colors and rolled into a shallow grave out behind the barn with no marker to tell her tale, no tree to shade her bones, into a depraved and cunning girl of fifteen. I was stunted the day he beat her to death, wounded like an animal that caught her foot in a trap, tethered to an anger for Jeb that matched the heat of the earth's inner core. I expected nothing good to come my way in life. I became, that day of my mother's death, a relic of a human being.

Why am I not as able to fall to earth as gracefully as my mother fell, as swiftly as my forest had fallen? I am only a handful of ashes. I long to be done with it and scatter in the wind.

The woman who calls me 'Mom' is still crying.

I cannot take you with me. You must wait for coyote to come and bring you home. The Chief whispers in my ears and disappears through the mother-of-pearl veil.

I reach for him but he is gone.

Chapter Eighteen

Raynie: Halloween 2001.

"You are so *gauche*. You need some serious help my friend."

True mimics her mother's favorite 'how-could-you-go-out-of-here-looking-like-that?' stance. She wags her index finger back and forth, chirps like a mentally disturbed chipmunk, one hand on hip, one foot pointed at the object of her disapproval. She doesn't like my Halloween costume, or, rather, lack of.

"That's not a costume. It's just your usual everyday bad taste in fashion."

"I'm trying to make a point here, duh."

I glare back at her.

"What point is that? That you're poor white trash?"

True doesn't approve of the army fatigues, combat boots, and Greenpeace shirt with 'Help Stop Global Warming' written across the front.

"You could have bought a costume when we were at the mall," she said, twisting around so she could view her butt in the mirror.

"Life is not about what you wear, but who you are," I say, not as convinced as I was when Tooley taught me that, by example. The principle applies out in the woods, a whole world apart from Southern California. Here, everybody seems to judge you by what you wear, before you even open your mouth.

"I didn't want to spend the rest of my allowance on a stupid costume," I said.

I wasn't about to remind True that Mom has cancer and my Granny Tooley got kicked off her land and almost died from heatstroke and a broken heart. True thinks the whole world revolves around her. "You simply do not understand my *modus operandi*. Stick that in your French pipe and smoke it," I say.

"That's not even French." She sticks her tongue out at me. "So what does motivate you, my dorky friend?" True asks.

"I will list them for you to make it easier for your pea brain to understand." I immediately feel bad for stooping to her level of criticism. But I continue: "One, get the message across that we need to stop polluting our world. Two, you don't have to spend a lot of money to enjoy a holiday, like Halloween. Three, I think for myself and don't buy into the whole consumer crap like some people I know."

I wish I'd never come over to True's, and I'm feeling mad at myself for letting her talk me into getting my belly button pierced at the mall, even though she paid for it with her allowance. That makes me a hypocrite to my code of ethics and a slave to her whims and demands.

The evidence is glaringly visible—a pink, throbbing little circle around the fake amethyst, my birthstone, where the woman in the jewelry store shot me with her piercing gun. It's beginning to itch.

"Trust me. This won't hurt," the woman had said, chewing her gum furiously the whole time. When she leaned over me, I could see that one band of her false eyelashes was slightly off-kilter and her thick makeup was hiding a world of ripe zits. Granny Tooley told me never to trust anyone who says 'trust me.' I had ignored my better instincts to please True.

I went under the gun first, as usual in our joint adventures. We both had three silver studs shot into our earlobes last year, which just about sent Mom straight up a tree. She made me take out the earrings and let the holes heal over. Being from a culture where women adorn their bodies, True's mom had no problems with ear piercings. I don't think Ashanti will feel the same about the navel piercing.

It hurt like hell for a few seconds, but I didn't make a noise or scrunch my face for fear True would back out of the deal and leave me alone in this unholy alliance, or should I say too holy.

"Now don't scratch it, no matter how much it itches," the woman with the gun said. True didn't even flinch. All she said was, *a quell prix beauté*, and closed her eyes like a guillotine was about to chop off her head.

"I don't want to be seen with you. I wish I had never invited you to come with me to the party." True is not joking. There is no telltale crinkling around the eyes to indicate a "just-kidding" laugh is about to steamroll down the track. She stands before the full-length mirror appraising herself in her Brittany disguise, in the new rosy bedroom with ruffled satin pillows. She assured me the décor is no joke, it's just the way she wanted it. She and her mom shopped for a week finding just the right shades of accent colors to go with the peony-pink walls and carpet.

Will the real True stand up? Or maybe this is the real True.

"Why am I *gauche*? Do you even know what that word means? And who appointed you the fashion police?" I gesture with palms up at the room that looks like a movie set from the late forties. I'm rarely critical of décor, but sometimes True gets on my nerves with her constant put-downs concerning my *drab* clothes and *dorky* behavior. I wish my mom hadn't agreed to let me spend the night.

Halloween was Wednesday, but it's Saturday and there's this big costume party True's been invited to with her *tres chic* friends at her new school in Irvine. She assures me that only the *enchantés* will be there. Why does she even want me there? To show how *enchanté* she is by contrast?

I wish we could go back to a simpler time when we belly laughed at the world, held hands and tip-walked our way through our troubles, when our biggest worry was maneuvering to get seats together in the school cafeteria at lunchtime. Not dealing with mothers who get cancer, and grandmothers who disappear and then are found almost dead in the desert. And fathers who don't answer your phone calls, threaten your mother, never come see you, and then moves to Mexico without even saying goodbye. And on top of that, a world full of people who hate you so much they are willing to kill themselves in order to blow you to little pieces, or make you afraid to open your mail because it might have anthrax in it.

"You can't go like that. Everybody will think you're a dweeb, and you don't even have a real mask to wear," True says, adjusting her blond wig with two wispy side-wings meant to imitate Brittany's little-girl do. I can't believe that Ashanti approved of the short skirt that practically shows True's underpants, and she has on so much mascara that she's squinting like a squid I once saw at Sea World just before he squirted all of his ink out into the water.

The three stipulations for Ashanti allowing True to go to the party are:

One. She be chaperoned by her big brother Delmar who will soon be shipped off for basic training in the Marine Corps and then on to *Operation Enduring Freedom*. Delmar says we're bombing Afghanistan back to the Stone Age in search of Osama bin Laden. True says he regrets signing up but had no choice when his folks found out he had dropped out of school. His punishment was to join the Marines and become a real man. (But I sidetrack.)

Two. True has to include Jason, to which she protested with

her screaming, kicking, foaming-at-the-mouth routine because he's not so *enchanté*. He's more of a loner like me. I'm glad he's coming since I seem to have more in common with him than I do with True.

Three. That the parents hosting the party be at home. (Ashanti has already called them to make sure.)

"I hope Ducky is coming," True giggles, as she exaggerates the boundaries of her lips with Ashanti's signature lip gloss, Big Apple Red. True and one of her new best friends, Bubbles or Bunny, or whatever her name is, who I have not yet had the pleasure of meeting, have been stalking this football player around school. He's all True talks about these days. She founded, then elected herself president of the Ducky Wald Fan Club. The members silk-screened shirts with his picture on the front. I doubt Ashanti knows about True's fall into the depraved world of groupies.

I give in and wear black Capri pants and one of Rudi's Hawaiian shirts. It surprises me that Rudi, True's dad, has such a colorful collection of shirts. The man is quiet and seems shy. He's short, pudgy, and balding, with big, soft brown eyes like a deer.

Rudi hardly ever talks, but when he does, it's hard to understand what he says. His accent is strong. He sounds like his tongue is too big for his mouth.

* * *

"Let's get a move on," Delmar says. He has lost a lot of weight since last I've seen him, still hard-bodied, but now gaunt. His eyes have receded into his head, making his forehead stand out. It gives his face a caveman appearance, and the eyes seem haunted, in a scary way, like dead vampire eyes. True says he's scared to death of going into the Marine Corps and shipping off to war.

The Burning Jacket

I can't believe this is the same person who taught Sunday school and was enrolled in a Christian college, a grade-A student.

Earlier today, True and I found paraphernalia and a stash of *cannabis sativa* wrapped in a purple velvet cloth hidden in the back of Delmar's closet. I am familiar with this plant because my father, Ray, is an advocate for the 'godly weed.' Ray even let me take a puff from his pipe one time. It hurt my throat and made me cough. True and I decided the prudent thing to do was to say not a word about Delmar's hidden stash.

We had pillaged Delmar's closet because True was looking for something that might give Jason's pirate costume a little flair. She found a red necktie to tie around his waist. I notice he didn't bother to wear the costume. Jason and I are of the same persuasion about the whole masquerade thing.

I have a queasy feeling in the pit of my stomach as we pile into Delmar's new Ford Jeep, a coming-of-age birthday present from his parents before they learned he had dropped out of school. He already reeks of Mary Jane.

Ashanti and Rudi have gone for a weekend retreat with their church; they've left Delmar in charge during their absence. I'm on the verge of panic but I don't know why. It feels like I stepped into a nightmare where I am the alien. This must be how Granny Tooley felt when she was thrown out of the woods and forced to interact with a world that has gone insane.

The flat metallic color of the tank-like Jeep exterior brings to mind a dense, matted pile of dung left by an animal chased through the dry sands of Africa, and the interior blue-gray looks like the thick leathery skin of a rhino. I feel the breath being sucked from my body as True and I are herded into the back seat of this mammoth steel trap. True sees my discomfort and gives me a surprising pat of compassion on the knee after we holster ourselves in with the safety belts.

We head north on Interstate-5 to Highway 55, entangling ourselves in a snake pit of slow-moving traffic as far as the eye can see. Everybody is on the road tonight, trying to escape the city for the weekend.

I feel trapped and try not to look at the passing traffic. It makes me dizzy. True has her back to the window and her legs up in my lap.

"Surprise," True says. We aren't going to a dorky school party. We're going to a Rave in the Anaheim Hills with Delmar's friends. She leers at me like an evil Barbie doll. My instinct to strangle her twists my stomach into knots as we pass through thoughtless urban sprawl. The orange haze around the passing car lights doesn't exactly invoke confidence that all is right with the world.

"I want a spider massage," True demands as she wiggles her legs up on my lap. They feel heavy and I push them down on the floor.

"I thought you were all a-twitter to see Ducky tonight." I glare at True and push her legs down again after she hoists them up again. A pearl forms in the corner of my eye, an uninvited tear, as my chin trembles. I don't want them to see me cry, I just want to go home. I want to be with Mom and Tooley. I miss them. I could call them on the cell, but if I did, I would lose True forever.

I'm stuck in the backseat of a car, headed for somewhere I don't want to go, and the only way out is to open the car door and throw myself onto the freeway. I think of the poor people who jumped out of the Twin Towers and how they must have felt.

"Trust me," says True. "This party will be way cooler than hanging out with middle-school dweebs, with the exception of Ducky." True makes the sign of the cross, and looks up. "I owe Delmar a favor," she says in a whisper, behind a shielding hand to her mouth. "He gave me money to buy those really neat shirts I showed you, and he really wants to go to this party instead of hanging out baby-sitting us."

True tries to put her legs on my lap again. I push them down this time with a little more force.

"Keep your damn legs to yourself." I want to lash out and start hitting and screaming like she does when she wants her way, but I remember a technique that Granny Tooley taught me and decide to use it. She learned it from one of her ancestors, a Native American holy man.

I close my eyes and take a few deep breaths.

Go to your center and see yourself as the all-encompassing ocean. The cleansing waves are your breath as they roll in and out, in and out, unending, and forever. Just surrender to your breath. I hear Granny Tooley's strong and steady voice.

True giggles and says, "There she goes again, lost somewhere in the emerald sea of her *satori* mind."

I ignore True and keep breathing. Eventually my body goes limp against the sounds of Steely Dan's *Two Against Nature* blasting from Delmar's state-of-the-art speakers.

I'm floating away to Oregon, to Tooley's forest, only it's not dark. The air is filled with a golden light. All the animals are there, including the raccoons. We are having a tea party. Then there is a flash of light so bright it jolts me from my body and melts the trees and everything around me. I float, like a ragged ash in a super-hot wind in aimless agony until a voice from somewhere says, "You didn't do it right. Get back in your body and leave again, only this time, leave through the top of your head."

I go back into my body and the light forces me out again, but this time I relax into my last breath and shoot straight through a hole in the top of my head. Every particle of me bursts into a song of light.

When I return to my body, there is a persistent flutter at the top of my head, like butterfly wings, and I remember that babies have a soft spot in their skulls that heals over and hardens with age. Maybe my spot is getting softer again. Maybe I'm developing the ability to time travel without my body.

"Wake up, silly girl. You were snoring. We'll have to arrest you for violating the sound control standards." True pats my face in mock concern. Delmar has changed the music channel to a Christian Rock station. *Jars of Clay* pounds its message of faith.

Jason comes into focus. He's kneeling on the front seat facing us, telling us about some boy in his class who *sucks* big time. Everybody *sucks* in Jason's mind. Squinty-eyed, I look at Jason from the periphery of that other space, still not having quite crossed the boundary back into reality. Jason looks like a beautiful prince. Due to a recent growth spurt, he's almost caught up to me in height. His muscles form smooth bulges under his post-grunge ripped jeans and plaid shirt. At first, he is perfect, as is everyone and everything around me, and then I step back through the looking glass into reality.

I find myself perversely attracted to this infantile nerd who spends most of his time playing stupid games on his computer. I wonder what it would be like to run my fingers through his thick, dark, curly hair and lose myself in his sleepy, thick-lidded green eyes, and what it would feel like to kiss him, all this while he's inhaling a king-size bag of corn curls, half of which are stuck in his braces in yellow gooey chunks.

"Gross," I hear myself say, referring not so much to the yellow mush, as to my bizarre, lascivious thoughts. *Puberty! That's what sucks.*

I've thought a number of times about True's soft kiss, so unexpected, so complete. She reminds me of hand-crocheted lace, delicate and vulnerable despite her recent obnoxious performances. Lately, I've detected a constellation of sadness reflected in her eyes, fossilizing like a million-year-old mosquito caught in a piece of amber, getting harder amid the masks of smiles, jokes, annoying behavior and increased shallowness.

I've been feeling big-boned and awkward around her. I want to hold her in my arms and rock her like a baby, and kiss her again, but of course, I can't. She would laugh at me and tell everybody that I'm in love with her. If her parents could read my thoughts, they would probably haul me off to jail as a sexual deviant, or send me to a Christian rehab center for homosexuals.

How would my mother feel if I turn out to be a lesbian? Rachael Carson was in love with Dorothy Freeman. If Rachael Carson, my heroine, loves women, why can't I? Mom would probably accept it. Tooley would be cool with it.

Maybe I should talk to Tooley about it, but this probably isn't a good time. She's been through a lot lately. She hasn't been the same since the heat stroke. The day the towers burned in New York was the day the sun turned on Tooley and nearly burned her to a crisp. She wasn't used to intense sunlight and one hundred-degree days. She likes rain and cloudy skies. She and Kevin and Kachina have moved in with us. She's having trouble adjusting to life in Orange County. She laughs sideways and says, 'Orange County is an oxymoron. There are no orange trees left in Orange County.'

The wildness has gone out of her eyes, like a campfire extinguished by buckets of water. I know she is burning inside with discontent. She complains about everything, mostly about neighbors living so close you can hear when they fart and what they watch on TV when the windows are open. She misses the giant Douglas fir trees climbing to heaven through rain-filled skies. To her, everything seems flat and dull here where all the buildings look alike and the smog covers everything with yellow-gray cotton candy that looks like it has been eaten and vomited up.

When she's really wound up she accuses Mom of being a rightwing extremist and a war monger because Mom said she thought it was the right thing to do—to go after bin Laden in Afghanistan. Tooley said this whole world doesn't seem real to her anymore, like it's all plastic. And she is really worried about Mom's cancer treatment. She doesn't say anything to Mom, but she tells me that the doctors are destroying Mom's body with chemotherapy, that the treatment is all wrong and she should be doing a carrot juice and herb fast and go somewhere where there is fresh air. She thinks we should all move back to the Oregon woods.

Sometimes Granny Tooley cries when she doesn't know I'm listening, and mumbles about how she can never forgive herself for leaving Gattita behind, sitting on the porch all alone in the rain that day she and the dogs drove away in Dorothy Ann. Both Mom and I keep reminding her that Gattita is safe and warm with Alisha but she seems to forget, or doesn't believe us.

Kevin and Kachina are shedding, and even though I have taken up the task of brushing them every day and vacuuming when I get home from school, Mom threatens to take them to the dog pound. She's allergic to dog hair.

After Granny Tooley's heatstroke, her driver's license was revoked. She was already so beaten down by then that she didn't even protest when Mom sold Dorothy Ann to a used car dealer in Bullhead City. I could tell that losing her old truck was a terrible blow. She rarely smiles. Her skin has taken on a slightly bruised shade of blue-gray, like a beached whale, and her hair has turned as white as newly fallen snow.

The one thing that brings a tiny glow back to my Granny's pale blue eyes is watching The Nature Channel or old Hollywood movies. Mom bought her a TV for her bedroom and Tooley is usually hunkered down in front of it wrapped in her jacket. Mom closes the door to Tooley's room when she goes by.

The Burning Jacket

She says it makes her too sad to see Tooley so depressed, all curled up and docile like the dogs that sleep at her feet.

A few days ago, while Mom was at the hospital getting her chemo treatment, I pressured Tooley for a story so she built a bonfire in the backyard. She wore the burning jacket even though it was eighty degrees outside. The neighbors called the fire department when they saw the billows of smoke and we got ticketed with a huge fine for illegal backyard burning. It wasn't worth all the trouble. Without the forest and the stumps to sit on, and the yearly ritual of spring burning, the stories were not forthcoming.

"Earth to Raynie. You didn't hear a word I said, did you? Where were you? I might as well have been talking to the wall." True looks exasperated. "Repeat what I just said," she demands.

"Go stick your head up your butt," I say. "I don't care what you just said. It was probably something stupid about your precious Ducky, and that is too boring to even listen to."

True sticks out her tongue, then sidles up to the door and turns her head to look out the window.

* * *

Delmar exits off Highway 99 at Weir Canyon and parks in an already crowded lot behind an old warehouse by Lakeview. I remember this area. I've been here with Ray. He took me to garage sales around here, back in the days when he still loved me. He said there used to be groves of avocado trees all around. Now, it's all concrete and ugly block buildings. We go up to an older building, with lots of steel and mesh reinforcement around the windows. Looks like it could have been an old jail.

"Just keep a low profile," Delmar shouts over the blast of music that shoots like a missile out the front door where people have gathered. "If anybody offers you pills don't take them. And buy only bottled water with the seal unbroken. Stick together. Here's fifty bucks for each of you in case we get separated and you need anything, and here's a spare key to the car in case the music gets too loud and you want to get away and go to sleep."

Delmar hands me the key with a look that says, 'I can trust you to be the responsible one.'

"Remember, what happens here tonight stays here. Right here. Clear?" We all nod our heads.

Jason does his characteristic shuffle whenever he finds himself in gatherings of more than three people. True smiles. Thank God she has taken off that silly wig.

"I'll meet you back at the car at two a.m." Delmar looks around while he was talking, obviously searching for someone. He waves to a girl with a black half-mask on her face. She's dressed like Princess Leia.

"See you goonheads later. Have fun. And behave." With those instructions, Delmar walks away and disappears with his friend into the dancing crowd.

The three of us stand just inside the front door for what seems like eternity. I feel as though I'm all arms and legs. The dangling miniature skeleton hangs on the charm bracelet Ray gave me two years ago, a souvenir from The Day of the Dead celebration in Mexico.

"Delmar is right. We need to stick together." I shout to be heard above the music. True acknowledges my plea with a shrug of her shoulders; I can't tell if she's in agreement. She tries to look blasé, but the color of her eyes has gone from brown to black, a dead give-away that she is excited and maybe a little afraid. Jason nods his head and points to the bathroom, not far from us. It looks like there is only one bathroom and it has a long line of gyrating people dancing alone waiting to relieve themselves. I watch him push his way through the edge of the crowd by staying close to the wall.

The Burning Jacket

People mill around with bottles of water in their hands. Some drink from paper cups. All are moving to the beat, like crazy robots turned on by a master switch. True reaches for my hand without looking at me, taking in the scene. Finally, Jason returns and reaches for my other hand. The three of us follow the growing funnel of people toward the center of the music. They are gathered around a giant synthesizer, a monolithic god, on a stage that is backlit with glowing red light. The stage is flanked by speakers that thrust the sound into the mass of bodies. The crowd is thickest in front of the stage, gyrating like they are being driven mad by the sound of a metallic beat that does not vary in pitch. I feel it penetrate my whole body as if it wants to own me. People, some in costume, some not, wave psychedelic green and yellow glowing wands above their heads. They seem mesmerized by the sticks, holding them close to their faces, and lost in the movement as the colors trace unearthly trails in the air. People aren't dancing with each other. The music leads them inside. They dance to their own individual rhythm, yet hold together as a unit by some powerful god present in the beat.

A giant screen behind the stage flashes changing scenes: mobs of people dancing, tigers running through a jungle, ocean waves rolling against sandy beaches. Colored strobe lights shoot from the stage and roam the crowd, as if searching for escapees. At each end of the stage are giant blow-up plastic icons from Alice in Wonderland—the White Rabbit, the Mad Hatter, and the Cheshire cat sway together in a dance macabre as laser lights dart around them.

"This music rules," Jason says. He bumps his hip against mine, and then circles out as if drawn to seek his center in the growing crowd, his arms swaying back and forth over his head. True and I look at each other in amazement. This zebra is truly changing his stripes.

The music is slightly off-key, pulsating at a faster rhythm

than my pounding heart. Faint recognition of an ancient and secret tempo, one that encapsulates a feeling deep inside of me, slowly rises up my spine and takes control of my central nervous system. The thought crosses my mind that this is a beat that emanates from the heart of the universe; a music that thrusts up mountains out of the sea and pressures coal into becoming diamonds.

Surprise ripples through my nerve endings in shock waves as I remember the dream or meditation I had during the drive here. I touch my head and remember the fluttering I felt just after I woke up. *Surrender, surrender, surrender* taps itself out in a metallic high-speed Morse code, this techno-god's truth so simple it seems clichéd. With closed eyes, I see throbbing hieroglyphs projected onto the screen of my eyelids in neon pink, red, and green.

I spot True over by the wall near the front door. She is buying a bottle of water from a man with a refreshment tray strapped around his neck, like one sees at ballgames. The bottle glows an eerie electric green in the darkened room.

True ponies over to me. "Here, have a drink," she yells, handing me the bottle. "Highway robbery. The thief charged me seven dollars."

"I'll get the next round," I say, downing half the bottle in one long guzzle. I didn't realize I was so thirsty.

"I have a feeling we're going to need a lot of this magic green water before this gig is over," she says, treating me to one of those True magic smiles that lights up her whole face. "That guy with the water is selling X for thirty-five bucks a hit. Shall we try it?"

"Hell, no. Are you insane?" I scowl at her. "Where's Jason?"

"I already told him I'd cut off his balls if he bought any pills. Shall we dance?" she says, laughing and tugging at her

The Burning Jacket

Brittany skirt. It slips down further over her hips to expose the glitter of her new piercing. I close my eyes and feel the repetitive beat, calling me to go deep inside and explore the muscles and nerves of the esoteric jungle of my own body. At the same time, I'm aware of the surface throbbing of my new navel piercing.

I must have lost track of time. I had been deep in a dream, on a trip to a far planet, but I'm still on my feet, moving to the beat. In Earth distance, I've traveled only a few feet from the source of the music. Molecules tighten their dance around me, gathering closer together. I can see and feel them slowing down. Even the air is tired and wants to rest. The only lights are the streaks from the wands people wave and the gigantic Disney figures whipping around in a man-made wind. Jason's face flashes before me in the crowd. He sees me and snakes closer.

"Check out the dude sucking on the baby pacifier. That really does suck." Jason winks at me. "I dig this kind of music," he says. "I mean, really." He takes my hand and pulls me toward him. The music has transformed him into Mr. Personality. The tension in his face is gone and his body is relaxed and graceful on the dance floor. He leans forward and kisses me, our lips barely touching. We step back and look at each other as if we'd never met before. I never noticed how blue his eyes are, with flecks of green, twin planet Earths.

I suddenly remember, "Where's True?"

I realize how tired and hungry I am, and more than a little irritated at Delmar for dragging us to this party under false pretenses, and then just disappearing and leaving us to fend for ourselves. I push Jason away.

"Give it a break, Toad," I hiss at him. Jason seems to be resting on the laurels of his first success and not bothered at all by my rejection. I bet it's the first time he's ever kissed a girl. He dances in circles around me and da-da-das to the music, his hands above his head like Anthony Quinn in *Zorba the Greek*. I saw the movie with Granny Tooley a few days ago, in her room.

"Last time I saw True she was fanning herself and motioning toward the front door. So I assumed she was going outside to cool off," Jason says. The crowd is thinning.

"Was she with anyone?"

"No, she was alone, I think."

"Come on. Let's go find her. Have you seen Delmar?"

"No. I haven't seen him since he dumped us at the front door and danced off with Princess Leia."

The keys to the car are in my pocket so I knew she wasn't in the car unless Delmar let her in, but we look anyway. Cars are leaving. People are laughing and milling around in the cooling breeze.

"Hey look up there." Jason points to a trail at the end of the parking lot that meanders to a hillside.

True is perched on the top of a big rock overlooking the warehouse looking down at us and waving her arms frantically to get our attention.

We run up the hill, hand in hand.

"I was hoping you guys would come up here." True is barefoot. A half full bottle of Boone's Farm wine cooler is by her side. "Here, have some. It doesn't taste half bad."

Jason chugalugs and looks at me.

"Go ahead and kill it. I can't stand the stuff," I say. Ray used to drink it when he didn't have anything stronger around the house.

The circles of mascara around True's eyes have widened. "I'm queen of the mountain," she says, falling back laughing and kicking her legs in the air, showing her underpants under her skimpy Brittany skirt.

I sit down next to her, Jason sandwiches me in the middle. We all hold hands and fall back into the spell of a rare, clear, night sky. We lie there, ignoring the hardness of the rock beneath our bodies, speechless in the face of such vast, unfathomable beauty.

"The stars look so close," True says, reaching her hand up as if to pluck one from the sky.

"Can you imagine that at one time the sky looked like this everywhere on earth?" I feel as if I'd seen it all before, in another lifetime. The Milky Way is a translucent, slurry smear across the sky, a luminous band of stars, planets, suns, and moons, millions of light-years away. I wonder if other beings are watching the Earth as we are watching them at this very moment.

* * *

The smell of eucalyptus wafts in on a breeze and awakens me. The chill of the night is gone. The moon is a faint shell in a rose-colored sky, the hills around reflect soft tints of sunrise that remind me of the colored pencil tones my mother uses for the backgrounds in her shell drawings.

The music has stopped. My mouth is dry and my stomach rumbles with hunger. It feels as if time has moved on without me. Where am I?

True and Jason are wrapped around me, asleep. I look down and see the warehouse. Only a few cars are left in the parking lot that is shaded on one end by a lone avocado tree.

"Wake up you guys. It's daylight and Delmar is probably down there looking for us." I could see crewmen carrying out sections of the stage and wooden dance floor, followed by a procession of pallbearers, four on each side, cradling the robotic oracle that had lured so many seekers into drunken abandonment such a short time ago. A metallic Bacchus, it's magic vanished in the light of day. What I see is a big, dull, metal box, all smoke and mirrors, like in the *Wizard of Oz.*

A siren wails in the distance. The sound closes in as it makes the rounds of the hills. A white ambulance with red stripes pulls into the parking lot below. Three paramedics jump out of the back, rolling a gurney, and run through the front door of the warehouse.

"Delmar! Oh my god. Something must have happened to Delmar! He wouldn't just leave us stranded all night."

True is already in motion, running down the hill in her bare feet, leaving her shoes behind. I grab her shoes and Jason follows close behind. All I can think about is the crunch of our footsteps in the dry, brittle underbrush, and how True's feet must hurt from running on all the thorny seedpods.

Only the ambulance and Delmar's car are left in the parking lot. We rush into the building. Gray light filters through the metal of the windows creating shadow prison bars on the walls and floor, daring us to cross them.

The three paramedics are hunched over, working on a body on the floor. "May be a weak pulse, eyes fixed and dilated," one of them says, as he shakes his head from side to side.

My heart stops beating.

"He's just a kid," another says, slightly breathless, eyes big with what looks like fear, as he sees us rush in. "You kids can't come in here. Stay back."

"Oh my God, it's Delmar!" True screams. She runs to him and pulls on his leg like she's trying to drag him away from the paramedics. The one with the big, scared eyes moves her away.

A paramedic with his hair pulled back in a ponytail puts an oxygen mask over Delmar's face while another starts an IV. They hoist him onto the gurney, wheel him out, and lift him into the back of the ambulance. Delmar looks like a rag doll, skin gray as old linen. Jason is behind me, twisting my shirt, restricting my movement, holding on for dear life.

"Oh, no! Delmar! Delmar! Oh, no!" True shrieks.

Two policemen are outside. One is tall with big ears, a sharp pointy nose, and the longest arms I've ever seen. He reminds me of Ichabod Crane in *The Legend of Sleepy Hollow*. He catches True with his octopus arms and holds her around the waist as, kicking and screaming, she tries to get into the back of the ambulance.

One of the paramedics motions for the officer to let True go with him. "Maybe she can help us figure out what happened to him. Are you friends of his?" he asks Jason and me.

All I can see of Delmar are the soles of his tennis shoes facing the back door of the ambulance.

"He's my brother," True sobs as she climbs into the back with Delmar. The siren burps a few times as the truck pulls out of the parking lot, and then screams a loud, grim warning for all to get out of the way, as it winds down the hill at high speed. The sound carries with it a finality, like a fatal blow to my heart, like a house that has just burned to the ground with all of my possessions inside.

"You kids know the young man in the ambulance? What happened here?" The other policeman asks. He looks like he spends a lot of time in a gym lifting weights, and he's got a crew cut. He reminds me a little of Ray, only he's younger and in better shape. He approaches Jason, who cannot seem to find his voice. Jason points to me.

"We'll need some answers here to inform the paramedics as to how to treat this young man. What happened? What was he taking?"

The policeman hovers over me, looks me up and down in disapproval, like he thinks what happened to Delmar is my fault. I shake my head and start to cry. "We don't know what happened. We were asleep up on the hill and we heard the sirens. Then we saw Delmar on the floor and they were working on him. Is he going to be all right?"

A river of snot is running down from my nose onto my upper lip. I wipe it on the bottom of Rudi's Hawaiian shirt. It seems like years ago that True was belittling my outfit in front of her mirror. I wish we had all gone to the high school party. Delmar wouldn't be lying in some ambulance with a needle in his arm and an oxygen mask on his face.

"Were you kids taking drugs? Did Delmar take anything? Any drugs or alcohol? You can tell me. Nothing bad will happen to you. We need to know what he took in order to help him."

"We don't know what happened. He brought us to the party with him and told us he would meet up with us later. Then he disappeared. We got tired so we climbed the hill and went to sleep. That's all I know." I sob and shrug my shoulders. It feels like a thousand tons of gravity is pounding me into the ground. The wheezing starts and I haul the inhaler out of the pocket of my Capri pants.

"I need to ask you again. Did you kids take anything or know anybody else who did? We need to find out what drugs he may have ingested. We're trying to save his life here," he said, defensively.

"The three of us were drinking green water in bottles, and it looked like that's what most people were drinking. It tasted like regular water. Delmar did tell us that if anybody tried to sell us X, not to take it. And the three of us shared a wine cooler. That was hours ago. Delmar smoked a little marijuana before he left home." My stomach is growling and I feel ashamed of my hunger in the middle of the unfolding tragedy.

"Okay. That's helpful. Are you all related?" he asks.

"I'm his brother," Jason manages to croak. "Raynie is a friend of the family." He points to me. "Where are they taking him? I want to go and be with him and True." Jason's voice sounds deeper, more grown up than it did before we walked back through the door and saw Delmar on the floor. Time seems to be moving in slow motion. All I can think of is getting to the hospital and being with True instead of standing here answering questions.

"He'll be at Anaheim Memorial. Is this your brother's car?" He points to the car like maybe it was stolen or something. The policeman walks over to the car. "It's locked."

"He gave me the keys," I remember and dig in my pants pocket. I hand them over.

"Do your parents know where you are?" We both shake our heads in the negative.

Both policemen look at each other and roll their eyes.

"How old are you? Where are your parents?"

"I'm almost thirteen and my mom knows that I'm spending the night with True, but she didn't know I was coming here. She thought we were going to a school party."

"What's your home phone number? We'll call her and have her meet us at the police station."

I panic. "You can't call her. She has cancer. I don't even know if she's home. She may be at the hospital having chemotherapy. I don't want to upset her." How could I have gotten into such a mess?

"I doubt that she is having chemo treatment on a Sunday morning." He looks at his watch as if to confirm the day. "Just give me your number. We'll figure it out," Ichabod says in a softer voice, like he really cares.

He dials, listens, and hangs up. "The answering machine," he says. We'll try her later, at the station.

"She could be over at her friend Duchess's house." I volunteer the phone number. I just want to see her and give her a hug. "She owns a bakery but she wouldn't be there on Sunday."

Jason tells the policeman that his folks are at a church retreat in Big Bear and won't be back until tonight.

"Didn't they leave you a phone number or name of the place where they were going?" the tall, skinny policeman asks. He tells us to call him Officer Bob.

"Yes, but they gave the info to Delmar. He's in charge while they're gone. We can get it from him if we follow the ambulance," Jason says, trying to bypass the police station and go straight to the hospital.

"Come on you two. Let's go to the station. Tell us the name of your church and we can track down your parents," they say to Jason as they escort us to the back seat of the police car.

"New Life Baptist Fellowship. It's in Irvine." Jason says and sighs in resignation as the policeman who looks like Ray talks into the radio asking the dispatcher to look up the phone number of the church.

We're in deep shit no matter what we do. And when Delmar wakes up, he'll be in a bigger pile than us. Police lights flash and the siren screams as we head back down the way we came last night, and get on Highway 91 West toward Anaheim, in the middle of Sunday morning traffic. I look at the blank faces of the passing drivers, not yet fully awake, coming home from a weekend off, or just leaving. An ordinary weekend for them, but a day that will brand my life forever.

After an eternity, we get off at Harbor. Officer Bob is on the radiophone but we can't hear anything through the partition. I see his head and shoulders sink down below the barrier. We take a right on La Palma and circle into the driveway of Anaheim Memorial.

Officer Bob gets out of the car and punches in a security code above a door that reads *Emergency Room.*

The Ray-like officer gets out of the driver's seat and opens the door on Jason's side.

"Change of plans," he says, with a well of sadness in his voice. "We came straight to the hospital. Looks like your brother didn't make it." He touches Jason's shoulder.

"Well, where is he then?" Jason asks. He won't let himself understand what Officer Bob has said.

"He died on the way here in the ambulance, son. They found an empty container of Prozac in his pocket, and there was evidence that he'd had a lot of alcohol. I'm very sorry. We've gotten in touch with your folks. They're on their way home. They're coming to the hospital to pick you up. Should be here in a couple of hours."

"We were able to reach your grandmother," he turns his gaze to me. "She's waiting for you at home. We have another car coming to take you home."

Before he even finishes the sentence a police car pulls up behind us and a young policeman who isn't even as tall as I am takes my arm to escort me to the backseat of his police car.

"But what about True? I can't leave her." I jerk my arm away.

I look to Jason for help, but his face is buried in his hands and he's sobbing.

The new policeman opens the back door of his car and helps me in, a little forcibly, over my repetitive lament of "What about True?"

True came out of the Emergency Room door as we pulled away from the curb. I hold my hand, palm out, against the glass of the window. She's shaking all over like she's having one of her fits, only this one is for real. She doesn't see me. She goes over to Jason and wraps her arms around him. His knees buckle and True keeps him from falling.

What I remember about the ride home is that it felt as if it would never end.

When we pull up in front of the house, Granny Tooley, Mom and Duchess are waiting, holding hands. The magnolia tree out by the curb is in full bloom. It seems odd to me that it should choose to bloom at a time like this. Its branches are full of birds singing long and complicated songs. I remember thinking that the birds shouldn't be singing.

I remember that when I hugged Granny Tooley she smelled of vanilla leaf and sage, just like in the old days when she lived in her real home in the woods. I remember thinking that nothing lasts forever. And my navel hurts where I got it pierced.

I have trouble breathing and Mom puts the inhaler in my hand. She is crying, and smells of cinnamon; she must have been at the bakery after all. I collapse into her arms, thinking that as long as she keeps baking God won't let her die.

I remember peeling off the Capri pants and Hawaiian shirt and taking a shower in the hottest water I could stand. I put alcohol on my belly button and it burned like hell.

I don't remember going to sleep, but when I woke up the next day, Erma Geddon was waiting for me on the floor beside my bed.

Chapter Nineteen

Molly: November 8, 2001.

I catch a break in traffic and take Ball Road down to Beach and then to Westminster Memorial Park. This is where Dad is buried. It's been too long... years, since I made the trek over to his grave. It used to be a monthly routine that involved too many flowers. He seemed to hang around there waiting for me. After a while, that feeling wasn't there anymore, like he had moved on, so my visits became fewer, until I just stopped going altogether.

Military as well as civilian burial services take place here.

Delmar is getting a civilian burial since he hadn't even made it to boot camp before he died. The circumstances around his death all lead to an overdose—a combination of Prozac, alcohol, and marijuana. True told Raynie that he had been terrified of joining the Marines, but had felt pressure from his buddies to join. He later regretted his decision and tried to get out of the contract without his parents finding out that he had dropped out of college. He was not able to maneuver the obstacles to getting released once he'd signed the papers without the help of his parents. He feared Rudi and Ashanti's reaction as much as he did being a Marine and going to war.

I think of Raynie and pray that she would come to me first if she ever found herself in such a double bind that the only solution she could see was using drugs or killing herself.

The statue of the Marines raising the flag at Iwo Jima

comes into view. I know that I should feel proud and patriotic but I have never felt that the violence that comes with conquest is ever justified. It's our innocent youth who are sent to fight that pay the price, not the leaders who make the decisions to go to war.

Duchess is doing a double shift at the bakery today so that Raynie and I can attend Delmar's memorial service.

Tooley is with us and we've come early to accommodate her fears about having to sit with people behind her. We hope to get seats in the last row. I am doubtful we will have success. The parking lot is full.

Tooley is in the backseat clutching the door handle. She also has a strong aversion, a full-blown phobia, about being a passenger in a car. She insisted on coming with us to support Raynie but she may have to wait outside the church.

Raynie, scrunched up and silent, is up in front with me. I haven't been able to coax a word out of her for several days.

The Santa Anas have blown in and the hoarse voice on the car radio is warning that the Topanga Canyon is burning.

According to the thermometer in the SUV, the outside temperature is eighty-two degrees, and it's only ten in the morning.

We haul ourselves out of the car and walk up the wide steps as the sound of bells tolling reaches us. It is only slightly cooler inside. The heat is strangely comforting. It seems to help console the grieving energy within the church.

Despite the fact that today is Wednesday, the church is crowded, overflowing with flowers and mourners. Three men in the back row dressed in marine uniforms yield their seats to us. I wonder if they are the recruiters. I accept for all of us, but Tooley has turned ashen. She sits, but looks ready to bolt at the least movement behind her. I tried my best to dissuade her from wearing the burning jacket but to no avail. She said Raynie wanted her to wear it to help give her strength.

THE BURNING JACKET

Grasped in her right hand is her walking stick. Sometimes she calls it her power wand for dramatic effect. The stick is decorated along the sides with carvings of what could be hieroglyphs. Her sage bundles and flute are safely hidden under my bed just in case she would not be able to resist the urge to spontaneously accompany the organist with a flute elegy, or smoke out the congregation with a purification ritual.

The jacket smells ripe, like aged cheese, in the trapped heat of the church. The bulky monstrosity is full of burn and moth holes. Tooley wears the old rag like a badge of honor. She used to wear it to burn trash at her place in the woods, thus the name. These days she wears the nasty thing almost all the time. I make her take it off when the thermometer goes above eighty.

One summer, in between my third and fourth year of high school, while visiting her in the woods, I hid the filthy thing in the bottom of the laundry bag. Tooley dropped me at the Laundromat in Roseburg while she made a trip to the feed store. I isolated the jacket in its own separate washing machine, and was about to press the 'fill' button when Tooley came back in and stopped me. She had suspected something when she didn't find the jacket in the truck. She raised her stick in the air, I thought she was going to hit me, but she mumbled a litany of words that I didn't understand and told me that sacrilege had been committed against the ancestors. She put the jacket on and walked out in a huff, leaving me stranded at the Laundromat. It was after dark when she came back to get me and the washed and folded laundry. That was the end of my visits to the forest. We didn't discuss it, but it was a mutual decision. I saw very little of Tooley until Raynie was old enough to visit her in the spring and summer.

All eyes are on the casket in front of the altar. Flanked by stands of red roses, the rectangular box is made of a smooth blond wood. It looks young like the lifeless body it embraces. A spray of red roses is draped over the mid-section of the casket.

There was a viewing yesterday evening, but when Raynie called True's house to find out where and when it would be, Ashanti answered and said it was best if Raynie didn't come to the viewing or the funeral.

Raynie calls the Shandaras every day since Delmar's death and asks to talk to True or Jason. Isabella, the maid, seems to be the only one answering the phone. Isabella says nobody is able to talk, and not to call anymore. I called once to try and find out what was going on. When I announced who was calling there was a hurried click and then a flat line buzz.

People grieve in different ways. Some need to do it privately, but to separate the girls at a time like this seems like cruel punishment. They both need closure on Delmar's death; they need to share their mutual grief in order to heal. That's what I wanted to tell Ashanti when she hung up on me. It seems that in her anguished mind she is somehow blaming Raynie for Delmar's overdose.

I called True's grandmother, Fenona, at the retirement center where she lives in Anaheim, and she told me that Delmar had been depressed for some time and had successfully hidden it from his parents. Fenona said that she had known about Delmar's dilemma about quitting school and his fear of going to war and fighting in Afghanistan but he had sworn her to secrecy.

"The president's hasty rush into war killed Delmar. Prozac was the weapon instead of a gun." Fenona cried into the phone. "I just want to go home to India," she said. She also said that one of Delmar's friends had been accidentally killed in a training maneuver at Camp Pendleton, in Oceanside, while in boot camp, and that had only heightened Delmar's fear of going to war.

An extremely obese lady dressed in a sheer, billowing brown dress is playing the organ near the altar. None of the hymns are familiar to me. The only time I remember going to church as a child was while attending bible school the summer of the third grade while Dad went back east for three weeks to learn some new techniques on making dentures. We learned how to make origami swans and the words to *Jesus Loves Me, This I know. Cause the bible tells me so.*

I still think of the blond lady at the bible camp, more so since I've been diagnosed with cancer. She told us stories about Jesus in a soft, musical voice. She was kind, gentle, and seemed so at peace. Would the miseries of life be easier to cope with if I were grounded in a strong religious faith?

Making art seems to be a religious pursuit for me. I feel centered with a brush or pencil in my hand.

The image of the woman in the waiting room at the hospital with the colorful scarf that hid a bald head enters my mind. She looked like an angel. Is it a religious faith that keeps her going, or something else?

The organ music stops and the church falls silent except for an occasional cough and shuffle, as people rearrange themselves in the pews.

The Shandaras enter the church. Like dark inconsolable brides, they walk down the central aisle. I'm so close to Ashanti I want to reach out and touch her, let her know that I can only imagine the pain of losing a child. She is dressed in a red silk sari, her hair drawn back tight in a bun. Rudi is dressed in a black suit with red tie. He is leaning against Ashanti as if he could not make it down the aisle without her support. True is dressed in a sari of blue silk. I've never seen her wear a sari. Her face is gaunt; she's lost weight. She's all eyes... heartbroken and beautiful. Jason is dressed in a black suit with a red tie like Rudi. He sees Raynie seated at the end of the row and touches her on the shoulder as he passes. Ashanti and True keep their eyes focused downward as if that's the only way they'll be able to make it to the front of the church without collapsing.

I've always thought Ashanti and Rudi were good parents with the bedrock of Christianity upon which to stand. They've seemed consistent and reliable in their interactions with their children. They've given them the best of everything. They may be too generous at times, lavishing the children with expensive gifts, but who is to say I wouldn't do the same if given their financial circumstances. What happened to Delmar had nothing to do with his upbringing. I agree with Fenona that the fever of impending war added to his depression and death.

Looking around the church at a scattering of young men and one woman in military uniforms brings home the reality that we are at war, a different kind of war than we've ever known, a war with no rules, one that our children and grandchildren will inherit.

Raynie's face seems tightly drawn over her bones, her jaws clenched. She's determined to not cry. She pulls away from me when I cover her hand with mine. She has hardly spoken in the last five days and stays in her room with hibernating Erma Geddon who went into her big sleep yesterday. Poor timing on the part of Erma's biology.

The minister stands behind the pulpit. His voice is small and humdrum, apologetic.

"He leadeth me beside the still waters." His gaze falls somewhere in the vicinity of the Shandaras while reading the twenty-third psalm but never meets their eyes directly.

I reach over and touch my left breast. It seems alien to me. Then I touch the soft, smooth silk of my scarf that hides my bald head. I started to shed, mostly on the pillow at night, after the first few treatments. Then hair came out by the handfuls. Duchess, Raynie and Tooley threw a coming out party for me, complete with my favorite dessert, Cherries Jubilee, and Duchess shaved my head. They all wanted to be bald in sympathy, but I told them I would never speak to them again if they stole my thunder. I wanted to look like the lady in the waiting room with the angel eyes. I found a scarf that almost matched hers and I got a pair of hoop earrings. My eyebrows and eyelashes fell out as well so I've been using more eyeliner and brighter lipstick. Tooley and Raynie say they like the new look, that I've become glamorous and mysterious, like an old star of the silver screen.

Hopefully, I'll be finished with chemo in a few weeks. Dr. Brewer, the oncologist, thinks I should have radiation treatments to be on the safe side. I'm not looking forward to that, but will probably follow his advice.

What caused some of my cells to become invading little Hitlers? From where comes this urge for certain cells to colonize? Some inner death wish?

Suddenly my thoughts turn to 9/11. My emotions were so tied up in my own personal drama with the news of a biopsy and learning that Tooley was in the hospital in Bullhead City, that I had no feelings left over to mourn our country's tragedy. Until now. Now I grieve those who died that day and the loss of freedom, of a way of life that will never be the same. Look what it has done to the Shandara family. A flood of tears draws the attention of a stranger in uniform seated near me. It feels good to let them flow. I cry for all of us.

More shuffles and coughs among the congregation bring my attention back to Delmar in the wooden box. Various people, mostly strangers to me, bring home the fact of how peripheral this young man was in my life. They go to the pulpit and say words of praise for him... How he was a wonderful Sunday school teacher to their children. How he always had a smile and a kind word. Everyone seems to be crying with the exception of Raynie. Her face is a dry, gray stone.

The congregation stands and the people reach for hymnals in the pews in front of them. Raynie holds the open hymnal but is silent. Tooley reaches over and shows me the page number. I mouth the words with no sound behind them. She sings in a strong, sweet voice, as if the song were an old friend, which surprises me. When did my mother ever go to church?

The pallbearers look like children playing at being adults. For some, this may be their first intimate encounter with death. They wear brave faces and do not cry as they carry the flower-strewn casket out of the church. They are followed by the family and the rest of the congregation. We all squint as the glare of the sun hits our faces. The pallbearers make their way down the steps with their heavy burden and carry it to the civilian side of the cemetery.

I stop Raynie from following the procession. She has her eyes on True. True does not look back.

"It's just for the family," I say. "This is how they want it to be. We mustn't intrude. Get in the car." I open the passenger door for her.

A cloudburst of tears pours from my daughter's eyes followed by thundering sobs. I hold her as she shakes.

"Why can't I talk to True? I didn't even want to go to that stupid party." Her words are staccato, sandwiched between gusts of breath.

As the SUV engine fires and the air-conditioner starts its task of trying to cool the increasingly stinking air, a volley of gunfire can be heard from over the hill on the military side of the graveyard. And then the keening sound of a lone trumpeter playing taps for a fallen soldier.

Chapter Twenty

Raynie: Christmas Vacation, 2001.

"Imagine a crisp, cold day. Just enough breeze to fan the fire. The sun is shining. We are in the woods seated at the conclave of chiefs," says Tooley as she stirs the air in front of her nose with her hand, determined to recreate the rich and complex odor of the forest, one of the ingredients that seems to be necessary for the telling of a story.

Tooley tries to entertain me, a half-hearted attempt, the best she can muster under the circumstances. Christmas is a week away and I'm out of school with no friends and nothing to do. I know Tooley misses her big trees and cabin with a fire in the woodstove, surrounded by all her animal friends. Plus the fact that Mom doesn't exactly make her feel at home here. She keeps hinting that maybe Tooley would be more comfortable in a home with people her own age. And that makes Tooley terrified of being put in an old folks home against her will; somewhere she can't have her dogs. She would rather die than live without her dogs. I know I couldn't live without Erma Geddon.

I hate Mom when she rags on Tooley like that. Mom's always on her back about something. She gripes all the time about dog hairs all over the house. It seems like Tooley spends most of her time brushing the dogs, and I spend my time after school vacuuming. We both bend over backward to be nice to Mom since she started the chemo treatments. She spends a lot of time in the bathroom being sick.

Tooley and I are seated on two lawn chairs with plump, flowered cushions, by the outdoor gas grill on the back patio. Even though it's hot, Tooley wears the burning jacket. Kachina and Kevin are lying on the concrete at her feet.

I'm trying, but I can't substitute the solid, heavy, yellow haze for a clear winter day in the Oregon woods.

"I can smell it. The dried peppery odor of yerba buena vines that have twined around the stumps in our magic circle and the homey smell of a wood fire. Can't you just see it and taste it?" Tooley attempts a smile and tries to convince me that we are back on her beloved land.

My head shakes involuntarily in the negative. I don't even want to play this stupid game.

She hands me a fork with a melted marshmallow she toasted over the grill. I blow on it and pop it in my mouth like I'm enthused about the whole thing, but the white drippy goo tastes like liquid cardboard with sugar sprinkled on it.

Tooley has had a hard time adjusting to living with us after her heat stroke. Ever since Mom started treatment, Tooley has stopped complaining about every little thing she hates about living in Anaheim, but I know living here has taken its toll. Her hair and skin have turned even wintrier, and her eyes are so pale you can hardly distinguish the irises from the whites.

In a few days, we will celebrate her birthday. No one seems to know the exact date of Tooley's birth, so we celebrate in mid-December. Mom says Tooley is somewhere between seventy and seventy-five, give or take a few years.

I haven't been able to concentrate long enough to decide what to give her for her birthday. I usually make something handmade. I may give her a scarf I knitted with yarn I spun this last summer on her spinning wheel. When the wheel arrived from UPS out of the blue, during the time that Tooley was roaming around the desert, I put it in the living room. Mom made me put it in the bedroom so she wouldn't have to see it. She said it reminded her of unpleasant things from the past.

Last year I made Tooley a prayer arrow out of a willow stick and the yarn I'd spun at her cabin, with a beautiful, wild turkey feather attached. Ray had given it to me several years ago. He said he found it down in a favorite canyon in Mexico. He said that one day he would take me there. Fat chance of that happening. He lives there and could have asked me to visit over Christmas holidays, but, of course, Mom probably wouldn't let me go even if he did invite me.

Granny Tooley's recent stories are lackluster compared to the vitality of the original family sagas she used to tell around our blazing campfires. The new stories are thinly disguised plots from the old movies she watches constantly. If she isn't piled up on the bed with the dogs, buried in a movie, she's watching the nature channel on cable.

This is our first foray out on the patio together since the fiasco a few months ago when we nearly burned down the neighborhood.

"Some of your ancestors lived in a beautiful and peaceful place called *Shangri-la,* hidden away in the mountains in Tibet, where the people and all the animals never get old and die."

Today's story is not a disguise but a blatant plagiarism. She's lifted this tale straight from *Lost Horizons* without even bothering to change the name of the place. I read the book a year ago and we watched the movie together last Saturday morning.

Faithful guardians Kevin and Kachina are snoring like fired-up chainsaws. They're getting fat. They don't get much exercise anymore. Tooley used to take them for walks around the block when she first moved in, but she's stopped doing that. The job fell to me, but I haven't walked them since Delmar's funeral.

Erma Geddon has gone to sleep. She went into brumation

just after Delmar went to sleep for good. I think she tried to stay awake as long as she could for my sake, but her natural instincts overtook her. She crawled under my bed and didn't come out. Mom insisted that she be put into her sandbox, so I tucked her in, and put the box back under my bed with no further arguments from Mom.

Before the chemo treatments made her too tired, Mom would pile us all in the car a few times a week for trips to the fenced-in doggie park off of Chapman, over in Orange. Before she got cancer, she was pretty uptight about keeping her SUV spotless. Now she tolerates the hair in the car, but still gripes about it if Tooley or I don't vacuum the car out as soon as we get home from the park.

Mom hasn't felt like doing anything much lately except work at the bakery and sleep. I know she wants to paint, but she doesn't have the time or energy. She only has one more week of chemo to go. I hope that if I ever have to have chemotherapy I'll look as good bald as Mom does. She has a pretty, well-shaped head.

I offered to go sit with her during treatments but she wouldn't let me skip school, and neither would the principal, Mrs. Evans.

Mr. Harrison has reinstated me as a piano student, I suspect because of constant pressure from Mom. Playing the piano is the only undertaking worth doing these days. I've been staying after school two days a week to practice on the big grand piano in the band room. It gives me time alone to not think about things, like if Mom's going to get well, and True not wanting to see me, and to prove to Mr. Harrison that I'm worthy of his time and attention. I wish I could join Erma Geddon under the bed and go to sleep for a hundred years, but playing the piano is the next best solution.

I feel so alone all the time. Even with Tooley and Mom in the same house, I miss them. I miss the way they were—the

The Burning Jacket

Granny Tooley who lived in the woods and loved everything about her life, and the Mom before she got cancer and divorced Ray. And Ray. I still miss Ray and blame myself for his moving to Mexico.

The language of music is a safer form of communication than words. Once a wrong word has flown out of your mouth, you can't make it fly back to the nest again. With music, you're off the hook. Nobody expects you to get a piece right the first time. If you hit the wrong key, it's okay, you just keep practicing until you get it.

I'm learning *Claire de Lune*. I love all the flats and sharps, and the way my fingers feel as they ripple over the black keys, like silvery waves covering everything in sparkling moonlight. And all the sadness and loneliness I feel seems to go to my fingertips and spill out into the sounds, to fly away and disappear in the air.

Regular classes don't interest me anymore, not even biology. I feel like a piece of wood matriculating through meaningless days, watching the clock until it's time to go and play the piano. On the off-practice days, I usually go home and watch old movies with Tooley. Sometimes we play music together. She carved me a flute and taught me how to play.

After numerous attempts, I gave up trying to reach True or Jason on the phone. Mom even drove me over to Irvine to True's house after school one day, a few weeks after the funeral. I rang the doorbell and their maid, Isabella, answered and said that nobody was at home even though both Rudi's and Ashanti's cars were in the driveway. She nodded to me with sad eyes as if she understood what I must be feeling.

"I'll tell the family that you stopped by." Isabella closed the door before I could say anything.

I miss True now more than ever. We always spent our Christmas vacations together, hanging out either at her house or mine, mostly her house. Ashanti was more comfortable with us being over there so she could keep a close eye on us.

Mom called True's grandmother, Fenona, and found out the whole family was making plans to move back to India. They were going to dig up Delmar's body to take with them for a proper cremation in the land of his birth. Fenona said that she was glad to be going home, she didn't want to live her final years in an old folks home apart from her family, as is the custom here in the United States.

I turn on the faucet and drag the hose over near the west wall to water the baby Hawthorne tree Tooley and I planted in honor of Delmar. We had our own ceremonial burial, only without the body. Tooley says the Hawthorne tree helps wandering souls find their way into the light, and that no negative energy stays around where a Hawthorne tree is planted.

Frankly, I don't feel like honoring Delmar. I think he was a selfish son of a bitch for taking us to that party so he could kill himself. I can only say this thought to myself. Everybody else would think I was a terrible person for thinking this way.

Out of the blue comes a sharp pain in my gut. It's True. She's kicking and screaming inside. It's really probably all the stale marshmallows I ate to cheer up Tooley.

Will True leave without even saying goodbye?

What did I do that was wrong? I think about the night of the Halloween party. What could I have done to save Delmar's life? Do the Shandaras blame me for his death? Maybe it is partially my fault. I could have said, NO. I could have refused to go to the party. I could have threatened to call Mom or Ashanti and tell them what was going on. True would have been mad at me but that would be better than Delmar dying. Jason would have probably stood beside me. I wonder why he doesn't call.

I feel like a lump of clay, with my emotions baked inside. It would take a hard smash with a hammer to break me apart and let the feelings out. I seem incapable of making a decision about anything, except playing the piano.

"Come on. I think you've watered that tree enough. We're going to the movies." Tooley turns off the faucet and takes the hose out of my hand.

"I don't want to go anywhere," I manage to chirp.

"I want to see *Harry Potter and the Sorcerer's Stone* and you're going with me because I'm supposed to keep an eye on you. You have to go and that is that. Marsha's going to drop us off at the theatre."

Tooley plays the Harry Potter card. I don't want to go but to resist Tooley would be useless, like trying to stop the Santa Anas from blowing.

She takes my hand and leads me inside to put on my shoes and comb my hair. We are followed into the house by the canine entourage that will wait patiently in Tooley's room for her return from Hogwart's School of Witchcraft and Wizardry.

Chapter Twenty-One

Molly: Christmas Eve 2001.

The morning light retains tinctures of reds and greens, saturated shades that promise rain. This Christmas Eve has staged its colors for a winter's tale. There is only a hint of the sulfuric odor of smog in the air. Last night's winds blew away the air's foul stench and replaced it with the smell of green things growing in a rich, forest.

The weather takes me back to those days in the forest of my early childhood with Tooley and The Chief. They didn't celebrate Christmas; their holiday was December 21, the Winter Solstice. Tooley lit pine-scented candles in her cabin to honor the returning of the light. We all wore crowns of fir and cedar on our heads, feasted on fruits, vegetables, and special cinnamon and raisin cakes Tooley made for the occasion. She and The Chief would snake their way around the trees playing flute and drum to keep the sun from falling from the sky and the trees standing upright. I usually watched from the sidelines with a certain amount of fear, reluctant to participate in what seemed to me, even then, either foolish nonsense or serious dark magic.

Today I am in a mood to toast all benevolent beliefs and holidays.

Despite having little energy and still carrying the lingering memory of the nightmare I had early this morning, there are things for which to be thankful this Christmas. My last chemo treatment was last week and radiation is still a question mark for the future. I have hope about a treatment in the form of a pill made from the bark of the Yew tree.

"Thank God for Yew trees!" I said to the two technicians, Sam and Shelley, in the oncology department. Sam is a smiling, bald-headed man who always had a joke to share. Shelly is a young and vulnerable-looking woman, shorter than my teenage daughter. I'll never forget their kindnesses. Every day I took them an Orange Sunrise coffee cake from the bakery, and the last day of treatment, they gave me a beautiful red candle that smelled like cinnamon. We hugged and Shelly said she hoped we would meet again, but not in this place.

The house is festooned with garlands of looping popcorn and cranberry strings that Tooley and Raynie hung above the doors and windows. Variegated green and white holly with red berries adorn the mantle of the gas fireplace with the log insert, along with bay-scented candles and a basket of giant redwood pine cones that Ray stole from Yosemite Park four years ago. I tried to talk him out of taking them; if caught the fine would have been five hundred dollars. But, for Ray, that only enhanced the excitement. He stuffed the giant seedpods under his jacket and walked out of the park looking very pregnant and smug, without a trace of guilt. I still feel pangs of remorse for displaying them, but it seems to be a wasteful act, after the fact, to hide them in the garage or throw them away.

I never talked about our actions that day with Raynie. She was eight at the time and saw it all. She's too bright to have missed the moral implications. Should we talk about it now? Does she see me as a hypocrite for punishing her for keeping a secret with her father when I was accomplice to a crime that was a much greater offense? (At least in her eyes it would be.)

Six giant Christmas stockings of various shades of red and green, knitted by Tooley, lay on the hearth waiting to be filled.

We will each take turns sneaking into the living room and playing Santa tonight. I bought new wooden circular knitting needles for Tooley, a pair of silver turtle earrings for Raynie, a new scarf to cover my bald head, and of course candy, nuts and fruit. Erma Geddon's stocking will be hung as an honorary gesture but will not be filled because she's asleep. In past years, Raynie was sad because Erma had to miss Christmas, but she hasn't mentioned it this year. Kevin and Kachina each have their own stocking. (Tooley made theirs bigger than the others.) I bought them each a leathery pig ear, and an artificial bone to chew on.

Tooley insisted that a real tree not be slaughtered and have its carcass drug into the house, so we bought a fake one at Sam's Club. She said the thought of a tree that had been murdered would ruin the spirit of Christmas. There was a bigger tree with the lights already on it that I had my eye on at Wal-Mart, but Raynie and Tooley are boycotting the store so, under penalty of excommunication, I don't dare shop there.

Tooley and Raynie strung red, green, and white blinking lights and hung shiny silver ornaments on the artificial tree. It looks kind of real, standing eight feet tall, topped by a wispy angel with a silver halo. The false tree has the advantage over the real thing in that it's fire proof and doesn't need water or shed needles.

Under the tree are more presents. The biggest box wrapped in shimmering gold paper with a fake poinsettia on the bow is my special surprise to my daughter. Inside is a card I made—a drawing of Raynie playing a piano. The likeness is weak, but I captured her signature gesture of years gone by: proud, straight and tall, not the curled up fetus of recent times. She slouches around now, reminding me of a giant comma or a sleeping puppy. I hope the new piano will help. That's all she seems interested in these days.

The Burning Jacket

The piano will be delivered this afternoon. Marsha will come over and let the moving men in. They will wrap the piano with a tarp and when I get home from the bakery, I'll adorn it with a giant red bow. I wanted to buy a baby grand but didn't have the money or space for it. Besides, something that extravagant might send the wrong message. I don't want Raynie to feel pressured to play. Upon the advice of Mr. Harrison, I bought an upright.

Raynie and I bought Tooley a few of her favorite movies: *Portrait of Jenny* and *The Bigamist*. There is a music book of Kohler's sonatinas for Raynie wrapped in red shiny paper and a silver bow.

Under the tree is Raynie's present for Ray. It's a drawing rolled up and wrapped in red Christmas paper, held in shape with two rubber bands. We don't know for sure where he is. Rumor has it that he is still living in Mexico. If this is true, I have another thing for which to be thankful.

Tooley has taken over the holiday cooking. She won't admit it, but I think she appreciates the instant fire when turning a knob on the stove. Today she plans to make an apple pie, cranberry sauce, and stuffing. After several days of protest, she agreed to cook a turkey, but not before she blew sage smoke on the plastic-wrapped, half-frozen carcass and played a particularly moody piece on the flute to thank and honor the bird for its sacrifice. I will bring home Christmas breads and rolls from the bakery.

It's raining now—a soft blanket that excludes nothing. I'm grateful for its rhythmic pattern, a muted shuffle, a graceful ballet to my ears. I need the rain, the yin, the feminine after having the poison of chemotherapy pumped through my veins. The rain surprised me with an unexpected longing for the green nourishing drizzle of Oregon.

I can better understand how Tooley must feel. She rails

against the sun and continually seeks out shadows in which to stand or sit. The child in me still believes that my mother is a sorcerer. I wonder if she had a hand in this unexpected rain on Christmas Eve. Sometimes I catch her blowing sage smoke at me while I'm napping, mumbling her hocus pocus under her breath. I vacillate between accepting her gestures as caring and still being frightened of them, or irritated. Still, I'm thankful she is here in my time of need. And this morning, when I had the nightmare and was frightened, she was there to hold me, like a mother is expected to hold her child.

Abandoning the kitchen table, I go out on the patio to sit in the bountiful downpour. My body is a sponge hoarding every drop as it falls on my parched skin. I turn my face to the sky and open my mouth to let it drip on my tongue.

Thank God, I'm alive.

The cloudburst has stirred up the smell of jasmine from a bush over by the wall that divides my yard from Marsha's. I can smell the sweet exotic flower as the rain caresses my skin and penetrates deeper into me to touch and soothe my nerves and lubricate my bones. How fortunate I am to be here on this amazing planet to inhabit this precious body, flaws and all.

It is enough.

Cells of living bodies are constantly dying and new cells are being born. The cycle continues, and I am thankful.

Like today's weather, urged on by a complication of factors and a great deal of mystery, I'm different than I was yesterday, and if blessed with another day on this earth I'll be different tomorrow. Everything in the universe is whirling energy in constant motion, changing. It used to be planted in my mind as a sure thing that the earth, with all of its inhabitants held to its surface by gravity, speeds around the sun in a sort of floppy, elliptical waltz. I no longer trust scientific fact. My DNA molecules spin around uncertain nuclei. Tomorrow, or even the next minute, cannot be taken for granted.

Bits and pieces of the nightmare I had last night fit in somewhere.

I'm watching a live magic show in a theater. The magician, dressed in his usual black cape and high hat, passes his magic wand over the head of a young woman with nothing on save a necklace of precious gems. She disappears into thin air. I realize the woman is the Julia of my dreams. The magician goes to a rectangular box, swirls his cape, and waves his wand over the box. He opens it. It's empty. He looks perplexed, closes the box, furiously swirls his cape, and waves his wand again. He reopens the box. It is still empty.

I panic and can't breathe. I don't want Julia to disappear. I need the illusion, the dream of her to exist. I realize that she is what keeps me going through all of this. She is my assurance that the world will spin around, and that we will continue our existence in some manner even after the body disappears, even if only in someone's dreams.

I awake from the dream with Tooley by my side stroking my arms and hands, soothing me. I welcome her touch, strong and reassuring and do not pull away.

"I don't want to die," I sob as she holds me.

"I know. I know. You must be so frightened. I heard you cry out." The smell of sage and rosemary that hangs in the air around Tooley, the odor I linked with black magic and occult rituals, the odor that used to raise goose bumps of fear on my skin, now calms me.

"You are not going to die, not now." Tooley looks at me, her faded eyes the color of her skin. I feel my body relax. I know with a certainty I've never felt before that she is telling me the truth.

"You know this?" I ask. "You know it is not my time to die?"

"Yes, I know this."

"Thank you."

Tooley went to the kitchen and brewed a cup of tea for me. The dream had brought up my worst fears and Tooley had banished them.

"This will make you sleep. It is chamomile and valerian root. Drink it."

Tooley held it out to me, both hands in front of her in blessing, the way a priest offers up a chalice of wine while the wine symbolically is changed into the blood of Christ.

"How do you know what you know?" I ask. The tea is delicious. She has added honey and a wedge of lemon.

"I don't know the answer to that. I only know what I know." She shrugs her shoulders. "I don't bother wondering how or why. It's a waste of time to try to second-guess the gifts that the Great Spirit gives us.

I asked her to lie down on the bed with me for a while. As I was dozing, I felt her frail body beside me as both miraculous and impermanent as a soft white cloud.

I used to pretend that I didn't have a human mother, that I had sprouted from a seed and grew roots from the ground, a tree, a Diana, but I'm beginning to see my mother in a new light. Being kicked out of the forest had snatched away her hold on the earth. I don't know if she will be with us much longer. Even so, she has a strength that transcends her body, a force as elemental as earth, fire, wind, and water.

The rain stopped suddenly. The sun is out. Soon all traces of precipitation will be gone; the drops and puddles will disappear like the magician's lady in my dream. With Tooley's affirmation of my life not ending yet, I can let Julia disappear back into the dream for now.

Things change in the blink of an eye. This is the human

condition: constant flux. My toes tingle with the awareness of this as *the* fundamental human paradox. We are in constant mourning for yesterday as we reach with longing for tomorrow. The ternary event that is today, the hiatus holding the present moment between grief and anticipation, is where lies the gods of true religion, nirvana, paradise, the still being within.

The buzzing of my cell phone on the counter interrupts my epiphany, but not before the impact of the 'aha' sends shivers up my spine, the same feeling I get when a painting comes together in just the right way.

"Where are you, Queenie? You were supposed to be here an hour ago," Duchess shouts in my ear ending the possibility of residing in this present moment for even a millisecond longer. "James called in sick, said he has the flu, and I can't work the front and finish baking the Christmas stollen orders at the same time. They need to be ready for pickup soon. Remember that we're closing at four? I need to get more Christmas shopping done. I haven't even bought your present yet!" I hear Duchess take a breath, but she continues before I can speak. "If you don't feel well, maybe Raynie could take a taxi over."

"I'm fine. I just let the time get away from me. Raynie and I both will be right over."

I hired Raynie to work at the bakery with me today partly so she wouldn't mope around the house. This is the second Christmas without her father and the first since first grade without True. The girls had always exchanged gifts on Christmas Eve.

Raynie is in the kitchen feeding the dogs. I hear the theme song from *The Sound of Music* coming from the TV in Tooley's room. Normally it would bother me that she is watching movies this early in the morning, but after last night's healing exchange it seems harmless to let her cope with life in whatever way she chooses… whatever helps her make it through her days.

"Raynie," I call out, "we need to head out to the bakery. Duchess is holding down the fort by herself and she needs us. And don't let me forget to pick up some Chanterelle mushrooms on the way home. Duchess is bringing her cousin who's visiting from Brooklyn over tonight for Christmas Eve dinner and Tooley wants to fix a wild mushroom quiche."

Raynie shrugs and stretches in slow motion with the graceful languor of a wild cat basking in the morning sun.

I give in to the present moment. I am here, if ever so briefly, watching my beautiful daughter greet the day.

It is enough.

Chapter Twenty-Two

Molly: Christmas Eve Afternoon.

The clock on the wall behind the counter looks like a frosted oatmeal cookie because it's surrounded by a string of frosty white dancing snowmen holding hands. The time is fifteen minutes until closing.

The shelves are bare except for a few loaves of sturdy, no-nonsense whole wheat bread sitting next to the bread slicer. We've sold everything else in the store that wasn't tied down or hanging on the walls. I stashed three Christmas stollen bulging with fruit and nuts for our own celebration, along with two Orange Sunrise coffeecakes and a dozen poppy-seed rolls.

We'll share the goodies with Marsha and her grandson, John, next door. They are coming to our house to open presents and have Christmas breakfast.

The last of the special orders have been picked up.

My body shakes from exhaustion and hunger. I didn't have time to eat lunch. I pour myself a cup of coffee from the dregs in the bottom of the pot, grab the last two thumbprint apricot jam cookies from the Santa sample jar on the counter, and sit down in a chair by the window. The lights are out at Swift Cleaners next door. They closed at noon. The parking lot is still half-full of cars. Weary last-minute shoppers pass the window, their gaits stiff and hurried, their faces holding a hint of anticipation. Perhaps arriving home to a glass of eggnog or a cup of mulled cider and the festivities to follow. The thought of soaking in a hot bathtub by candle light and sipping a good brandy entices me to finish my coffee and cookie and get moving.

I hear laughter from the kitchen. Clean up time. The music begins. Not the usual Marvin Gaye collection, but the soulful sexy sounds of Barry White's "Can't Get Enough of Your Love." Raynie bought the album last July when she read that a marine center in England played Barry White music to encourage the sharks to mate in captivity. The throaty voice is a soothing, pleasant relief from the jingle-jangle of Christmas music that's been playing non-stop around the mall for a month.

Barry White brings to mind what is missing in my life. My thoughts turn to John Graham, the doctor from the garage sale. It feels as if an icy continent separates us, but in reality, we are practically neighbors. Every day that I stepped foot into the hospital for treatment I was afraid, and at the same time hopeful, that I might run into him. It wasn't the right time and probably still isn't, but I might give him a call after Christmas to wish him a Happy New Year. He's probably involved with someone else. But he did give me his card, and what's the harm of saying hello?

What's this? A heart that skips a beat at the mere thought of the man? One would think that after being so unlucky in love my brain would monitor out these foolish longings. Tooley says if you don't follow your heart life isn't worth living. She may be right.

Shuffling, crashing sounds, then giggling comes from the kitchen. Duchess and Raynie must be dancing. My heart warms to hear my daughter laugh again.

Empty coffee cup in hand, I walk back behind the counter to get ready to close up. I take the money out of the register and put it in the bank deposit bag next to my gun that's hidden in my purse behind the unfolded pink pastry boxes. The cigar box that holds the surplus of cash is bulging with bills. I stuff those, too, in the bank deposit bag. I'll run by the bank on the way home and make the usual deposit.

The jingle bells attached to the front door announce the arrival of a customer.

Damn. I forgot to turn the sign around to CLOSED and lock the door.

"We're closed," I say as I stand. My skin bristles like a porcupine sensing danger. A man in a Santa suit and mask, followed by two elves with caps pulled down low over their foreheads swagger toward the counter in a take-charge manner.

As Santa nears the counter, I see the flashing colored lights of the ceramic Christmas tree on the counter reflected in his eyes.

"Ho, Ho, Ho, give me all your dough." Santa, flanked by his two elves, pulls a gun out of his pocket and points it at me. The two elves laugh, like they think it's funny, like it's an April fool's joke. *Oh, God, let this be a joke.*

I smile. "It is a joke, right?"

"Don't laugh at me, bitch." Santa waves his gun in the air. "I want the money. Now!"

My blood becomes a rushing ocean pounding against the shore of my skin. It's not a joke. I'm not aware of reaching for the gun under the counter but I can feel it in my hand. With no conscious thought on my part, my arm rises and the gun aims itself at the barrel of the gun pointed at me. The trigger is pulled. I just want the other gun to go away.

The only thing I see now is my own gun in my hands, pointed and blocking my view. It's not working. It's not firing. All I hear is the roaring in my head. There are dark spots before my eyes, like clumps of dirty snow, and I'm in a dark tunnel. I keep pulling the trigger trying to make it fire. *Did I put too much oil in the chamber?*

The paper man with the target on his chest moves toward

me, just like at the shooting range. I feel the kickback but the gun isn't firing. Still, my finger pulls the trigger. Then I stop. Barry White has stopped singing, but "I'll be Home for Christmas" plays on the outdoor speakers.

Santa is lying on the floor over by the front door. He seems so far away. The empty day-old bread rack is on top of him. Why?

The elves are gone.

I feel as if I'm looking through the wrong end of a telescope. Santa looks tiny. He isn't moving. His beard is red instead of white. Blood is oozing out from behind his head and shoulders. It's spreading like a deep, red cloud in a murky sky, onto the gray tile floor. The wall behind him reminds me of a canvas with Jackson Pollack-like splatters in alizarin crimson… not my favorite color. It needs to be cleaned up before a customer comes in and sees it.

The gun is still in my hand and pointed in Santa's direction.

Duchess and Raynie stare at me from the kitchen door with frightened looks on their faces.

Police sirens wail in the distance, getting louder as they close in on the mall. My eardrums throb and my head aches from the sound. The shrill noise of the sirens stops and car doors slam. I want to shoot to make the sound go away.

"We called them," Duchess says. She stares at me with a look I can't read. "Are you all right?" She walks over in slow motion but does not touch me. Her arms are spread out with palms facing me. "You can put the gun down now, Queenie." She holds out her hand and I give her the gun. It's too heavy to hold any longer.

All I can think of is that I have to stop the blood from staining the tiles of the floor, and the walls. I grab a towel and start walking over toward Santa.

"Don't touch anything, Ma'am, this is a crime scene." A policeman comes through the door. His voice sounds like an old phonograph record, dragging and distorted, or like a muzzled hound baying in the distance. The officer looks like a kid. He frowns and holds one arm out straight to keep me from getting closer to Santa.

The fake Santa in the window and his sleigh full of brightly wrapped presents, led by plastic reindeer, looks comical. I realize that I am both laughing and crying and can't stop. The red and green lights on the sleigh are blinking like stop-and-go traffic lights.

Raynie stands at the door to the kitchen with her cell phone in hand.

Two policemen are bent over Santa. One has his hand on Santa's neck. After a minute, he shakes his head in the negative.

"This is a coroner's case," he says. "Call the team."

Duchess is talking with one of the policeman. Another one puts up yellow tape with the words "crime scene" in black letters across the front door. I can hear static and then a loud voice from the radio of one of the three police cars pulled face-in at the curb. I can't make out what they are saying but it sounds urgent. Two more policemen are outside.

Onlookers stop and look through the window. I'm upset because I don't have any Christmas cookies left to give them. The policemen are shooing the "Looky Loos," as Ray used to call them.

The muted sound of a cell phone rings from somewhere in the forbidden zone near Santa. One policeman bends down and follows the ring to one of Santa's side pockets. The phone is playing a familiar song: "Hey, Good Lookin'." It makes me smile. It was Ray's favorite song to dance to at our country swing dance classes. He was stiff and never kept time to the music, but we had fun.

"Hello, who is this?" The policeman kneeling near Santa holds the phone to his ear.

"Dad, it's Raynie. I'm surprised you still have your same cell phone. Something has happened at the bakery. Mom shot somebody. Grams said you were in Mexico. Where are you?"

My daughter's voice sounds loud, but shaky. She is not supposed to call him. I go over to tell her to hang up, but Duchess leads me away and motions for me to sit in the chair she dragged out from the kitchen and placed behind the counter, over by the pastry case.

The police officer stands, frozen. His face is a puzzled mask as he looks over at Raynie who is still standing in the kitchen doorway with the phone to her ear. The distance between them is only fifteen feet but it seems like an eternity of space.

The policeman says something into Santa's phone that I can't make out. Raynie screams and lowers herself to a sitting position against the doorframe with the phone still against her ear. I see her body shake, and I wonder what horrible thing Ray is saying to hurt her feelings. He could at least be nice at Christmas time.

I get up, go over, and squat next to her on the floor.

"Get away from me!" Raynie kicks at me and screams in little short bursts—she's wheezing—and drops the phone to push me away with both hands and feet. "I hate you. I hate you."

Raynie knocks me back on my bottom. Duchess comes, lifts me up, and leads me back to the chair. Raynie keeps kicking and screaming at the air.

"Leave her alone right now. She needs to deal with this in her own way."

"Deal with what?" I ask in bewilderment. "I just stopped us from getting robbed and possibly killed. Why is she mad at me? Doesn't she know that Santa will be fine when he stops bleeding?"

The jingling bells at the front door announce the arrival of two men and one woman with CSI insignia banded on their upper arms. The young woman puts on plastic gloves and takes the gun from Santa's side, shakes her head and comments to her partner, and then puts it in an evidence bag. I'm familiar with crime scene investigations from programs I used to watch on TV with Ray, before I stopped loving him.

One of the policemen bends over the body and takes off Santa's mask. The face looks familiar to me. It's hard to tell with all the blood.

"Oh, my God!" Duchess tries to hold me down but can't. I get up and run over to the body on the floor. It's Ray. *How did that happen? Is this a nightmare?* I want to wake up but I'm trapped in a corral with wild horses stampeding across my chest. I can't breathe.

"Get Raynie out of here." She is still sitting on the floor gasping into her inhaler. I don't want her to see her father lying on the floor. "He isn't really dead. He's just pretending, isn't he?" I hear the voice coming from me but I don't recognize it. Someone else is inside my body, talking.

"Yes, he's very dead," the officer who is still holding Santa's cell phone says. "We can't determine yet how many bullets were fired into his body. I take it that the deceased was your daughter's father? Your husband?"

How could it be Ray? It isn't possible. I'm aware that my legs are not supporting me; Duchess is holding me up. The floor is soft beneath my feet. It feels like I'm walking on a mattress. "We're divorced," I manage to say.

"Let's go sit down. We have some questions."

Duchess drags two more chairs from the kitchen and places them by mine.

"In the kitchen," the policeman says. "Away from the body."

I want to sit up front at the table by the window but that area is sectioned off as part of the crime scene, and blood is splattered on the table and chairs. I still have an overwhelming urge to wipe the wall with bleach and water.

Duchess and the officer drag the chairs back into the kitchen. He sits down across from me, a notebook and pen in hand. "Is this your gun?" He points to my gun, which has been bagged. "A Smith and Wesson hammerless snub-nosed .38."

He says it like a half question, half statement of fact.

"Are you the one who fired the gun?"

"Yes," I say. "I got a permit because I transport money to the bank very day."

"Are you aware that you fired five times?" His voice is even, like he's trying to remain neutral, but his face looks troubled.

"No. The gun wouldn't fire, so I kept pulling the trigger." My body is quaking and threatens to erupt. I want to tell everyone not to get too close to me. They could be in danger when I explode.

"It's not unusual to think the gun didn't fire. When your adrenalin kicks in it plays all kinds of tricks on you." The policeman nods his head. "When that happens it's hard to think. You're in a 'flight or fight' syndrome and using only about ten percent of your brain." He writes something down on his notepad.

The doorbells jingle again. I hear someone say, "The coroner is here." A heavyset man with no hair on his head walks through the door followed by two men with a gurney and a body bag. This has gone far enough. I want to wake up. *Why can't I wake up?*

"Did Santa have the gun out and pointed at you?" The policeman taking notes looks up at me with concern in his eyes.

"Yes. He was walking toward the counter, and the elves were on either side of him, and he asked for my money and pointed the gun at me."

"Can you describe the gun, please?"

"It was big... silver." I shrug my shoulders, a Raynie and Ray kind of shrug. "I don't know. It was big."

"Did you know that the gun was a toy? That it was a cap gun?"

Now I really need to wake up. "I don't want to be here." The two men are carrying the body out the door on the gurney. One of the policemen is talking to Raynie. She has her hands over her face. Duchess is up near the front door talking to another policeman. She's gesturing with both hands. I must not forget to take the three poinsettias on the counter home with me. I can put one on the dining room table for our holiday dinner tonight and the other two out on the patio.

"Did you get a good look at the elves? Were they carrying guns?"

"I don't know. I don't think they had guns." I remember something. It startles me and I don't want to tell the policeman. In a pocket somewhere in my brain I must have stored a memory of the shoes the elves wore. They were the same kind of shoes that Ray's teenage buddies wore that day I saw them together at the liquor store over on Lincoln, and again at the garage sale, black sneakers with silver stripes.

"They had on black sneakers with silver stripes." I blurt it out.

"I think that will be all for now. You are free to go home. It will take us several hours to finish our business here, but there is no need for you and your daughter to stay. Take her home and get her calmed down. We'll be in touch. You may want to leave by the back door to avoid the news reporters."

The SUV is conveniently parked in back. That seems like the wrong choice of words. Nothing may be convenient ever again. I hand Duchess the keys when she holds out her hand for them. Somehow, Duchess manages to coax a silent, slumped over Raynie into the back seat of the SUV, and pours me into the passenger's side in front. I feel shapeless, like a bead of mercury.

As we pull around in front, I see the Channel 5 News truck parked by the curb. A woman I recognize from the news is holding a microphone and interviewing one of the policemen.

"It's after seven. Too late to be on the six o'clock news. It'll be on at eleven." Duchess shakes her head. "We'll be plastered on every TV screen across America by tomorrow, but we'll get through it." She reaches over and touches my hand.

I remember only bits and pieces of the ride home. We take surface streets. A small gift. I don't think I could deal with freeway traffic tonight. I don't know what time it is, but it is dark out and the cars on Lincoln all have their lights on. I don't know why, but it seems strange, like they turned their lights on to spotlight me. It's all so confusing and I can't seem to sort it out.

We turn right onto Sunkist. All the houses are decorated with Christmas lights and some have manger scenes lit up, or an occasional reindeer with blinking lights that make it look like the reindeer are running. They seem like bizarre props in a carnival fun house with trick mirrors that distort reality.

The ride home feels like purgatory. No one speaks. It starts to rain as we pull into the driveway. Tooley is at the front door wearing her burning jacket. She's pinned a bouquet of little silver bells with a red ribbon to the front. I find this hilarious and laugh.

Raynie jumps out of the car and runs and buries her face in the stinky wool of Tooley's jacket. Tooley half carries her into the house and closes the door before I even get out of the car.

"Here, take one of these and don't ask any questions." Duchess puts a tiny white pill in my hand and breaks the seal on a bottle of Evian water in the car. I swallow the pill and drink, thankful for anything that holds a promise of ease from the progressive realization that the world is a different place than when I awoke this morning. I finally manage to stop laughing.

The soft innocent rain of this morning that blessed me with its luscious grace and deemed me a child of God, seems like centuries ago. Now I am a murderer and the rain feels like acid on my skin.

Duchess walks me to the front door and hugs me. She puts the pillbox in my hand.

"Give one of these to Raynie if she needs it. We'll pass on dinner tonight, but I'll check with you in the morning and see how you are feeling. I'll get my cousin to follow me over here to bring your car back."

"But what about Christmas morning?" I ask, still hopeful that this was all a nightmare and we can at least celebrate Christmas morning.

"Let's wait and see how you and Raynie feel tomorrow."

"Yes, that would be good," I say, wondering if anything will ever again be good.

The first thing I see when I open the front door, pushed against the wall, is a bulky rectangular shape covered by a tarp with fake snow thrown over it. The piano. It looks like a coffin on a pedestal.

I give Tooley one of the white pills with instructions to give it to Raynie to calm her down. Tooley handles it as if it was a weapon of mass destruction, and gives it back.

"I fixed her some hot chocolate with some calming herbs and she's in her room resting. Duchess called and told me what happened at the bakery."

Tooley hands me a cup of warm chocolate. I don't remember anything ever tasting so good. For a moment it feels like life is normal and nothing bad happened today.

"I put a shot of brandy in it. Thought you might need it."

She pats my hand. "It's not your fault you know. Some people are just asking to be taken out. The bastard set you up so you would be the one who would have to live with the consequences of his actions for the rest of your life. I know about these things." Tooley stares out into the rainy night as though she was as far away from this world as the moon.

The angel that sits atop the tree is lit from below giving it an evil "Chucky" doll appearance. Every breath that billows from my lungs feels like an act of treason.

I go into my bedroom and undress. Even my clothes feel like traitors as they fall to the floor. I want to burn them as partners in a terrible crime. It crosses my mind to take a shower but I can barely make it to the bed.

In honor of the big holiday we celebrate as the birthday of Christ (which it really isn't of course; I think he was born in the spring), I had put red sheets with green trim on my bed. I slip under the covers and feel as though I have dived into a sea of blood, Ray's blood. I cannot swim in this dense fluid but neither can I escape.

Just before the merciful God of sleep renders me unconscious, I hear Ray laugh and say, *Gotcha.*

Chapter Twenty-Three

Raynie: New Year's Eve 2001.

I wish I had taken the half of sleeping pill that Mom offered me earlier and just knocked myself out. Instead, I waited until I heard her soft snoring and sneaked into the liquor cabinet to pour myself a snifter of her expensive brandy. I'm on my third refill, but it doesn't seem to have any effect.

    I lift my glass to Dick Clark. Mom said she used to jitterbug to reruns of American Bandstand when she was a kid.

    They are starting the countdown now to 2002.

    Ten... nine... eight.

    I lift my glass again and swirl the liquid around. It's heavy, like cough syrup, and has the color of chestnut skins. I see the reflection of the silver ball as it drops through the brandy in the glass. I take another sip. A little smoother now.

    The crowd is laughing and throwing confetti and blowing horns. They look cold. I can see their white steamy breath in the air.

    Seven... six... five. I hope Tooley isn't watching this. She'd be upset about all the trees that had to die to make the confetti.

    I miss her. Tooley took the dogs and went down to visit her new friends at the Golden Acres Retirement Spa down in Desert Hot Springs. I heard her tell Mom that sometimes all the "negative vibes" around here are too much for her to take.

    Mom's response (and I quote), "Why don't you get away

for awhile, explore California. You could hop on a bus or join a senior citizen group and go traveling. We're all just getting on each other's nerves right now. You can burn your sage bundles all you want and it won't make things better. We both need time and space. Raynie goes back to school in a few days so she doesn't need you to be here for her."

The conversation made me nervous. No matter how lousy I feel, just having Tooley around always makes me feel better. I don't want her to go anywhere. She might start roaming and never come back.

But I don't blame Tooley for taking Mom up on her offer. She practically asked her to leave. I would leave, too, if I could, but it doesn't matter where I am. I can't escape from myself. And besides, I can't leave Erma Geddon right now. She's asleep and I need to watch over her so nothing bad happens.

This has been the longest Christmas vacation of my life. I can't wait for school to start and I can take music lessons again from Mr. Harrison.

I e-mailed True yesterday and Jason about an hour ago, but no response. This is the first time I've tried to contact them since Ray died a week ago. I didn't get to see him after they took him away on a stretcher all bundled up in a black bag, like a mummy. After his autopsy, they released his body to Gram and Gramps Rogers. Mom said they had a small memorial service for him in Bullhead City. We were not invited.

      Four... three... two. I wish I could stop the ball from dropping and make it go back the other way.

"Stop." I hear myself shout. I want to turn back time to when Ray was alive, not lying in a pool of blood because my mother, who has cancer, had shot him in the face and killed him. I want to be a little girl again and go visit Granny Tooley in her magical place in the woods. I want to tip-walk on the beach with True when she truly was my best friend. I want to go back before 9/11 when we all felt safe and the Twin Towers gave a silent promise to stand tall in the sky forever. Now, the pictures on TV of black, gaping holes in the ground almost make me vomit. I want Delmar to be alive, and I want the Shandaras to stop blaming me because he died.

"One! Happy New Year!"

The crowd's gone wild and the music is playing really loud. I raise a toast to "Auld Lang Syne" and drain the remains of the brandy snifter.

I can't turn back the clock. I can't raise the dead.

I hide the snifter under the bed when I hear Mom knock on my door.

"Come in."

"Happy New Year, sweetheart," she says, her voice thick and drowsy, as she comes over to give me a hug. "Why don't you turn off the TV and get some sleep."

"Happy New Year, Mom." I touch her bald head and think I feel hints of whiskers of hair breaking through her scalp.

"Everything's going to be all right," she says and smiles.

I feel a little dizzy.

When Mom leaves and shuts the door, I grab my pillow, roll around on the bed, and giggle until I cry, the way True and I used to do over the slightest funny thing.

I'm glad I stayed awake to usher in 2002.

You only get one chance to do that.

Chapter Twenty-Four

Tooley: February 2002, Desert Hot Springs.

"Here comes the princess with the Technicolor eyes."

When Willard smiles, it looks like his face is melting, in a charming kind of way. He reminds me of a bulldog, Bugsy, who lived on Jeb's farm when my mother was alive.

Willard wears a perennial smile even though arthritis bombards his body constantly. At first, I had trouble looking into his eyes, which he beams on me in frequent overdoses. They are a pale mint green and remind me of the floor tiles in public restrooms. But now they add to his offbeat charm.

The sun keeps trying to go back to bed this morning. Willard and his sidekick, Parker, are wrapped like mummies in their bleached white bath towels issued to them by Golden Acres Retirement Center Spa. Willard pulls a poolside lounge chair close to him and pats it for me to sit down.

"I don't know why the hell we rush to get up and out here so early. It's always cold and windy until around eleven."

Parker is a spare little man who complains about everything. Whenever I see him, he looks like he's lost more weight. Even his body is trying to escape his constant nagging.

"We got here early because we pay big bucks for spa privileges, all of three dollars a day and you didn't want to waste money by missing a few precious hours of daylight, remember?" Willard says as he smiles and snuggles down in his chair with feet up, soles facing the pool. "Wait for awhile and the sun will smile down upon us." He pats my hand and I half-willingly sit down next to him, not my usual response to requests of any kind from men, but Willard is nice and Goody and I want to borrow his jeep this afternoon to go over to Palm Springs to the swap meet. We love taking advantage of his good nature, mostly because it makes him feel needed. That's what we tell ourselves.

He may not let us borrow the jeep after last week's fiasco. Goody backed into a Rolls Royce in the parking lot of the Goodwill store here in Desert Hot Springs. The driver of the Rolls was an old dame with platinum blonde hair and long red fingernails. She looked like Gloria Swanson. She came over and glared at us with scary, dark, made-up eyes, cell phone to ear. Goody jumped out and spun around the woman like she was doing one of her roller-skating routines. The performance made me dizzy.

"Why the hell is a Rolls Royce parked at Goodwill? If your car weren't so damn big, I wouldn't have hit it. Stay over in Palm Springs where you belong!"

Goody's "subversive" behavior (the term used by the policeman at the scene) cost her her driver's license. He said someone eighty-five years old with such a smart-mouthed attitude shouldn't be behind the wheel of a car. I've been the designated driver since the incident even though my license was taken away when I had the heat stroke last year. It's worth taking the chance. What are they going to do, throw two old ladies in jail?

Goody is my best new pal. We met a month ago when I took the bus from Anaheim into Los Angeles, to Hollywood and Vine. Goody was roller-skating on the sidewalk in front of Grauman's Chinese Theater, gliding over the handprints of legendary Hollywood stars. Barely five feet tall and weighing in at eighty-five pounds, she impressed me as a person who hadn't bought into the whole twenty-first century technical/commercial scene or followed the usual social norms of people her age. My first impression turned out to be right. While living on the grid, she plays with it doing whatever she can get away with to stay enthused about this mostly heartbreaking condition we call life.

I began having my affair with buses just after Ray's death. At Molly's suggestion, when things got too tense in the house, I hopped on a bus and went to Hollywood. I left the dogs in my room or out in the yard with Raynie to watch over them.

Raynie never talked much after Ray's death, but I sometimes heard her talking to the dogs, or to her sleeping Erma Geddon. Maybe she felt they were more trustworthy than humans, which is a belief I share as well.

I had started to tell Molly a number of times about my past, but she still isn't ready to hear it. I see my own pain reflected in my daughter's eyes every time I look at her.

Molly can't bring herself to go back to the bakery. Duchess and the man they hired to bake, I can't remember his name, took over her chores. She said it was only temporary, until she could walk into the room where she had committed murder, and not want to run out screaming and vomiting.

Before I left, Raynie was attempting to learn a Beethoven Sonata that sounded heavy, dark, complicated. The little classical music I've been exposed to confuses me. A lot of it seems overblown and pompous, with confusing melodies that do not connect directly with my heart. One of the few exceptions is Debussy. When Raynie plays *Clair de Lune*, the sounds are like a force of nature. She merges with the music in some magical way, moonlight rippling over everything within hearing range. She transforms herself into the waves of the sea in *Le Mer* and grieves for a dead princess in *Pavane.* If I request Debussy, Raynie will stop playing or launch into one of her heavy-handed sonatas as if in defiance of any kind of authority.

I'm used to simple music that I can play on my flute,

inspired by wind buffered by the rustling of leaves in tall trees, the baying of wild coyotes and dogs, and the subtle rhythms of growing plants. I miss the monochromatic beat of The Chief's drum as he accompanied my spontaneous melodies to the sound of the spirit of oneness nurturing itself.

Anyway, the dogs and I were bumping around Molly's house, in the way, and not bringing anything positive to the mix, so I escaped by bus and went on adventures while Kevin and Kachina stayed behind and lounged around the pool or stayed in my room and waited for me.

At first, it was difficult getting used to the cramped space on the bus, with people sitting behind me and next to me, but I just closed my eyes and pretended that The Chief was sitting beside me and eventually the fear went away.

The day Goody and I met, I had plunked myself down on a bench in front of Grauman's Theatre to eat a peanut butter sandwich and watch the people walk by. Goody skated up and sat next to me.

"What's a sweetheart like you doing in a dump like this?" she asked in a Bob Dylan voice. We shared my sandwich and the talk came easy, like friends reunited after a long absence.

We soon realized that we share a mutual love of old Hollywood movies, particularly ones with Ida Lupino and Jennifer Jones. Goody is a minor celebrity herself. She ice-skated in Sonja Henie's touring show, Hollywood Ice Revue. Her real name is Goodrich Shindrel.

She's the reason I moved (part-time) to Golden Acres. I had never had a playmate as a child, or a best friend growing up—with the exception of The Chief, but that relationship was far too complicated to be a simple friendship. Goody and I giggle and have fun. She distracts me from my problems and brings a breath of fresh air to my life.

Goody used to ride in on the bus from Desert Hot Springs

to Los Angeles and spend a night or two in a motel, go see movies and take a bus back to the desert. I brought her back to Anaheim to spend the night with us once, but she found the house "stifling" and my family "dreary."

I don't really live at Golden Acres per se. I bought a used trailer, at Goody's suggestion, and Willard pulled it up in the back parking lot behind the building. They let seniors squat there for free and pay three dollars a day to use the spa, and they allow dogs. There are several other campers around me, mostly snowbirds from Canada. I took some money out of my savings account in Roseburg, the account I'm mostly saving to give to Molly and Raynie, the one I haven't told them about yet. So here I am enjoying carefree days, soaking in warm pools with new friends. There is something about soaking in hot mineral water that makes people open up and want to share their life stories.

Kevin and Kachina like it here. Goody and I take them for long walks in the mornings and evenings, and we sit under crystal clear skies and watch the stars come out.

When it gets too hot for the dogs to stay in the trailer during the day, I head north and park the camper somewhere cooler. I hope I don't get caught driving without a driver's license. The thought of going back to Molly's for good gives me the shivers. I like having options.

We celebrated Goody's birthday last week. Willard treated us to a night at The Follies over in Palm Springs, and then we came back to Golden Acres for ice cream and chocolate cake. Parker suggested we make it a special birthday party and commit mass suicide out by the pool.

Goody confessed to me later that it wasn't really her birthday. She just wanted a little extra attention. "Sometimes you have to pretend you're happy and excited, make up something that gets your blood flowing. And the trick is, you have to be ready to surrender it all in an instant when the time comes."

Goody is a wise woman.

Parker doesn't like her, but then he doesn't like anybody who is having fun. He calls her the bitch on wheels.

I sometimes hang out in Goody's room when it gets windy and cold. Dogs are not allowed in the rooms but we sneak them in. They are becoming experts of subterfuge. The rooms are sort of depressing, all California fake glitter and gold. The furniture is chipped and the mattress is lumpy. But the thing I like most about Goody's room is the life-sized sculpture of a black bear carved in wood that stands in the corner by the back door. We found it sitting by the curb at a luxury home in Palm Springs one day when we had borrowed Willard's Jeep. Goody and I managed to haul it into the back seat. You find all kinds of wonderful things over in Palm Springs. Rich people's trash.

A pair of doves in a gilded cage graced the lobby with their presence when I moved here. Goody shared my strong opinion that birds should not be kept in cages. We stole them one night and released them up in the canyon. The birds were replaced a few days later with a tropical fish tank. Goody wanted to return the fish to the ocean but I talked her out of it with the argument that they might not live until we got them to the ocean, and the manager would probably replace the fish with something even more offensive.

Living in a camper, in a parking lot out in the desert, brings me closer to the life I lived in the forest, with the constant wind in the palm trees and the cooing of doves that nest in the fronds, and the complicated songs of nightingales. At Molly's, too many man-made things distract me and kept me separate from nature. When the air-conditioner was on, all the windows had to be shut, and the sound of the motor in the swimming pool drowned out the bird songs. Cars with motors racing and radios blasting rap songs gave me adrenalin rushes.

Never good at playing roles, it was exhausting to try and be someone I wasn't. Put me in a city isolated form nature and I am lost, unknown to myself.

I belong to the gentle rains of Oregon and the complex balance of give and take of a forest environment. The rich odors of leaf decay, the sounds of the wind, rain, and coyote howls, the light as it filters through high trees. These things are all part of me. They kept me grounded and were constant reminders that I have a place in this great circle of being.

Here, where steel monsters on wheels define the pathways, and plastic gadgets are the gods of modern kitchens, I am lost to myself.

Willard smiles and winks at me. "This is the life. Nothing to do but sit in the sun and look at pretty girls."

A gust of cold wind blows his plastic bottle that used to hold Golden Acre Spa water into the pool. I take off my bathrobe and wade into the tepid water of the kidney-shaped pool that smells like rotten eggs, sporting my new swimming suit I found at Goodwill for a dollar. I throw his bottle back up to him. He gets up and does a canon ball into the water, splashing the cursing Parker. We both get out of the pool and grab one of Parker's skinny arms to launch him into the water.

"More like buttermilk sky eyes if you ask me," says Parker, after he recovers his breath from being dunked underwater.

"What are you talking about, old man?" asks Willard.

"Tooley's eyes. They don't look like Technicolor. They look like buttermilk." He scrunches up his face.

Goody jumps in beside him. "You wouldn't know beauty if it bit you in the balls. Her eyes look a hell of a lot better than those rat turds you call peepers."

I'm shivering from the wind. The sun hasn't come out yet. "Let's go plant some trees," I suggest.

"I'm not going anywhere. I'm staying right here until the sun comes out," Parker shakes his head vehemently in the negative. "Why the hell are you planting deciduous trees in the desert? They'll never grow here."

"You don't know what's possible until you try," says Willard. I can tell he would rather sit in his chair by the pool, but he doesn't want to miss out on an adventure. "Let's stop at the coffee shop and have a turkey burger before we go. I'm buying."

"Race you to the coffee shop." Goody takes off at a fast walk over the smooth and sometimes slick concrete around the pool. Willard takes my hand. I resist at first, and then relax, as we swing our entwined arms back and forth like kids at play.

Chapter Twenty-Five

Molly: Early March 2002.

Ten o'clock in the morning and the temperature is already in the mid-seventies. The garage door is up, the side door to the backyard is open, and two fans move the air around the studio. My drawings are tacked up against the walls in order of execution, all created during the last month and a half. The arrangement feels like a retrospective of a lifetime of work even though they were done in such a short time. I feel like I'm on speed dial.

There is a progression that I'm not sure I understand or even want to totally comprehend. These works are part of an ongoing process. It's important not to make a big deal about any one of them.

The drawings feel like gauzy wrappings around a butterfly chrysalis. When the butterfly emerges, the casings will fall away having served their purpose of bringing the butterfly to wing. The whole body of work is a cocoon of atonement. Not sure what this means, I only want to get to the bottom of things, find a truth that can only be told in paint. Because I am incapable of putting the craziness that happened into a logical sequence of words.

Those first days after Ray's death I could use only pencil and ink on large pieces of rag paper. I did contour drawings, mostly of hands, my hands, with no thought to light and shading other than the variation of line that suggests ever so slightly the illusion of turning in space, which gives the impression of being able to leap off the page, fully formed as a three-dimensional being. I would stare at my hands for hours and touch the pencil to paper without taking my eyes from my hands, not looking at the paper except occasionally to reposition my pencil at the end of a line that turned inward.

I tried, but abandoned the seashell drawings I was working on before I killed Ray. As strong as they seemed at the time, they didn't make sense anymore; they were too pleasing to look at. No more paintings to match the sofa in the living room.

The first drawings I made, a few days after Ray's death, were just those simple hand studies. My mind prevented me from feeling anything other than protective numbness. Denial, I suppose. I could not bring myself to think about the incident, or work on anything that involved more than one form at a time, and I could work only in black and white. The thought of adding color confused me to the point of not being able to draw at all. My thoughts isolated me from others. In those early drawings, I seemed to be grasping for something, anything that made sense trying to survive.

Since the shooting, I've been holing up in the studio most of the time. I get up at five in the morning and bring my coffee out here to draw. I didn't even go in and eat breakfast with Tooley or Raynie. And then Tooley moved out.

I couldn't face Raynie, still can't. Raynie's silence, the baffled look on her face when she looks at me is not one of blame, fear, or even hatred. It's more like she's surprised the world is still turning and surprised her mother is a murderer. At some point, we both stopped trying to interact with each other. She goes to her room when she sees me coming and locks the door. She hardly ever talks. Yesterday, I was passing her bedroom and I heard her whispering to Erma Geddon, who is still asleep under the bed.

"Life is not fair, Erma." I heard her say. A lesson we all learn, but usually not so young and not in such an extreme manner. I think the best thing to do is honor her wishes and leave her alone; give her time to heal.

Raynie spent her birthday with Tooley down at the spa in Desert Hot Springs. Tooley and her friends Goody and Willard picked her up for the weekend and brought her home. I gave Raynie turtle socks and an Orcas whale charm for her bracelet. Raynie thanked me politely but didn't seem enthusiastic about getting a year older.

She comes to the studio door and mumbles goodbye with a piece of toast in her hand. She is bent from the weight of her backpack full of books.

"Off to school?" I ask. "Have a good day. I'll see you after school. If you're not coming straight home, call me and let me know where you are," I say.

Raynie looks at me with that surprised noncommittal expression she wears these days.

"I have an extra lesson with Mr. Harrison today after school," she mumbles and slouches out with the heavy load on her back. She is interested in little else other than her music and Erma Geddon. This month Raynie has been taking two lessons a week in preparation for her recital in early April. She's working on a Beethoven sonata. It's a bit beyond her ability, but she seems to be getting it, little by little.

Eleven weeks have passed since Ray's death and I haven't been able to step one foot into the bakery yet. Duchess and James are handling everything. James learned how to make my specialties, and rumor has it that his Orange Sunrise coffeecake equals mine. Duchess seems happy with the arrangement. I think she and James may be sweet on each other. There is a throaty slowness, like honey in her voice when she says his name or talks about him. Duchess hired a young college student to cover the counter in the afternoons. The girl is friendly and smiles a lot. Customers seem to like her. I've discovered that I am dispensable. Only a small part of my ego wants to protest this fact. But for the most part, I need the freedom to paint.

The shooting doesn't seem to have hurt business. In fact, our customer base has increased. People must have a morbid curiosity about crimes scenes. Duchess tells me that people come and stare in the windows or come in with others and point out the exact spot where Ray's body fell.

The policeman who interviewed me the day of the murder called a few weeks ago to tell me the two boys who had held up the bakery with Ray had been detained and confessed to having been there with Ray. They said it was supposed to be a joke he was playing on his ex-wife. Ray had been staying with relatives of the boys down in Tijuana and decided to come back and surprise his ex-wife and little girl for Christmas. I hate him for his intentions, whatever they were.

I follow the progression of the drawings on the wall. They began to change after a few weeks. I started adding charcoal, smudging it around, not really as shading, but more to balance some interior need. I added touches of white acrylic paint to break through pen and pencil lines to achieve the illusion of light penetrating form, or to alter the width of a line, also suggesting more light on the form. The hands are getting bigger.

I take frequent breaks and go out to smell the roses in bloom The intense red reminds me of Ray's blood. My heart aches. How I wish I could take back that moment I aimed the gun and fired.

Marsha is here. She says she came over to clean my house. I think she is watching one of Tooley's old movies. I hear theme music to *Splendor in the Grass.* Martha has the sound turned up loud enough to wake the dead. She won't admit she is hard of hearing.

I look at the drawings and think about what happened that day at the bakery. *If I had hesitated and thought for one minute, would I have pulled the trigger? There was something about the shoes of the elves that seemed odd, like I'd seen them before. And Santa's voice when he said, 'Ho, Ho, Ho, give me all your dough.' Wasn't that voice familiar?*

In mid-January, the gun started to appear in the drawings. The same Smith and Wesson hammerless snub-nosed .38 that I had in my hand the day Ray died. The gun appears as if in free fall as it twists and turns and plunges down the pages in profile, then muzzle aimed outward on the page at the viewer, then handle facing out. Different parts of the gun are exaggerated, foreshortened, and distorted. The drawings look like they should be framed as one, but they're too big to frame together. I hang them frameless, side-by-side.

Hands dart into the page, diagonals that create movement and a menacing kind of dialogue with one another and the object of contention. The gun is finally deconstructed into one cubistic form and becomes the central image on the page, presented in both profile, front, and back views simultaneously.

The hands begin to touch the gun. One finger at a time caresses the dissected and reformed object, leaving snail traces of cobalt blue on the handle of the gun, on the muzzle, the shapes spread out like a fan in their Picasso-like structure.

By the end of February, a mysterious thing happens. The drawings take on a numinous quality and seem to pulse with a glow of sadness and tenderness. They stand alone in the world as a presence, as if they had created themselves.

The flower-like gun reminds me of the Indian goddess Kali, the life-giver and destroyer. The many hands that surround the gun seem to represent the instruments by which we do our work in the world, and somehow they have become symbols for karma. Our actions done in the past influence our present and future actions, making us responsible for all we do.

I think Duchess would be proud of me for tapping into such a cosmic principle without her guidance. On an intellectual level, I know next to nothing about reincarnation and karma, but I feel in my gut that the killing of Ray will reverberate through many lifetimes like tidal waves.

I've had several dreams about a child.

A little boy runs to the end of the path of a big yard. A large, elaborate house is in the background. He calls his mother's name. She and a man are carrying suitcases to a car. She turns and waves goodbye and tells him to be a good boy. He runs toward her, crying, but she gets in the car and locks the door before he can reach her. She tells him through the thickness of glass that his babysitter will be along soon and to wait for her and not be any trouble, and she will bring him a new toy when she returns from her travels. He waits on the curb, looking up and down the street for any signs of life. He feels abandoned and betrayed.

It hits me like a freight train. The little boy is Ray. And I killed this little boy as surely as did his parents kill his spirit, abandoning him to the care of young girls who became mother figures for him.

A week ago, the drawings begin to change again.

When I started drawing the hands there was no conscious thought on my part about them being offenders. I didn't really think of them as anything other than shapes with which I was obsessed.

Now, the hands start to become knobby, with hairs drawn in sienna pencil on the knuckles. Why? My hands are not hairy, and I'm still using them as my model. The reason, I tell myself, is that I wanted some red tones to balance the cobalt blue of the smudges on the gun. But there are new stirrings deep within my heart, an awakening as if from a long sleep, a metamorphosis in progress. These are predatory animal hands and they belong to this body that moves me around.

The hands grow long fingernails that gradually curl and become claws, changing gradually. There must be fifty separate drawings of this transformation—in each iteration the hands grow more hair until sienna is the dominant color on the page. I add thumbprints of cadmium yellow in places to avoid the illusion of negative and positive space, like objects on a background. The thumbprints look like the eyes of wild animals peering out from the page. I add a slight bit more cobalt to keep a balance of cool and warm colors.

The word I've been searching for over the past several days comes to me: Lycanthropy—the mythical transformation of a person into a wolf. Are the hands in my drawings becoming those of a werewolf? In the first drawings, the beastly fingers surround the Kali-like gun image. As the drawings progress, the hands begin to touch the guns, shyly at first and then in the newest drawings, the hairy claws grasp the gun firmly. I laugh, and for a moment, the sound scares me as it turns into a howl-like lament that seems to go on a little too long.

Marsha is at the studio door with a dark look on her face.

"What in the hell is going on out here?"

Marsha looks at the drawings on the wall and shakes her head. "I think you need to take a break from this foolishness and go back to work. You're driving yourself crazy."

"If we could transform ourselves into anybody or anything we want to be whenever we wanted, don't you think that would be exciting? It would certainly keep the blues away," I say. Marsha clutches the doorframe.

"I am becoming my alter ego, a werewolf." I open my mouth wide and belt out a howl that sends Marsha back inside the house. "Wait, I'm just kidding!" I call out.

Marsha comes back to the edge of the door.

The Burning Jacket

"I had a dream last night that I was a wolf loping over hill and dale under a full moon. It was so freeing," I say.

"Don't tell anybody else about this," whispers Marsha. "And please don't share this with Raynie. She's traumatized enough without worrying about her mother turning into a werewolf."

"Does she talk to you?" I ask. "She barely mumbles anything to me."

"No, Raynie doesn't talk to me, either. She's silent, like my grandson. Maybe it's a phase teenagers go through. He's too busy in his room on the computer to give me more than a good morning, thanks for dinner, and good night. I'm not one to seek out the help of a shrink, but I think in Raynie's case you both need to talk to a professional."

"You really think Raynie needs to see a counselor? You don't think the school counselor is enough?"

"She's had an overdose of misery this last year. It wouldn't hurt to let her talk to a professional. And you two avoid each other like the plague. You're strangers living in the same house. I say, look into counseling for the both of you."

Marsha comes and shoos me into the house. "Leave your guns and werewolves for awhile. Take a rest and I'll make you a concoction of your mother's soothing tea."

Chapter Twenty-Six

Raynie: Early March 2002, Anaheim.

This has been the longest morning of my life. I'm in Mrs. Headley's Algebra class. I'm shaking with the heebie jeebies. That's what Mrs. Headley calls it when students fidget. She hasn't noticed me yet. My eyes are frozen to the hands of the big clock on the wall. Listening to each tick of a second gone by makes my body want to levitate from the chair. At 9:45, I will ask for a hall pass. I plan to meet True in the girls bathroom. It's almost time. An audible sigh of relief escapes my lips and Mrs. Headley frowns at me.

True called me on my cell last night from a telephone in a convenience store to say that she was spending the night in Anaheim at her Grandmother Fenona's apartment. She would be there all day, without Ashanti, to help Fenona pack to go back to India. They were finally moving. True said that Ashanti wanted to leave right away after Delmar died but it took a while for Rudi to wrap up his business—some kind of import/export company. I never really knew what he sold.

Sounding like the old True I know and love she said, "Hey Turtle Breath, meet me in the girl's bathroom at fifteen minutes before ten o'clock sharp. I can't stay long, so be on time."

My body feels like an accordion that has unfolded too fast as I rise and slink up to Mrs. Headley's desk for the pass. Her back is turned to me as she chalks out a complicated swirl of letters and equal signs on the blackboard. It looks like a mini-tornado of letters and numbers brewing. She doesn't even turn to look at me as I grab a pass and tiptoe out the door. It feels like every eye in the room is on me.

Math is beyond my comprehension these days and I welcome any excuse for a break. True calling me is something I've dreamed would happen ever since the day Delmar died.

I want to make a dash for the bathroom but I'm playing it cool, walking at a normal pace down the long, wide hall that smells of sweaty sneakers and fruity hair gel. Strawberry seems to be the popular flavor this month.

Halfway down the hall the girl's bathroom comes into view. My legs seem to have a mind of their own and they break into a trot. No one else is in the hall.

The entry to the bathroom is a long curve so no one can look in from the hallway. There is no door. And there are no doors for the stalls, only side partitions.

A gloved hand juts out and curls around the partition on one of the stalls. The fingertips have been cut off and long, phony, red fingernails are exposed. One of the fingers sports a big, fake emerald ring. The hand waves a long piece of white toilet paper.

"I surrender, G.I. Joe."

A voice that sounds like Tokyo Rose is followed by "Surprise!" as True jumps out of the stall and says, "Boo!" She runs over and throws herself in my arms.

"I've wanted to see you so much, but Ashanti guards the phones like a hawk and she took my cell phone away; Jason's too. And I guess the truth is I wasn't ready to make contact yet or I would have found a way."

I nod my head, incapable of words. We both cry and hug each other.

"I just had to come and say goodbye. We're leaving in a few

days. I've missed you, my little lizard." She messes up my hair.

"Ashanti sort of went crazy for a while. I guess we all did after Delmar died. She wouldn't let me or Jason out of the house, not even to go to school." True blows her nose on the toilet paper surrender flag.

"I've been miserable thinking that maybe Ashanti blamed me for the whole thing," I say. True is sitting in one of the sinks and I'm leaning against the one next to her. She seems so frail. She has lost even more weight since the memorial service. I feel huge and looming next to her.

"It's not so much she blames you, as what you stand for. She blames the United States for killing her child, her **only** flesh and blood child at that. She says the whole country and everybody in it is all messed up. She thinks this place is godless, without a soul, where her son felt forced to quit school and sign up for a war that made no sense, and she doesn't want her remaining children to grow up here just to get killed in another stupid war. She says the United States isn't a democracy anymore and that George Bush is another Hitler and planned the attack on the Twin Towers so he could go and invade countries in the Middle East." True hops down from the sink and stands close to me.

"We just dug up Delmar's body and when we get back to New Delhi we'll have a ceremony by the banks of the Yamuna River and cremate him in the Hindu tradition so that his soul may be released by the fire to new life. As you've probably surmised, Ashanti has forsaken Christianity for the religion of her ancestors. She has forbidden any of us to go to church anymore." True pulls a pack of Gitanes out of her pocket and lights one.

"When did you start smoking? Don't you know those things can kill you?" I try to take it out of her hand and she jerks away from me.

The Burning Jacket

We used to watch Mr. Roth, the drama teacher, smoke these during rehearsal breaks when we were in the play, *Men Are Like Streetcars*. True had a crush on him and it was her dream then to be an actress and smoke foreign cigarettes.

"I just need them for now. I'll quit soon. I've been under such heavy guard, this is the only fun I have anymore. Ashanti would shit in her pants if she knew I smoked." True turns and blows a puff of blue smoke in my face. "Raynie, I'm so sorry about the way I treated you. I didn't mean those things I said about your clothes and I'm sorry I called you a geek. I was jealous of all the freedom you had. It seemed like your Mom let you do pretty much whatever you wanted and I was under Ashanti's thumb all the time. I've always envied you. That is until a while ago." She frowns and bites her lip.

"You mean about my mom killing Ray?" I feel my fists clench. "I was there and I still don't know if it was an accident or if Mom knew it was Ray and saw an opportunity to take advantage of the situation to get rid of him once and for all. I don't know if I can ever trust her again, or forgive her. All she wants to do is hang out in her studio and stare at her hands and paint those horrible pictures of guns and werewolves."

True puts her cigarette up to my lips and I pull the spicy smoke into my mouth and throat and then swallow. A convulsive cough sets us both to giggling and out comes my inhaler. True imitates the sucking sound it makes when I breathe into it and we both double over with laughter.

"Must I teach you everything, Little Grasshopper? Don't inhale, silly. Just blow the smoke out of your mouth." She rumples my hair again. I forgot to brush it this morning.

True frowns. Her eyes are wide with trouble. "Okay, here goes. I should have told you this a long time ago, but I knew how much you loved your dad and missed him after he left, so I kept it to myself. You must not blame your mother for what she did. If she did know that Ray was the robber that day at the bakery, and I'm not saying she did, she shot him to protect you." She heaves a sigh. "Your dad was a real asshole." I start to interrupt and she holds up a hand to stop me. "When you and I started growing up, we were around ten when it started, he would come on to me when you weren't around. That's why I always wanted you to spend the night at my house and why I always made sure I was never alone with him. I never told Ashanti or she would have ended our friendship."

She took a final puff from the cigarette and flushed it down the toilet. Just in time. A girl came in to use the bathroom. True and I each went into a stall and pretended we were going to the bathroom until the girl flushed, washed her hands, and left.

"I need to know more. How could my father have come on to you? Is this just one of your theatrical tricks?" My face was pulsing with heat. "He never once touched a hair on my body," I hissed.

"I would never have told you before, but now you need to know so you can forgive your mother. He tried to kiss me and stick his tongue in my mouth. He even stuck his hand down my shirt one day."

"Ashanti told me that your mother caught him in a motel room with a girl that was only slightly older than us. He liked young girls. Now you know. How long would it have been before he got drunk one day and started doing that crap to you?" True came close and tried to hug me but I pushed her way.

"Raynie, I'm sorry but I've got to go. Fenona will get suspicious if I stay away too long. Don't hate me. Just remember that I love you. I only thought you needed to hear the truth. I'll write to you when I can. I miss you already. You'll always be my best friend."

My fists unclenched and I grabbed her and sobbed into her silken black hair that smelled like jasmine.

"Don't leave. You can come and live with us," I say hopefully.

"I can't. I have to go. My family needs me now. But maybe when this all blows over you can come and visit me in India."

Her odor lingered for a while after she left, a gift, like an unexpected warm breeze on a frozen winter's day. True cracked the hardened shell around my heart wide open. I shivered and went into one of the stalls and sat and cried and sucked on my inhaler until I heard the bell ring for lunch.

Students fill the bathroom and two Hispanic girls see me doubled over in tears and ask if I am all right. They help me stand up and splash water on my face and escort me to the school nurse. I didn't want to go back to class and I didn't want to go home, so I told Mrs. Brady, the nurse, that I needed to rest awhile, until my music lesson with Mr. Harrison.

Chapter Twenty-Seven

Raynie: Same Day 2002, Afternoon.

"Stop! Raynie concentrate! This is a very emotional piece."

I don't have to look up to feel the gathering storm on Mr. Harrison's face. "You're banging out Debussy like it's a beer barrel polka. What happened to that special touch?"

Sunspots stream through the windows of the music room; miniature flying saucers. They have come to rescue me from myself. Pulsating circular rainbows pierce me like blinding arrow shafts. The notes on the sheet of music on the stand are floating spots and my ears are hives filled with buzzing bees rendering me deaf to the notes I play.

Mr. Harrison has decided to go with *Claire de Lune* for my recital piece. He says I have not progressed enough to do Beethoven's *Moonlight Sonata*. A burden has been lifted from me. The thought of playing the sonata in recital had me in knots.

My fingers feel dead and the keys are hard to push down and the buzzing in my ears is deafening.

Your father was an asshole. True's words hiss in my ears.

"Haven't you memorized this yet? You've been working on it long enough that you should know it by heart."

Mr. Harrison stands behind me. I can feel his breath on my back, a hot wind of disappointment.

By heart. By heart? I know nothing by heart. Whenever I

THE BURNING JACKET

feel I know something by heart I destroy it and it disappears forever.

"Let's start from the beginning. Remember, make it smooth and worthy of the moonlight that the composer was trying to capture in the music."

I stop playing and fumble for the inhaler in my backpack as my breath comes out in labored gasps. The air conditioner must not be working. It's hot, and the tiny flying saucers have reproduced and multiplied, monopolizing the air and making it hard to breathe. They swirl in front of my eyes. The piano keys are a puzzle of black and white in jumbled planes and angles.

"Let's do this. I only have twenty more minutes. I have to take my wife to the doctor." Mr. Harrison looks at his watch.

His wife probably has cancer like my mother did. Because of me, he might not get her to the doctor in time and she'll die.

"She'll die because of me. It's all my fault." I ball my hands into fists and strike out at the piano. Pieces of me fly off into the air with each blow to the keys. I need Tooley's jacket to hold me together.

"Raynie, what is the matter with you, child? I'm sorry I was harsh with you. Stop beating the keys with your fists, and stop crying. We'll work on this piece when you feel better."

I turn and look at him as if gazing at a dark reflection of myself melting in a deep well of water. I wish I had on my wetsuit, all alone in the ocean with no people around, only the sea creatures softly bumping up against me to hold this thing called me together.

I have the vague sense that I'm not supposed to do what I'm doing, but what is it that I'm doing? Fists like hammers are beating the keys in time with a high shriek that sounds like it's coming from deep inside of me.

Mr. Harrison is on his cell phone. He looks worried. I hope he's not going to be late for his wife's doctor appointment.

Mrs. Brady, the school nurse, comes in. She says to Mr. Harrison, "You're lucky I was still here. How long has she been like this?"

"About fifteen minutes. I can't get her to stop."

"Call her mother and tell her to meet us over at the Emergency Room of Anaheim Memorial. Raynie was in my office earlier today and she seemed okay, just a little tired."

"Raynie, everything will be all right. We're here for you, sweetheart. We're going for a little ride, okay?"

Mrs. Brady has a kind smile. She reminds me of Mrs. Marple, the grandmotherly detective on *Mystery*.

My teeth hurt from shaking. They click inside my head like a metronome wound too tight. It hurts when they grab my arms and carry me to a car. Mrs. Brady rides in the backseat with me. Mr. Harrison is driving and talking on his cell phone to his wife.

The screams continue from somewhere inside the car, like the siren on the ambulance the day they took Delmar to the hospital. Mr. Harrison drives down State College and takes a left on Chapman. The car pulls up in front of a door that reads *Emergency Entrance*. This is where they took Delmar to die. Am I going to die?

A hefty young man who reminds me of an early version of Ray meets us at the door. He smiles and hoists me into a wheel chair.

"Let's go for a ride, young lady."

"Dad? I'm sorry. Even if you were an asshole. I still love you." He doesn't look like he believes me. Long ribbons of high-pitched shrieks leave gold and silver streamers tunneling down the hallway from the sides of the wheelchair.

This is where Delmar died.

"No, No. I'll die if I stay here." *Claire de Lune* ripples in the air gilding us all in moonlight madness.

A woman sticks a needle in my arm.

Chapter Twenty-Eight

Molly: Same Day 2002, Anaheim.

Mrs. Brady is waiting for me in the lobby of the children's psychiatric ward.

"What happened?" I ask in a voice that sounds like the ocean filtered through a seashell.

"She's been through so much. We, uh, I should have seen this coming." Mrs. Brady shakes her head and touches my hand. "I know little more than when we got here. Raynie fell to pieces during her music lesson and started beating on the keys and screaming. Mr. Harrison called me. We brought her here and they wheeled her away. A nurse just came out and told me they'd given her a shot to calm her down and she's sleeping." Her lips tremble, yet she tries to smile for my benefit.

Fell to pieces. What a strange thing for a school nurse to say, as if Raynie fell off of a shelf and shattered to bits, a fragile, brittle object like a delicate piece of china. I never would describe my daughter as fragile or brittle. She is so well put together. "She is dealing with some difficult things and just needs time to heal her wounds," I say, with perhaps more confidence in my voice than I'm feeling.

Mrs. Brady looks shocked at my words. She looks at the floor and shakes her head. "I have to go now. Please call me at home and let me know how Raynie is doing, and call me anytime if I can be of help."

She writes her phone number down on a piece of paper and puts it into my hand. I watch her walk away with shoulders stooped as if in defeat, and out the big double doors. She looks much older than when I saw her last. I guess as school nurse she blames herself for not noticing the precursors to this sort of thing. What sort of thing? Has Raynie really fallen to pieces?

I announce to the nurse behind the desk that I am Raynie Rogers' mother and would like to see her.

"She's sleeping now. We gave her a sedative to calm her down. You probably won't be able to talk with her today. Dr. Grill will come out to the lobby and find you. It shouldn't be too long." The nurse's voice is cool, matter-of-fact and judgmental.

The impact of what the nurse just said barely had time to soak into my brain when a young man with a shock of black hair comes over and offers me his hand to shake.

"I'm Dr. Grill. And you are Raynie's mother, Molly?" He smiles.

"Yes, doctor. Is she all right? Can I take her home?"

He hesitates.

"What I would like to do is transfer her over to Orange County General to the children's psychiatric ward for evaluation and some much needed rest." He looks at a chart in his hand. "From what I've been told, Raynie has recently experienced some overwhelming losses. She may need help sorting it all out. What I would like you to do is sign a seventy-two hour hold for her on the psych ward so she can get some distance from what's going on in her life." He holds out a form and hands me a ballpoint pen.

"But I want to see her now. I need to know that she is okay." I can't stop the tears.

"Let's go in. She's asleep and won't wake up, but you can be with her." We walk down a corridor of rooms covered with white curtains that remind me of niches in a mausoleum. "We'll take her over to County General by ambulance. Believe me. She needs this kind of attention right now. She shouldn't be going home. She needs a break from her usual environment to begin working through her grief. What often happens in cases like this is that the child blames herself and is struck down by guilt."

The doctor pulls aside the curtain to one of the niches and my daughter lies there, eyes closed, her face frozen in a frown. Her eyelids are red and puffy. Her hair falls on the pillow around her face, like a deliberate arrangement in a funeral home. How could I not have noticed the extremity of her pain?

"Is she breathing?" I go over and touch her hand. "Does she have her inhaler? She needs it to breathe when she's upset."

"She's breathing easy now. And she has her inhaler for when she needs it. Best to not wake her. She really needs to sleep. We have your phone number and we'll call to keep in touch about how she's doing."

He steers me away and out into the hallway before I even have time to kiss Raynie on the cheek. I write my name on the release form and hand it back to him. He pats me on the back.

"I hope you are getting counseling to deal with your own grief." His eyebrows go up as if he's asking me a question.

I shake my head. I don't know what to say. It would sound crazy to tell him that I'm dealing with murdering my ex-husband by drawing pictures of guns and werewolves.

My poor Raynie. If only I had been paying attention.

"Well, good luck to you and Raynie." He smiles and shakes my hand again and walks away, down the hallway of niches where nurses and technicians come and go as if the world is not falling apart, as if this was a normal day. People moan in pain behind white curtains. Others talk in whispers

I exit the double doors to the lobby. Space opens around me and I feel as if I'm in the middle of a muffled and strained silence of a De Chirico painting. For a second I'm walking on the marble floor of some ancient architectural ruin, among stone statues. Some statues standing, others sitting and the rest crumbled, body pieces lying on their sides, their flaws reflected in the marble floor, silently waiting their turn to be seen in the emergency room.

"Mrs. Rogers." A nurse behind the desk beckons me over. "Raynie was asking for a tool jacket when she came in. She said she needs it. If you know what she means could you take it over to County General? She may want it when she wakes up. They'll be taking her over there soon. If you have it with you, I'll take it in to the emergency room."

I shake my head in the negative. "I'm sorry, I'll have to find it and bring it over. She must have meant her Grandmother Tooley's jacket. She loves that jacket."

Where is Tooley's burning jacket? I'm sure Tooley must have it with her at Desert Hot Springs. I wasn't at home when she moved out, but I can't imagine she would leave it behind. I'll have to try and track her down. I can call the Spa and hopefully they can find her.

I feel estranged and out of touch with both my daughter and my mother. Do I even know who they are? I was so wrapped up in having cancer and my own guilt for killing Ray, and spending all my time in the studio doing my art that I ignored the hard times they both must have been going through. Raynie lost her father for God's sake. And Tooley lost the only home she ever knew or wanted. And I chose to block all of that out.

* * *

On the way home from Anaheim Memorial the song "I Fall to Pieces" by Patsy Cline sings itself over and over in my mind.

Duchess's old Ford van is in the driveway. My legs feel wooden and uncooperative as I try to walk up the sidewalk to the front door without wavering.

The Burning Jacket

Marsha and Duchess greet me, each with tears and a big hug.

"This isn't your fault," Duchess says, as if anticipating my thoughts.

"I should have paid more attention to her, spent more time with her. She acted like she didn't want to be around me. I thought if I gave her space and time she would get over it." I'm aware of a throbbing headache and an overwhelming need to peek in on Erma Geddon.

I go to Raynie's room and check under the bed. Erma is there. She has been awake for a few days. "It's time for you to go outside for a while and get your sea legs again. You've been under this bed long enough."

Erma follows me to the back patio and eats three big leaves of lettuce and a tomato. It seemed she slept longer this year than last. I wonder if it has anything to do with the gradual global climate change. Another thing to add to Raynie's burden of worries.

Erma looks at me as if to ask, "Where is she?"

"She'll be back soon." I say. I put a kiss on my finger and touch Erma's head with it. She stretches slowly and heads out to her burrow under the tool shed.

Marsha leaves.

I wish Duchess would leave. There is something I have to do.

But Duchess knows me too well. She is out in the studio with all the lights on, taking my drawings down from the walls. She has them neatly stacked in a pile on the floor.

"What the hell are you doing?" I yell.

I go over to the last remaining drawing on the wall and rip it down the middle. It falls in two pieces. "Look at this shit. This is what I've been doing while my daughter was falling to pieces, and I didn't even notice because I was so busy trying to be an artist. What a crock of bullshit." The torn drawing beneath my feet is being watered by my falling tears. It's one of the drawings where the hands start touching the gun.

If only I hadn't pulled that trigger, Ray would be alive and Raynie would not be unconscious in some hospital bed in a psychiatric ward.

"I didn't want to keep her from Ray to be spiteful. I was afraid of him; afraid he would take her away or do something to her. He was so angry. I didn't know what to do."

"I know. I know. It wasn't your fault, Queenie. You were just protecting your daughter from a madman. You didn't know how sad she was, how deeply his death affected her. None of us did. You're not a shrink. How would you know?" Duchess wipes my tears with a painting rag stiff with dried acrylic paint. "Step off of your drawing or I'll have to use force. I really like this one. Maybe we can patch it. What do you think?" She laughs.

I stomp on the drawing a few times, and reach down and tear it into pieces and scatter them like pieces of confetti. We both laugh.

My body lightens. My bones feel loose and young again for a moment. I think of the radiant woman in the hospital lobby with the colored scarf. She wouldn't have centered her whole identity around some silly drawings she'd made, or hold on to anything else of this world for that matter. She was probably beyond caring about things and matters of the ego. She seemed free, prepared to accept imminent death.

"What were you going to do with those drawings? Tear them all up the minute I leave?" Duchess asks.

"Probably," I manage to laugh. "But just tearing up one did the trick. I feel better." I walk over to the stacked drawings and am surprised at the thickness of the pile. I've done a massive amount of work in the last few months.

Duchess holds one up and looks at it. "These are really good," she says.

I shake my head in the negative.

"Queenie, you are not in a state of mind to make judgments right now. Am I going to have to drag these to the van and take them home with me or will you be a good girl and not destroy them?"

"I'll leave them alone. I'll call you first if an urge to rip them to shreds overcomes me. Thanks for saving me from myself."

I watch as Duchess backs her van down the driveway and waves goodbye. A sense of relief fills me, a heavy burden lifted, if only for a moment as I look at the stacks of drawings and then at the bare walls of the studio. I feel at once a sense of an ending and a beginning. I must have known at some level that my daughter was not dealing well with her grief, that she must be angry at me for taking her father away from her forever. Now the issue is out in the open. We will both have to deal with it.

Raynie is strong. She will pull through.

I almost forgot. I need to call Tooley right away and see if she can come back and stay with us for a while, and bring the burning jacket for Raynie.

I hope Tooley can forgive me for driving her away.

I stand in front of the mirror in the bathroom and rub my head. I have hair now. Not much, but it's coming in curly.

Chapter Twenty-Nine

Tooley: The Day After Raynie's Breakdown, 2002, Anaheim.

It was springtime up in Oregon at Jeb's farm where my mother and I lived. He took us in because we had nowhere else to go. I must have been around two when we moved in.

I'm in the twilight zone, half-dreaming and half-awake.

Calendula, a tall, lanky, yellow, wire-haired mutt, leads me through a grove of trees to a clearing.

She came to our door one frozen night in December just after my third birthday. Jeb called her a stray and wanted to shoot her, but Mama won the argument this time. She fed her and took her out to the barn to sleep with the goats and cows. The dog took on the role of my protector, and, when nights were warm enough, Calendula slept under my bedroom window.

As we walk through the wooded area, I look up at the dog and grab on to the collar of fur around her neck for stability and to keep pace with her. The terrain is bumpy. Calendula leans down and licks my face once in a while as reassurance that she will always be there for me.

We leave the stand of trees just as the sun comes out and throws soft light on a meadow filled with tiny white butterflies with purple eyes on their wings. They look like flying wild violets. Meadowlarks sing. The sun catches the flowering currant in the meadow and the plants look as if they are on fire with magenta flames. The yerba buena has come back in

THE BURNING JACKET

abundance. In a few weeks, Mama will harvest enough to dry for winter tea and leave the rest to spread new roots for next year.

Mama appears from the core of the swirl of butterflies. It is as if they had fluttered her into existence. She stretches and begins to sing and twirl with arms outstretched and eyes to the sky, naked as the rising sun.

'Mama, Mama, you're here,' I cry with delight. She smiles, bends down, touches my face, and says, 'Daughter, I never left you. I am always with you. Now you know what you have to do.' I reach out to hold her, but she disappears.

I open my eyes, not to the sight of my mother, or the sound of meadowlarks, but to the staccato of the swimming pool giant worm that eats the debris off the sides and top of the water. I'm back in Anaheim. The smells of yerba buena and sweet woodruff, the perfume that clung to my mother, linger in my mind.

You really were here, Mama.

A painting of a zebra on the wall hangs here in the jungle room, the extra room that became my room. The sheets and pillows are zebra-striped. A zebra rug lies on the floor in front of the bed and a large stuffed zebra sits on a trunk, along with a lion, tiger, and a large gorilla with a red heart that reads 'Kiss Me.' The concept of theme rooms seems indulgent. I learned at an early age to be a survivalist and to utilize everything found in the woods or things that people throw away as junk. It seems odd to decide how you want a room to look and then go out and spend a lot of money to make it look that way. I feel confined in this room surrounded by stuffed animals. No space to stretch. No fresh air. The animals only remind me of my wild friends in the woods, who I miss.

Kevin and Kachina snore in sync at the foot of the bed. Their eyelids move rapidly and their bodies twitch. I wonder if they are both having the same dream.

I was soaking in one of the hot tubs at Golden Acres last night with an interesting woman from the San Juan Islands. Until they got old and moved to Desert Hot Springs, she and her husband woke early every morning and threw themselves into the icy waters of Puget Sound at Orcas Island. I admire and envy her former life. What a great way to start the day.

One of the desk clerks at Golden Acres fetched me out of the hot tub and told me to call my daughter in Anaheim right away.

"Mom," Molly's voice said, "Raynie's had a breakdown. I need you. Can you come, tonight if possible? Raynie's asking for the burning jacket. I'm sorry; I wouldn't ask if it wasn't really important."

"Of course I'll come," I said right away. "You don't need to apologize. I'll ask Willard to drive me, and I'll bring the jacket. See you soon. Don't worry. Raynie will get through this. I know she will."

Both Willard and Goody decided to go with me. They would have no part in spending the night in Anaheim, but they had each other for company on the drive back. I put on the burning jacket, packed a few things, and rounded up the dogs. They sat in the back seat of the jeep with me.

The wind had picked up and blew little swirling devils of sand by the side of the road. The white windmills twirling in the Banning Pass look like grasshoppers with three wings, and strike me as omens of hope that my granddaughter would soon be well.

Long, refrigerated produce trucks from Mexico barrel down the highway toward Los Angeles. The grinding gears of the big trucks labor up the hill and sound like stretched out, elongated, wild animal growls.

My lips chant a healing mantra for Raynie. Willard looks worried and Goody is unusually quiet. I don't think we said three words during the drive. The dogs wrap themselves around me.

THE BURNING JACKET

Molly met me at the front door. I took off the jacket and handed it to her. She held it with three fingers and dropped it into a large plastic bag. Then she kissed me and gave me a prolonged hug.

"I'm sorry I have to go but Raynie may wake up and need this. No point in you going since you've had a long ride. There might be something good on TV. I'll be back as soon as I can." Molly kissed me again and left.

Goody and Willard were still outside in the jeep. They declined the invitation to come in for something to eat or drink.

"Call me when you want to come home and I'll pick you up," Willard offered. He put his hand over mine, which was resting on the driver's side window. He gave it a comforting pat.

It surprised me that I was beginning to think of the old camper, the spa, and my friends at Desert Hot Springs as home. I hugged them goodbye through the car windows and watched them drive away.

I went straight to Raynie's bedroom and performed a cleansing ceremony with sage bundles. I added twigs of rosemary for forgiveness and to remember the good days. I'm glad I remembered to bring my flute.

I smoked some of the sorrow out of the room; there is so much of it. Erma Geddon crawled out from under the bed to see what was going on. There has been too much negative energy to get it all with one smoking. I'll repeat the ritual.

Erma Geddon followed me out to the back patio and sat next to me while I played a special song that I felt spoke to her loneliness and sorrow for Raynie. I stroked her intricate shell and she nestled next to me.

"Raynie loves you. She just needs a little time out." Erma listened, eyes filled with concern.

That was last night. Today I must deal with unfinished business. My eyes fall on the pendant on the dresser. Last night, on the drive here to Anaheim, I cut it out of the hem of the burning jacket.

I get out of bed with dread to face the day, not knowing what condition Raynie is in, not knowing what Molly's response will be when I tell her what I have to tell her. Every bone in my body aches.

My mother's words echo in my head and heart.

You know what you have to do.

Chapter Thirty

Tooley: Same Day 2002, Anaheim.

"Good morning." Molly mutters the greeting meant to bestow blessings on everyone one meets, a once powerful word that has become meaningless through habitual use. Molly's eyes are red and swollen.

"Good morning to you," I return the blessing with deliberation. She looks like she didn't sleep last night. "Here, have some coffee." I hand Molly a cup from the freshly brewed pot. One thing we agree on, we both like strong coffee.

"Um. How is it that the smell of coffee can reassure us even in the midst of dreadful things?" Molly throws me a half thank-you smile as she sticks her nose over the cup and breathes in the curls of steam.

"That's because coffee is an herb, and herbs are our allies, given to us by the Great Spirit to help us live healthier, happier lives. And to help take us out of the world when our time comes." I said the wrong thing. I can tell by the slight curl of her lip that she has misinterpreted my words. "I didn't mean...."

"Forget it, Mom. You don't have to apologize. I'm just glad you're here."

"How was Raynie when you went to the hospital last night? Did you give her the jacket?" I ask, yet risking again an affable start of the day by mentioning the jacket.

"The nurse said that she couldn't have visitors."

Molly recoils within herself. She sits with feet tucked under her like when she was a little girl. "The nurse said she was resting and that she would give her the jacket. You should have seen the look on the woman's face when I handed her the old rag." Molly throws a sardonic smile at me that strikes a blow to my heart. *Touché*, I think, but this is not the time to keep count. This is the time for me to tell the truth.

As if in sync with my thoughts, a red-tailed hawk lands on the windowsill and pecks on the windowpane. This hawk has come to me before in times of hardship. I believe it is my mother in spirit form. I caught glimpses of her the day the loggers came. It was circling in the rain above my head. And before that, a long time ago, she was there the morning to steady my hand and intent. She had guided me through my deadly mission.

The hawk nods her head as if to say, *Don't hesitate, go on and tell her.*

"Mom, I know how close you are to Raynie. She loves you very much, and if your jacket makes her feel better, I'm glad for that." Molly puts her hand over mine on the table. The contrast is startling—her smooth skin like butter against paper-thin ashes. How did I ever get this old?

Molly pats my hand and takes hers away. "You've lost more weight since I've last seen you. I think you should see a doctor while you are here."

"I will," I say to shut her up about the matter, but we both know that it will be a cold day in hell before I subject myself to false medicines that use artificial poisons in the name of healing.

"Speaking of the jacket," I change the subject, "I have something to tell you."

Molly stiffens, gets up, and says she will fix breakfast. "How about two poached eggs on that new whole wheat bread Duchess invented; the one with sunflowers, flax seeds, and orange peels?" Molly puts a skillet on the stove hoping to distract me from telling her what she thinks is another silly lie.

"No, Molly. You must sit down and listen to me. It's important. I will tell you only the truth, even though it may sound like fiction to you. You must believe me." The look on her face changes from irritation to anger.

"I'm not sure I want to know the truth after all these years. What could you possibly tell me now that will make up for all the years of lies, of never really knowing who you are, who I am, or where we came from?" She stares at me without blinking. My eyes lock in and do not look away.

"Just sit down and promise you will listen and not interrupt."

She pours us each another cup of coffee and sits, arms folded across her chest as if to guard her heart.

I feel myself going back to a time and place I've tried to forget and long to remember. I tell stories so I won't have to deal with the 'real' one that defined my life, the one that belongs to this dubious reality that seems to be the one that counts the most in this world, the real history of Tallulah Running Bear Winters, the little I know of it.

"I'll start with what happened to my mother so you will better understand why I did what I did." The red-tail hawk circles the back patio in slow motion.

It was Easter morning, that special day when Christians all over the world celebrate the resurrection of Christ. I was five years old. My mother had made me a beautiful white dress with a print of little red roses all over it to wear to Easter services at church. We were in the kitchen. I was turning around and around showing off my dress and we were both laughing, excited. Mama braided strands of sweet woodruff into my hair. I climbed up on a kitchen chair and she got out her needle and thread to make some final adjustments to the hem.

Jeb came in from milking the goats and cows, ready for breakfast. He saw us laughing and having fun, and breakfast wasn't ready. It set him off. He never wanted anybody to be happy. He was always so miserable.

'Doesn't Tooley look pretty in her new dress?' Mama was bent over my hem putting in the finishing stitches when Jeb hit her so hard she fell over backwards and hit the back of her head against the wood cook stove. He just kept hitting her until she stopped crying. She never got up.

I saw this all from atop the chair, a scene that is burned into my brain, a scene that in the past I would have done anything to keep from being unearthed. I tried to bury it in a hole that reached to the center of the earth's core. I tried to fill my mind with other stories and pretend it never happened.

I ran to her.

'Mama, Mama, please wake up.' I had seen dogs and cats and other farm animals go to sleep and not move. They would disappear into a hole in the ground and never be seen again.

There was blood all over her. Jeb bent down and put his hand on her neck.

'She's dead,' Jeb said in a normal everyday voice, closing her eyes with his hand.

'Don't touch her! Don't close her eyes. She won't be able to see.' I said and jumped off the chair and started beating him in the leg with my fist. 'Don't you ever touch her again.' My voice sounded like the bleating of a newborn calf. Jeb threw me across the floor and against the wall. I got up and ran out the kitchen door. Calendula was outside barking, waiting for me.

'Stop that dog from barking or she'll be next,' he yelled. Calendula knew from experience to stay clear of Jeb. It had only taken one good kick from his boot for her to learn that lesson.

We both took off running for the grove.

We hid behind the trees and watched the house while Jeb

The Burning Jacket

dragged my mother's body outside, wrapped in a beautiful quilt she had made for her bed.

Mama had been a wonderful seamstress and made quilts and clothes and sold them to the people in town. Jeb paid no attention to her endeavors. He called it women's work and as such, in his mind, it was not important. But that's how she made her spending money.

The quilt that became her funeral shroud with its colors of the rainbow was what Mama wrapped me in on icy days when we couldn't go outside. She would swaddle me and read to me, or make up stories. When Jeb was not within earshot, she told me stories about my real father, Running Bear, and what a brave and beautiful man he'd been. He was killed in a car accident on Interstate-5 while driving down to California to find work in the vineyards. He died when I was a baby. She said he would rock me in his arms and sing songs in his native language. He was from a coastal tribe. I don't remember which one.

Mama said Jeb had been kind and generous at first, and invited us to stay with him on his farm. His wife was dead, he had no children, and he was lonely. We lived with him but he and Mama never got married.

Jeb's kind nature didn't last long. By the time I was walking, he complained about everything and yelled a lot. Occasionally he would slap Mama across the face, usually for not having a meal ready on time. When my hands could reach the top of the stove I would help cook if she was running behind.

Molly got up and turned off the coffee pot and when she sat down again I continued. "Back to the killing," I say.

Jeb dragged my beautiful mother in her colorful quilt back out behind the barn. Calendula and I crept to the end of the stand of trees that was a stone's throw from the barn, for a better view. Jeb dug a deep hole in the ground next to where all our pets and farm animals were buried. He dragged the quilt over to the side of the grave, then kicked the quilt with her body in it with his boot. She rolled into the grave and he covered her up with dirt, patting the mound down with the back of his shovel.

'Ashes to ashes and dust to dust. Good riddance to bad rubbish,' Jeb said.

I had to put my hand over my mouth to keep from screaming. Calendula knew not to make a noise; she licked the tears from my cheeks.

Calendula and I walked back through the thicket of cottonwoods and alders and hid out down by the stream all day. My new Easter dress was muddy and wet where we had waded upstream to a good place to drink water. We both sat by the bank shivering until dark, when it got too cold. I didn't know what else to do so I went back and slept in the barn between two bales of hay with Calendula on top of me to stay warm.

"Mom, I'm so sorry you had to go through something so horrible." Molly comes over and hugs me around the head. Her tears are wet on my cheek. "How long did you stay with him?"

"This is only the first half of the story. I need to tell you the rest." My voice is weary and I feel an urgency to get it all out before my voice gives out.

"Are you sure you want to tell me now? We can wait until later, if you want to rest," Molly says.

"No. I have to tell it now." The hawk is over in the orange tree, swaying as if to invisible music. "Let's go sit outside on the patio." The hawk will give me strength to finish my story.

Despite the warmth of the sun on the patio, I feel cold, as if I am reliving that night—the coldest night of my life.

I stayed with Jeb seven long years after he killed Mama. I

The Burning Jacket

was about Raynie's age when I left. He never touched me or my dog after the killing. Calendula died of old age about six months before I ran away. I buried her out behind the barn near Mama's grave. And I put a stone at the head and a stone at the foot of Mama's grave.

When the people from the church noticed that Mama had disappeared and I didn't come to kindergarten and then first grade they came around to check on us. Jeb told them that Mama had run away with another man and had left him alone to raise her daughter. He told them that he was going to home school me and instill good Christian values in me so I wouldn't turn out to be like my heathen mother. Back in those days, they didn't have social workers checking up on people all the time.

People from the church were extra nice to me and Jeb. They would bring prepared dinners out to the farm. I never said a word to anybody about what really happened.

Things went along okay until Jeb's "accident," as he called it, just after my twelfth birthday.

Molly sighs as if in anticipation of more bad news.

A herd of wild horses lived in the hills just beyond the back pasture. A mare I named Jesse was among them. Jesse was my friend. She would come to me and let me pet her for a ransom of carrots. We visited every day. We were kindred spirits. I could smell the wildness in the air around her. She knew I longed to be as free as she.

Jeb went up to the hills to try and catch the horses, they were the last wild herd in the area. He wanted to take them to town to sell them at the horsemeat market. He didn't need the money; he just couldn't abide their freedom.

They spooked when he tried to herd them into the fenced pasture. They stampeded and kicked him until he was unconscious. I should have left him to die that day. My life would be so different if I had.

He missed lunch and dinner. I knew he was around the farm somewhere. His truck was parked in front so I knew he hadn't gone to town. His old horse, Chestnut, was saddled and standing, untied, alone by the barn door. Calendula and I went looking for him around twilight. I walked around calling his name. Then I saw him beyond the fence where the wild horses lived.

I should have left him there to die, but I couldn't. I ran back and called Doc Moody. He came out with an ambulance and they took Jeb to the hospital. He had a broken arm and some broken ribs. The worst injuries were to his head and face. Doc Moody said if he had lain out there in the cold all night, without treatment, he probably would have died. I wished I'd never found him.

He stayed in the hospital a good two weeks. I was glad to have the place to myself. I spent a lot of time at my mother's grave; the grass had long grown over it. I weeded around the head and footstones, and scattered flower petals over her.

When several members of the church brought him home from the hospital, Jeb looked to be in pretty bad shape. A long red scar traversed the right side of his face. It looked like an imprint of a hand, outlined by raised angry ridges of hard skin. He seemed to be proud of it; he called it the hand of God.

The kick that left him disfigured had also altered his speech. When he tried to talk, scattered vowels punctuated by occasional guttural hard sounds flew out of his mouth, like bullets. Crazy, incoherent sounds. He never spoke when others were around, he spoke only to me. After awhile his gibberish made sense.

The day he came home the doctor told me to feed him soft baby food for awhile, so to welcome him home I fixed fried pork

The Burning Jacket

chops, mashed potatoes, corn bread and coleslaw. I watched with twisted pleasure as he struggled to cut his meat with the arm that wasn't in a cast. He couldn't really chew. Most of the food landed back on his plate, a mess. He managed the potatoes and some of the stewed tomatoes. I didn't offer to help.

A few months after Jeb's return home, Doc Moody came out and cut the cast off his arm. I was sorry to see it go. The first thing Jeb did was to go up to the hills and poison the pond where the wild horses drank. When I went up later that day to give Jesse some carrots, she was lying dead, close to the pasture fence where we always met. Horses were down everywhere. They were all dead.

I vowed revenge.

It had been a simple plan, really, one that I could carry out easily and no one would be the wiser for it. An eye for an eye, as Jeb would say.

The idea had been in the back of my mind, and now came forward, like an old friend I hadn't seen for years. It took my breath away, and gave me goose bumps. The idea had formed itself in my mind, like an insect caught in a spider's web, the day Jeb killed Mama, but it had lain dormant all those years until I was old enough to carry it out.

Molly takes a sip of her cold coffee. She is silent and tears fall into her cup. She nods for me to keep talking.

The gentle sound of the rippling water down by the creek soothed and cleared my mind. There were no doubts or second thoughts. It was as if I had been born again once I decided to carry out my plan.

Mama had pointed out the deadly hemlock many times when we went down to the creek to harvest watercress and mint. 'Don't mistake these for the wild carrots and parsnips,' she told me. *'See, they are taller than all the other plants.' Mama's voice had been soft, like the flow of water from the creek. The white flowers arranged in umbrella-like clusters towered above my head. 'Remember the hemlock has purple spots all along the large smooth stems and it smells old and musty, not fresh like the mints or wild carrots,' she warned.*

I pulled up the hemlock, making sure I got the deadliest part, the bulbs, gathering as much as I could carry, half dragging the heavy plants along the trail from the creek back up to the potting shed.

I hung them from the rafters to dry next to the herbs that had been gathered for teas: lemon balm, peppermint, sage, and oregano.

The hemlock had a strong smell of dead mice that overshadowed the pleasing aromas of the other herbs. The deadly alkaloids were dispersed in all parts of the plant, but most of it concentrated in the seeds and bulbs. From these, when dried, I made an infusion. I didn't worry that Jeb would be suspicious of the brew. He always drank the teas I made for him, and he couldn't taste or smell anything after the accident, so he wouldn't detect the fetid odor or bitter taste.

I carefully pulverized the dried root and seeds in Mama's old mortar and pestle in the potting shed. She would mash bundles of dried herbs in the stone basin, sift the leaves into clear plastic bags and label them peppermint, chamomile, lemon balm. The tonic smells of the hanging plants had always reassured me. As long as the wonderful smell of herbs, and Mama, were by my side, the world would be a good and safe place.

When there were enough pulverized materials for a strong infusion, being careful not to let any of the dried powder touch my skin, I poured the powder into a plastic bag and put it on a shelf in the kitchen for morning tea.

The Burning Jacket

The next day I got up at dawn to make the brew while Jeb was out milking the animals and feeding the chickens.

Without a word, Molly comes over and hugs me. Her face is a landmine of sadness.

The tea was deep amber, the color and thickness of sorghum. I had made a special breakfast of bacon, eggs, and buttermilk biscuits, and had waited for him with steady heart and head. Even though he had no sense of taste, he always wanted a big breakfast.

When I heard him stomp on the porch and scrape the mud off his boots, I got a little shaky, but then steeled myself, and never doubted what must be done.

Out of habit, he walked into the kitchen and went to the stove. He bent over as if to smell the bacon, a tribute to his lost senses. I watched out of the corner of my eye as he poured himself a cup of tea and sniffed the contents of the steaming cup. The kitchen was saturated with the cloying smell of the hemlock, like overripe fruit and rotting grass, with a familiar musty odor of dead mice.

'Dad blatt it!' Jeb said. 'What crazy concoction have you brewed up this morning, girl?' He slurred and drooled as he hurled his misshapen words at me.

He was used to my different brews, sometimes containing wild grasses and common garden weeds. And even though he was resistant to change, I could tell he enjoyed, if he enjoyed anything, the mushrooms I would add to omelets and soups in the fall.

'What kind of tea is this?' Jeb asked again. 'It's as thick as molasses.'

'Something to make us strong and healthy,' I said with a smile, one that was not forced. 'Just something different to spice

up the dull routine of our lives. It has honey in it to make you sweet.'

I sensed Jeb was in a tolerant mood and that I could get away with this kind of backtalk. Why shouldn't he be happy? He'd just killed my favorite mare and all the other wild horses. And he'd left them out by the pond to rot. If he had detected my sorrow, he would have felt proud, even overjoyed, by his evil deed.

When Jeb was in a bad mood, he would pout and throw his food on the floor. He viewed my natural curiosity about plants as laziness, just an excuse to roam the woods and meadows to get out of work. 'Idle hands are the devil's workshop,' he would say.

'You're just like your mother, willful and self-indulgent. God rest her sinful, half-breed soul.'

I could tell his mood had turned sour when he started thinking about my mother. I wished he would drink the tea and be done with it.

'She was never satisfied with the simple things, always lusting after something new. That's why she up and left us, abandoned her only child.' He jerked his head in my direction.

I think the horse kicked the memory of what he'd done out of his head. I think he really believed his lies.

'You're goin' turn out just like her if you're not careful. You got those wild, restless hawk eyes just like her.'

Jeb buttered a biscuit and took a crooked bite. It took him forever to chew his food.

'The Lord loves a plain and frugal man,' he said, in honor of himself as he lifted the cup of tea and drank with lips that veered to the left of his face. I almost gagged from the stench. Some of the liquid dribbled, like thick tobacco spit, down the front of his cotton long johns and overalls.

After about thirty seconds, Jeb fell to the floor, drooling even more than usual. His eyes had always frightened me. They *held a certain mad intensity, but I stared at him and didn't look away. They became glassy and seemed to look through me to a place far away. I was scared but I couldn't look away.*

The poison moved quickly through his body. First, his legs stopped moving, then he had trouble breathing. He tried to say help me, but it came out as heeee yaa.

'This is what God thinks of you.' I walked over to him and spit in his face. 'This is what you get for killing my mother who was the kindest, most beautiful person in the world. You never deserved her. She never loved you.'

I spit on him again. 'This is for killing the horses. Jesse was my friend and you couldn't stand that. She was a magnificent horse, all afire with a mahogany sheen when the sun hit her coat. Your evil heart could not understand anything that beautiful and free. I hope you rot in hell.' One last spit for good measure, but I don't think he felt it.

I'll never forget the feeling of relief when he took his last breath. Mama's spirit was in that kitchen with me, spinning and dancing in circles. I looked out the kitchen window and saw a red-tailed hawk circling in the sky.

"Some people don't deserve to live, but it puts a heavy burden on the hearts of those brave enough to take them out of their misery and stop them from hurting other people," I say after a long silence.

The hawk circles the yard one last time, looks in my direction and flies away. Even though the sun is warm out on the patio, my body is shaking and chilled.

Molly speaks so softly I can hardly hear her.

"I had been trying to understand the image of who I think myself to be with what I did to Ray and for the life of me I could not reconcile the two until now. Now I know what gave me the courage to pull the trigger."

Molly looks more relaxed than I've seen her look in a long time. In my presence, she always holds a resistance in her chin. That defiance is gone now.

We are all contradictions. We are made of opposites. We live between two poles. Remember the yin and the yang? We do our best to meet somewhere in the middle, with no blame. But sometimes we are called upon to make terrible choices.

"Mom, I keep racking my brain trying to figure out if I knew it was Ray when I fired the gun. I honestly don't know."

"In the heat of the moment how could you know? You were protecting yourself and your child. You didn't know the gun was a toy. You didn't know the man wouldn't shoot you and everybody else in the bakery. People do all kinds of crazy things. You did the right thing. Stop blaming yourself for something you had to do. Nobody else blames you."

"Well, that's not true. Raynie blames me."

"She'll come to understand it wasn't your fault. Why would a grown man disguise himself and point a toy gun at someone he knows has a registered gun and was trained in how to use it? Ask yourself that. Maybe he wanted to die and wanted you to suffer the consequences for the rest of your life for shooting him. Perhaps he was trying to get even." My body shivers with cold even though the temperature has risen.

"That thought has crossed my mind. Maybe he did want to die and punish me at the same time." Molly shakes her head and notices that I'm shaking. "Let's go inside and get you warm."

She puts an arm around me and walks me into the house. She feels solid and strong this morning; it's like I'm leaning against a Douglas fir tree in the forest.

"There is more to the story, but I think I'll rest first," I say. The telling of a story that could never be told has left me relieved, like going to confession, but drained of energy. My legs barely make it back to the zebra room to collapse on the bed for a nap.

Chapter Thirty-One

Raynie: Rehab, March 2002.

"Digs are cool. Looks handmade."

The girl sits down beside me and touches my jacket. She arrived here the day before yesterday and hasn't been to group yet. Her room is at the other end of the hall, but I watched them bring her in kicking and screaming.

When your time comes to wear the jacket it will protect you and keep you strong as it has me, and all of the women in our family before us.

When the girl touches my jacket, I don't go into panic mode and think she'll try to take it away. *This must signal an improvement in my behavior.* A few days ago, one of the nurses tried to take it down to the laundry. I staged a fit that rivaled, maybe even surpassed, True at her finest.

The staff is always talking about our behavior—they say things like 'her behavior regressed today,' or 'she shows improvement in her behavior.' Other favorite phrases are 'check your attitude,' or she's 'acting out.'

The TV room is empty except for the two of us, and Denise who is always here, curled up in a chair like a homeless cat. She's watching *The Young and the Restless.* Denise is all skin and bones. She's taller than I am and weighs around eighty pounds, if that.

Usually there are more people in here watching the soaps

or working on a stupid puzzle of an old sailing ship at sea that pitches through dangerously high waves. It makes me nervous to look at it. The puzzle is almost finished. Then we'll get a new one. I hope I won't still be here to work on the new one.

"My name is Magellan," the girl says, holding out a long, tapered, honey-colored hand with fingernails that have been bitten to the quick. I hesitate, not sure that I can trust a handshake, not sure if a handshake will suck me into a deep dark hole. "That's okay. I understand," she says. "You got to be careful. I usually don't like people shaking my hand or huggin' me up, being all friendly right away. It's cool." She laughs revealing a hedge of straight white teeth. "What's your name, baby?"

"Raynie."

"Raynie. That's a pretty name. Like rain falling. What are you in here for, Raynie?" She looks me straight in the eyes. I stare back at her and she breaks the gaze first. Tooley taught me never to be the first to look away.

Magellan's eyes are brown when she looks directly at me. But when I watched her in profile, when she was looking out the window, they looked like blue clouds. This confuses me. She could be what Tooley calls a 'shape-shifter,' a spirit that can take on different physical forms. Some shape-shifters you can trust and some you can't, according to Tooley.

I miss Tooley. We talked on the phone this morning. I've been here seven days and haven't seen either her or Mom yet. They both wanted me to be released and come home, but the shrink and I decided I should stay a few more days, go to group, get a little more perspective on my life. I miss Erma Geddon like crazy, but I want to be well when we meet again. I'm not ready to face my life yet.

Magellan's eyes still hold the question. *What you in here for, Raynie?* I don't have the energy to get into the whole entangled nest of snakes that is my life. I give her the brief cause of my fall, the plain, simple facts. "I pounded on the piano keys and screamed during a music lesson. Next thing I knew here I was."

"Nah, nah," she laughs. "You don't end up in here for punchin' out no piano. You musta done som'um more than that." She shakes her finger at me and laughs again. "You was a naughty girl, but it's okay, you don't have to tell me. It's cool. You in your Raggedy Ann coat."

Even though the only things in the TV room are the TV, two big sofas, three overstuffed chairs, and some metal folding chairs around the table with the puzzle, the room feels messy, cluttered with unspoken words and regrets. It all feels sticky on my skin, like molasses. I want to take a shower and wash it away.

This room is the gathering place where we tell each other stories about what brought us here. We tell our tales of woe here and in group, over and over again, at first with surprised looks on our faces, as if we can't believe we did what we did to wind up in here, but after a while the reality sinks in and the shock gives way to boredom. Our sins become dried up dog turds on a neutral sidewalk. It's easier to talk about things here than it is in group. No therapist telling you to check your attitude.

The walls are painted a shocking swimming pool blue, adding to my sense of bewilderment about why I agreed to stay here a few more days when I could be at home by the pool with Erma Geddon. They won't let me wear my Save the Earth shirt in here. They say all of us in here shouldn't worry about anything except getting well. I asked the counselor in group how we can get well if we destroy the earth. She avoided the question by telling us all to take a breath and check our attitudes.

"Looks like Nikki is gettin' ready to divorce Victor again." Magellan says and shakes her head. "No matter how much of the soaps you miss, nothing new ever really happens. It's always the same old drama. Just like life, I guess. One minute you're perfectly fine and the next you've jumped off the high dive into an empty pool."

Most of the girls I've met in here seem perfectly normal except for the fact that many of them have tried to commit suicide, or cut their arms with razors, or are on drugs, or refuse to eat.

"I like your name. How did you get the name Magellan?" I wrap my jacket tighter around me, trying to make conversation, but not at all sure I want to get to know this girl. She's tall, thin and hard, but with a certain natural grace. She looks older than me, maybe sixteen. And she looks different than most of the girls I've met here. Most seem floppy and boneless. They tend to throw themselves in chairs rather than sit. Magellan seems in control of her body.

"A dad in one of my foster homes used to call me Magellan. You know, after the great explorer. He said it was because I was all over the map. The name just stuck." She laughs. "I liked him. Boy did I like him. Too bad his wife didn't like me." She laughs and shows her teeth. "That was a good home. They even had an automatic dishwasher."

I suddenly feel a need to get away from this girl. I go over to the window with the burnt orange, flowered curtain that reminds me of vomit. This hospital is badly in need of an interior decorator. None of the windows open. Even breathing in the smog would be preferable to the heavy air of guilt and self-loathing that permeates the room.

When I go to group and hear other people's stories, I see that behind the drama the patterns of our lives are so similar. We blame ourselves for things that are not our fault, things we couldn't do anything to fix or change.

My thinking is interrupted by the hexagonal, thick, chicken

wire that covers the windows. It reminds me of cells in a beehive. I get sucked in and am unable to look away. The dizzying pattern sends me on a downward spin of self-loathing; the clichéd old mantra of *it's all your fault* beats inside my pounding heart. When first I got on this train I couldn't get off by myself, but today I'm able to turn and move away from the window.

I walk down the hall to ask the nurse on desk duty for my inhaler. I take a few puffs and then give it back to her. I go in my room and shut the door.

* * *

I'm on the floor, sitting in the lotus position wearing the burning jacket. In here with me are Tooley and the ghosts of all the women who wore the jacket before her, reinforcing my God-given right to be in this world.

I go deep inside and watch the sea rise out of the dark to meet a rising sun. An image of a lone turtle with the sun reflected like two rosy pearls in her eyes lights up my mind. When I come back to reality, I go to the nurses' station again and ask for a pencil and piece of paper to write down the insights that came to me during meditation.

1. It's not my fault that Mom kicked Dad out of the house.
2. It's not my fault that Mom got cancer.
3. It's not my fault that Mom killed Dad.
4. It's not my fault that Delmar died.
5. It's not my fault that Ashanti blames me for Delmar's death.
6. We can't control everything that happens to us, we can only control our attitude toward it.
7. It's not my fault the planet is screwed.

THREE

Chapter Thirty-Two

Tooley: Fall 2002.

I feel like a building in shambles waiting for the wrecking ball to smash me to pieces. I wish the heat stroke had taken me. I don't really wish that because then I wouldn't have had 'the talk' with Molly or been able to give Raynie the burning jacket when she needed it most.

A relentless ache seems to have invaded every bone and muscle of my body. This kind of constant reminder makes me all too aware that I am a spirit in a mortal body. The pain drives my focus of who I am away from my body and leads me to the real me, which is a place of no space and all space that resides deep within and without, a mere presence that needs no physical form in which to manifest. It is compassionate joy that makes us more than physical beings and unites us to all living beings on earth, even the stones. If the purpose of the pain is to remind me of my vulnerability as a passenger on Mother Earth, then it is working. For some of us, I suppose, the way out is through physical suffering, otherwise we wouldn't ever wake up to the truth or be willing, until the pain gets too great, to leave this wondrous and beautiful planet.

The hospital elevator announces itself with a precise ding. The doors part. People indifferent to one another, each involved with their own particular worry, file out of the steel box. I see their angel selves with my heart's eyes. Molly nudges me to get on. My legs won't move. I don't want to go.

"Mom, we've missed the last three elevators. This is a busy place. There are always going to be other people getting on."

I close my eyes and step forward.

That wasn't as bad as I thought it would be. Only two people on board with us. They get off on the second floor and we realize that the elevator is going up rather than down to the lab. A man with shorts and running shoes gets on. Molly's face flushes with shades of red. She runs her hands through her now short and curly hair. She has already had one haircut since the chemo treatments. Luckily, she was able to bypass radiation. She had her six-month check-up and shows no sign of the tumor.

Short hair becomes her. It makes her face softer and her eyes bigger. She has a beautifully shaped head. And her facial expressions seem more honest than before. No pretense. What you see is what you get. In this moment she cannot disguise the expression of joy and excitement she feels about seeing this man on the elevator.

"Well, hello. How are you? This is a pleasant surprise." The man extends his hand to Molly and holds it for a minute longer than seems necessary for a casual greeting.

"Hello, Dr. Graham. I'd like you to meet my mother, Tooley Winters. Mom, this is Dr. John Graham." She presents him with a flourish of her hand like she is introducing a knight of the round table. "Looks like you've been running," Molly says, with a smile that transforms all the cares of her world into a work of art displayed on the canvas of her face.

"You remember my name! I wasn't sure you would remember me from the garage sale." He looks at his feet and puts one foot on top of the other, like a little boy.

The elevator slows and stops. The door opens on the fourth floor.

"This is my stop. I have to scrub in for surgery, but I would still love for you to call me, whether it's about the rock equipment or not. We'll catch up," he says, as if he and Molly were old friends.

He looks Molly full in the eyes. I can see the exchange of vital energy, a closed circuit between the two of them.

"Yes. I'll call you soon."

The door closes and Molly presses the B button for basement. She glows. I am free of pain for a moment as I catch my daughter's millisecond of joy.

"It's funny, but I feel like I just ran into an old love of mine. Someone I've known forever, even though I've met Dr. Graham only once and that was just for a minute. Do you believe that love can live forever?"

This is one of the few questions of a philosophical nature my daughter has ever asked me. I must be careful with my words.

"You were both lit up like five-hundred-watt light bulbs. There is no doubt that you two have a strong connection. I do believe that love transcends death."

I smile at Molly and think of The Chief. Then I think of my mother who has been beside me for the last few weeks.

"There were too many things going on before. I couldn't deal with a relationship. Still don't know if I can."

The elevator stops and we get off. It feels like we are in a vault in the bowels of the earth. I walk stiffly to the desk and check in to have my blood drawn, already knowing without clinical proof that my condition is terminal. My body diminishes a little more each day. There is no need for blood tests, but I allow them to grope for a good vein for Molly. She needs to know that she has done all she can. I make things more difficult for her by refusing to take the medication the doctor recommends. Poisons, all.

I turn to speak to my daughter as the technician calls my

name. "Don't put off calling your friend, no matter what's happening in your life. You deserve some happiness. Don't worry about me and Raynie. We'll both be okay no matter what. Always."

Raynie is the comeback kid. She came home from the hospital six months ago. She lacks her old bravado and the expectation that life should go her way. That attitude seems to have been replaced with an understanding, a truce with the world that shines from her eyes, a knowledge that life is not fair but is still worth living with enthusiasm and gratitude for every day the sun comes up. I have much to learn from her. Learning comes slowly to me without the forest and all my plant and animal friends.

When she first got home, Raynie announced she would not be playing the piano anymore and asked Molly to sell it so she wouldn't have to see it every day and feel guilty for not practicing. There was no discussion and, seemingly, no remorse.

The piano was gone the next day.

The technician draws my blood up into a syringe and then puts drops of it on a glass slide. He smears it across the rectangle of glass. The spread out blood looks pale pink instead of red. He puts a Band-Aid on the puncture wound.

"Please wait in the lobby until the pathologist takes a look at your slide and blood count. I'll call you when they are ready." He looks at me with concern.

I go out to the lobby that has filled with people. Molly saved me a seat next to her; our backs are against the outside wall. She's reading a magazine that showcases homes in the Pacific Northwest. The page is open to a ranch style house in a wooded area. It has high ceiling beams and big French doors that look out at the Columbia River at the base of Mt. St. Helens in Washington.

"This is where I want to live," Molly says. "I'm tired of the freeways and the pollution. Baking coffeecakes no longer interests me. I've hardly set foot in the building for the last ten months. Duchess and James have offered to buy me out. They seem to have a good partnership going, in more ways than one, except Duchess isn't ready to tell me about their romance yet." Molly stops to take a sip of coffee from a paper cup. "Mom, would you like me to get you a cup of coffee?"

I shake my head no. Coffee tastes like battery acid and food tastes like cardboard.

"I want to be somewhere with a view of a mountain, a body of water, clean fresh air, and be near a town where everybody knows each other."

Molly says all this with a determination I haven't heard before. Often, her voice echoes a kind of confusion. The image of someone jumping on a horse and trying to ride off in two directions comes to mind. Her statement about what she wants comes out with crystal clarity; her voice speaking her truth with conviction, a voice I can believe. I pat her on the shoulder, a small recognition of this great achievement.

"Speaking of small towns. We need to go up to Roseburg and pay a visit to the bank to retrieve the money from my savings account," I say. "There should be enough money in there to fund Raynie's college tuition and to help buy you a house anywhere you want to live."

Molly looks at me with surprise. "You never told me you had money in a savings account."

"I never told anybody. It was an inheritance from my mother. It's a long story. I'll tell you about it soon."

"Mom, you should spend it on something you want, maybe a little place in the woods back in Oregon. Or maybe you could live with me somewhere in the country and we could build you a cottage out back with lots of trees around it."

My daughter is in denial. The only place I can look forward

to is a home in the ground, hopefully, beneath a Douglas fir tree.

"Mrs. Winters? Would you please come with me? The hematologist is here and would like to talk with you." The technician motions for Molly to come too.

We walk into a cubicle where two men are hovered around a microscope. I feel the walls closing in on me. I don't remember their names as they introduce themselves. One is the pathologist and the other is a hematologist. They look alike in their white lab coats. Their eyes avert my direct stare. They turn to address Molly.

"Her white count is very high. She has blast cells in her blood that should only be found in the bone marrow, and she is very anemic. Has she been bleeding?" The hematologist asks Molly.

"I don't know. Mom have you been bleeding?"

"Not much. Just a few nose bleeds," I shrug to downplay this little charade. I had a nosebleed a few days ago that took all day to stop but I don't tell them. They will want to pump poisons into my bloodstream to fix things.

"As I said, blast cells are immature white cells that belong in the bone marrow but not in the bloodstream. We're going to want to take a sample of her bone marrow to confirm the diagnosis," says the hematologist, "but we're pretty sure she has acute myelocytic leukemia. We've already scheduled the bone marrow test and can do it now."

The pathologist looks up from the microscope and nods his head in agreement. A nurse comes in with a hospital gown. She pats my shoulder and with a smile says, "Follow me, dear."

"I'm not doing this. I know a woman who had a spinal tap and it paralyzed her. I'm too old for this nonsense." I walk out of the cubicle and wait in the hall for Molly.

"She'll die without treatment. She needs blood transfusions and possibly chemotherapy," I hear one of the doctor's say.

"I'll take her home and talk to her. This was all out of the blue. I'll call. We can reschedule the procedure," she whispers, not wanting me to hear, but I hear everything.

There was no conversation on the way home. Molly was crying and she was driving way over the speed limit.

At the stoplight on Harbor and Lincoln, the Anaheim ice skating rink is on my right. Goody and I had talked about making a day of it sometime. She wanted to show me her moves on the ice and teach me to skate. I wish we could have done that.

My feelings about my impending death are mixed—sad about the things I never got to do, the people and creatures I love that will be left behind. What will happen to Kachina and Kevin? Molly and Raynie will miss me, but they will walk their path strong and true until their time comes to depart. I am grateful and proud to have been part of their lives. I'm thankful that I was given the opportunity to spend time here for a short while. I wouldn't trade any of it, the good and the bad. I bless the tiniest spore and colony of algae that grow green on tree branches, but I ache to be in my mother's arms once again. I have waited long enough.

Chapter Thirty-Three

Molly: December 2002.

We are driving on Interstate-5 headed north to Oregon. Raynie is next to me in the front seat but constantly turns to look back at Tooley who is stretched out in back with her eyes closed. Her breaths seem few and far between. Kevin and Kachina are snuggled around her, fast asleep. There are three shovels and a box of black plastic bags in the back of the SUV, along with an ice chest full of sandwiches and sodas.

The radio's weather report announced that chains are required to cross the Siskiyou Pass into Oregon, so we stop in Shasta at a gas station convenience store.

Willard and Goody are trailing us in the Jeep. They pull in behind us and Willard gets out and walks over to the SUV.

"I've got to buy some chains," Willard says. "I suppose they'll have some here in the store. I guess I better gas up as well." He looks at Tooley in the back seat. "Hello my beauty with the Technicolor eyes." He touches the freezing cold glass of the back window as if in blessing, tears in his eyes, and then walks into the store.

Raynie has gone to the bathroom. I look at Tooley while the gas tank is filling. Her eyes are open but I'm not sure she is awake.

"Would you like to stop for a bite to eat?" I ask Willard. He shakes his head no and wipes tears from his eyes with a Kleenex.

The Burning Jacket

"Let's just pick up some snacks here and eat in the car while we're driving. I don't think we can afford to take the time."

Raynie comes back and lets the dogs out for a pit stop and to stretch their legs while Willard goes into the store for snack food.

"Are we in Shasta?" Tooley wakes up and looks over at the snow-covered mountain for proof. "This place reminds me of The Chief," she says in a whisper.

I see her eyes change, like two planets that have gone retrograde in their celestial paths. A smile crosses her face, a smile of anticipated reunion no doubt.

I'm selfish. I'm not ready to let her go, but what choice do I have? She refused treatment. The truth is, it probably would have done little except prolong her suffering a few more months.

Tooley told me the story of how The Chief had disappeared on Mount Shasta during the Harmonic Convergence. At first, I didn't believe her, but after living with Tooley these past months, I believe anything is possible. I just hope she can hang on and not disappear until we get her back to her final earthly destination, her beloved forest. We need to make three stops first: the bank in Roseburg, Alisha's Café, and the old farm where Tooley's mother is buried.

About a week ago, Tooley finished the story she had begun telling me about Jeb killing her mother and burying her out by the barn and then how she poisoned Jeb when she was twelve years old.

Tooley said her mother, Fanny, told her a story about four pots of gold buried at the end of the rainbow. Tooley wasn't sure how old she was when the stories began, but she thinks it was around the time she was four or five, shortly before her mother was killed. That was when the felted wool jacket appeared. Tooley remembered that the jacket was clean and smelled new.

Her mother hid the jacket in the back of Tooley's closet so Jeb wouldn't see it. She told Tooley there was a map hidden inside the hollow of a pendant in the shape of a key and the pendant was sewn into the hem of the jacket. She told Tooley to always keep the jacket close to her and never let Jeb see it, and to never give it away. The jacket was her security in this world.

At first, I thought Tooley was reverting to her old lies, or hallucinating from the pain of the leukemia sucking the life from her in giant slurps. But then she showed me the pendant, shaped like a key, and the old weathered map drawn in ink on a piece of lined notebook paper stuffed inside the hollow of the pendant.

The map showed that the gold was hidden on Jeb's farm, down in a culvert at the base of the weeping willow tree where the goats used to graze. A good-sized, heart-shaped river rock was placed at the site. Directly under this rock was the place to dig.

Tooley said that Fanny told her about an old friend, Rebekah, whom she had gone to school with in St. Louis. The women had stayed in touch by writing letters after Fanny moved to Jeb's farm. Rebekah knew Fanny was having a hard time making ends meet. One day, a mail truck pulled up to the house and the deliveryman came to the door with a heavy bucket. Four buckets total, if Tooley's memory was correct. The man said the buckets were for Fanny specifically, and she had to sign a piece of paper to get them. A letter was attached. The letter was from Rebekah, explaining that she had married the son of the vice president of Standard Oil and the buckets were a present to celebrate her good fortune. Tooley said she remembers her mother dragging the four heavy buckets down to the culvert, one at a time. Jeb was away, he had gone to town that day. Fanny told Tooley they needed to hide the buckets before Jeb got home.

After the repeated stories about the gold at the end of the rainbow and remembering what she had seen as a child, and the

The Burning Jacket

secret jacket in the closet, Tooley put on the jacket after she killed Jeb and then ran away.

It wasn't until 1980 that Tooley and The Chief went back for the gold. The old farm was still there. A few windows had been broken out of the house. The barn was in need of repair, but still standing. The land was off the beaten path and behind three sets of gates, isolated enough so that few people had wandered there.

Tooley and The Chief found the pots of gold with no trouble. They hauled out three of the buckets and reburied one just in case they needed an ace in the hole for later, as Tooley told the story. The Chief sold the gold for a soaring price of six hundred and forty dollars an ounce and gave the money to Tooley to put in a savings account in the bank at Roseburg. She didn't remember the exact amount but it was a little over a million dollars. She said she always kept a reserve of ten thousand dollars in twenties, fifties, and hundreds in a black plastic bag under her bed in the cabin. She rarely dipped into it while she lived in the woods, but it came in handy when she had to leave the forest and hit the road.

Tooley called the bank last week and told them she wanted to close her savings account and have the money transferred to her daughter's account in Anaheim. A bank official said the total account was now worth over two million dollars. She would have to come to the bank and sign papers and show some identification in order for such a large sum of money to be transferred.

I almost fainted when Tooley mentioned the amount of money she had squirreled away. She said the president of the bank had advised her to diversify her holdings, but Tooley refused to support a "corrupt system." It had taken some hard talking for The Chief to even convince her to put the cash in the bank.

After we fill up, chain up, and eat, we caravan out of Shasta, Willard and Goody behind us. Tooley is sitting up in the back seat now. She managed to eat half a tuna sandwich and crackers while Goody cheered her up with a lively dance in the parking lot of the filling station. Dolly Parton's "Nine to Five" was piped outside from a speaker in the store. The other customers seemed to enjoy Goody's dance. Some of them applauded.

"Look out the window!" Tooley laughs with delight.

As we turn to get back on I-5, two juvenile coyotes romp together in the snow in the center island. The dogs are already asleep, they don't notice.

"That's what these old bones have been missing... my playful coyote friends."

Tooley takes her flute out of the pocket of the burning jacket and gifts us with a whisper of a "Coyotes Playing in the Snow" song. The notes are shaky as they roam the scale up and down, mimicking running then skipping, then notes that sound like jumping.

"How far are we from the border?" Tooley asks with a voice that cradles a vital anticipation.

"Not far. Yreka and the border are next, and once we get there, it's only a hundred and twenty miles to Roseburg."

The word Roseburg comes out of my mouth like a latent sob. I want time to stand still or move backwards. I want to relive my childhood with the Tooley I have come to understand and trust. There was never a question of my love for her. I just didn't know what made her tick. I didn't know what she had been through, what incidents crafted the eccentric person she is today. The lies, the paranoia, the attachment to the burning jacket, all were ways of coping with the crushing blows life had dealt her. The jacket is the only tangible thing that links her to the mother she lost at an age when a mother is needed most.

The Burning Jacket

A couple of days ago I asked Tooley why she never allowed the jacket to be washed even after she took the pendant with the map out.

"This old rag carries within the essence of what is good and right in this world of insanity that man has built up as protection," she said. "Protection from what you may ask? Oh, Molly, if we realized who we really are, we wouldn't need all the stuff we are all so attached to. Our possessions wouldn't be our protection, they wouldn't mean diddley squat. We wouldn't have to fight and drop nuclear bombs on each other if we knew that we are, and have always been, a part of each other, a part of the whole; call it God, the Great Spirit, Energy, Allah, or whatever. This jacket is my legacy from my mother. Her energy fills every woolly fiber with love and kindness toward all creatures."

"What about all those stories you told Raynie? None of that family history was true."

"I told those stories about the jacket to Raynie so she would have something tangible as a reminder of who she is and where she came from. What difference does it make that I made most of it up as long as her belief in its truth makes her strong in the face of darkness. I never knew my mother's last name or anything about her family, so I had to wing it."

"Mom, I wish you had told me the truth earlier."

"I tried, Molly. You wouldn't let me. People carry around bibles for inner guidance and strength. Somebody made up those stories, but our society doesn't go around calling them liars. They embrace the bible as something to live by, something to lean on in hard times. I don't wash the jacket because I'm afraid all the holiness, the magic that was my mother, the energy of her presence, would wash away and the jacket would fall to pieces."

I thought about my attachment to the Julia of my dreams. How an intrinsic part of me needs Julia to have been a real person. Are not my dreams just stories? Are they not all lies? And what about my compulsion to make art? The drawings and paintings are all products of my imagination. Stories. Lies.

A light snow falls as we approach Yreka. We stop for another break. Tooley has to go to the bathroom. Willard pulls in behind us. When he sees Raynie and me trying to help Tooley out of the back seat he comes over and scoops her up in his arms and carries her into the bathroom. He waits outside while I help her sit on the toilet, get up and pull up her pants. I covet this closeness to her and want to hang on and never let go. For some strange reason I think of the lyrics to a Joni Mitchell song, *"you don't know what you got till it's gone; they paved paradise and put up a parking lot."*

Willard is waiting, along with Goody, at the bathroom door. He carries Tooley back to the car like a baby in his arms, his forehead touching hers. Goody holds her hand. It is obvious what a close bond the three have formed in such a short time. It's hard for them to let her go.

Willard places Tooley in the back seat. Raynie covers her grandmother with the burning jacket Willard tucks the afghan around her for added warmth. Tooley knitted the afghan, the color of autumn leaves, for Raynie when she was three-years-old. Raynie insisted Tooley take it with her to her grave.

The summit of the pass is a whiteout, a blizzard. I turn on my headlights and crawl downhill towards the Oregon border and Ashland. As we descend, the snowfall lightens. Headlights shine on each separate snowflake, soft white angels, each with its own pattern but part of the whole.

A smile breaks across Raynie's face as if she read my mind. She reaches over and touches my shoulder. She already knows what I am just beginning to understand.

Chapter Thirty-Four

Tooley: Late Afternoon, December 2002, Oregon.

"Granny Tooley, wake up. We're here at the bank and we need to go in before it closes. Do you want Willard to carry you?" Raynie had the car's back door open; she's shivering in the cold rain.

"No, just help me up. I don't want the people in the bank to get suspicious about what we're doing."

I slept the whole way here from the border with the dogs wrapped around me for warmth. They cried when Molly tried to shut them in the back with the shovels.

The shovels, instruments that bring home the reality of what we are about to do, give me goose bumps. But it is time to move on. My feelings are mixed. I'm at peace with my decision and so very thankful that my family and friends understand and are willing to make it happen, but letting go and leaving them behind is torture, albeit a temporary one.

Molly promised she will take care of Kevin and Kachina and not drop them off at the dog pound as soon as I'm in the ground. A trust has built between us. She will not betray my wishes.

The clean moist air, scented with fir and pine, fills my lungs. The smells are old friends giving me strength for the next step in the journey towards home.

Focusing all my attention, I manage to get my legs and my

butt out of the car with the help of Molly and Raynie flanking me. I try not to show that they are carrying most of my weight.

I announce myself to the bank teller and she points to a man dressed in a black suit sitting at a desk that looks a hundred miles away from where we are standing. I've seen this man before, here in the bank, but can't remember his name.

"Hello, Mrs. Winters. We haven't seen you for quite a while. I'm Jack Yakers, remember? I'm the person whose been trying to get you to diversify your holdings all these years in order to achieve a higher return on your investment, but it seems you've done all right for yourself with just the savings account."

Yaker's hair had been black when I first met him; now it is gray. He's speaking in an extra loud voice, like some people do with the very elderly. He pats the back of my hand. It's a good thing Goody stayed out in the Jeep with Willard. When people play the "little old lady deaf card" with her she hams it up and makes them repeat what they've said until they are shouting and uncomfortable. Then she laughs and says, "I heard you the first time."

"Mr. Yakers, this is my daughter, Molly Johnson and my granddaughter, Raynie Rogers Winters."

Molly dropped Ray's last name when they divorced and Raynie decided to keep her father's name and add mine. It all seems too complicated, this naming game. Jack Yakers, Mrs. Winters, Molly Johnson, Raynie Rogers Winters.

Names: words that identify a person to others, and to themselves. My name is Tallulah Running Bear Winters, but not for much longer. This impressive moniker confused me for quite some time. I didn't feel big enough or wise enough to step into it. Who is this Tallulah Running Bear Winters? Not knowing her history, I made one up. The animals and plants don't ask your name. They know who you are without naming.

The Burning Jacket

Everyone is looking at me like they want an answer. I'm bone cold but Molly insisted that I not wear the burning jacket into the bank. She said it would call unnecessary attention to myself.

"Since I can't persuade you to keep your money with our bank, I'll need you to sign this release in front of Mrs. Doby here, our notary public, and we'll transfer the money to your daughter's account in Anaheim. Yes, I have the routing number right here." He puts on a pair of glasses. "I just need to see some valid identification with your picture on it, even though I know who you are."

I show him my old driver's license that a friend of Willard's had helped doctor up so the date is current.

Valid identification. Another confusing and funny thing. I find myself suppressing a laugh. A person needs a piece of paper with the right numbers on it to be valid in this society.

But not where I'm going!

In a shaky hand, I sign the paper. Yakers makes a copy and hands me the original. Without looking at it, I stuff the paper into the pocket of Molly's brown winter coat that I wore into the bank to make a more respectable impression.

"Don't you want to know what the account is worth?" Jack Yakers asks.

I take the piece of paper out of my pocket. The numbers are blurred. I hand the paper to Molly.

"Two million, three hundred forty thousand dollars and ninety four cents," she says in a whisper.

"Congratulations to you, Mrs. Johnson. Your mother is most generous. She must love you very much. Take care of yourself, Mrs. Winters, and come back and see us sometime."

Yakers shouts at us as we leave the bank.

I manage a faint wave of my hand as Molly and Raynie haul me out of the bank before the three of us fall over.

It is getting dark. The rain could turn to snow tonight.

Molly, Goody and Willard huddle by the SUV to plan our strategy, with me in a sitting position in the back seat. Raynie is walking the dogs.

We decide it is too late to go to Jeb's old farm tonight. I hope my mother's grave hasn't been paved over in the last twenty-two years. That part of Oregon is so remote that development has been slow.

"Let's go have a celebratory last supper at Alisha's," I say, "and then check into a motel. There's a Comfort Inn near the café."

Apparently, they had been waiting for me to make the decision.

* * *

The Liar's Café hasn't changed much. Billows of excitement and gratitude expand my chest and breathe for me. Willard helps me walk into the restaurant, almost on my own two feet.

Alisha does a double take. "Tooley! What a surprise! I'm so happy to see you!" She hurries to clean off the table that stands close to the brick wall.

I no longer need to sit with my back to the wall, but I sit down to acknowledge her thoughtfulness.

The place is full with a dinner crowd, mostly loggers and sheep farmers. Some faces I recognize without ever having known their names. Alisha brings over a chair with a soft cushion and I sink what's left of me down into it.

"It took me a minute to recognize you, Tooley. It's been more than a few years."

The Burning Jacket

Alisha is startled by my skeletal appearance. But of what importance is it now how my body looks? My flesh will soon be compost for the fir trees. I am overjoyed to be back and on the last leg of my journey. Soon I will be home.

The restaurant is warm and cozy. I look over at the fireplace and my heart skips a beat. I see her sleeping. "Gattita! My chaquita bonita Gattita," I call softly.

Her ears perk up and Gattita looks around. She spots me and stands up, stretches, then saunters over to the table and rubs against my legs as if we had never been separated. Willard reaches down, picks her up and puts her in my lap. She purrs so loudly that the others laugh.

"She certainly looks well fed." I rub her round belly. The day I left her in the pouring down rain, sitting on the porch of the cabin, seems a lifetime ago. Leaving her was one of the hardest things I've ever had to do. The others see the joy I feel at this reunion because they are all smiling at me. Willard's eyes are welling with tears that hesitate to fall.

I am whirling in circles with Mama, around and around in my new white Easter dress with the tiny roses.
It's raining. It's raining. It's raining.

"Would you like to order the usual?" Alisha asks.
"Yes. Granny Tooley and I would like a garden burger and a hazelnut milkshake," Raynie says as she winks at me.
Everyone followed suit and makes the order unanimous.

In my mind, I am already in the forest, ahead of the others. The spicy scent of Douglas fir trees fills my being as the trees sway in rhythm to the beating of my heart.
It's raining. It's raining. It's raining.

"What happened to Annie and her baby, Raoul?"

"Well, Raynie, you would be proud of Raoul. His fleece won first prize at the Black Sheep Festival two years in a row in Eugene, and Annie has given birth to two more potential prizewinners. I've enjoyed having them as part of my family. I bought a spinning wheel, but haven't had time to learn to use it yet. I'm saving that for my retirement, when the time comes, but my daughter is taking classes and she's getting really good at it." Alisha looks at me. "Tooley, do you still have that wonderful spinning wheel The Chief made for you? Boy, that was a beauty. If you ever want to part with it I'll be glad to buy it from you."

There was an awkward silence. Alisha, sensing her mistake, turned red.

"Granny Tooley gave me her spinning wheel." Raynie smiles and puts her hand over Alisha's. "We kind of want to keep it in the family."

"Of course. Of course. I understand. Have you been out to the old place yet, where your cabin stood?" Alisha looks confused by another awkward silence.

"No." I say in a whisper. "We plan to go out there tomorrow and take a look."

A last look.

"Well, my nephew and I drove out there the other day hunting for late chanterelles and the Doug firs are growing back where the lumber company replanted. Still small, but they'll grow."

"Did they clear cut everything out there?" Molly asks, and then looks at me.

"No, they left a stand of old-growth trees up on the far side of the hill straight up from where your old cabin stood and off to the right about a hundred yards." She looks at me. "There's some wild turkeys up there and some chickens running around. I suspect they're from your old brood, Tooley."

The Burning Jacket

Gattita falls asleep in my lap, still purring in her sleep.

I manage to get down a few sips of milkshake but the bite of sandwich sticks in my throat and I spit it out into a paper napkin. The others pretend they don't notice. Willard eats the rest of my sandwich and Raynie drinks the rest of my milkshake.

"Good to the last drop," Raynie says after two loud slurps with her straw. She looks at me and laughs. "Remember when I was little and I always used to do that when we came in here?"

"Of course I remember. It was part of our dining ritual. When you first came in you would head for the counter and set all the stool tops spinning."

"Granny Tooley, you remember everything!"

"Yes I do, child. There are gaps here and there, but I remember most of it."

The Chief and I, along with all our animal friends, are lying on our backs up on the hill watching first the moon and then the stars come out.

It's raining. It's raining. It's raining.

Alisha hugs me goodbye and I thank her for being my friend and making such a wonderful home for Gattita.

I pet Gattita on her head between her ears the way she likes it, and Willard picks her up and puts her down on the floor over by the fireplace.

As we leave, Alisha says, "You come back and see us. Don't be a stranger."

Never more will I be a stranger.
It's raining. It's raining. It's raining.

Chapter Thirty-Five

Raynie: Next Day, December 2002.

The rain hammered all night and the wind howled wild in the trees outside the motel. I didn't get much sleep sharing a bed with Tooley. She barely moved all night. Every time I dozed off, I would catch myself and wake up to check on her, to make sure she was still breathing. Mom and Goody shared another bed and Goody was snoring loudly. We got Willard a separate room because he needed his sleep. The brunt of today's hard labor will be on his shoulders. Mom offered to get Goody a separate room but she insisted on being close to Tooley.

I feel like we're playing out a scene in a movie and when the director says "cut" it will be all over. Tooley will take off her death mask, we'll all go home, and Tooley and I, along with the dogs, will go into her room and watch one of her favorite movies.

Mom makes coffee in the motel room and Willard comes over for cheerios, milk and bananas. We decide not to take time to eat at a restaurant. We need all the daylight we can get. We look at Tooley and silently agree that we are running out of time.

I cannot swallow the cereal. It won't get around the aching lump in my throat. Despite Tooley's reminder that death is as natural as breathing in and out, and her promise that she will always be with me even if I can't see her, I cannot imagine life without her here in this world. The thoughts cascade through my brain and fall down my cheeks as tears. She won't be here to celebrate my fourteenth birthday.

We pack our things and haul them out to the car. I don't want to leave the motel. Maybe if we stay here we can avoid living out this day, a day I know I will never forget.

* * *

We're on the long driveway that leads up to Jeb's old farm. It's more like a muddy track than a road. Someone put gravel down a long time ago, but most of it has been absorbed into the earth. The potholes overflow with rainwater. I look back at the three shovels. How in the world are we going to dig in this mud? How are we going to find great grandmother Fanny's grave? I pull out my inhaler and take a pull. Mom reaches over and pats me on the arm.

"Hang in there, Raynie. Once we get her to the forest where she wants to be, I think things will go easier."

We're in the lead with Willard and Goody in the Jeep following us. We come to the first of the three gates Tooley told us about. A rusty and bent FOR SALE sign, riddled with bullet holes, lies slanted on its wooden post in the ground by the side of the road. It looks like something ran into it and knocked it half-mast.

We stop and Willard gets out and untangles the chain wrapped around the fence and gate latch. He opens the rusted white gate that spans the width of the road and motions for us to drive through. Then he closes the gate again. He comes over to the SUV and pokes his head in the window on the driver's side.

"Thank God there wasn't a lock on the gate. Why don't you let me lead?" he says to Mom. "The road from here might get pretty bad. We don't want to get stuck in the mud."

Willard blows a kiss to Tooley in the back seat. She

attempts a smile in return and he walks back to the Jeep. We wait for him to pass us.

"Was that The Chief smiling at me through the window? I haven't seen him in years." Tooley achieves a half-smile.

I look over at Mom and she bites her lip to keep from crying but it doesn't work. She wipes her eyes with a Kleenex before she goes forward.

We make it through the second and third gates, dodging potholes and managing not to get stuck.

"I remember opening those gates the day I was in such a hurry to get out of this place. None of them ever did have locks, but the chains were heavy and hard to open," Tooley says. Her voice is a hoarse whisper.

"Granny Tooley, you're safe now. Jeb's gone and he can't hurt you anymore," I say.

"Yes, you're right. Be gone with him. I've carried him around too long. We're here to get Mama and take her with us, and then I never have to lay eyes on this place again." Tooley nods her head. "The old place doesn't look too different from when I was here with The Chief. Back in 1980. As far as I can see. Which isn't very far."

So many words strung together have worn her out. Tooley sinks back on the seat and closes her eyes.

So here we are at the scene of the crimes. My great-grandmother's death at the hands of Jeb. Jeb's poisoning by Tooley.

I think Tooley was brave and I'm glad she killed Jeb for taking her mother away from her, and for killing the wild horses. I think I would have done the same thing. Maybe it's wrong to feel that way but some people don't deserve to live. I think about True and what she said about Ray in the girl's bathroom at school. Now I understand what she meant.

Most of the boards to the front porch of the cabin are

missing, and a few windows are broken, but the house doesn't look too bad for having stood empty for so long. I shiver at the thought of going inside. Maybe murdered people's ghosts are hanging around in there. I think everyone must feel uneasy; no one suggests we go inside.

"Granny Tooley, look. That must be Great-Grandmother Fanny's old potting shed. It's covered with blackberry vines." I point to a small building, a pathway overgrown with mossy seashells leading to it.

"Mama takes me to the beach and we collect pretty shells when we can get away. I'm helping her build a path," Tooley says with the excitement of youth in her voice. She seems to be going backward in time, to her childhood. I wonder if that is what happens to all people when they die.

Mom is silent in the driver's seat. She cries intermittently. I know how she feels. The grief comes in waves. I'm fine for a while and then this really sad feeling rolls up from my stomach and flows through my heart and makes me cry. And then it ebbs again until the next wave hits.

Molly motions Willard to drive back to the barn. Both cars manage to find a flat spot of grass and Willard and Mom circle the cars around so they face the road. In case they get stuck in the mud, it will be easier to get out head first. The roof of the barn looks like it will cave in any minute and the whole structure leans to the left.

I get out and open the back door on the passenger side. I whistle for the dogs to get out, do their business and take a little run.

"Look! there's Bugsy, and, hey, there's Calendula!" Tooley palms the back window. Tears run down her dry, old cheeks. She mistakes Kachina and Kevin for her first pets, the playmates and protectors of her childhood.

"Be sure and dry off the dogs with a towel before you let

them back in the car. They are going to be wet and muddy," Mom says. She wears a wool cap that Tooley made for Mom when she was bald. The cap is colored various shades of green with a few threads of red running through it for highlights. Mom's hair is coming in dark brown and curly.

Business as usual, I think. I find the thought both odd yet comforting. It *is* business as usual. People die every second somewhere. It's as natural as being born. The thought of Mom taking care of everyday things, and seeing her hair grow back reassures me that life will go on.

Willard comes with an open umbrella to get Granny Tooley out of the back seat.

"Sure you don't want to wait in the nice dry car and we'll go look for the grave?" he asks.

"No. I need to go see Mama. I need to tell her who you all are. If she sees me first she won't be frightened by strangers."

I put one of Tooley's arms around my neck and Willard does the same on his side, holding the umbrella with his other hand. I can tell movement causes her pain.

We go and look for the head and footstones of Great-Grandmother Fanny's grave.

"Look. There's Calendula's grave," Granny Tooley says. "I remember I put a bucket, with her favorite rubber ball inside, on top of where I dug the hole. Jeb was just going to burn her on the trash heap, but I stopped him."

Her voice holds a trace of hatred. Is there a rule that says you have to forgive everybody before you die? Some things are impossible to forgive.

"Calendula is under there." Tooley blows a kiss in the direction of the lump in the earth that is covered with weeds. "Sorry I don't have time to dig you up and take you with me, but I know that you are in the hands of the Great Spirit." Tooley starts to smile, but a grimace of pain overrides it.

The Burning Jacket

The dogs go over and sniff the ground as if they can smell one of their kin down through the layers of earth.

"Here's the headstone," Mom calls out. I can barely hear her in the pounding rain. She and Goody are standing in the shadow of the slant of the barn next to a rectangular rise in the earth. It's as if the old barn is leaning toward the grave, trying to protect Fanny from the elements.

Willard and I carry Tooley over to the mound in the earth. Her body shakes. Whether from the cold, illness, or anticipation of being with her mother, it's hard to say.

"Let's take you back to the car to stay warm and we'll dig," Willard suggests to Tooley.

"No, just put me in the barn so I can watch. I'll be able to see through the gaps where some of the boards fell out," she croaks.

Willard carries Tooley into the barn while I run back to the car for blankets. She's wearing the burning jacket. The oily, dirty wool repels the drops of rain. Willard props her up against an old seat that looks like it could have come out of a tractor.

"You stay in here with her and make sure she stays warm enough," says Willard.

Goody and Mom have already started digging. They are struggling. They can barely get the shovels heads into the hard, wet ground. Willard motions them away and points to the barn.

"This will go faster and easier if you let me do this alone."

Willard starts digging. He's very old to be so strong. He must be as old as Granny Tooley, but we're not exactly sure how old *she* is.

Willard struggles for about a half an hour. He's hindered by the mud that keeps caving in around the shovelfuls he has just dug up, but finally he reaches pay dirt.

"Bring me one of those blankets. I've got what's left of her bones." Goody stays with the sleeping Tooley while Mom and I run over to the grave. "She wasn't buried all that deep," he says, with a quiver in his voice.

The handmade quilt Tooley told us her mother had been wrapped in had disintegrated, all but a few rotten shreds. The earth around her body was gray, the color of ashes. You could tell that when she was rolled—or kicked—into the hole that she landed on her side; some of her bones overlap. Her skull is intact, but has a spider web crack in it.

Mom and I spread the blanket on the ground and Willard gently hands the crumbling bones up to us. We lay them in the blanket, roll it up, and carry it to the back seat of the SUV. Willard carries the sleeping Tooley from the barn and puts her in the backseat. He places the blanket with Fanny's bones on top of Tooley and folds her arms around it. She opens her eyes briefly, sighs, and smiles. And the sky smiles with her. The rain lightens for a brief moment.

We all look up.

Willard hurriedly fills in the hole as best he can.

"We have one more stop to make while we're here," Mom tells Willard.

"On our way back down the hill, not far from the road, there is a culvert with an old weeping willow tree. Something is buried there that Tooley wants you and Goody to have," Molly says.

Good for Mom. She's going to give Willard and Goody the other bucket of gold.

Willard places two shovels in the back of the SUV, puts the third in his Jeep and leads the way back down, watchful for the signs of the culvert and weeping willow.

The rest of us wait in the SUV with the heater running on high while Willard digs up the bucket of gold coins. We see him come over the rise of the hill with the bucket, smiling as he climbs the fence and walks toward the SUV with his heavy burden in one hand, shovel in another. He has on a western hat that acts as a rainspout. The rain pouring down in front of Willard's face makes me laugh.

Willard puts the bucket in the back of the SUV along with the shovel.

"That bucket goes in the Jeep with you," Mom tells him. "I don't know how many pounds of gold coins are in there or what it is worth, but Tooley wants you and Goody to split it. A little nest egg for your golden years. Tooley told me to tell you that."

Willard laughs and leans in through the window to kiss the sleeping Tooley on the cheek.

Chapter Thirty-Six

Molly: Same Day, Mid-Afternoon.

The directions to Tooley's old cabin are fuzzy in my mind. I haven't been back in these parts since I was sixteen—when Tooley caught me about to wash the burning jacket at the Laundromat in Roseburg. I wish I could go back in time and change things, but I'm thankful that we have come together for this ending.

We could all go to jail if anybody finds out about this, but it's worth it to me to honor my mother's final wish. She asked to be buried with her mother's bones, entwined in the roots of a Douglas fir tree.

"Go through town and take a left at the stop sign onto Oak Knoll where the freeway bridge crosses," Raynie says. "This is the way we always used to come."

I vaguely remember. My stomach growls loudly. We ate breakfast at the motel six hours ago. It seems like twenty-four. I wasn't sure we could find Jeb's old farm, let alone Fanny's grave and the bucket of gold, but we did. No wonder I'm hungry. The others must be as well. We have peanut butter sandwiches in the ice chest.

"Should we stop and eat some sandwiches?" I ask Raynie.

"It's not that far. Let's wait until we get there." Raynie seems excited to be going back to the woods where she spent such wonderful time with her grandmother. They bonded so strongly. I'm sad to think of how Tooley and I pushed each other away. But we are beyond regrets now.

I look back at Tooley. She's snoring softly as she hugs the blanket of bones. The dogs have their heads on the blanket as if guarding a treasure.

"See, there's the turn for Oak Knoll up ahead. After that, it's only five miles to Granny Tooley's. I hope I recognize the place with all the trees gone." Raynie sounds unsure.

"Raynie, are we doing the right thing?" I look at her.

"Of course we are, Mom." She reaches over and touches my shoulder. "Wouldn't you want me to grant your final wish? It's not hurting anybody. You know how hard it would be for Tooley to die in a hospital with tubes sticking out from everywhere. This way she'll be surrounded by everything and everybody she loves, including her mother."

"You're right," I say. I'm aware of my jaw tightening and then loosening again.

Thank God the rain has stopped, even though the sky is covered in a blanket of clouds. I pray for the rain to hold off for just a little longer, until we get Mom and Fanny in the ground. I surprise myself about how matter-of-fact and normal it all seems. As if it is the *natural* thing to do.

I check the mileage gauge to keep track of how far we travel on this winding county road. Trees flank both sides, mostly Douglas fir with a scattering of Ponderosa pine and Madrone. There are bare spots from clear cuts all the way down to the blacktop.

"See the 'deer crossing' sign full of bullet holes up on the right? We should come to a sharp curve in the road right after that, and then we take the first turn off to the left."

The dogs are awake, whining and restless, looking out the back windows. They know where they are. I slow down and put on my left blinker so Willard doesn't run into me.

"That's it!" Raynie points to a side road.

The gravel on it is new. Alisha had said logging trucks needed to get in and out.

I'm nervous. What if there are people back there? What if we get caught?

A few miles up the graveled road Raynie calls out, "There's the conclave of the chiefs! We're here. Let's stop now and eat. This is where Granny Tooley and I built our fires and toasted marshmallows."

I remember the old Doug fir stumps arranged around the burning circle. There is no evidence of the remains of the cabin or outbuildings.

I park the SUV and Raynie and I and the dogs get out to stretch. Willard stops the Jeep, gets out and walks over to me. We both look at the hillside replanted with trees. They are only a few feet tall. Undergrowth vines are giving the little trees a good race for survival. The land reminds me of stubble on a man's face.

Willard points up the hill and to the right, to the stand of old-grown Doug fir that Alisha said had been spared.

"I'm gonna have to carry her up there. Can you and the girls bring the shovels and tarp? And I sure would like a sandwich or something before I start digging."

I'm glad I wasn't the first to suggest eating.

I haul out the ice chest and Raynie gets the dog bowls out and fills them. The dogs are too busy checking things out to be interested in food.

"I bet Kachina is looking for Snooky, the big Rhode Island Red that laid an egg for her every morning," says Tooley in a whisper. She is too weak to get out of the SUV. It is clear she is finished with the process of eating.

The rest of us seat ourselves on the tree stumps, eat our sandwiches, and drink Coca-Cola.

"The Conclave of the Chiefs," I say out loud. I can feel the energy of the earth rising up through my feet and giving me strength for the task to come. This earth energy is what Tooley must have felt, what made her strong when she sat on these stumps and lifted her stick in the air to chant to the wind. Back when I was a little girl, I used to think she was crazy.

I look over at Raynie. "What are you thinking?" I ask.

"I'm thinking about all the bonfires we had here, and the marshmallows we roasted, and of the stories that Granny Tooley told me about my ancestors." She has tears in her eyes. "All of her animal and plant friends would gather here to listen to her. She would tell them stories about their ancestors too, and play songs that she composed for them. Everything was alive for her, even the stones in the ground."

Goody tells the story about when she and Tooley stole the doves from the lobby of Golden Acres and freed them up in the canyon, and how they hung around in the trees to hear a song Tooley composed for them. When the song was finished, they flew away.

"There is something special about my princess. I always feel young around her. I'm going to miss the way she makes me feel." Willard looks toward the SUV and Tooley, and then down at his watch. "If we want to get out of here before dark we'd better get started. It's time to stop talking and do."

Willard trudges up the hill to dig a hard grave, his shoulders bent in sorrow. Goody, Raynie and I return to the SUV to check on Tooley. She is unconscious and barely breathing. We sit with her in silence, soothing ourselves by touching her, not wanting to let go. We sit there until Willard comes back an hour later. Even though it is only three in the afternoon, the light is beginning to dim. The rain will return soon.

"Grab the two shovels. Raynie, will you carry the blanket with Fanny's bones?" Willard asks.

"I will be honored to do so," says my brave and beautiful daughter. I am proud that she has inherited the best traits of my mother.

I'm so thankful for Willard. He has been a wonderful friend to Tooley. And Goody was the girlfriend she never had while growing up. We could not have pulled off this caper without the two of them.

Willard picks up Tooley's frail body and carries it up the hill as if she weighs no more than a feather.

"Spread the afghan out beside the hole," he says to me softly. He has dug a deep, rectangular grave. Around the top side of the hole are ferns and Oregon Grape bushes, wild hellebore and dormant vines of yerba buena. He has lined the hole with branches of Doug fir trees and pinecones.

Willard lies Tooley's body down on the afghan ever so gently and kisses her on the cheek. He takes the burning jacket from her body and hands it to Raynie. Raynie takes off the sweater that Tooley made for her and wraps the jacket around her. The gesture seems like the ending of one royal reign and the beginning of a new one. It was decided by Tooley, Raynie and me that the jacket should skip a generation and go directly to Raynie.

From his pocket, Willard takes out a hypodermic needle and fills it with a mixture of Phenobarbital and Dilantin that he got from a veterinarian friend.

"This should take my princess to heaven," Willard says. No tears. Willard is smiling. "If anyone opposes what I am about to, do speak now or forever hold your peace. A few more hours and she will leave us under her own steam."

We all sit down on the cold, wet ground and touch Tooley's body while Willard delivers the drugs intravenously into an arm that has little left but bone. We all cry as Tallulah Running Bear Winters takes her last breath.

"Fly home, Granny Tooley. Fly to your mother's arms. Go back to the Great Spirit," Raynie says through her tears.

The dogs come over and lick Tooley's face. They softly whine their farewell.

Tooley still holds the blanket of bones. I place a bouquet of Anaheim violets next to her head. Willard and Goody pull fistfuls of rose petals out of their pockets and scatter them on Tooley's body. It looks as if she is disappearing.

Raynie puts a drawing of Erma Geddon beside Tooley. "I know how you loved her," she says.

Willard rolls up the afghan. He jumps down into the grave and we hand the precious cargo down to him. He places Tooley on the bed of Doug fir branches. Then Willard grabs some vines to hoist himself out of the hole. Goody, Willard, and Raynie shovel the rich loamy forest soil back into the grave.

I double over with grief and fall on my knees, covering the grave's bare earth with moss, twigs, Douglas fir boughs, ferns—to make it look like the earth had never been disturbed. And because I want my mother to be warm.

Please, God, don't let my mother be cold.

Raynie comes over and holds me.

"Don't worry, Mom. We've still got each other." I sink into her arms.

Tooley wanted no graveside eulogy. She may have thrived on ceremony during her lifetime but stated with no hesitation that she wanted a peaceful non-eventful death. No drama, she told us.

Raynie plays her own version of *Pavane for a Dead Princess* on the wooden flute Tooley taught her to play.

Goody does a strange little jig and sings *After You're Gone*.

I notice a silent and discreet gathering of animal friends nearby in honor of Tooley's passage. In the clearing one hundred yards away stand seven white-tailed deer. The dogs are glued to the gravesite, still whining softly, and have no interest in chasing the deer. Farther up the hill, a lone coyote watches us. He remains silent and motionless until we all stand to leave and then he howls, turns, runs up the hill and disappears.

"I can't believe she's gone," I say to Raynie.

"She isn't gone. She is part of this forest, this whole ecosystem. She will be compost for the trees. She will live in every creature and plant. She will live in the wind and the rain. They have all been waiting for her to return to them," Raynie says.

My daughter is so wise.

I turn around and we walk down the hill hand in hand. I see a red-tailed hawk circling in the sky directly over Tooley's grave.

So. There it is. Her mother came and took Tooley home.

FOUR

Chapter Thirty-Seven

Molly: April 2003.

I'm standing in the middle of the showroom at the Lasson Gallery on North Main in Santa Ana, waiting with Angie, the gallery owner, for her crew to bring in my work from the back room.

It's finally happening. The show was postponed twice, once because of Raynie's breakdown and then again, when Tooley died. Now, today, my show is being hung. The opening is tomorrow. The sharp smell of freshly painted walls and the glisten of polished hardwood floors add to my excitement and give the whole affair a professional feel. The long wait is over as Angie's two helpers, young, muscular, aspiring artists hired to hang her exhibits, carry in the paintings and drawings.

The work looks brand new to me. I feel brand new. My energy has returned and my hair has grown back thicker and darker after the chemotherapy. It's been a year and seven months since my first treatment. The oncologist says I won't be out of the woods for five years, but I refuse to think anything other than positive thoughts about permanent remission.

I shiver with excitement and worry that the paintings won't be strong enough to hold the massive expanse of the white walls. And I worry that people won't come, that they will stay home glued to the TV. Bush has just invaded Iraq.

I used the meditation technique Raynie taught me before I

drove to the gallery today. Raynie said she learned the technique from Tooley. I imagined a vast ocean and the world at peace. It helps relieve, but not banish, the sense of doom that hovers over me whenever I think about how my paintings will be accepted.

These same two men came to my studio two weeks ago and loaded my drawings and paintings into the gallery van to take to the framers. They handled the works as if they were pieces of gold.

I decided to show nine of the gun and hand drawings and three large canvases I painted after Raynie came home from the hospital. Like the drawings, they are mostly black and white with touches of color. The paintings are loaded with paint, producing luscious, creamy, bold brush strokes that stay on the surface and also take the viewer on a journey deep into the canvas, creating an ambiguous space that makes the paintings come alive with a certain sense of crossing a boundary to another dimension.

At least that is how I view them. I hope others will understand what I've tried to do. I have a tiny nagging fear that my artwork will come across as little more than therapy.

As the men carry in the art pieces, Angie directs where each should be hung. She is like a policeman in rush-hour traffic. Angie is petite, pretty and young, but speaks and acts with no-nonsense authority.

This is the first time I've seen the pieces since they were framed. The framers did a great job. I won't know until they are on the walls whether the work will hold the space. At first, I resisted Angie's insistence that she be in charge of the placement on the walls. I wanted the pieces to hang chronologically, but she had other ideas. I didn't quite follow her visual reasoning, but have to admit after seeing the arrangement that she was right.

In the studio, as I was working on them, the predominant

overall feeling they conveyed to me was a dense sorrow, but here in this space, they look powerful, almost luminous, like they could take flight. I inhale a deep breath of relief.

"Your use of color intrigues me," a man with a pen and pad says to me. I turn to look at him. A photographer is taking pictures. I hadn't noticed the two men enter the gallery; too much hammering and shuffling of pieces as the hanging process continues. The man with the pad stands in front of the three big paintings already up.

"Your work reminds me of Susan Rothenberg's sparse yet exquisite and relevant use of color."

Now I recognize the man. He is Rex Taylor, art critic for the *Los Angeles Times*.

"I am more than pleasantly surprised by the work," he says. "I've heard the story that goes with the paintings—about the shooting—and to tell you the truth I wasn't keen on covering it."

He waves his hands in front of the work on the walls. "I didn't expect this much power in the drawings, and the paintings, my God, they need no story." He shakes his head and stuffs his hands in the pockets of his tight jeans and walks away from me to look around.

Rex Taylor is slim and delicate, with salt and pepper hair. I see him jot something down on his notepad from time to time, as he steps forward to look up close and then stands back at a distance from the walls. He does this several times.

"What led to your choice of such a limited palette?"

He walks back and stands by my side as we look together.

"It wasn't a rational choice. I couldn't deal with color at the time. My world had lost its color. Only occasional glimmers now and then shone through a veil of darkness."

Was I being overly dramatic?

"The only time I didn't feel depressed, once the numbness and the import of what I had done soaked in, was when I was working in the studio. So I guess the process of making art saved my life."

"Sublimation at its shining best," he says with a wry smile.

"Are you making fun of me?" I ask, following the question with a nervous laugh.

"Not at all. You've translated your feelings into a stunning body of work. Your exhibit, with photos of the paintings and drawings, will be featured this weekend in the Art section. I'll leave you alone now. I need some time to just look. Thank you for talking to me. May I call you if I have more questions?"

"Of course," I say, aware that my voice sounds like I have just swallowed a birdcall whistle.

* * *

Opening Day. Duchess called this morning and read my horoscope to me.

Do you remember that dream? The dream that fell off a train headed for glory? Your dream derailed and ended up in the bottom of a canyon. In the interest of getting all your other goals and responsibilities safely to their destinations, you had to let it go. But today you can hitch that dream back on track. I can't imagine why you wouldn't.

I'm wearing black pants with a white shirt and a tailored jacket. I have on a pair of Raynie's black leather shoes with a slight heel and a stylish strap. They are barely worn. I can only get her in a dress and heels once or twice a year. I was going to wear red high heels to mimic the contrast of black and white with the limited color in my paintings, but Raynie talked me out of it. My black pants are a magnet for Kevin and Kachina's hair. I used a sticky roller when I left the house but I'll do it again when I get out of the SUV at the gallery. I take the dogs to the

The Burning Jacket

doggie park almost every afternoon and it's impossible to keep their hair from clinging to the car seats. I can tell they still miss Tooley, but they are attached to both me and Raynie. I've come to love them. They now sleep with me.

I'm disappointed that Raynie isn't coming to the opening with me. She has chosen instead to attend a protest rally with John, Marsha's grandson, against Bush's invasion of Iraq. They've gone to other peace rallies together. This one is down in Santa Monica. I dropped them at a bus stop this morning on Ball Road. John is seventeen and seems reliable. I just hope the demonstration remains peaceful.

Raynie has grown taller and more graceful this last year. And has exchanged a youthful naiveté for a quiet kind of gentle wisdom. This morning she dressed in her usual attire of khaki pants and a blue shirt with an image of a killer whale. The message across her chest read, *Save The Whales.*

It's just as well she didn't come with me. She would probably be bored. She's lived with the work for too long. For her, my art is probably a constant reminder of her father's death. I have to admit that I'm glad to finally get it out into the world so I can be done with it, too. It's time to start a new series. I've been thinking of doing some large canvases based on the old seashell drawings. The ones I began several years ago.

So much has changed since then. I sold my half of the bakery. Duchess and James bought me out. Since Tooley's death, I've been thinking seriously of moving to Oregon. Despite the bad air, Raynie wants to finish high school here, and then go to college in San Diego to study Marine Biology. She refuses to leave Erma Geddon. Erma wouldn't be able to live in Oregon; it's too damp and cold for her. So I've put my moving plans on hold until Raynie graduates and goes off to college. She could always come to Oregon to visit during school breaks.

Marsha and I are in the SUV driving down Main Street

headed south to the gallery. I talked her into going with me. She said she has never been to an art opening before and she's afraid she won't fit in with the high-falutin' crowd. I told her I wasn't sure I would either and that I needed her as my anchor.

"Is your doctor friend going to be at the opening?" Marsha asks, reading my mind.

Dr. John Graham had called me the day after we had seen each other in the elevator at the hospital when Tooley was having her blood checked. We met for lunch several days later. The conversation didn't flow easily. Things seemed awkward. I was dealing with Tooley's refusal of medical treatment and her insistence of going back to the woods to die. I told John about Tooley not trusting medical doctors, but, of course, nothing about our plan to let her die her own way. John leaned on me to force her to get medical treatment, even though he knew the disease was terminal. I lied to him and told him that Tooley wanted to go back to Oregon for treatment and I was going with her and would be gone for several weeks.

He called again and we had dinner together after Raynie and I returned from burying Tooley, but I'm not a good liar. I told him Tooley had died despite the treatment, and had been buried in the cemetery next to her mother's grave. When he asked where in Oregon she was buried, I said, 'a small town near Portland.' I broke out in a cold sweat and didn't say much the rest of the evening. When he called the third time, I told him I wasn't ready for a relationship, but wanted to remain friends. We talked on the phone several times after that but neither of us had much to say.

"I don't know if he's coming," I answer Marsha. "We're not dating, but I did send him an invitation."

We are not the first to arrive at the gallery. People are mingling in groups in front of the pieces hanging on the walls.

The Burning Jacket

There is a buzz of conversation. Occasionally someone looks up at one of the paintings, but mostly art openings are an excuse to dress up, drink free champagne and wine, eat hors d'oeuvres and socialize.

The gallery is festooned with flowers of every variety. I'm drawn to a bouquet of a dozen yellow roses surrounded by purple violets. I notice a card addressed to me. I open it and read, *Sorry I can't make your opening. I'll catch the show sometime while it's still up. I wish you the best, your friend John Graham.*

I recall the many dreams I've had about a soul mate that brings me violets. Maybe in the future, if and when I am ready to have a partner, and if he is still unattached... a lot of ifs, maybe too many.

A constant parade of people come up to me and comment on the paintings. Those I know hug me, and those I don't introduce themselves and shake hands. I'll never remember all the names.

I am thrilled and surprised to see four red dots on the white labels on the wall. Each red dot means the piece has been sold. One drawing and all three of the paintings. Angie allows her favorite buyers to come in before the show opens and select the ones they want to purchase. The paintings each have a price tag of twelve thousand dollars, and the drawings are priced at five thousand. More riches to add to my generous inheritance from Tooley, and the money from the sale of my half of the bakery. There will be no problem sending Raynie to school anywhere she chooses to go. And having money allows me to spend my time doing what I want to do, which is paint.

Duchess glides over. She's dressed up in a long, flowing cotton skirt with an Indian print, a throwback to the seventies. James is close by her side. Duchess holds out her hand and flashes a diamond on her ring finger. "We've decided to make it a true partnership." Duchess is glowing. "He's an Aquarian and my Venus is in Aquarius. It couldn't be a more perfect match," she says. James looks proud of this fated accomplishment.

I spot a huge bouquet of sage and rosemary on a white sculpture stand at the end of the wall. I recognize Raynie's handwriting: *Although I cannot be with you in my Tooley costume to burn sage and purify the gallery, I am with you in spirit. Blessings for a successful show, love from your mother.*

My eyes fill with tears of gratitude for having the privilege of being the mother to such a magnificent, thoughtful daughter.

And Tooley. My mother. She *was* a work of art. Her creativity and connection to the earth guided her through all the hardships she had to bear in life. She lived and died true to herself.

I am truly happy in this moment. I know it won't last.

It is not only a joy, but also a burden to view the world of nature not as perfection, but as a potential work of art.